THE PHOENIX QUEST

An Isle of the Phoenix Novel

Greg. S. Baker

www.isleofthephoenix.com

The Phoenix Quest
An Isle of the Phoenix Novel
Greg S. Baker

Copyright © 2019
Printed in the United States of America

ISBN: 9781690989912

Second Edition
Independently Published
Cover Design: Simone Torcasio Art

OTHER BOOKS BY GREG S. BAKER

Christian and Christian Living

- *Fitly Spoken – Developing Effective Communication and Social Skills*
- *Restoring a Fallen Christian – Rebuilding Lives for the Cause of Christ*
- *The Great Tribulation and the Day of the Lord: Reconciling the Premillennial Approach to Revelation*
- *The Gospel of Manhood According to Dad – A Young Man's Guide to Becoming a Man*
- *Rediscovering the Character of Manhood – A Young Man's Guide to Building Integrity*
- *Stressin' Over Stress – Six Ways to Handle Stress*

Biblical Fiction Novels

The Davidic Chronicles

- *Book One - Anointed*
- *Book Two - Valiant*
- *Book Three – Fugitive*
- *Book Four – Delivered*
- *Book Five - King*

Young Adult Adventure Novels

Isle of the Phoenix Novels

- *The Phoenix Quest*
- *In the Dragon's Shadow*
- *More to come…*

www.TheDivineIngredient.com

DEDICATION

To my four children, all of whom are growing up faster than I care to contemplate. A father couldn't be more proud. All of you have become avid readers, and as your father, I wanted you to have good, clean adventure stories to spark the imagination, share lessons of life, and inspire you along the journey of your own adventures.

I love you, each and every one of you.

ACKNOWLEDGMENTS

In any work of this magnitude, there are plenty of people who have contributed greatly of their time, talent, and money to make this all happen. I am grateful to them all.

Specifically, Liberty, Kevin, Faith, Keith, and Debbie for all their hard work and help.

A special thanks to Craig and Paula St. Amour for their support of this project and to my incredible grandmother (Granny) who taught me the importance of keeping family close.

"A good name is rather to be chosen than great riches, and loving favour rather than silver and gold." – Proverbs 22:1

"If I take care of my character, my reputation will take care of me." – Dwight L. Moody

"It takes many good deeds to build a good reputation, and only one bad one to lose it." – Benjamin Franklin

THE ISLE OF THE PHOENIX

In the Year of the Lamb, 33rd Year of King Emeth's Reign

THE CITY OF KHOL

1. Roy's House
2. Seth's House
3. King Emeth's Palace
4. Burk's Stables

5. The Naming Plaza
6. Justice Yosher's House
7. The Singing Cathedral

CHAPTER ONE

I woke to an entirely new world outside. The sound of a woodpecker banging its head incessantly against the wooden window frame roused me to the wonders of a new year. I had fallen asleep on the windowsill the night before in a futile effort to watch the world being transformed; but like every other year I had attempted it, I had fallen asleep anyway. Everyone did. It was impossible to watch the Rebirth of the island, but waking up to new wonders more than made up for it.

I lifted my head and speared the annoying bird with the Evil Eye, but of course, it had no effect. I didn't have such power, and the bird merely eyed me right back with a baleful expression. "Shoo!" I muttered irritably.

It wuked loudly, the sound grating in my ears, and then it beat its stupid head against the frame in rapid succession before flying off, much to my satisfaction. That's when I got a really good look at the new world outside my window.

I blinked in wonder. The snow covered, rolling hills of the day before had been replaced by a thick rain forest. Birds of all kinds called to each other, and I could distinctly hear the tinkling sound of a brook as it wound its way through the trees not too far away from my house. The temperature had changed too. Yesterday, the lingering effects of a bitter winter had allowed a few patches of snow to remain in shaded areas and the temperature to drop below freezing at night. But now, sweat rolled off my face profusely, and I could feel my thick coat becoming damp with my own sweat.

I shrugged out of the heavy clothing, anxious to get outside and really take a good look around. This was the first day of the new year and King Emeth would be throwing the annual Phoenix Festival in celebration. There would be all sorts of opportunities for mischief over the duration of the three-day event, and I wasn't about to miss any of it—but first, I wanted to explore the new forest outside my window.

Tossing the coat, boots, extra pair of socks, and mittens onto the bed, I donned a light shirt, trousers, and a light pair of walking boots instead. Once I finished dressing, I dashed out of my room and into the common room of my family's small cottage. My mother stood at another window looking out at the new terrain.

"Roy," she called as I darted by her, "where are you going?"

My mother's penetrating voice stopped me in my tracks. I sometimes wondered if she didn't have a Word of Power at her disposal. That was foolish, of course, for neither my mother nor my father possessed a surname and so could not have a Gift.

"Going exploring is all," I said, rotating around on one foot. "Did you see all the trees, Ma? We haven't had this many trees in five years!"

Mother turned to smile at me. Though she was getting old in the way all parents got, she still looked beautiful. She stood perhaps six inches shorter than I, but had the ruggedness associated with all farmers on the island. Her hair had been tied off in a long ponytail, and only a few strands of her brown hair had turned gray. Wrinkles, however, had begun to form under her eyes. Farmers had a rough life. Every year their fields underwent a dramatic transformation, and sometimes that meant they would need to clear the land before they could plant crops or find viable water sources to water them.

"I see them," she said. "The sawmills will be happy, but your father is not. He's already out looking for clearings." She sighed. "At least we can sell the timber, though with so many trees, I doubt we'll be able to sell the wood at a premium."

"Uh-huh," I agreed absentmindedly, anxious to go. I just wanted to explore—before my father dragged me into the work.

She noticed and smiled. "Go on, get out of here. But don't stray too far. I suspect Father will be wanting to find you before too long."

I nodded in agreement, but winced inside. She had read my mind. I hated work. That was probably the only problem with the new year. The world changed, but everyone had to practically start over—unless you lived in the city. The only things that never changed were the human built structures. Blacksmiths, stables, weavers, and the like had a significantly easier time adjusting to the yearly changes, seeing as their livelihood was protected, mostly, by being in the city. Not so for the farmers. Farmers who lived in the surrounding country had to adapt the most.

Realizing I was hesitating, I blurted, "Okay, Ma!" I darted outside before she could think of anything else to say.

The moment I got outside, the musty, humid air hit me, and I instantly began to sweat even more. I wiped away moisture beading on my brow, but it hardly made any difference. So I chose to ignore it and turned to the world around me.

The newly appeared trees grew practically right up to the large porch Father had built around the entirety of our house. They formed a thick canopy that allowed for sparse light to penetrate. Thick foliage covered much of the ground under the trees, vines hung in clusters like draped curtains from branches, and thick moss clung heavily to rocks and trees.

Yes, it was a whole new world.

I loosened my collar and looked around for a good vantage point. Two years ago, when the Phoenix had been reborn, remaking the island, the city of Khol and the near countryside had been hedged in by gigantic mountains. On a whim, I had climbed as far up as I could on the nearest peak. I had been able to see for miles all around. That had been incredible, though Father had complained that farming on mountain slopes was practically impossible and transporting water from the high mountain lake had been grueling work. I looked for something similar, some hill or mountain that I could climb to get a good look at what the Phoenix had bestowed upon the isle this year. I saw nothing that would work.

I did, however, see Seth winding his way through the trees. "Seth!" I yelled. "Over here."

Seth lived on the farm next to my parents' and was probably my best friend and favorite partner in crime. He spotted me, waved, and jogged a winding course through the brush to me. "Roy, do you see all the trees!" he burst out as if I wasn't practically standing under one. "There are trees everywhere!"

Seth stood about an inch shorter than my six-foot height. We were both seventeen, though I had filled out much more than Seth had. Seth still looked like a skeleton, though he could eat like a horse. In contrast, I had put on muscle and weight over the last few years to the point where I now rivaled my own father pound for pound. My black hair resembled a mop, waving about the top of my head, and I was seriously considering getting it cut short for this new environment. I could already foresee how attractive my hair would be to tics and fleas. The rain forest looked as if it bred those small menaces in entire colonies.

Few would call me handsome. My weathered face made what I was obvious to anyone at a glance: a poor farmer. In fact, probably the only physical feature I possessed that would catch a girl's eye would be my bright blue eyes.

Seth emulated the farmer's look as well as he could. He cared little for personal appearances and usually let his ragged brown hair do what it would. In fact, his hair looked like he had slept on rocks. Part of it was matted to his skull and other parts stuck straight up.

"What happened to you?" I asked, gesturing to his hair.

He looked sheepish. "I thought maybe I could stay awake on the roof. I'm telling you, roof tiles don't do your neck any good." He rubbed the offending spot with one calloused hand.

I grinned. "You tried to wait it out on the roof?"

"Yeah." He looked rueful.

"What if you fell off?"

"I tied myself to the peak with a rope."

That was too much. I doubled over laughing. Seth's face clouded over, which only set me off into more gales of laughter. "That is so stupid, Seth!"

"You have a better idea? Nothing we've ever tried has allowed either of us to stay awake during the Rebirth. I thought maybe a little altitude would help."

That only made me laugh again. Irritated, he shoved me, and I fell against one of the new trees growing next to the porch.

"Ouch!" I complained, rubbing my shoulder. "No call for getting mad. I didn't mean anything by it."

"Shut up." Seth was looking at the tree and the porch roof. "Hey, what about climbing this tree? I bet we can reach the lower branches from the porch roof."

I stepped away to get a better look. Various parts of the porch had been buckled in by the newly grown trees—and would require repair soon. It had been for this very reason that my father had built the porch to surround the house. Only the porch needed repair, not the house. "I think you're right. Let's do it."

No one could claim that my intelligence rated among the brightest in Khol, but I had one thing going for me: I never gave up. So, once determined to climb the tree, I was determined to conquer it or break a leg trying. Seth and I climbed atop the porch roof and then regarded the tall tree and its leafy canopy above. I calculated which branches I would need to reach to climb to the top and soon began my climb. Seth, bravely—or foolishly—followed me.

It took perhaps thirty minutes of careful and laborious climbing before I could stick my head above the canopy enough to look around. Seth joined me a few minutes later.

The sun was much brighter up there and only a few wisps of clouds dotted the blue sky. To the west, we could make out the bay that spilled out into the Endless Ocean. From this position, I could just make out the Dragon's Breath—a thick fogbank that surrounded the entire Phoenix Isle about fifteen miles or so offshore. The fog hid incredibly treacherous waters that prevented anyone from leaving the island. In my seventeen years of life, I had never heard of a successful escape from the island. In most cases, those that tried simply disappeared completely and absolutely. Only wreckage ever washed ashore. Most of the time. Sometimes people did too, alive and from beyond.

We could also see the spires of Khol, though little else of the city, hidden as it was behind the towering trees. I picked out what looked like the towers of the Singing Cathedral and of the palace. Although some of the towers might have been guard towers built along the wall. I idly wondered what those who lived there thought of this new transformation.

"Wow," Seth gasped, looking toward the south. "The trees go on forever!"

I turned to look in that direction and nodded. They did seem to stretch on and on, though perhaps ten leagues away, a forbidding mountain range poked up out of the rain forest. The mountains, of course, had no names since they had not been there the day before. The shape of the island never changed, so someone had gotten around to naming the ocean, but why name specific landmarks on the island when they would simply be different the next year?

Only one other feature of the island never changed. "Have you ever thought about going to see it? The Phoenix's nest, I mean," I said, pointing toward the very center of the island. I tried imagining what the nest might look like, but could not. Few people had ever seen the nest, and much of what anyone knew lay wrapped in secrecy and legend. Regardless, the nest was always located in the exact center of the island—or so everyone said.

"He's just a chick right now," Seth mused, "but in a month he'll be full-grown again. Maybe he'll even fly this way. I sure would love to have one of his feathers. Do you believe in that stuff? Do you believe that if you could get one of his feathers that you would then have a Gift? I sure would love a Gift!"

Not really knowing how to respond, I shrugged, which made the thin limb I stood on shake slightly. I stilled my body. "I'm not really sure what I believe. I would certainly love a Gift. Who doesn't? But the Phoenix is rather picky about who gets one." I refrained from shrugging again, but I was a bit perturbed by the notion. I didn't feel it was at all fair.

"What about the ashes? I've heard that ink made from the ashes of a Phoenix is powerful enough to give someone a Word of Power. All you have to do is write the word on your skin somewhere and the Word becomes part of you. I'd love a Word of Power."

"Oh? And what Word would you chose?"

"Strong," Seth replied instantly. "Then I could be strong enough to do anything. What about you?"

I thought about it for a moment. Honestly, I didn't know what I would want. All the words that came to mind seemed pathetic for one reason or another. Not sure what to say, but unwilling to leave it at that, I said, "I'd want 'fun.' Then I could pull pranks on everyone!"

Seth grinned. "You're evil, Roy."

I sighed in mock agreement. "I know."

Just then a dark cloud lifted out of the branches of a distant tree and began moving erratically toward us. I watched it curiously, not sure if this was a natural phenomenon of the rain forest or some aspect of the island itself.

"What's that?" I asked, pointing.

Seth turned to look and frowned. We watched for a moment more as it moved inexorably in our direction. Finally, I could make out specific details and fear gripped my heart.

"Seth, that's not a cloud."

"What?"

"Strix!" I shouted the dreaded name.

Strix were bat-like birds that swarmed their prey, taking bites out of the flesh of anything that moved with their fang-like teeth. The reason it had taken me so long to recognize the danger was because they had changed right along with the island. Last year they had been huge creatures with a wingspan of nearly five feet in length. They had hunted in small groups, as their size could not support a larger colony. But with the Rebirth, they had been transformed into a much smaller creature, roughly about the size of my fist. That would not be a problem in small numbers, but these strix had formed a colony that numbered in the hundreds. They would strip the flesh off their prey in minutes.

We were their prey.

"Hurry!" I shouted at Seth, who just stood there looking dumbfounded at the approaching strix. "Get down! Get down!" I couldn't move until Seth did. "Move!"

Finally, Seth moved. He ducked down below the leaves and began as rapid a descent as he could make. I did the same. I slipped almost immediately, losing my footing and my grip. I came down on top of Seth, who grunted as he was knocked loose too. We both fell, slamming into limb after limb. Fortunately, the branches were thick enough this high up that I finally managed to grab a branch and halt my descent, but only after banging my chin on it. Seth managed to do the same, but I could see blood flowing from a cut across his brow.

"Seth? You okay?"

"Yeah. I think so," he said shakily. "Why'd you have to fall on me?"

"Like I did it on purpose," I said defensively, finding a branch to brace my feet against. I tried controlling my heart since it seemed determined to pound itself right out of my chest.

"Roy, you're bleeding."

I looked down into my friend's scared eyes. "So are you."

There was a tense pause as we digested that bit of terrible news. Strix could smell blood, and it whipped them into an awful frenzy.

"Oh, ashes. We're in trouble," Seth murmured.

Just then the swarm dropped into the trees around us, and we were dodging strix from everywhere. We yelled ourselves hoarse as we flailed wildly about. We succeeded in striking a few of them hard enough to stun them into senselessness. They fell like fluttering leaves down through the branches of the trees.

But we were taking damage too. I got bit on the tip of my nose by a blue-headed strix with beady, black eyes. I yelled in pain and smacked it into the trunk of the tree. It fell from sight in a puff of bluish feathers. Another one bit me on the elbow, getting away with a small hunk of my flesh.

That made me mad!

The only thing Seth and I had going for us was the thick foliage of the rain forest trees. The denseness of the leaves and branches prevented the flesh-eating strix from maneuvering effectively. I managed to twist around and place my back against the trunk of the tree and brace myself enough to free up my hands for combat. Screams of pain and rage from Seth told me he wasn't faring well.

I spotted two strix coming at me in formation. They wove their way through the trees, making their run at my face. The black-headed one took a slight lead over the redheaded one as they suddenly twisted and dove right at my eyes. I ducked at the last moment and both of them plowed into the trunk of the tree. They made little "plop" sounds upon impact before falling toward the ground, stunned. Strix were not known for their intelligence.

While I was distracted, another took a bite out of my ankle. "Yeow!" I screamed, kicking at the darting strix. It dodged and came back for another bite. I kicked again, nearly losing my perch.

There were too many. For every one that Seth and I managed to hit, two more took its place as they slowly managed to penetrate the leafy tree and get at us. In desperation, I scrambled downward, slipping on branches, breaking some, and generally making my way down through sheer force of destructive energy more so than with any real finesse.

I lost sight of Seth at some point, though I could hear him above me now, thrashing about in his own battle with the vicious little birds. Another got a nip in on my finger, which really hurt. It also made me angrier. I stopped climbing and swung at the hovering beast, managing to smack it away. Unfortunately, the branch I was holding on to could not take the stress of my violent swing and it broke, causing me to flail desperately for some other handhold that didn't exist.

I fell.

Only I didn't fall far. The ankle of my right leg had somehow gotten wedged between two thick branches, and though my ankle twisted with my fall so that I did not break it, it was still firmly caught between the two. My head smacked the trunk of the tree—upside down. I saw bright lights for a moment as I dangled over empty space and a stab of pain ran the length of my body.

It took the slow thinking strix a moment to reorient on me since it seemed my fall had momentarily confused them, but when they did, I could practically hear them licking their chops at the helpless hunk of flesh dangling tantalizingly before them. And I didn't even know if they had tongues or chops!

The strix darted in for the kill, and that's when a thick plume of smoke rose up through the branches, engulfing us all. I began coughing violently, becoming disorientated quickly. I looked down—er...up in my case...or was it still down?—and peered through the smoke. I saw my father throwing wet wood on a blazing fire he'd built at the base of the tree. Another plume of thick smoke billowed upward, causing me to cough more. Above me—or below me, whatever!—I could hear Seth coughing likewise.

"Pa!" I cried. "You're killing us!"

The wide face of my father floated in the smoke as he looked up at me. "It's the only way to drive the strix away, Son!"

Indeed it was. The strix, having even less liking for the smoke than I did, had flitted away, leaving me dangling, but alive—or at least until the smoke killed me. "Pa! They're gone!"

"Not quite yet, Son. Hang on."

Oh, funny. Several disrespectful thoughts flashed through my head as I dangled helplessly in the tree, but they didn't stay long. If it hadn't been for my father's quick thinking, I would be strix food by now. I had enough sense at least to be grateful for that.

Finally, my father kicked the logs of the fire away and threw a bucket of dirt over the flames, which doused the smoke more effectively than water would have. The smoke began to dissipate, and I began to breathe easier.

The strix were gone, but worse than those evil creatures eating me into tiny bits was the fact that I had to be rescued by my pa. I'd never hear the end of it. Father took stock of my awkward position and frowned in perplexed anxiety. "How ever did you manage that, Son?"

I groaned, embarrassed, hurt, and rather put out by the whole ordeal. And that's when Seth climbed down to my level. He took one look at me hanging upside down and burst out laughing. Caught as I was in the tree, I couldn't even take a decent swing at him, and my glower only sent him into more gales of laughter.

CHAPTER TWO

I touched the dark purple bruise on the side of my face and winced in pain. "Leave it alone," Ma said as she walked beside me. "You'll only make it worse."

I grunted sourly and slowed up some as we wove through the new jungle. The bruise on my face wasn't the only thing that hurt, but none of it so much as my injured pride did at that moment. I really wasn't looking forward to having to explain it to my friends.

Lam, my pa, glanced at me, frowning. "Don't drag your feet, Son."

"We've got time," I grumbled. "There's another hour yet before the sixth bell."

My father's wide shoulders never wavered as he picked his way through the jungle. His hair had long since started to gray, but he still retained more power in his frame than most men I knew. He wielded a machete that I didn't even know we owned and used it to cut away vines, leaves, branches, and underbrush to ease Ma's path. His corded muscles bulged with each swing, and he seemed tireless.

Our farm lay a half mile from the south entrance of Khol, but with the Rebirth we had to make a new path just to get there, making the going somewhat slow. Still, Pa plowed ahead nearly as quickly as if strolling along a paved road, leaving cut branches and vines in his wake.

"I don't want to be late," Lam said. "And neither do you. If we have to stand in the back, you'll be the last to the food."

That did add a bit of haste to my steps. My stomach growled in anticipation. Ma noticed and chuckled, causing Pa to laugh as well. They understood me all too well.

"This will be a good year, Ruth," Lam said. "I just know it."

"Aye, the Year of the Lamb," she answered. "It's always been a good year afore."

"The ground is fertile, despite all these Abyss-spawned trees. Once we clear enough space, I think we'll bring in a good crop this year." I looked up when I heard the hesitation in my father's voice. "Maybe even enough to carry us through next year," he finished.

That ended the conversation as surely as if someone had cut our tongues out. Next year would be the Year of the Dragon, the most dreaded year of the Phoenix Cycle. In my seventeen years of life, I had only lived through the Year of the Dragon twice. The first when I was but four, which I hardly remembered. But I had vivid memories of the last one six years ago. I still had nightmares of that year.

A short time later, we emerged from the jungle onto a wide cobblestoned court that had been built before the huge southern gate of Khol. The Moon Gate. Anything that wasn't manmade would change with the Rebirth. Centuries ago, the kings of Khol had paved over practically every inch of the city, including a wide courtyard in front of the gates. This prevented the land from changing too drastically near houses, shops, and other structures, significantly reducing the damage to the city itself. At the fringes of the courtyard, many of the cobblestones bulged upward, disrupted by the root systems of the new trees that grew right to the very edge. In a few days, men would come to cut down the trees close by and repair the stonework.

A huge stone wall, nearly forty feet tall and at least twenty feet thick, towered above the courtyard. I had heard once that the walls were seven miles long around the edge of the city. A good part of the city abutted the bay, and the walls came practically to the water's edge, the only notable exception being the docks.

Two guard towers bracketed the raised portcullis, and a steady stream of people, carts, wagons, and horses made their way over the cobblestones and into the city. I knew most of the people, seeing as they were our neighbors in nearby farms. A pair of guards loitered beneath the gate, absently watching the people coming in. There were dangers to be wary of, but mostly they were looking for people they did not know. People who might be from the southern city of Taninim. That was where the real danger to the city lay, as many strangers from nearby villages and towns had been arriving for days in anticipation of the Phoenix Festival. But that had stopped yesterday. Only a fool would be caught out in the open during the Rebirth. Most of those entering the city on this day were local farmers that the guards knew on sight.

Seth was already standing under the gate when we walked up. "'Bout time you got here," he said by way of greeting.

He had a bandage wrapped around his left hand and a bit of plaster stuck to his cheek where one of the strix had taken a fair bite out of him.

I turned to my parents. "I'll catch up with you later."

My father shifted to look the pair of us over. "Fine, but stay out of trouble." He waved the machete in our faces. "I mean it. If you don't, I'll tan your hide good—and I don't care how big you are. You hear me?"

"Yes, Pa," I said as meekly as I could. I glanced at the two guards standing nearby. They were grinning back at me in a way that made me want to punch someone. "I'll stay out of trouble."

Pa glared at me as if he didn't believe a word of it. I swallowed. "You better," he growled. "If the constable has to visit us one more time—" He bit off whatever else he intended to say and just shook the machete violently mere inches from my eyes.

"Leave off, Lam," Ma said. "You've made your point."

"We'll see," he grumbled.

As my parents disappeared into the crowd, I heaved a sigh of relief. Just thinking of the constable made me nervous. The chief law enforcer of Khol possessed a Word of Power that could cause people to submit immediately to any threat against him, even against their will. The man didn't even need to wear a sword to do his job.

I shuddered again and put the man firmly out of my mind. Perhaps now I could find a bit of fun before the Gathering took place. That would cheer me up.

One of the guards chuckled loud enough to draw my attention. "You'd think, Roy, that you would learn to stay out of trouble. I've seen your father handle an axe. I wouldn't want him angry with me."

I swung about to look at the young man, at least five years my senior. "It's my problem, Jair. Don't worry about me."

Jair adjusted his helmet and his spear then shrugged. "Just trying to be friendly."

Muttering under my breath, I grabbed Seth's arm and pulled him into the city proper.

"Hey," he protested. "Don't get angry with me! I didn't do nothing!"

I let go of his arm. "Sorry. I never thought I would get away from them." I gestured toward where my parents had disappeared. "My Pa has had me cutting down trees since he *saved* us from the strix."

Seth winced. "I know the feeling." He looked at his calloused hand—one heavily bandaged—and shrugged. "But we're free now. Come on. We need a good spot at the Gathering."

"Maybe we can find Vin first," I suggested.

"He knows which way we would be coming, Roy. Come on. I want to see the princess."

"You always want to see the princess," I muttered, but I allowed him to tug me into a fast walk. We took Lion Street into the heart of the city.

Khol had been built at the edge of a bay. The bay emptied out into the Endless Sea to the north, but the bay itself was a prime source of fish for the city. The city sprawled along the coast in a crescent moon shape, and the only unwalled portion of the town lay directly to the west where the docks were. Directly ahead I could see the towering spires of the Singing Cathedral, a massive circular structure that housed, among other things, the university. Two miles to the north stood the palace, taking up the entire northern spur of the town. Several towers and spires of the palace could be seen even above the two and three-story buildings that lined the street.

I plowed ahead with Seth, making our way through the crowd converging on the Naming Plaza where the Gathering would take place. Not everyone would come, of course, but the traditional announcement of the new year by King Emeth kicked off the Phoenix Festival—and free food—so it was generally well attended. Besides, with so many people around, the opportunities for a bit of mischief abounded.

I touched the tip of my nose as we walked and winced. I hated strix. Still, even that reminder of our misadventure of the morning was lost in the bustle of activity around us. Much of the conversation I overheard centered on all the trees. Wood meant fuel, and fuel meant industry. Industry meant profit. People were excited.

We passed hawkers trying to capitalize on the influx of people to the city and shouting their wares overtop of one another. Everyone seemed to be gaily dressed, some in costume for the pageantry later on. Farriers worked on horses in stalls, blacksmiths banged away at their forges, and curriers worked on leather saddles. There were musicians at practically every corner regaling people with songs and stories; masons roaming about doing little, but taking inventory of the damage the Rebirth had caused; and seamstresses doing brisk work selling costumes for the festivities.

More people than at any other time of the year had crowded into Khol, and I let it wash over me. Opportunity abounded. "Perhaps we should get a costume," I suggested. "It would be funny to sneak into one of the pageants."

Seth shook his head. "You know how seriously they take that, and too many of the City Servants will be there watching. They'll truss us up and throw us in a cell faster than we could breathe."

I grunted. Seth was right. It wasn't a good plan. "A costume still might come in handy."

"Maybe," Seth allowed. "What about pulling the wheel pins on a couple of wagons? The wheels would come off, and if we picked the right wagon, we could block an entire street! That would be funny."

I thought about it. Finally, I shook my head. "No, I saw that happen once and a man got caught underneath the wagon, crushed both his legs. I don't want to hurt anyone, just have a bit of fun."

"Guess so," Seth said, looking a bit glum. "I still think it would be funny."

"What would be funny?" a voice asked from just behind us.

I gave a violent start and whipped around, my heart in my throat. "Vin!" I gasped. "You nearly made me swallow my tongue! I thought you were one of the Watch!"

"Sorry." Vin grinned at us. That, added to his baldhead and tight skin, made him look something like a gaping skull. At sixteen he loved to trail along with Seth and me, having long ago shunned most of the other young men in the city. He was a stalky lad with nearly the muscle mass to rival my own. He had a devious mind and absolutely loved the mischief we got into. I often had to rein him in on his wilder notions. At the moment, he wore a flamboyantly colored red shirt and odd-looking blue trousers. A wicked looking dagger hung from a rope belt.

"Where did you get that?" I asked, pointing at the dagger.

"Found it," he said shrugging.

Seth scowled. "You stole it, didn't you?"

"What of it?"

I poked Vin in the chest. "You know what they do to thieves. Why would you steal anyway? The City Servants make sure everyone gets food and clothes."

Vin's grin slipped away. He plucked at his garish shirt. "You call this good clothing?" He snorted. "I look like a clown."

Vin was a street waif, orphaned years ago when his parents had both come down sick and died. Vin had been sick too, which led to his baldness. Not a hair grew on his body, not even eyebrows. He could live in one of the shelters provided around the city, be fed and clothed, but he disdained it. Instead he lived on the streets, salvaging what he could find and thieving the rest. My parents didn't like him, but I felt sort of sorry for him, and so I'd allowed him to tag along on our escapades. Besides, no one knew the city better than Vin. That knowledge had allowed us to escape any number of instances when the City Watch had shown up too early.

I decided to change the subject. "We were trying to think of what we could do for fun."

Vin's grin reappeared as if conjured. "I know what we can do."

"Oh," I asked interested as I dodged around a cart full of bolts of cloth. "What?"

"Her." Vin pointed.

I followed his finger and spotted Skinny Minnie talking to another woman at the corner of Lion Street and Ox Street. To say that she was skinny would be an understated description of the girl. The girl was downright emaciated. She wore a long, off-white dress that fell in straight lines around her body. Her long face looked like someone had squeezed a banana too hard. Her thick brown hair framed her face in such a way that made her look even skinner—if that was possible. I suppose if she put on a bit of weight, she might turn into a pretty girl, but for whatever reason, she was rail thin. Even her arms stuck out like sticks, practically all bone. I knew her well. She had been the target of numerous pranks over the years, and remained one of my favorite sources of fun. Mostly because I couldn't stand her arrogance. The girl thought she was better than anyone else just because King Emeth had made her his ward after her parents died.

Vin more than agreed with me. Every year on the last day of the Festival, King Emeth selected an orphaned child to make his ward. He would then see to it that the child had a good education and was apprenticed to a suitable trade when old enough. None of the wards actually lived in the palace, but they did get to live in the Old City, the part of the city where only the City Servants could live.

Minnie, for whatever reason, rubbed me the wrong way. But if I had a benign dislike for her, Vin had a downright hatred for the girl. He, as he often liked to point out, had never been chosen to be a ward of the king. The year he might have been eligible, Minnie had been chosen instead of him.

"Did you have something in mind?" I asked.

"Every day between the sixth bell and the seventh, she goes to the Sun Gate to deliver something to the guards there. Normally she's accompanied by a few other girls, but during the next two days she'll be alone. We could catch her as she is making her way to the Naming Plaza either tomorrow or the next day." Vin's dark eyes gleamed evilly.

"And do what?" I asked warily.

Vin eyed me sideways. "I don't know. Teach her a lesson."

I shook my head. "I don't mind putting her in her place," I pointed out, "but I won't hurt her. You understand?"

The bald youth nodded sullenly. By this time we had walked near where Minnie was still talking to the other woman. Minnie spotted the three of us, and her lips compressed tightly as she followed us with her eyes.

I couldn't resist. "Hey, Skinny Minnie," I called, grinning. "Are you going to be part of the pageant tonight? You would make a great troll!" Trolls, of course, were anything but skinny, but the incongruent image sent all three of us into gales of mocking laughter.

Skinny's face paled—always a sure sign I had gotten to her—and she glared back fiercely. "What happened to your face?" she retorted. "See yourself in a mirror and get into a fight?"

My laughter cut off abruptly, and I came to a dead stop, turning toward her. But the woman Minnie had been talking to stepped around the younger girl and glared at us. "Get out of here, you delinquents, before I report you to the Watch!"

That was enough to send all three of us scampering away. I didn't hear any laughter from Minnie, but I imagined it. "Oh it's on!" I muttered. "We'll trail her tomorrow night and see if an opportunity to make her cry presents itself."

Vin nodded soberly, his features dark. I wasn't too pleased myself. The woman had called us delinquents, perhaps one of the worst things that could be said to a youth in the city. There weren't many, but once someone was charged with delinquency and so Named, they couldn't find a job, they couldn't be apprenticed, they couldn't buy anything on credit, and hardly anyone would trust them. Most who were so Named would leave the city and never return; but those that did stay lived worse than vagabonds. I didn't much like being taken for such. Minnie would pay for causing that remark.

Seth slugged me on the shoulder. "It's a plan. But right now, we need to hurry! Come on! It's almost the sixth bell."

Vin looked confused.

"He wants to see the princess," I explained.

Vin's grin came back. "She is quite pretty," he admitted. "Too bad she'll never notice the likes of us."

Seth rolled his eyes. "You just wait. One day I'll get a Gift and then she'll notice me."

I slugged him back. "Keep dreaming, farmer!" I dodged another punch, and we ran off toward the Naming Plaza hoping to get a good vantage point to watch the pageantry and the Gathering Ceremony.

The plaza was already packed with people except for the cleared space at the northern portion. That would be where the king and his family sat, slightly above a raised platform where the annual Phoenix pageant would be performed.

I was tall enough to see, but Seth grumbled at having to step up on his toes. "There's got to be a better spot than this," he complained.

Vin looked around. "There," he said, pointing. "That's Master Finley's goldsmith shop. There is a back staircase that leads up to his apartment above his shop. His youngest daughter got married last spring and moved out. He doesn't use her room anymore, and it overlooks the plaza. We could watch everything from there."

"Finley won't mind?" I asked doubtfully.

"He'll never notice. He and his wife will be too busy minding the shop underneath, what with all these people clustered about."

I nodded. "Lead the way."

Vin took us on a circular route of back streets and allies until we reached a cobbled alley behind Finley's shop. The building, like all buildings in Khol, was made with brick and stone. We found the staircase easily enough and hurried up to the second floor door. Sure enough, the door was unlocked, and we made our way to a room that harbored dusty furniture, a reminder of a time that would never again come for Finley. The window, however, provided an excellent view of the plaza.

We were just in time.

"There she is," Seth whispered excitedly. I looked. The royal family was arriving from where Lion Street continued on toward the north. They rode in an open carriage to the cheers of those lining the streets and buildings. A roar of approval erupted from the plaza below as people began catching sight of the king.

King Emeth, a widower for many years, sat in the front seat alone, while members of the King's Guard walked along side of the open carriage. I couldn't make him out much at that distance, but he looked regal enough in his stately robes and the Phoenix Crown on his brow. Two others sat just behind him.

One was Prince Bain, a young man roughly the same age as Seth and me. I had never really met him, but he had never struck me as the sort you would want to go out and have fun with. I couldn't ever recall seeing him smile before. He had a reputation for being a fierce swordsman, but drawn to a brooding, black disposition. People had a hard time relating to him, unlike his father whom everyone loved.

Beside Bain sat Princess Kyrin. Even from this distance, we could all tell how beautiful the girl was—though little else. She was several years younger than her brother, but rumor had it that any number of suitors had already been lining up to court her. Seth would be one of them if he had his way. By the Phoenix, I would be too, but I had enough sense to realize how absurd the notion actually was.

The carriage came to a stop, and the three walked directly onto the raised platform and to the three seats sitting above the audience. They would have a front row seat to the pageantry from an angle that allowed the people to watch them as much as they did the pageant. Watching the king and his family, of course, was as much fun as the pageantry, so the people approved of the seating arrangements.

Bain and Kyrin took their seats, but King Emeth remained standing in front of his chair, waiting. A few moments later, the bells from the Singing Cathedral pealed over the city, marking the sixth bell, the eighteenth hour of the day. The bells had a soothing quality to them, and the crowd hushed in anticipation.

As the last note faded on the humid air, the king raised a hand. "Welcome, dear friends," he called in a voice that carried easily across the entire plaza. "In accordance with tradition on the first full moon after the Spring Equinox and the Rebirth of the Phoenix, I proclaim this new year to be the Year of the Lamb!"

A vast cheer rang out over the pronouncement. When it died down, King Emeth continued, "May this year be one of bounty and blessing. I call upon all citizens of Khol to see sacrifice as an act of beauty, a measure of our hearts, not merely a duty to perform or an act of necessity, but one of pleasure. If all of us join in this, we will be prepared to stand against anything that would harm us or destroy the ideals of the Phoenix."

A dramatic hush fell over the people as the king turned to an aging man, one known far and wide as the king's Blesser, though, strangely, no one seemed to know his name. The king gestured while saying, "We will now seek the Blessing for the new year."

The older man climbed up on the platform and turned to face the crowd. He held his hands up and began speaking in a soft voice that I had to strain to hear, "May the Blessing of the Phoenix be upon all the people of Khol, and may this be a year of bounty—" he hesitated "—and enlightenment."

A simple Blessing, but potent. The power the man possessed was well known. When he Blessed something, things tended to go right. I had high hopes for this year. The king's Blesser didn't always bestow such a straightforward Blessing. Only that slight hesitation had caused me to frown. The crowd below, however, erupted in cheers once again.

King Emeth raised his hands, patting the air for quiet. When he had it, he announced, "Now, let the pageant begin!"

As he sat down to more cheering, the players of the pageant began to emerge onto the platform. The first player, dressed as a red Phoenix, regal looking and majestic, stood peacefully on the platform looking over the crowd like a benevolent ruler. He spread his wings and began reciting the Phoenix Canticle in high chant, his voice washing over the crowd, stilling even the most fidgety of children. Music underscored the words, lifting the chant into flows of tones and notes that riveted the mind.

"I am the offspring of the light, birthed in light 'er the sun was created. Before the first drop of sunlight touched the earth, my birth heralded creation and joy. Sent to watch, sent to Gift, sent to be, I am the sentinel of righteousness and peace."

The man continued his recitation, and I listened, entranced by the cadence and pure joy of the words. But then the Dragon appeared—a player dressed as a black, serpent-like creature with a mouth full of teeth—to challenge the Phoenix for the right to rule the world.

The Dragon wished to enslave mankind and dominate them. The Phoenix wished to see the world free of the Dragon's evil touch. A battle ensued whereby the island was created and the Dragon trapped in the Abyss on the island. So long as the Phoenix lived, the Dragon was trapped on the island.

In a horrific rage, the Dragon smote the island, poisoning it and bringing forth corruption. The Dragon's Breath, a misty barrier, sprung up around the island, trapping the Phoenix with the Dragon. Men would come, shipwrecked from Outside, but washed ashore and trapped here, unable to leave.

The Phoenix, to prevent the corruption from contaminating the land forever, made the ultimate sacrifice: dying each year to be reborn in its own ashes. Such a great sacrificial death rekindled and replenished the land, pushing the Dragon's Breath back out to sea where it would slowly encroach on the land over the next year until a new Rebirth pushed it back. Thus began a cycle of death and rebirth that kept the Phoenix and the Dragon ever imprisoned on the island; but such an imprisonment protected the world beyond the island from the Dragon's direct touch.

The Dragon spawned evil creatures from its own blood to disrupt the balance and slay the Phoenix: elves, trolls, ennedi, strix, anansi, cockatrices, and satyrs appeared to kill and devour the Phoenix. In response, the Phoenix brought forth goodly creatures, born from its own ashes, to restore the balance: simurghs, unicorns, finrir, gnomes, hibagons, lamassus, and sylphs.

Great was the Dragon's rage, so he struck at the heart of the Phoenix by reaching out and touching the hearts of men, corrupting them by bestowing mighty Gifts upon those who would worship the Dragon. Men who would dominate and destroy, defile and control. Those men rose up and laid waste to the island, seeking even to murder the Phoenix once and for all and set their master free.

To counter this, the Phoenix sought goodly men, men of purity, men who held true to a servant's heart. To them the Phoenix bestowed Gifts of his own, and balance was restored once again. Evil men were defeated and driven to the far south where they nursed their anger and vengeance. As long as the Phoenix lived, men of good and right would always win out.

The pageant ended to thunderous applause. The players took a last bow as the musicians played a triumphant theme to conclude the play. I clapped enthusiastically as did Seth, though Vin only scowled. He found very little that interested him other than getting into trouble.

"That seemed better than last year," I commented.

Seth agreed. "Whoever played the Phoenix did a wondrous job." Seth's voice sounded awed. "I wonder if I could ever become a player."

I grinned. "Sure, you could play one of the sylphs."

Seth shot a glare at me. "Only girls play that part."

"Yeah? So?"

That earned a punch to my arm, but I only laughed. "Let's get down there before all the food is gone!"

The end of the pageant signified the start of the end-of-day feast, and already men and women were serving the crowd from the backs of carts and wagons at the edge of the plaza. I could smell it from the top of the goldsmith shop, and my mouth watered.

Seth and Vin nodded enthusiastically. As we retraced our steps to get down to the plaza floor, Vin said, "Tomorrow, you guys going to meet me so we can fun Skinny Minnie?"

I had almost forgotten about her. "Sure," I said as it all came back to me. "I owe her for that remark about my face."

Vin's smile reappeared. "Great. Think of something good though."

"I always do," I said modestly. I was the brains of this little operation.

CHAPTER THREE

"**R**oy!" Seth hissed at me from just ahead. "I see her!" I tried to peek around Seth, but my angle was all wrong. We stood in the entrance of an alley, near the center of Khol on the last evening of the Phoenix Festival. Our wounds from our battle with the strix had generally healed, and we had thoroughly enjoyed King Emeth's generosity. Now we wanted a bit of memorable fun to cap it all off.

"You see Skinny Minnie?" I asked.

"Yeah, she's alone too."

"Told you," Vin said smugly from behind.

"You weren't right yesterday," I pointed out without looking back at him. "She wasn't alone then."

"But she is now, and that's all that matters. Where's she headed?" That last was directed at Seth.

"Can't tell," my friend replied, peering out. "Maybe the Naming Plaza? That's where everyone else is going."

I thought about the route Skinny would have to take. She wasn't taking the main route, but a more direct route through back streets. This would be our last chance to fun her, so I really needed to figure out her route. I thought of it, and my mind settled on a devious plan. I glanced back at Vin, who knew the city better than me or Seth. "She'll have to pass by Burk's stables, won't she?" I asked, a tone of utter cunning bleeding through my voice.

The sun hung low in the west, giving enough light to see by, but by this time the lamplighter would most likely be making his rounds before it got too dark, lighting the oil lamps along the main streets.

In the deep shadows, I could just make out Vin's baldhead. It seemed to glow a bit. He blinked, but when what I had in mind dawned on him, a sinister smile crept over his lips. "Perfect. I know how we can get there before she does. Oh, this will be great!"

Seth looked a bit perplexed, but he followed as we turned and dashed back down the damp alley. Usually, a few vagabonds occupied various corners, but most, if not all, had gone to the city plaza to take advantage of King Emeth's generosity and gorge themselves on free food and drink; so we encountered no one as we dashed through the back streets of Khol.

Vin knew exactly where to go. He spent much of his time wandering around the city, doing everything in his power to avoid anything that remotely looked like honest work. Frankly, I thought he put more effort and energy into being lazy than he would working. But I couldn't fault him much. I tried doing the same thing—if not quite to the degree my friend took it. Vin was a thief, a braggart, and a liar—if not on his way to eventually becoming a detestable drunk. Vin was exactly the sort of person my mother always warned me against. But, to be frank about it, I didn't care. Vin was a lot of fun, and I wanted some fun. I could keep his wilder impulses under control, so I didn't worry.

We quickly navigated the city and reached Burk's stables ahead of Skinny Minnie. Burk owned the oldest stables in the city, inherited from several generations of his forefathers. As the city had expanded, Burk's stables found itself more in the center of the city rather than being located at the outskirts with the other stables. This worked out well enough for those looking to transport goods just between points within the city.

Because of this, Burk owned mostly pack mules, good for pulling carts and wagons. The mules themselves lived on the ground floor, but the manure was carted up to the second floor and dumped into a disposal shoot that, once full, could be released into a wagon waiting below on the street. I knew of this because my father often bought manure to fertilize our fields in years when the land wasn't so fertile. We would drive a wagon under the shoot, Burk would release a lever, and the manure would spill into the wagon bed. It was a good system, and now it would be the source of some quality fun.

We arrived in plenty of time and surveyed the street. Everyone had gone to the Festival, so the street looked deserted. The street lamps had already been lit, so the lamplighter had come and gone too. Perfect.

"We've got to get her to walk under the shoot," Vin said.

"Why don't we block off the street so that the only place she can walk is right underneath?" Seth suggested.

I looked more closely at the situation. "She'll probably get suspicious if we try that. We need to keep her distracted so she doesn't realize where she's walking. Grab a couple of those sticks by the wall. Vin, you hide up the street. Let her pass you. Seth, you hide a bit down the street. Once she is near the shoot, both of you come out. Yell at her, wave your sticks around. She'll have no choice but to retreat under the shoot. That's when I'll pull the lever." I grinned.

Seth and Vin grinned right along with me. Vin rubbed his hands together. "That'll teach the tramp. She thinks she's better than everyone else."

I nodded. She was the king's ward. Rumor had it that the king himself was once an orphan, but I had never met anyone who knew for sure. "Just don't get carried away," I warned. "Remember, she is the king's ward, and the last thing we need is the king getting involved personally."

"It's not fair," Vin muttered. "She's always got her nose stuck up, looking down at the rest of us."

Actually, I didn't think she did that...much. I had nothing personal against Minnie. She was just an easy target of opportunity. Because she didn't have parents, she lived at the mercy of the king; but the king was too busy to deal with minor matters of pranks, so Minnie had become one of my favorite sources of entertainment over the last seven years or so. I even had a secret rating system. If she just got angry, then it was a minor success; but if she cried, then I had really scored.

"Get into your places, hurry!" I shooed my cohorts away and went to find my own position by the lever. I could see the bulging sides of the manure shoot, so I knew there would be plenty of the foul stuff to dump on her head. Oh this was bound to make her cry for sure!

I looked up the street in time to see Minnie coming our way. She wore a pale red dress that still made her look like a stick. I shook my head in wonder. I didn't know how anyone could get so skinny.

I hunkered down behind some water barrels so she wouldn't see me and waited for the show to begin. It didn't take long. The moment Minnie came even with the stables, Seth and Vin stepped out and began advancing on her.

"Hey, Skinny Minnie," Seth shouted to get her attention. "Wanna dance? I brought my own stick. See?" He held the stick up and waved it rather threateningly.

Minnie stopped in her tracks, her eyes going a bit wild. "Stay away from me, Seth! I mean it!" Her voice rose into a high pitch.

"Where you going, Skinny? You can't get away from us."

That prompted her to look behind where she saw Vin advancing toward her, his own stick sweeping from side to side. "Just let me go," she pleaded.

I snickered softly. She had no clue.

Seth and Vin advanced toward her on the opposite side of the street from the stables. In order to back away from them and retain as much distance as possible, Minnie began to edge toward our trap.

"Let you go?" Vin said, his voice dropping and his tone menacing. "Not until we teach you a lesson, girl."

I frowned at that. That seemed a bit too much. Well, I could handle Vin. We would spring the trap, and then I'd hustle Vin away, laughing.

Terrified now, Minnie backed all the way under the manure shoot. Oh, how perfect! I jumped to the lever and pulled. The spring-loaded door at the top of the shoot was pulled away, and piles of smelly, icky, and gloopy manure fell right on target.

Minnie screamed as the stuff hit her, plastering her hair to her face, running down her cheeks and off her nose, staining her dress, and piling up at her feet. There was more manure than I had expected, and Minnie was practically buried in the stuff. Oh, what joy!

All three of us began to laugh and laugh as Minnie began to cry, struggling vainly to extricate herself. I couldn't help it. It was just too funny. What perfect revenge for that comment about my face!

Seth dropped his stick, holding his sides as he laughed. Vin, however, edged forward, poking his stick at the goop around Minnie, shoving some of it more firmly around her shoes and dress. He didn't laugh so much as grin wickedly.

That, plus Minnie's sobs, sobered me up some. I looked into Minnie's eyes for the first time and saw something there that I had never seen before. I had pulled other pranks on her, but this one was by far the most humiliating. Something there in her eyes made me feel uneasy. She didn't look angry as her tears mingled with the manure on her cheeks. She looked resigned, as if the life had been sucked right out of her.

Suddenly, I felt a bit guilty.

"Come on guys, let's get out of here," I urged. I didn't want to look at her eyes anymore.

Seth nodded. "Yeah…before the constable shows up."

Vin, however, seemed uninterested in leaving the scene of the crime just yet. He started poking Minnie with the stick, trying to push her over. She tried to push the stick away, but her sobs only made her body shudder and shift some of the manure around. Her efforts were largely futile.

"Vin!" I ran over to him and jerked him away from Minnie. "That's enough. Let's go."

"I don't think she's learned her lesson yet," he shot back, yanking his arm out of my grasp and advancing on Minnie once again. She cowered, unable to flee.

I went to stop him and that's when he did something completely unexpected. He pivoted and smacked me over the head with his stick. The branch broke over my hard head, but the blow had enough force in it to knock me on my backside. I sat down hard, dazed by the blow.

"Vin!" Seth protested. "Why'd you do that?"

"You broke my stick," Vin accused me. He looked around. "Gimme yours," he demanded of Seth.

"You're crazy!" Seth shouted back.

About that time, the constable arrived with four of his men. In such a large city, it never ceased to amaze me how often I ran into him. I wondered if the man followed me. Seth and Vin took one look at them and bolted like startled deer. Two of the men drew billy clubs and gave chase, but the fleet young men would soon disappear in the dark allies. The other two and the constable came over to where I was struggling to regain my feet. They caught my arms and held me still so the constable could look me over. He glanced at Minnie and his hard face softened in compassion. "Miss, did this delinquent do this to you?"

Despite the knock to my head, I shuddered at the use of that word. The last thing I wanted was to be officially labeled a delinquent. I opened my mouth to protest, but Minnie looked up with a tear-stained and grimy face to fix her eyes on me. I snapped my mouth shut. Silently, I pleaded with her to not turn me in, to let me go.

She nodded. "Yes."

The constable echoed her nod, his more grim. "And the other two?"

"Yes, but he's the ringleader," she said, pointing a quivering finger at me.

I started to protest, but the constable spoke a Word of Power and suddenly the ringing in my ears clanged loudly. I blinked, trying to focus as the world spun around me. I hadn't heard the Word spoken, but it had effectively silenced me.

"You best not say anything, delinquent." The constable considered me like one would an unwelcomed guest. Turning to his remaining men, he said, "Help Minnie and see that she gets back to her home safely. I'm taking this oaf to see Justice Yosher."

My entire body turned cold despite the stifling humidity in the air. Justice Yosher possessed the Inner Eye and could peer into the very hearts and souls of men. Her judgment on matters was final. Not even the king questioned it. I tried to protest again, but my mouth wouldn't work. I could only provide token resistance as the constable dragged me away.

He didn't even seem to notice my weak protests.

* * *

Justice Yosher indicated a chair in the common room of her house. "Have a seat, Roy."

I looked nervously over my shoulder, but the constable still stood by the door, effectively blocking any escape attempt I might make. Even if I could overpower the constable, evade his reputed deadly sword arm, and make it to the door, I knew he could stop me with but a spoken Word. Like the king, both men possessed a Word of Power, a Gift from the Phoenix. The king could cause anyone to speak the truth by merely placing emphasis on some version of the word "truth." The constable could negate intention by emphasizing various forms of the word "no."

The king's ability was substantially stronger. You merely had to be in range of his voice to be affected. The constable's Word of Power only worked on those acting against him directly.

Still, it made him very formidable. I always wondered why he bothered to carry a sword. He never had to use it.

"Please, Roy," Justice Yosher said softly, "sit down. I have no intention of hurting you."

I sank into the chair since it seemed foolish to remain standing. I turned my attention to the woman who would no doubt seal my fate. She looked radiant in her blue dress. Somewhere in her forties, she could easily be mistaken for a woman much younger. Unmarried, dedicated to her service to the city and the Phoenix, she was held in awe by the entire population of Khol for the strength of the Inner Eye she possessed.

I squirmed in my seat, unsure what it would feel like when she laid bare my soul. I suspected a burning sensation would start in my heart as she peeled all the layers of my soul back. I set myself to resist with all my strength.

She suddenly smiled, and her perfect white teeth showed. "Roy, you have nothing to fear. I have already looked into your heart. I know you. It is done."

I blinked, surprised. "That didn't hurt."

She chuckled and swept her blond hair back off her ears. "Knowing someone's heart is always easier than telling it to them, Roy. It will be my words that bring pain, not my power."

"I don't understand."

She sighed and sank down in the chair opposite me. A small table with a vase of flowers sat between us. Other than a shelf full of scrolls and old tomes, the room was decorated with a scattering of wall pictures. One of them showed a huge red bird of a noble bearing. It was a painting of the Phoenix, I gathered.

She spoke, drawing my attention back to her. "It is hearing the truth of yourself that you will find most painful, Roy.

Everyone does. Most people cannot accept who they really are. In fact, in most cases, they really don't even want to know." A sad smile graced her lips. "Unfortunately for me, this means I have few real friends."

"You seem nice enough," I said, meaning it. So far this had not gone nearly as badly as I had expected.

"Thank you, but you may change your mind after you hear what I have to say."

I shifted uncertainly, saying nothing.

"Roy, I have looked upon your heart with the Inner Eye. There is no secret of your character that is hidden from the Eye. Although I cannot read specifics, I can determine the general character and disposition of those I look upon. In your case, Roy, there are several things you need to hear. Regarding your character, you are lazy, rebellious, and disagreeable."

"No I'm not!" I disagreed vehemently.

She raised a pretty eyebrow at me. I'd opened my mouth to protest when the truth of what I'd just said dawned on me. I snapped my mouth shut.

"Do you not try to get out of as much work as you can? Do you not disobey your elders in matters where you think they do not understand? Do you not disagree with what I am saying right now?"

"No—I mean, yes…er, that is no…" I grunted irritably, flustered. Had I just agreed or disagreed? Angry, I muttered, "I'm not as bad as all that!"

"Are you saying that you are not a negative person?"

"No!" I hesitated. "Yes! I mean…" I growled low in my throat, frustrated. The woman could twist a word like a top.

Then she struck while she had me backpedaling. "Do you remember Alice from three years ago? Your little prank cost her half of that year's crop."

"Now that wasn't my fault. Vin—"

She cut me off. "What about Luke's barn?"

"That was an accident. How was I supposed to know the fire would—"

"And then there was the anansi spiders you put into widow Dora's house. She and her daughters had nightmares for weeks until someone realized what was causing them."

"No one can prove I did that," I said emphatically, my heart racing. I knew she knew I had done it. All she had to do was look into my heart. Still, a bluff might work. One could never tell. I had liked that particular prank. The anansi spiders had been tiny that year, but because they fed off of fear, they caused irritation, nightmares, and anger, even so small. I had laughed for days at their irrational antics.

"The spiders were also sucking their blood, Roy. They got very sick."

"How was I supposed to know they'd do that?" I blurted, realizing only belatedly that I'd just admitted to the crime.

She sighed. "You are seventeen, Roy. That is an age where adult responsibilities begin to intrude on your life. Do you not resent these responsibilities? You seek your fun at the expense of others, teasing them, playing pranks on them. In effect, you are a bully."

"No, I'm not! I'm just having fun. I don't mean anything by it." My face began to turn red. I did not like hearing this.

She smiled slightly. "Every bully I've ever talked to says the same thing, Roy. No bully sees what they do as wrong. You're just having fun. You don't mean anything by it. This, Roy, is the definition of a bully. You act without thought of the way your pranks make others feel. You don't know what the consequences of such behavior is, so you take no personal responsibility for those actions. To you, it is just fun and games."

I opened my mouth to protest again, but an image of Minnie's defeated eyes popped into my mind, stifling my words.

Justice Yosher nodded. "Yes, you have treated Minnie badly. I have not looked upon her, but I suspect she is broken. You, Roy, are partially responsible for her broken spirit. Right now you are trying to deny this, trying to dismiss your role in this tragedy—and that is the core of your problem. You have good qualities too, such as loyalty and determination, but they are overshadowed, driven deep and hidden. And it is why I have no choice but to Name you Delinquent."

My heart fell into the pit of my stomach. I shook my head, trying to deny it. "That's not fair," I managed to whisper.

"Is it not? You don't think the truth is fair? Shall I lie then to empower you to continue in your destructive ways? No, I shall not."

Her eyes bore into mine, and I dared not object further under such scrutiny. Deep down, I knew it to be true.

"Do you know what this Naming means, Roy?"

I nodded, a turmoil of emotions churning in me. "A Naming is both a reputation and a responsibility—or a punishment. You have Named me Delinquent. Few will trust me. Most will shun me. I will be a vagabond or an outcast." Each of my words was said in utter bitterness. In my entire life, I had never felt such emotional pain. I sat there listlessly, the weight of the entire world crushing me into my chair.

She nodded in agreement with my assessment. "This is true. But it is not all the truth."

Something about the way she said that last statement caused me to look up, a quiver of hope rising into my heart. "What else is there?"

"A bad Naming is something to overcome. This Naming need not define you, Roy. There is an alternative."

I stared at her, hardly believing what I suspected her to be hinting at. "You mean a Gift, don't you?"

"I do. This is the Year of the Lamb. The lamb represents many things in our culture, but primarily it depicts sacrifice and responsibility. Maybe this is your year. If you were to be given a Gift from the Phoenix, you would be given a new Name, a surname. Mine is Yosher. I am Justice Holly Yosher. Holly is my birth name, but when the Phoenix gave me the Gift of the Inner Eye, I was also given the surname of Yosher, which means 'right.' The title of Justice is something bestowed upon me by King Emeth as a City Servant. Regardless, whatever I was before I received the Gift has now been erased."

"But the Phoenix only gives few people Gifts. How am I to get one?"

"You must go to the Phoenix himself. You must go to the nest. There you will find out if you are worthy of a Gift."

"A Quest," I whispered. "You want me to go on a Quest to the Phoenix's nest?"

"I don't want you to do anything, dear. I am telling you of an alternative. A Quest is wrought with danger. The interior of the island is overrun with creatures of both good and evil persuasion. Humans only live on the coast or near the shore as it is much more habitable for us—and safer during the Rebirth— but every year the interior is completely changed when the Phoenix is reborn, so there are no maps, no roads, and no easy way to the nest." She paused, obviously wondering if she should say anything else. She did, and I wished she hadn't. "The last Quest was three years ago, and the Quester never returned."

I swallowed hard. "Did you go on a Quest?"

"No, dear. The Phoenix came here and granted me my Gift. The only man alive today who has successfully completed a Phoenix Quest is King Emeth." She nodded over to her shelf of books. "I have histories that tell of others, but the only one I know of today is the king."

"The alternative is to live with your Naming?"

"I'm sorry, dear. That is the reputation you built. It is more your Naming than mine."

I nodded. It was as I suspected. I sat silently for a time, thinking. I didn't want to live with this Naming. I could leave, find one of the other human settlements along the coast and start over, but a Naming had a nasty habit of following a person. I doubted I would be able to run from it. No, if I wanted it to change, I would have to earn it. I made my decision.

"I will go on the Quest," I told her as emphatically as I could.

She smiled. "I knew you would. Now you must go to the king. All Questers are granted three boons before they begin."

I started. "You want me to begin right now?"

She laughed. "Not quite. It will take a week for all the details to be worked out. Your intent needs to be presented to the king and the court, then the city must be told." She paused. "And only then, when you are officially called, can you go before the king and receive three boons from the Phoenix Throne."

"Still, that seems awfully soon," I hedged.

"We'll announce your intent to the king tomorrow. Before you know it, you'll be off."

Then my rebellious nature won out and I asked, "Why not make the announcement tonight?"

She raised another pretty eyebrow. "You have an apology to make and some manure to shovel first."

"Oh."

CHAPTER FOUR

I glanced nervously at the imposing doors that led to the King's Court. My parents, Ruth and Lam, walked behind me, just as nervous as I was. They'd tried desperately to talk me out of venturing on the Quest for the better part of the last week, but the more they begged me, the more determined I was to go through with it. They knew about the Naming, they knew that I would essentially be an outcast or a vagabond, but they also knew the dangers of a Quest. To them, living as the dregs of society was a much better fate than I would find in the interior of the island on some foolish Quest.

That last statement, said in all sincerity, still irked me. Foolish or not, now I wanted to go just to prove them wrong. Somewhere in the back of my mind, I understood that my reasons for going were stupid, but I shoved those thoughts as far back in my brain as I could. For me, there was no turning back.

Since I was of the age where I could make those decisions for myself, my parents grudgingly fell silent in their appeals. Mother wept tears, of course, and Father looked sternly disapproving, but I had armored my heart against all of it. I meant to show the whole lot of them that I wasn't a Delinquent.

The two guards at the doors eyed me with something akin to respect. I puffed out my chest at that. After all, it had been three years since the last Quest. I must be tremendously brave.

Or stupid, my father's unspoken thought somehow slipped into my head and rattled around uncomfortably. I threw a sour look at him, but he only looked baffled and sad. It had to be his thought, though, for it certainly hadn't been mine!

Turning back to the matter at hand, I nodded to the guards, who suddenly looked less impressed and more mischievous. Uncertain, I decided to ignore them both. One flung open the doors, and the other stepped inside immediately in front of us. In a booming voice, the second guard proclaimed, "Your Majesty, the Quester comes!"

That sounded all too official. Inside, the dull roar of hundreds of conversations cut off all at once. I straightened my plain looking leather tunic and adjusted my linen trousers, not that it made much difference, but I was feeling decidedly nervous again.

A herald responded, "The Quester may approach the king!"

The two guards stepped to one side, holding their pikes straight beside them. I noted their brandished armor and the Phoenix symbol emblazoned on their breastplates. Even their helmets gleamed. I readjusted my own drab clothing until a polite shove from my father sent me forward.

I slowly made my way down the center of the King's Court. The Court was rectangular in construction, with the doors and throne being on opposite sides of the long ends. Two rows of marble pillars reached high to the vaulted ceiling above on either side of the large central aisle. The wings of the Court held the crowd that had come to witness the beginning of my Quest. Hundreds of people lined the wings between the pillars, each watching me with expressions that ranged from curious to malicious. I snapped my eyes forward, trying to block the crowd out. I did spot, however, Seth and Vin moving through the crowd parallel to me on the right-hand side. I felt better immediately.

The central aisle had been overlaid in blue marble tiles, polished to a high sheen. I walked over them, my heavy boots clopping loudly. I cringed with each step as the sound seemed to echo through the chamber. At the far end of the Court, two gold-toned thrones sat on a raised platform. One of them, the Queen's Throne, remained empty. The queen had died many years ago. In the other, the Phoenix Throne, sat the king, waiting for my approach.

In his late fifties, King Emeth looked every inch the benevolent monarch. His iron-gray hair was encircled by a small circlet of gold, the badge of his office, and his smile seemed friendly, encouraging. This put me at ease a bit, and I straightened my steps, walking a bit more assuredly.

The Court staff stood arrayed around the thrones, but I tried to keep my eyes on the king only. I'd heard stories of some of the men and women who watched me approach. I didn't even want to meet eyes with any of them. One, the son of the king, Prince Bain, stood just to his father's right, behind the throne. I shuddered as he watched me like a hawk or one of the strix I had so recently fended off. That's when I noticed Justice Yosher standing farther off to my left, the king's right, but near the end of the raised platform. Her presence did give me some assurance. Despite what she had Named me, I knew her to be a caring woman.

Finally, I came to a halt, and my parents and I bowed low before the king. I then spoke the words I had been instructed to say. "Your Majesty, I come seeking three boons of thee so that the Phoenix Throne may aid me in my Quest."

Emeth nodded. "Indeed," he said, his deep voice carrying through the entire Court, "by ancient tradition, each Quester may seek three boons from the Phoenix Throne to aid him in his Quest. But first, Quester, do you understand the nature of your Quest?"

"I will seek to find the nest of the Phoenix and thereby be granted a Gift."

King Emeth frowned. "The Phoenix is under no obligation to grant you a Gift, Son. You understand that the failure of your Quest will mean that Justice Yosher's Naming will stand. You will be Named Delinquent for your many indiscretions. Having undertaken such a Quest myself, I know the hardships you will face, the danger. Is this Gift you seek worth risking your life over? I see in your parents' eyes that they do not wish you to go."

I licked my dry lips and considered. My natural instinct was to offer an obnoxious quip, my way of dismissing the danger before me; but I suspected such a course would not be profitable. Instead I said, "I am prepared to face these dangers. Justice Yosher has justly Named me, but she also said that I do not have to let the Naming define me. I hope to earn a different name on this Quest. I want to prove that I can have another name, a good name."

Out of the corner of my eye, I saw Yosher smiling slightly. That gave me hope. The king nodded gravely at my little speech. "Then receive your boons, Quester." He waved his hand and a man stepped forward. "The first boon is our Blessing."

I recognized the man who came to stand just in front of me as the same Blesser who had given the Blessing at the Festival. He was a slight man, his hair thinning, but his gray eyes were penetrating as he stared at me. He reached out and laid both hands on my shoulders. The man possessed the Blessing. When he Blessed a person, an object, or an endeavor, good things tended to happen. Coincidence turned favorable and chance meetings could become lifesaving events.

I felt a tingling in my body as the man said, "May the Phoenix Bless you and this Quest. May this Blessing be a shield from the Dragon's attention."

My confidence soared. I just knew I would complete my Quest now. A Blessing was a potent power that those with such a Gift rarely gave out, as it cost them something terrible, though exactly what that cost was I did not know. That bit about the Dragon's attention bothered me. Despite the pageant every year, I suspected the Dragon was nothing more than a myth. So why bring it up? Tradition? Regardless, I felt both honored and a bit unworthy. The strange man stepped back.

King Emeth motioned to a young woman who stood somewhat in the background. "The second boon is that of Foresight," the king announced.

Everyone knew of the Seer, Beth Chalom. The Phoenix had granted her the Gift of Sight. Of all those in Khol with the same Gift, it was said that hers was the most powerful. Emeth had moved quickly to include her in his Court. She practically flowed across the marble floor as she approached. Not ugly, not pretty, more handsome than anything, she exuded a sense of vibrant anticipation. Her white dress rustled softly against the tiles as she came to a stop before me. She carried a white staff, the symbol of her office. I smiled at her and she returned it.

Closing her eyes, she looked deep in herself, using a different Sight. Then she spoke in a musical tone, "Your way shall be fraught with danger, this is easy to see, but your fate shall be decided when you give up that which you hold most precious for that which you hold in disdain. Failure may be the path to success, and success may lead to failure. The choice will be yours."

Beth bowed slightly to me and glided away. I blinked in her wake, feeling confused. Some of my newly found confidence drained away. What kind of prophecy was that? That could mean anything! More importantly, it could mean nothing at all. I scowled at my feet, wondering if Beth Chalom was nothing more than a fraud. I glanced surreptitiously around and saw others nodding sagely, as if they understood it any better than I did. Yeah right. Year of the Lamb, huh? What did this prophecy represent? Stupidity? I shook my head in amazement.

My thoughts were interrupted by the king. "A potent prophecy, indeed, Quester." But even he looked uncertain. Emeth cleared his throat and continued, "The third boon is of thy choice, Quester. Ask and if it be in our power, we shall grant it thee."

Of the three, this was the one I thought to be of most value to me. Few people ever got the chance to ask for whatever they wanted. I had spent a lot of time earlier in the day thinking of what I would ask for. I had wrestled with a variety of things, such as a sword from the king's armory—they were reputed to have powerful properties forged into them—a finrir, hunting hounds that made great companions, and perhaps even a pardon of my Naming. The last, alas, would not be granted, I suspected, and I would still be required to go on the Quest. Ultimately, I decided upon a request that I felt sure would help me the most.

I cleared my throat and stepped a bit closer. "Your Majesty, for my third boon, I request a companion of my generation to journey with me on my Quest."

A shocked murmur rippled through the crowd. I knew my request was unprecedented. No Quester before had ever taken someone with him, but I hadn't heard anywhere that it would be against the rules—if there were actually any rules. Still, I held my breath as the king considered my request. I had framed my request carefully. I didn't want to name anyone specifically, because I doubted the king would agree to that, but by leaving it open ended, the king could ask for volunteers. Stipulating that whoever joined me must be from my own generation effectively made it impossible for some responsible adult—like my parents—to come along. I didn't want to be mothered, bossed around, or looked down upon. This was my Quest. Still, I didn't want to go alone either, but I felt certain that at least one of my friends would agree to be my companion, thus doubling my odds of success.

Emeth stood up from the throne and there was a rustle as everyone straightened in response. He came to the edge of the platform and looked first at me then at the people lining the wings of the Court. "You have asked wisely, Quester. It may not be within my power to appoint someone, but it is in my power to ask those assembled here if any would join you of their own free will. If none do, then you forfeit the boon. Do you understand?"

I hadn't anticipated that last condition. Still, the response was more than I could have hoped for. I nodded my agreement.

"Very well then," King Emeth said, raising his voice so that it echoed throughout the Court. "The Quester has asked that a companion of his own generation accompany him. Is there any here who would join him in his Quest?"

Dead silence greeted the request.

I shifted to look around, my heart in my throat. I spotted Vin, standing slightly behind an elderly couple. Our eyes met, but he only smirked and slinked back into the crowd where I couldn't see him. The treacherous villain! Well, I hadn't really counted on him anyway. The one person I wanted was Seth.

I found him several paces away from where Vin had been. He stood there frozen, and I could see an internal battle waging within him. *Come on, Seth!* I urged silently. *Come on!* I felt I could do this if he came along with me, but to do it alone scared me. I had boasted confidently to Justice Yosher and even my parents, but that all hinged on Seth coming with me. He was my best friend. We had grown up doing everything together. I needed him!

But then his head fell, and his eyes fastened on the floor. He would not look at me. He would not join me. He had betrayed me.

I felt sick inside. Worse, I had wasted my third boon. The prophecy would come to nothing, so the only thing that really mattered was the Blessing. It would have to do—but I knew it wouldn't be enough.

Finally, the king coughed into the silence. "It seems, Quester, that there is none who—"

"I'll go," a soft voice cut in. The voice was so soft, in fact, that it took a moment for it to register. Both the king and I looked toward the source and saw Skinny Minnie stepping forth from the crowd. She cleared her throat and repeated in a stronger voice, "I'll go."

"No!" I burst out before I could stop myself. "No way!"

The king cut me off with a stern look, and I practically swallowed my tongue. I choked and my father pounded me on the back. Embarrassment, anger, and incredulity warred for dominance in my heart.

King Emeth ignored me and focused on Minnie. "Do you speak *truly*, Minnie? This young man has done great evil to you. Why would you go with him?" Everyone in the Court could feel the power of Emeth's invoked Word of Power. He was compelling Minnie to tell the truth.

Minnie straightened under the power of that Word. "Yes, I want to go. The reasons are my own, and I would like to keep them."

She wants to murder me in my sleep, I thought frantically. I had to stop this. I had to retract my request. No way was I going to go on my Quest with Skinny Minnie trailing along behind me, looking for an opportunity to stab me in the back or poison my food—or at least slow me down. I opened my mouth to protest, but the king spoke over me.

"I appreciate your bravery, and indeed, you speak truly, but I fear it would not be appropriate. Certain conventions must be followed, and it would be unseemly if the two of you were to venture into the interior alone, unmarried."

I choked on that last word, and Father obliged by pounding me on the back again. Everyone ignored me. *By the Dragon's eye, this is my Quest!* I thought fiercely, trying to bring myself under control.

"I understand," Minnie said softly, "but I would still go. I would aid Roy in his Quest."

"I must forbid it unless a third should join," the king announced.

Fat chance of that happening. I stopped choking, feeling as if someone had just saved me from drowning. That's when another voice, strong and clear, said, "I'll go with them."

Everyone looked. Prince Bain had rounded the throne and come up behind his father. His hard face looked resolute, his blackish eyes determined. He carried himself like a prince should, sure and competent. The sword at his side was more than decoration.

"Bain?" the king asked surprised. "What is this?"

Bain looked at me and then at Minnie. "I think, Father, that this Quest is no longer about one person. I too need to go—for reasons that are also mine. I will act as chaperone, and I am of their generation, thus meeting the requirements of Roy's boon. Forbid me not in this, Father, I beg."

Oh, but I certainly wanted to forbid him. My Quest had just been hijacked! I felt betrayed, misused, and somewhat abused by the entire experience. No matter what the outcome of the Quest would be, this had been my moment to shine. All eyes had been on me, but even that had been stripped away. I knew any protest would fall on deaf ears. I had asked for a companion. If the king allowed Minnie and Bain to go with me, I would have two.

"Very well, Bain. You may go," the king said. He glanced at Minnie. "You may both go, and may the Blessing of the Phoenix be upon you all."

The traditional words officially ended the Court audience. To me, it sounded like the clap of doom.

CHAPTER FIVE

The thick rain forest began right at the edge of the city—or at the edge of the cobbled courtyard that lay beneath the shadow of the Moon Gate.

I stared at it, finding that the novelty of so many trees could wear off quickly when faced with having to tramp around in them for an unknown amount of time. The thick air clung to everything, and visibility was reduced to yards instead of miles. The sounds of insects, birds, and other creatures filled my ears. I decided I didn't like the rain forest—not one bit.

"Ready?" Bain asked, standing beside me.

I glanced at him, still uncertain about both his decision to intrude on my Quest. We were of the same height, though I might out-mass him. His dark eyes seemed to waver slightly when I glanced at him, but eventually they firmed. I was, after all, only a farmer and he a prince. He wore a soft leather cap that hid a shock of reddish hair, cut short. My mother had cut my hair short too in anticipation of tramping through a bug-infested forest. "No sense in giving them a nest," she said as she cut away at my mop of hair. Bain had dressed in a black tunic and black trousers. He wore soft leather boots that appeared to be resistant to mildew and dampness. A sword in a black sheath was strapped to his side. They had given me a sword too, but it didn't look nearly as impressive as Bain's.

"I guess," I answered. "Seems we have to begin sometime."

"We've tarried long enough. Once the boons are granted, we have three days to begin the Quest. This is the third day."

As if I didn't know that. Still, I didn't feel like getting into an argument, so I just nodded. I looked behind me. Skinny Minnie stood nearby, filling up the space—as much as a skinny girl could—like the trees of the rain forest encroaching on the city. Her presence certainly made me uncomfortable, and I took a step away. She wore a serviceable brown dress and carried what looked to be a heavy pack over one thin shoulder. My own pack of provisions was heavy enough, but hers looked heavier. Her long brown hair had been weaved into a single braid that fell down the length of her back. Having it pulled tight against her scalp made her look less skinny.

Beyond her stood what looked to be the entire population of the city. King Emeth, other courtiers, my parents, and anyone else who mattered or didn't matter had come to bid us good-bye. They filled the courtyard before the Moon Gate, and even the walls were lined with people. No one cheered, however. They just watched.

I would have preferred a more low-key send-off, and no doubt that would have been so if I were going alone. But alas, Prince Bain was going and so everyone had to be there.

King Emeth stepped forward. "Go with our Blessing and may you find success on your Quest—and be careful."

The word 'success' brought to mind Beth Chalom's prophecy, and I found my eyes seeking her out. She stood off to the side, and the moment I looked, our eyes met. I looked away first. There was something downright disturbing about that woman's eyes.

"Yes, Father," Bain replied, "we will."

Just then a small girl of around fifteen flew into Bain's arms, hugging him fiercely. "Do you really have to go?" she pleaded.

"Yes, sister, I do," Bain replied softly, hugging her back. "I will be safe. The Phoenix will watch over us."

I now recognized Princess Kyrin. For whatever reason, I had completely forgotten about her. She had not been at Court when I had gone to claim my three boons. Kyrin's brown tresses fell to her waist. She was a beautiful girl who would one day turn into a stunning woman. Kyrin stepped back from her brother, wiping tears from her face. Then she turned to Minnie and hugged her as well. "Watch him for me," she ordered. "Please."

Minnie's features softened. She bent low to reply, but I could hear her words clearly. "Of course I will, Kyrin. You have my word."

Kyrin stepped back, glanced at me, and then retreated to her father. I felt slighted. *What? No hug for me?*

Well, I'd said my own good-byes, so there was no reason to delay things any longer. "Time to go," I ordered gruffly. I waved one last time at my parents, who waved back sadly. Then, not looking back, I trudged boldly into the jungle.

I could hear the other two following me, but I was determined not to look back. We walked in silence in a southerly direction for perhaps two hours, directly into the heart of the wilderness. We had to move slowly as the branches from the trees hung low to the ground. Their giant leaves hindered our progress as well as visibility. When we passed through a clearing, tall grass often filled it. The stalks felt rough to the skin and left me insanely itchy. At other times, the canopy above became so thick that little grew on the ground and our pace quickened as a result.

In general, however, we found we could walk straight if we were careful and only occasionally had to detour around a tangle of vines and moss-covered trees that couldn't be pushed through. My skin became clammy, and I quickly learned to be careful where I shoved some of the foliage out of the way or my hand would come away with insects clinging to it.

Birds burst from their hiding places if we ventured too close, usually scaring the fire out of me. Snakes slithered out of the way on occasion, making me nervous about where I stepped or placed my hand. Much of the ground was moist and the moss on the trees wet, leaving stains on our clothing. Our feet soon felt uncomfortable and moist with sweat. Overall, I didn't like it much.

When I could, I would follow a trail as long as it went generally south. Some looked to be game trails, and at other times the thick brush petered out, allowing us to walk practically unimpeded.

Then Minnie caught up to me and walked alongside as we navigated through the trees. "Roy, do you know where we're going?"

I glanced at her from the corner of my eye. It didn't seem like she hated me. When I had apologized to her after dousing her with manure, she had been so upset she couldn't even look me in the eye. At the time, I had been grateful for that. I still felt guilty for what I'd done. Justice Yosher had a way of making one wish they'd never even been born, and Minnie could cause all sorts of twisted emotions with one glance of her hurt doe-like eyes. But now, her face glanced at me in curiosity, not anger.

I stopped so quickly that Bain nearly collided with me. He grunted, muttering something about idiots. Minnie took two more steps before stopping and turning around to look at me. I could take it no longer. I demanded, "Okay, what is really going on here? Why are you two here?"

Minnie and Bain exchanged glances. I decided to pin one of them down. "I don't get you, Minnie. I did all those terrible things to you, and then you volunteer to go with me on my Quest. Do you really want to help me, or are you just looking to get revenge?"

"I came to help, Roy."

"Why?"

"I have my reasons. I know you don't like me, and I'm not overly fond of you either, but I offered to help you on this Quest, and I mean to see it through. I have no intentions of getting revenge."

I frowned, not sure if I could believe her. "You're not going to tell me why you're really coming?"

She shook her head. "But I promise that I want to help."

She'd be in the way as far as I was concerned, but I decided not to say it. I couldn't send her back anyway. She'd just ignore me. Deep down, however, I was a smidgeon grateful. No one else had offered to come with me. Even Bain had only offered to come after Minnie had committed. In effect, Minnie had been more a friend to me than anyone else. It shamed me. But I would be dead before I'd admit it.

I looked at Bain. "And you? Why are you coming?"

"I've got my reasons too," he replied gruffly, folding his arms across his chest. "They are no concern of yours."

"Now don't get all princely on me. This is my Quest. I'm in charge."

He surprised me by nodding. "I agree. But Minnie's question is still valid. Where are we going? You must find the nest and see if the Phoenix will grant you a Gift. Fine. But how do we get there? We know that the nest is in the very center of the island, but which way is that?"

"South," I said shortly.

"Oh? Which way is that?"

I pointed.

"Are you sure?" Bain asked. There was a slight level of condescension apparent in his voice.

"Of course I'm sure," I protested.

"I can't see the sun from here. I can't see the Endless Ocean. All I see are trees. How do you know you haven't strayed?"

"I just know!" But I didn't. Could he be right?

Minnie solved the problem. "I brought a compass," she said softly.

I looked at her. "You have a compass? Where'd you get a compass?" Compasses were very rare. They could only be made with a certain metal, so few people had access to one. I hadn't thought to procure one for two reasons. First, they were rare and very, very expensive. Second, I never thought it would be difficult to determine which way was south. But Bain had a point—as much as I loathed to admit it. We couldn't see the sun and we had no other landmarks to follow.

Minnie explained, "I asked King Emeth for it yesterday. He was glad to let me have it." Of course he had been. She began to dig around in her pack for it.

Bain chuckled. "At least one of us is thinking."

I shot him my most menacing scowl. Minnie fished out the compass and we gathered around to see. I was appalled. The arrow on the compass pointed off at a sharp angle to the direction we had been traveling.

"Looks like we've been traveling more east than south," Bain commented.

I sighed, feeling defeated already. "Fine. I was going the wrong direction." I glanced at Minnie. "Good thing you asked for the compass."

She smiled, and it did wonders for her face. "Why, Roy, that almost sounded like a compliment!"

I snorted. "Yeah, well, we'd best be going."

We changed directions and headed due south. So far, this was a lousy Quest. The entire rain forest looked essentially the same. Occasionally, we passed a gurgling stream or by a large rock that would protrude from among the trees, but if not for the compass, we would have gotten lost quickly. Sweat gathered on my back where my pack pressed against my shirt. I felt sticky and clammy. Insects buzzed around us and regardless of how many times I swatted at them, they persisted in coming back. Within a couple of hours, all three of us were dirty and sweaty, we'd been repeatedly bitten, and we were ready to go genocidal on every bug species in existence.

"If this is a rain forest," I grumbled at one point, "where's the rain?"

"I don't think we would like the rain," Minnie replied shoving a leaf many times larger than the size of her head out of the way.

"Why not?"

"Not sure, but it looks to me that if everything gets wet, it will slow us to a crawl."

"If it gets rid of these bugs, I'll take it," I said fervently.

"Good point."

I felt halfway amazed. We had just had a normal conversation. I didn't quite know what to make of it. I opened my mouth to say something when a faint roaring noise reached my ears. "That's not a dragon, is it?" I demanded, coming to a dead stop.

"Of course not," Bain said, though his hand had gone to the hilt of his sword. "Don't be dense. Everyone knows there is only one dragon."

"The Dragon in the Abyss," Minnie confirmed, licking her lips nervously.

"Maybe," I said, "but if there is one, then there may be more." I drew my sword and edged forward. No one could ever claim I lacked courage. Minnie followed more slowly and Bain brought up the rear. He too had drawn his sword.

The noise continued to grow until at last I recognized the sound. "That's a river!"

We hurried forward, and, sure enough, we came across a roaring river that cut from the west to the east, right across the direction we wanted to go. The river looked to be a good ten yards wide, much wider than any of us could jump. The vegetation seemed thicker, probably because of more light from above. We paced the river for a bit until we found a suitable clearing.

Minnie immediately sat down on the bank, stripped off her boots, and sank her feet in the water. "Oh, that's much better," she said, sighing in contentment.

Bain and I looked at each other. He shrugged. "We could use a break."

I appreciated that he was letting me make the final decision. "Yes we could."

Moments later we joined Minnie on the bank, immersing our hot feet in the cool water of the river. I cupped some of it in my hand and drank slowly. I felt somewhat refreshed immediately.

After we drank our fill, Minnie began chatting. "I was thinking about dragons—or more appropriately the Dragon of the Abyss. Do either of you know anyone who has ever seen the Dragon?"

I shook my head, but Bain pursed his lips. "My father never spoke of his own Quest; and every time I asked him about it, he would get evasive. Something bad happened to him. I don't know what it was or what happened, but whenever I mention the Dragon, he gets angry. It's the only time I've ever seen him mad. He has forbidden me from speaking of it."

Minnie looked interested. "I didn't know that. Your father has been so good to me ever since my own parents died. I would have starved if it wasn't for him." She sighed. Looking at her skinny body, I wondered if the king hadn't nearly been too late. She continued, "My parents used to warn me that if I wasn't a good girl, the Dragon would eat me. I wondered about that. I wonder how much of the Phoenix Canticle is true. Do you really think the Dragon created the fog to trap the Phoenix? And us?"

I shrugged. "I don't know. My Pa used to scare me the same way, and I heard that anyone who attempts to leave the island ends up shipwrecked on hidden reefs in the fog. But he thinks it is the Phoenix's fault. If its Rebirth didn't change the structure of the reefs in the fog, we could map it and eventually leave the island if we wanted."

"How is that the Phoenix's fault?" Minnie demanded. "The fog is what hides the reefs. Get rid of the fog and we would be able to safely navigate through. It's the Dragon's fault."

"That's just how my Pa thinks. I don't think he's ever liked having to clear the land each year just to plant crops. The Phoenix makes life hard for him. Anyway, who's to say that the Dragon is even real. The fog could just be a naturally occurring thing. Maybe the world ends on the other side."

"No," Minnie disagreed. "I've met someone who came from Outside once. He was shipwrecked and stranded here, but he told of lands beyond the fog." She hesitated. "When he heard of Taninim, he wanted to go there. Said those people there might help him escape the island. He didn't understand why we don't want to escape. If the Dragon worshipers kill the Phoenix, then what happens to the island? Will it sink into the ocean?"

I shuddered at the thought of that distant southern city and the evil people who resided there, but as far as I knew, the Dragon didn't really exist. It was just a myth.

Bain, however, looked thoughtful. "I don't think you need to worry about that," he said. "There is something that protects the Phoenix from harm."

"What?" I asked curiously.

"I'm not sure. There are legends of a Guardian, but they're just myths too."

"You don't think any of it is true?" Minnie asked.

Bain shrugged. "I think there is something out there. My father hinted about it once. He said the Phoenix is protected. I don't know what he meant, and he refused to talk about it."

I kicked my feet in the cold water, digesting all I had heard. I wondered if whatever protected the Phoenix—this Guardian— would try to prevent me from getting to the nest. Then I thought about the Dragon. I wasn't convinced that the Dragon actually existed, but my doubts had taken a blow from what Bain had said about his father. Did some vile beast really exist? Was it waiting to consume all mankind? And what of those people in the south? Did they really worship an evil creature like the Dragon?

My thoughts were interrupted by a compelling voice. "Hi there!"

All three of us turned to see two human-like creatures standing in the shadows of the trees not too far away. The roar of the river had effectively drowned out any sound of their approach. I wondered why I wasn't more startled by their sudden appearance; but on second glance, I didn't think there was anything to fear. They looked harmless enough.

"Whacha doin'?" the slightly taller of the two asked. They looked to be about half our size, reaching up to perhaps my waist. They had long, unruly hair that fell around pointed ears. Both were dressed in simple smocks that looked to have been cut raggedly at the bottoms. A rope cinched it about their waists. Greenish, tight trousers fit all the way to their tiny, bare feet.

"Just taking a break," I responded.

"Whereya goin'?"

"To find the Phoenix nest." It never occurred to me that I shouldn't tell them.

They clapped their hands in glee. "A Quest?"

"Yes."

"Sounds like so much fun! Whacha got there?" the strange, little man asked, pointing to our packs.

"Just supplies for our journey."

"Food?"

"Yes."

"We have gift!" the other suddenly exclaimed. "Come see!" He held out his tightly clenched fist.

We couldn't see well, so all three of us got up and walked over.

"Gift for you! To aid in journey!" he exclaimed, holding out his hand, but keeping it closed.

We stared at his clenched fist, waiting for him to open it and show us this marvelous gift. I couldn't believe our fortune. To run across such a wondrous gift so soon meant the Blessing given to me as my first boon was working! Just then something out of the corner of my eye caught my attention, pulling me away from the closed fist and the wondrous gift within.

Instantly, the spell was broken. I blinked, coming to myself and saw six more elves hauling our packs away into the jungle, two each to a pack. "Elves!" I cried. For now I knew them. Elves could spellbind their victims with their voices and rob them blind. They were the worst thieves on the island and would steal anything they could—whether they needed it or not.

I shoved Bain into Minnie to break the spell on them. They collided and fell. Minnie let a small gasp escape her lips as she tumbled to the ground. I gave them no further heed, already darting after the two elves trying to steal my pack. I drew my sword and yelled, refusing to give them an opportunity to speak or cast their enchantment on me. Elves were not the bravest of creatures—unless the Rebirth had made them significantly taller than the average human. Fortunately, the Rebirth had only granted the elves half stature this year.

The two I bore down on screamed and scattered, running every which way and chattering incessantly. I'm no swordsman, so my wild swings didn't have a chance of catching them. I hesitated over my recovered pack, swinging my sword at empty air, not sure which one to chase. Then they were gone and we were alone.

"Elves!" Bain roared, climbing to his feet and shaking his head as if coming out of a daze. "I should have known!"

Minnie came to her feet more slowly. She looked shaken. "I couldn't even think. Their voices were so compelling," she said.

"It's how they steal," Bain muttered. If anything, he was more furious than I was. He glanced at me. "You broke their spell. How did you do that?"

I considered. "The Blessing. I was thinking of the Blessing when I got distracted. The moment I did, the spell was broken. I saw them stealing our stuff and just reacted."

Bain nodded. "Yes, the Blessing is a potent ally for us." He looked at my pack, which I'd recovered. Theirs were gone, stolen by the elves. His face contorted in frustration again. "But you saved the wrong pack!"

I started. "What? This one's mine."

"Idiot! Minnie's had the compass in it!"

I looked around, chagrined. It was true. The compass was gone, and it was vital to this Quest. Without it, we would get hopelessly lost. "Where would they go? We need to track them and recover the compass!"

But Bain was already shaking his head. "It's no good. Even if we can find them, there would be way too many for us to handle. They also hide what they steal, so even finding them doesn't mean we'll find the compass. We have to go back."

"What? No!" I cried.

"We have no choice. Without the compass we are lost. We need to go back and get another one. We also need more supplies. The filthy elves stole two-thirds of our food—and our boots!"

I gaped at him. Our boots? I glanced at the riverbank, and, sure enough, all three sets of boots were missing. That would make things more difficult for sure, but I had been raised on a farm. Running around barefoot was nothing new to me. I glanced at Bain's feet, noting how soft they looked and then at Minnie's.

She noted my scrutiny and shuffled, embarrassed. Her feet looked—well they looked serviceable. She had grown up on the streets of Khol.

My mind settled down as I accepted our situation. "You go back if you want, Bain. This is my Quest, not yours. I can't go back now. I won't go back. Besides, if we are quick enough, we can catch the elves before they get too far away." I looked around. "They went that way. I'm going, no matter if you're coming or not."

That said, I resolutely started off, following the riverbank toward the west. I would be burned to ash rather than see those vile elves steal from me. I meant to get that compass back no matter what—barefoot or otherwise!

Behind me, Minnie and Bain exchanged a long glance. Finally, Minnie said, "I'm going with Roy."

I heard it and my heart leaped.

Bain stood in place for a time watching us go. Finally, he swung his sword viciously at an unoffending branch, slicing it clean off. Then he rammed his sword into his sheath and grudgingly followed us.

Together—more or less—we went in search of the elves.

CHAPTER SIX

I marched determinedly west along the riverbank, my bare feet slapping the hard ground resolutely. Strangely, my feet felt better than when I wore the boots. They felt dryer for sure. We often had to veer away from the river as the vegetation became too thick to pass through, but we plowed on resolutely.

This was the direction in which the elves had retreated, taking our supplies, so their holt had to be somewhere in this direction. An elven holt was the center of their nefarious activities. As creatures of the island went, elves were among the most despised—right after trolls. In truth, I didn't know what I would do if we couldn't catch them before they succeeded in returning to their holt. It would be incredibly dangerous to try and go up against an entire tribe of elves.

"It's getting dark," Minnie warned. She walked behind me, doing a reasonably good job of matching my furious pace. Bain brought up the rear again, fuming and casting both of us angry glances. He was already favoring his tender feet. I ignored him.

"If we wait until tomorrow," I explained, "they will reach their holt. I don't know how we'll get the compass back then."

"We'll also be unable to follow them in the dark," she pointed out.

I ground my teeth together in frustration and plowed on. It just wasn't in me to give up. "Let's see if we can catch them. Those packs are heavy. They couldn't have gone far."

"Are you planning on killing them?"

I blinked. "I hadn't given it any thought either way," I said slowly. "I suppose if they don't return our stuff or they attack me, I might. They're just vermin."

Minnie frowned, but said nothing further about it. I didn't know why her silence irritated me. Did she doubt that Bain would kill if given the chance? Why should I be held to a higher standard?

Deciding that all women were an unsolvable riddle, I tried to cast the thought from my mind and focus on finding the elves before they could reach their holt, or I developed blisters on my feet.

That's when I heard voices up ahead.

I froze and so did Minnie and Bain. Motioning to them, I pointed into the trees ahead. The roar of the river still drowned out most of the sounds of the forest, but just over a slight rise and behind a copse of trees, I could hear faint, but fierce arguing.

Using the roar of the river to mask our approach, we edged forward until we could peer through the branches. About a dozen elves were clustered around our packs, arguing over every item they pulled out.

"Whacha got?" they cried over and over to each other.

"Gimme that!" they would demand, often forgetting one item the moment their eyes fell on another.

Since they were not talking to me or my companions, we didn't feel the compulsion of their voices, thankfully. A rising anger dulled my thoughts as I watched our things being haphazardly tossed about, tugged between two arguing elves, or discarded for something more interesting.

I studied the scene in the deepening gloom. We needed to act fast before the fading light made it impossible to retrieve our things. I glanced at Bain who crouched beside me. He took in my look and understood perfectly.

Slowly, we unsheathed our swords, set ourselves, and then threw ourselves through the branches at the arguing elves. I yelled something akin to a war cry and descended upon the elves like strix on tasty flesh.

The elves scattered immediately, chattering in their high-pitched voices in an effort to enchant us. Fortunately, so many of them speaking at once had the net effect of canceling each other out. I didn't think it would work anyway. I was simply too angry.

I swung my sword at one of them, but the thieving runt dodged agilely and ran around in seemingly random directions. I froze, trying to focus on one of the elves, but they resembled a flock of chickens finding a hungry dog in their midst. They dodged each other as much as they did Bain and me, confusing us and making it nearly impossible to track them individually.

Bain seemed bent on trying though. He ran around after them, shouting and swinging his sword with much more competence than I could, but he seemed equally as ineffective.

Then something hit me from behind, and I staggered forward. I glanced back to see an elf struggling to knock my legs out from under me. I reached down, plucked him off, and swung him around to face me.

He grinned and said, "Whacha got?"

Enraged, I threw the elf away, lest his voice enchant me. The smallish creature flew through the air with an excited, "Whoopee!"

That didn't work out as I'd hoped. to try something else. I dropped my sword at my feet, and instantly several of the elves veered in my direction to try and snag it. The first elf that came within range received a fistful of knuckles square in the face. The elf staggered back into one of his fellows, and they both fell to the ground.

I pivoted and kicked another who let out an "Oomph!" followed by a very weak sounding, "Whoopee," as he too went flying through the air. These elves certainly didn't weigh all that much!

I plucked two more off the ground that were trying to grab my sword and conked their heads together. Their skulls made a dull sound when they connected and their eyes rolled up in their heads as I let go. They staggered away in ever-widening circles until they collided with separate trees and fell over backward.

Another tried to sneak between my legs. The elf managed to grab the hilt of my sword, but I yanked him off the ground, and he dropped the heavy sword. He grinned at me with huge, blinking eyes. Angered, I pivoted and threw him as hard as I could into the nearest tree before he could say anything. His excited whoop ended abruptly as he crashed head first into the tree trunk.

Amazingly, the elf found his feet and staggered off into the forest. Between battling more elves, I vaguely noted that the dazed elf seemed to meander through the trees for some distance before smacking face first into another trunk some distance off. He fell over backward, disappearing from my sight.

Seeing my success, Bain threw down his own sword, attracting even more of the milling elves. He bashed one over the head and it walked away blinking in confusion. Bain tossed one through the air, but that one too seemed to delight in the sensation, shouting, "Whoopee!" as he went.

Then we both had our hands full as we kicked, punched, and flung the elves that tried to snatch our swords. This went on for some time, until, finally, they just melted into the trees and were gone, leaving our stuff scattered everywhere.

Exhausted, I sat down heavily and put my head in my hands. I had never been in such a battle before. Oh, I'd had my share of fights with other boys growing up, but the tenacity of these elves had been disheartening. They had just kept coming and coming, no matter how hard I punched them, kicked them, or threw them into trees.

Still, we had succeeded in rescuing our things. I lifted my head and looked around. Bain had also sat down, his chest heaving with exertion. Minnie, who I hadn't seen at all during the fight, walked around collecting loose objects in the failing light.

"I've never fought a tribe of elves before," Bain said. "That was kinda fun!"

Minnie paused in her collection. I noticed she had already put her boots back on. "This wasn't the whole tribe. This was a thieving party. A tribe of elves could have as many as a couple hundred elves in a holt. Just be glad they weren't armed."

That brought my head up. "Armed? You mean they have weapons?"

Minnie nodded. "They rarely attack people—just steal from them. But if they feel threatened, they will fight viciously."

I didn't want any part of that! "Did you find the compass yet?"

"It's not in my pack anymore, and I haven't found it out here yet."

Both Bain and I climbed painfully back to our feet and helped in the search. We found our boots and gratefully put them on. Then we set out to collect everything we could find before we could no longer see.

A bit later, we met to compare notes.

"Anyone find the compass?" I asked.

Both shook their heads helplessly.

"Burn it all to ash!" I yelled angrily. "You mean the elves still have it?"

"That or it is lying around here, and we just haven't found it yet," Minnie said hopefully.

"But if the elves got it, they took it to their holt!" I cried. "We'll never find it!"

"We'll have to search more in the morning," Bain said.

I opened my mouth to argue, even though I knew it to be foolish, but I was too upset to care. Just then, something rustled in the underbrush. All three of us turned around to see an elf staggering in our direction. He seemed dazed and disorientated.

He came to an uncertain halt and looked up at us with big, blinking, unfocused eyes. "Hi'ya!" he said loudly. "Anyone see where those thieving elves went?"

I looked at Bain, who looked at Minnie, who looked at me. "Get him!" I yelled.

Bain and I piled on the dazed and unresisting elf. We shoved him to the ground, pinning him there. He just continued to stare up at us, and I realized he must have been one of those who'd had his head knocked around during the fight.

"Don't let him speak!" Minnie cried, rummaging through her pack.

I clapped my hand over the elf's mouth. This didn't dissuade the elf over much for he said, "Whoomp a goomph?"

Minnie came up with a wad of cloth that we stuffed into the elf's mouth. Still, the elf tried again, saying, "Ooum amph ollemf?"

I considered the situation. "We need to tie him to a tree so he can't get away. He'll know where the elf holt is."

Bain produced some rope from his pack, and we tied the unresisting elf to a nearby tree. The elf continued to blink his large eyes. Clearly, the knock to his head had dazed him.

Once done, Bain said, "You're not really considering going to the elf holt are you, Roy. I've heard stories about those places. We wouldn't stand a chance there."

I ran a hand through my short hair. "We'll think of something. I'm not giving up. This is only the first day!"

And with that, the last of the light faded away.

We stood there, hardly seeing each other in the deep gloom. Minnie finally took charge. "You two collect some firewood and get a fire started. I'll see about cooking us something to eat."

My stomach growled in agreement. It has been said that the way to a man's heart is through his stomach. I didn't know how true it was, but if Minnie could ease my hunger, I'd gladly let her boss me around.

Bain and I collected wood that we found mostly by feeling blindly around. We found some rocks that we maneuvered into a fire pit of sorts, and Bain took out his flint and steel, managing to ignite some kindling. Before long, we had a nice cheery fire that lighted up the space around us.

Minnie fetched water from the river and with ingredients from her pack, she made a mouth-watering stew that Bain and I slurped up enthusiastically. Minnie watched us eat, a small smile gracing her thin lips. I had to admit, if I had to do this alone, the best meal I would have been able to manage would be cold jerky—and even that would have been prepared by my mother.

Each of us had a bedroll and a blanket. We spread them around the fire, and after checking on the elf—who had fallen asleep and was snoring into the cloth jammed in its mouth—we banked the fire more thoroughly, climbed into our bedrolls, pulled the covers tightly over our heads to keep out the bugs, and fell promptly to sleep.

In retrospect, we probably should have set a watch in case the elves came back or some other nocturnal creature happened upon us. But as the Blessing would have it, I slept peacefully through the night without interruption.

Morning came abruptly as the rain forest came alive with its normal daily activity and noise. Someone shook my shoulder, but I slapped the hand away, grumbling, and rolled over.

Memory came back in a flood, and I sat up straight, looking wildly around me. Minnie knelt beside me, smiling. "Time to get up."

I didn't see why, but the sudden smell of cooking eggs convinced me otherwise. "Where'd you get eggs?"

"I raided a couple of nests in the area. You would be shocked at the number of bird and snake nests you can find if you are looking for them."

I glanced over at the cook fire. "Those are snake eggs?"

"Some of them. Trust me, you won't even be able to tell the difference."

Bain came back with an armload of wood for the fire. "'Bout time you got up," he grumbled. "I don't know why he got to sleep in longer."

Minnie didn't say anything as she left my side to stir the eggs. I decided to ignore Bain too. Instead I looked at the elf still tied to the tree. He returned my look with his big, blinking eyes. He still looked dazed. I wondered if something wasn't right in that elf's head.

A sudden thought caused me to frown. "Hey, how are we going to question the elf if we can't let him speak?"

Bain rolled his eyes, "Now he thinks about that! Dolt!"

I stood up and clenched my fists. "What's wrong with you, Bain?"

"His feet hurt," Minnie said.

"His feet…" I trailed off. Oh. We had walked some distance without our boots, and though Minnie and I were somewhat calloused to it, Bain hadn't been.

"And I'm itchy, sweaty, bug-bitten all over, and a snake tried to crawl in my blanket last night! I hate snakes!"

"It's true," Minnie said. "He yelled, jumped around like a madman trying to learn to dance, and stomped his blankets to death."

I grinned. It didn't surprise me at all that I'd slept right through the show. I slept very soundly. "Did you kill the snake?" I asked.

"It got away," Bain grumbled, throwing the wood down violently next to the fire.

Minnie seemed unruffled. "Thank you, Bain."

He stormed off, muttering to himself. Now that I was paying attention, I could see how he favored both feet as he walked.

Minnie forked some of the eggs onto a small wooden plate and handed it to me. She said, "So how do we communicate with the elf? I suppose you have a plan for getting the compass back if we find the holt?"

"It depends on how the holt is laid out," I lied, stalling. "I'll need to get a good idea of the layout and where the compass might be before I can come up with anything definite. For that, I need to talk to the elf."

"Elves aren't people, Roy. They are part of the island. They don't organize their holts the way we do. From what I know, it is all just anarchy. They make use of whatever environment they find themselves in. I suspect their holt is in the trees this year."

"If they're not people, why were you so concerned if I killed any of them?"

She gave me an unrecognizable look. "You think that killing anything, human or not, is how you are going to solve your problems?"

"This is self-defense," I protested.

"How? We attacked them."

"We did nothing of the kind. They attacked us!"

"When?"

"Back there! Where they stole our stuff!"

"They attacked us or stole from us?"

I snapped my mouth shut and glared at her. Frustrated and angry all over again, I retorted, "I don't need a lecture from you, Skinny Minnie!"

She stiffened, her eyes going flat. I found this more unsettling than her lecture. Her eyes now reminded me of those of the humiliated girl covered in manure. Both of us turned away from each other.

Bain limped back into camp. He looked at us, no doubt feeling the tension in the air. "I scouted around some. Those elves hardly left a trace anywhere. I have no idea where they went, and I didn't find the compass lying around anywhere either. We're burned." He sat down next to the small campfire and accepted a plate of eggs from Minnie.

I refused to give up. "We still have that elf," I said, pointing. "He'll know where the holt is."

"The moment we take the gag out, he'll enchant us with his voice," Bain protested.

"What if one of us plugs our ears? He—or she—could then watch the other two. The moment anyone looks enchanted, he—or she," I threw a quick glance at Minnie, but she continued to ignore me "can break the spell by pushing the other two. That seemed to work the last time."

Bain considered. "That might work, but even if we do find out where it is, what good will it do? Taking on the holt will be difficult. They will protect themselves."

"One thing at a time. First we find out where the holt is. We can scout it, get an idea of what it might take to get back the compass, and then make our decision."

"You really don't want to go back to Khol, do you?"

"Not on your life."

"It may very well be my life," he grumbled. "So who plugs their ears?"

"I will," Minnie volunteered, still without looking at me. "You two will need to make a plan based on what he tells you."

I saw no sense in arguing with her, so I nodded. "Let's do this."

Minnie found some more cloth in her pack—I began to wonder what else she had in there—and stuffed them in her ears.

"Can you hear me?" I asked in a slightly raised voice.

She shrugged. "I can see your lips moving and hear you vaguely, but it is muffled. I've no idea what you said."

I turned to Bain. "That should work. Come on, let's talk to the elf." We walked over to the still blinking elf. "Okay, elf, your friends stole something from us that we need to get back. All we want to know is where your holt is so we can recover it. We don't intend to hurt you. Understand?"

The elf just blinked.

Bain snorted. "This must be one of the stupid ones."

Warily, I bent over and took out the gag.

"Hi'ya!" the elf said brightly. "Do'ya got anything to eat?"

I looked at Bain and Bain looked at me. "Do you feel spelled?" I asked.

"No."

"Me either. That's good." I looked back at the elf. "We'll get you something to eat in a few moments. First tell us where your holt is."

"Where elves live!" he replied.

"We know that. But where is it?"

"In trees!" he explained excitedly.

Oh this would take some doing. "Look—do you have a name?"

"Yes'sirree!"

"Good. What is it?"

"I be elf!"

I wasn't getting anywhere. "What about your friends—the other elves—do they have names?"

"Yes'sirree!"

"What are they?"

"They be elf!"

I ground my teeth together in frustration and looked at Bain. "This isn't working."

"You think? Maybe he can point out which way to go at least."

Good idea. I turned back to the elf. "Look, elf—I can't just be calling you that. Let's see...I'll call you Eddie. Eddie Elf. Now, Eddie—"

I broke off because the elf's eyes stopped blinking and he stared at the two of us in absolute wonderment. "You...you have Named me?"

"What?"

"You Named me! I am Eddie Elf! I am Eddie Elf!"

I looked helplessly at Bain. I had no idea what was going on. He sighed. "Dolt! You just Named him."

"So?"

"You just gave him a separate identity, a name. None of the creatures of the island have separate identities except humans. Except him now. Because of you. Now you've done it, genius. You've probably messed up the entire harmony of the island. The Phoenix will never give you a Gift now!"

"I didn't know!" I protested, still confused. I looked at Minnie, but with her ears stuffed with cloth, she just looked back, uncomprehending. I just couldn't wait to hear what she had to say about all this. Yeah, right.

Stifling my growing apprehension, I plowed on. "Uh, Eddie, can you point out the way to your holt? We need to find it."

"Yes'sirree! I'm Eddie Elf!"

"Uh, good. Which way is it?"

The elf shrugged.

Bain rolled his eyes. "Dolt! His hands are tied."

Oh. "I know that!" I cried, chagrinned.

I reached down to untie the elf enough to free one arm when Minnie suddenly shoved me. Hard. I staggered sideways, nearly slamming into a tree. I missed it and sat down heavily on the ground, surprised.

"Minnie!" I protested. "What are you doing?"

She pointed to her ears and then said, "You were trying to release him. You looked enchanted."

I choked on that. Somehow I doubted I looked *that* enchanted. I spotted her small smile and frowned. Had she done that on purpose? I climbed to my feet, stuffed the gag back in Eddie's mouth, pulled the cloth from Minnie's ears, and explained, "I'm going to free him enough so he can point out the direction of the holt."

"Oh," she said.

Grounding my teeth again, I reversed the steps to the point where I could free the elf's arm. "Now, Eddie, which way is your holt?"

He pointed directly across the river. "It be thataway!"

Finally. I looked at the others. "Okay, we'll go thataway and check it out. If the Blessing holds, maybe we'll find a way to recover the compass."

So far, my Quest was turning out to be an unmitigated disaster! I turned back to consider the elf. I found it interesting that the elf hadn't tried as of yet to control us with his voice. We'd given him plenty of opportunity to do so, so I wondered why he hadn't. Did it require more than one elf?

And what about this business of the Naming? I too had been Named, though my Naming was the entire reason why I was on this Quest in the first place. The elf, however, looked to be enraptured by the entire notion. What had I done?

Just then, Minnie shoved me again.

I let out a high-pitched squawk of surprise as I tumbled over onto the ground. "Minnie!"

She shrugged and pointed to her ears.

Ooh, this was going to be a long Quest. I just knew it.

CHAPTER SEVEN

Eddie Elf showed us a place where we could ford the river, and we trudged south toward the holt. We gagged Eddie just to be on the safe side, but I wondered about that. Eddie seemed enthralled over his Naming and didn't show even the slightest intention of trying to escape or do us any harm. He walked along next to me like a puppy, often glancing up at me in a sort of adoring, huge-eyed manner that made me extremely uncomfortable.

Minnie thought it funny—naturally—but Bain found it distressing. He kept predicting disaster, and I began to wonder if my innocent Naming had not doomed the island to utter destruction in some sort of twisted fashion. *Delinquent indeed*, I thought bitterly.

We walked for an hour or two when it started to rain. Within the space of fifteen minutes, everything was waterlogged. The ground became spongy as water found its way through the canopy above, often collecting in huge drops that infallibly found their way down the back of my shirt or hit me squarely in the eye.

It did drive away the bugs, or at least most of them, and our packs were waterproof, but our clothes were not. Soon, even my boots felt soggy, and I began to regret my wish for rain. I'd rather have the bugs!

Sometime after that, Eddie led us to a rise in the rain forest, a hill of sorts. He attempted to point with his shoulder toward the top since his hands were still tied behind his back. We all stopped and I removed Eddie's gag. "Elf holt there!" he proclaimed proudly. "Whacha waiting for!"

I stuffed the gag back in, though that hardly deterred the elf from trying to speak. We moved back some to a more defensible and hidden spot and gathered close together. The river had been left behind long ago, so only the rain helped to drown out any sounds we might make.

"One of us needs to go up there and scout around," I said. "But I really don't know what to look for. Anyone have an idea?"

"Maybe Eddie knows," Minnie suggested.

"Don't call him that!" Bain hissed. "Don't encourage him."

"It doesn't seem to be doing any harm, and he seems to appreciate the Name."

"It's unnatural," Bain muttered, shuddering.

I pulled the gag out of Eddie's mouth. "Where do you keep the things you steal?"

The elf brightened, eager to help. "In elf holt!"

Bain snorted, and I felt like bashing the elfish runt's face in. Minnie giggled. "You both deserved that," she said.

Maybe we did. I replaced the gag in Eddie's unresisting mouth and considered our options. "We all can't go. Someone has to stay and watch Edd—the elf. Who should stay here?"

Minnie shrugged. "I can stay if needed. I'm not exactly looking forward to crawling around on the wet ground."

"Then I'm staying too," Bain declared. "I'm not leaving Minnie unprotected. If those elves find us, they won't just be trying to steal our stuff. They'll be out for blood since we've now invaded their territory."

I didn't know what to make of that. I couldn't see how it mattered either way. If he was right, staying behind wouldn't make a lick of difference. However, I wasn't about to suggest that we put Minnie at risk, so I just shrugged. "Fine then. I'll go."

I removed my pack and gave it to Minnie. Then I took off my sword and gave that to Bain. He looked confused. "If you're right," I said with exaggerated patience that brought a deep frown to Bain's lips, "it won't do me any good; but if you two are attacked, you might be able to work together and get away. Anyway, it will only get in my way if I have to start crawling around."

He accepted the sword with a short nod. Well, I was as ready as I was going to be. "May the Blessing be upon all of us," I said.

"Indeed," Bain agreed grimly.

I set out. I didn't know how far up the hill the holt was situated, so I began by circling the base of the hill, hoping to see something from below before I ventured up. The base of the hill turned out to be much wider than I anticipated, and I could see nothing on top.

The rain continued to fall, soaking my clothing and getting into my eyes. I wiped it away and began a slow ascent up the hill, keeping my eyes open for anything out of the ordinary. I moved slowly from tree to tree, trying to utilize the hunting skills my father had tried to instill in me.

At the top of the gently sloping hill, I got my first look at the elf holt. Whatever I was expecting, I wasn't prepared to see the largest tree I'd ever seen in my life. The base of the tree itself was large enough to fit a nice sized house within. The branches that came off the tree would make the trunk of any other tree envious. Interestingly enough, the lower branches hung just off the ground. I could see ropes or ladders dangling at various places to aid in ascending or descending the tree. The elves didn't have houses. They had a huge tree in which lived the entire tribe of elves.

I immediately realized that this could present a problem. If the compass was somewhere in that tree, sneaking around up there would be near impossible.

From my position, I could see scores of elves swinging from branch to branch. Some looked female and others, smaller, might be children. However, through the rain and the thickness of the leaves on the tree itself, I couldn't be sure of anything.

Now what? I thought about waiting for nightfall. Perhaps the elves would all fall asleep, and I could sneak in without waking any of them, find the compass in the pitch black of the night, and escape by finding my way back down, all without alerting any of the sharp-eared elves to my presence. Yeah right.

"Whatcha doing?" an elf's voice asked directly behind me.

I froze, immediately taking stock of my emotions and feelings. I didn't feel enchanted by the voice. This seemed odd because the first time I had encountered the elves, they had captivated all three of us immediately. I wondered if I was somehow immune now. I silently thanked the Blessing and slowly turned around.

An elf stood there in the rain looking up at me in curiosity. He seemed somewhat different than the ones I'd fought on the other side of the river. For one thing, he had a bow slung over one shoulder and a quiver of short arrows sticking up behind his back. For another, he seemed more muscular and serious.

This was an elf warrior, a defender of the holt. I licked my lips and decided to see if I could beat the elf at his own game. I replied, "Standing."

He looked me over, scratching at his jaw. "Why'ya standing?"

"Why'ya asking?" I retorted.

The elf scratched harder at his jaw. Apparently, he was taking the question seriously. "I be'a looking for trespassers!"

"I'm not a trespasser. I'm just standing."

He rubbed the other side of his jaw and slowly removed his bow from his shoulder with his free hand. "Why'ya standing?"

"Why'ya asking?"

"I be'a looking for trespassers!"

"Well, I'm not trespassing. I'm just standing."

The elf blinked and slowly removed one of his arrows from his quiver. "Why'ya standing?"

Uh-oh, this wasn't working. We would go round and round until he simply put an arrow in my heart. I gauged the distance between us and realized I wouldn't be able to reach him before he could nock the arrow and shoot.

Panic began to creep into my heart, and I did the only thing I could think of. I ran.

"Hey! Where'ya going? You be'a trespasser!"

The only real direction I could flee that would allow me to put something between me and the elf's bow was right at the elf holt. I dodged around the tree I had been hiding behind and ran under the huge branches of the elf holt.

An arrow zipped by my shoulder as I dodged around and jumped over the large root system that supported the gigantic tree. Perhaps my dodging of the roots or the rain affected the arrow's accuracy, but the elf missed. Thank the Blessing for that! Other elves hooted and called out as I ran around the gigantic tree. Again, too many of the voices meant they effectively canceled each other out, so nothing they said felt compelling to me.

I continued my run around the trunk of the tree, but skidded to a stop as a dozen elves ran toward me from the opposite direction, brandishing clubs of some kind. I frantically looked around for some escape route, but saw nothing. Everywhere I went, I would be vulnerable to the elves' bows or clubs. I looked up, smiled grimly, and leaped up to grab the lowest hanging branch of the tree.

The elves hooted louder, and a few, who already stood on the branch I was attempting to climb, ran over to try and stomp on my fingers.

"Hey! Ouch!" I yelled as one hopped gleefully up and down on my tender digits. It hurt, but fortunately, the elves didn't weigh all that much, so there wasn't a lot of force behind their stomps. I hauled myself up, rolled over onto the wide branch, and knocked two of the elves off in the process.

They tumbled toward the ground, shouting, "Whoopee!" as they went.

I didn't wait to see what they might say once they hit the ground. I looked up for another branch and began climbing.

The entire tree came alive as elves rushed around in seemingly random directions, most just trying to get out of my way. The warriors, however, had found a trespasser, and they seemed to lack the humor of their counterparts.

Another arrow buzzed by my ear to smack quivering into the branch above me. Fear lending speed to my efforts, I pulled myself up onto another wide branch and ran down it toward the narrower end where it would be easier to grab the rounded branches above me.

More arrows followed me, but the leaves, branches, and other elves all seemed to conspire to get in the way. I knocked a few more elves off my branch and suddenly skidded to a stop as a female elf and her child stood in my way. Neither looked especially terrified of my presence, but the female's large eyes tightened in something that might be anger.

She opened her mouth, and I clapped my hands over my ears just as she began to speak. All I heard was, "Whatch—"

But even that much made my head swoon as an almost inexplicable desire to answer whatever question she had asked came over me. So, it did take more than one to enchant a person. Fortunately, I hadn't heard the whole question, so I was able to fight off the compulsion.

Keeping my ears covered, I spun around and ran back the way I'd come, desperately looking for some escape route or hiding place.

There was none.

A score or more of the elf warriors converged on my position. Two of them tackled me from behind. I fell toward the hard wood of the branch and had to let go of my ears to try and break my fall. I managed to, but then more elves arrived and I was overcome.

They piled on top of me, shouting, biting, kicking, and punching. I felt the blows, but panic overcame any pain I might have felt. I heaved my body sharply upward in an attempt to throw my attackers off. A few did tumble off, but a few more jumped right on in. In moments, they had my arms and legs pinned.

Suddenly, they all fell silent as one warrior stepped up on my chest and looked down at me. "Whatcha doing here?" he asked.

Instantly, I stopped struggling. "I came to get our compass back," I answered truthfully. It never even occurred to me to lie.

"Theres'a more of yous?" he demanded.

"Sure. Bain and Minnie are waiting down the hill. We have one of your elves captive."

This sent them to whispering among themselves. I was content to wait. Eventually, the elf questioning me said, "We have pretty gift on ground! Would you'a like to see it?"

What good fortune! Of course I wanted to see it. "Oh yes! I would love to!"

They helped me up, and I followed as we all made our way to the base of the holt tree. Once there, I stood patiently, waiting for them to show me the gift. They chatted among themselves for a bit until one turned to me—he may or may not have been the one who first addressed me—and asked, "Where be'a the other of yous?"

I obliged by pointing down the hill where I had left Minnie, Bain, and Eddie. "They're down there."

About a score of the warrior elves set off in the direction I'd indicated. I watched them go and then looked at the rest of the elves, waiting for them to show me their gift.

One walked up with a closed fist, holding it out before him. "Gift for you!" he called.

My eyes focused on his closed fist in anticipation, and the elf continued to hold it forth so I could watch, I waited patiently for the small fist to open and reveal the wondrous gift.

Suddenly, I blinked and the world around me shifted. The elf before me lowered his empty hand and walked away to meet the others who were returning. I found myself sitting in an uncomfortable manner and tied to one of the large tree roots that projected from the ground near the trunk of the massive elf holt. The rain had stopped, but here under the holt tree, the ground was dry anyway.

It took me a bit to realize what had happened. I'd been enchanted by the elves' voices. *Burn it all to ash! I am a dolt!* I silently berated myself. My body began to ache from the scuffle up in the tree. Come to think of it, my body had gone through quite a bit over the last week or so since the strix, and now that I wasn't doing anything at the moment, my body decided to let me know all about it—in excruciating detail.

The returning crowd of elves approached in my direction. I could see Minnie and Bain towering over the smaller elves. Each wore a sloppy grin, though Bain also looked a bit worse for wear as he happily followed his captors. I sighed, they had been compelled too! And it was all my fault.

The elves led my companions to the same projecting root and had them sit down. Soon they were tied up next to me.

I looked around for Eddie, curious what they would make of the elf we'd held captive. I soon spotted him walking among his fellow elves. Strangely, his hands were still tied and the gag remained in his mouth. Apparently, no one had thought to free him.

Soon Minnie and Bain blinked in confusion as they came out of the compulsion. They looked around, got their bearings, and fixed on me.

"Well, genius," Bain began, his voice dripping with sarcasm, "looks like your plan worked." He sported an ugly bruise on the right side of his cheek. "We all made it to the holt. Getting captured is a great way to get our compass back. Got anymore bright ideas?"

Minnie looked a bit disheveled, but uninjured. She also looked scared, but not panicky. I suddenly admired her fortitude and ability to bear up under stress. Having been someone who frequently brought stress down upon her, I'd never before appreciated this quality in her.

She caught me looking and asked, "Are you okay?"

"Just a bruised ego," I complained.

She smiled a bit at that admission and looked over at the elves that were once again rifling through our things and exclaiming over every little thing they pulled out. A few even began heated arguments, tugging the items this way and that.

The only odd thing was Eddie. He walked among his people, apparently content to remain tied up and gagged, his huge eyes blinking furiously. Eventually, he wandered over and stood before me, looking down at me with those adoring, blinking eyes. I didn't know what to make of it, so I just looked away.

Eventually, a troop of the warriors came up and formed a half circle in front of us. They didn't seem to notice that Eddie was caught in the circle with us. "You be'a trespasser!" one of the large elves proclaimed. "Trespassers must die!"

Uh-oh, that didn't bode well.

"How'ya want to die?"

I didn't feel particularly compelled by that question, so I blurted out, "Um, of old age!"

That set them back. They murmured among themselves for a bit. Finally, they came to a consensus. The elf turned back to us. "Choose'ya the death you prefer!" He held up an arrow. "Arrow!"

Two of them held up my sword. "Sword!" A third held up a rock. "Rock!"

That last sounded painful—or at least more painful than the other two methods. Bain cringed away from the elves, trying to become part of the root he was tied to. I just sat there speechless, feeling helpless. But Minnie frowned, seemingly only mildly concerned about this development. She looked over at me and asked, "Why aren't they compelling us to answer?"

"What?" I asked distractedly, keeping an eye on the three potential means of my death.

Minnie tried again. "They aren't compelling us to answer. Why not?"

"Um, because they don't need to? Hey, maybe if we don't answer them, they'll just stand there and do nothing."

"How long can that last?"

"A bit longer than answering!"

"Obviously they don't need to compel us or they would, but it seems strange that it comes and goes."

I thought about it some. I tried to find a reason for why the compulsion worked sometimes and not others. It did seem that it required at least two of them, but there were more than two confronting us at the moment. It was a puzzle, and one I frankly didn't care to answer at the moment, not with my imminent death about to descend upon me.

"What about Eddie?" Minnie said.

That unexpected question scrambled my thoughts. I finally looked over at her. Out of the corner of my eye, I could see Eddie hopping about at the mention of his name. He still remained between us and the rest of the elves who still hadn't thought to release him or even notice him.

"What about him?" I asked.

"Maybe he can help."

I severely doubted it, but anything to stall would be preferable than death by any of the options the elves were offering. I glanced at Bain who looked to have not heard anything Minnie and I had said. His wide eyes were staring at the elves in abject horror. Oh well. It takes all kinds.

I addressed the talkative elf. "Good elf, before we can choose the means of our death, we must first apologize to one of your own whom we have mistreated." I nodded to Eddie. "Perhaps you can untie him for us so we can apologize?"

No one moved. They just stared back at me.

I tried again. I mentally scratched my brain, trying to figure out a way to get them to release Eddie. Finally, a thought swam to the top and I offered, "He has my rope and gag!"

That got their attention. They turned to Eddie, shouting, "Gimme!"

They tore the gag out of his mouth and ripped the rope off his hands. Freed, Eddie raised his hands up and immediately shouted, "I'm Eddie Elf! I'm Eddie Elf!"

Every elf froze, looking at Eddie in abject wonderment. It was as if he had enchanted the entire tribe with his voice. One of the warriors moved closer and asked, "You have Name?"

"Yes! I am Eddie Elf!"

"How you get Name?" the other elf asked, amazed, and evidently not doubting it.

Eddie turned and pointed at me. "He gave me Name!"

Every one of the elves suddenly turned and looked at me with a mixture of awe and astonishment.

Eddie raised his hands high again. "I am Eddie Elf. I am king! I am King Eddie Elf!"

A chorus of voices rose to join him. "Eddie is king! Eddie is king! Eddie is king!"

I looked around in amazement, not understanding what was going on.

Minnie laughed. "How wonderful! Roy, you gave him a Name. No elf has ever had a name before, so you just made Eddie king of the elves!"

I gaped in openmouthed astonishment. "That's all it took?"

Minnie nodded. "Apparently for the elves that's all it took. Even among humans, only someone with a surname can be king. It fits."

Bain licked his lips, glancing at us then at the elves. "So does this mean they won't kill us?"

As if hearing that, Eddie turned to look at his three captives. Suddenly, I felt a sense of apprehension. We had kept Eddie tied up for better than a day, and I didn't like the look of self-assurance that Eddie now demonstrated. The elf king placed his hands on his hips in an imperial way and demanded, "You want go free?"

"Yes!" I agreed, nodding vigorously.

"You want stuff back?"

I hesitated slightly, not sure how far to push our luck, but Minnie jumped in. "Yes! And the compass your people took."

Oh well, might as well shoot for the moon. "And that," I agreed.

Eddie nodded. "It is done!" He looked back at the other elves who all watched him intently. "Free trespassers! Bring stuff! Bring compass!"

A mad scrambled erupted as the elves all sought to obey at once. They untied us and we stood slowly to our feet, trying to be as unthreatening as possible. Eventually, our packs, gear, and swords were all piled at our feet. I rubbed my hands together, trying to bring life back into them after having been tied awkwardly to the tree root.

"Thank you, King Eddie," I said.

Eddie nodded enthusiastically. "We bring compass!"

Soon another elf turned up with the small metal compass clutched protectively in one hand. He presented it to his king. "Here compass!" he exclaimed.

Eddie took it and brought it to me. He proffered it in one hand. "We square?"

"Huh?"

Minnie stepped over. "I think he is asking if this makes you even. You gave him a Name, and he is freeing us and returning all of our things."

"Oh." I straightened, trying to look as regal as possible. I reached out and Eddie dropped the coveted compass into my hand. "We are square," I agreed.

"Good!" he exclaimed. "You leave! Trespass no more! Death to come back to elf holt!"

He certainly seemed to be taking charge, and that adoring look he had been throwing my way seemed to be quickly dissipating. I nodded. "We will not come back." As long as we got to leave, I didn't care what his requirements were. "If it is all the same to you, King Eddie, we will travel south from here. Our Quest takes us toward the Phoenix's nest."

A certain amount of whispering among the elves followed my statement. Eddie held up a hand and everyone fell silent. He looked us over, his large eyes still blinking, but I could see a hardness there that hadn't existed before. He nodded. "Follow new river south!"

"The river is to the north," Bain argued. "We just came from there."

"Different river!" Eddie explained. "Follow south to mountain! Be warned! There be trolls in the mountains!"

"Trolls?" I groaned.

"Trolls!" Eddie agreed. He pointed toward the south. "You go now!"

We gathered our things and set out. We had our compass. We had our freedom. We had our lives. All things told, I could stand being banished.

As soon as we reached the base of the hill on the south side, I looked over at Minnie. "That was smart thinking, bringing Eddie into this. How did you know?"

Minnie shrugged. "I didn't. I only knew that he seemed friendlier since you Named him."

I gave a wry chuckle to that. "If having a name is so important to them, then I wonder why the other elves didn't demand that I give them a name too."

Bain snorted. "If you had, the world would no doubt be ruled by elves!"

"I didn't mean to cause such a ruckus. I only thought it strange to keep calling him 'elf.'"

Minnie nodded absently, looking away. "Well, you seem to be pretty good at Naming people," she said.

I detected something in her voice that sounded off. I glanced at her, but she continued to look straight ahead. I shrugged, dropping it.

Bain chimed in. "I'm just glad to get out of there. But do you know what my father will do once he learns there is now an elf king?"

I shuddered involuntarily. "You really think it's such a bad thing?"

"Did you see the way all the elves jumped to obey Eddie? What if he gets the notion to attack some of the human settlements? Minnie explained it to you. The creatures of the wilderness are tied to the island. They don't have individuality, but now one of them does. You may have just doomed us all. That one elf might be able to rally all the creatures against us humans!"

I stared at Bain, trying hard to comprehend the situation as he saw it. I couldn't imagine the doomsday scenario he evoked, but something deep in me warned that someday Eddie could be a real problem. Well, it would be a problem for another day—or for someone else.

"And that's not the worst of it," Bain grumbled.

"What do you mean?" I demanded, dreading his answer. I wasn't sure how much more evidence of my stupidity I could take in one day.

"We're heading directly into troll country."

This time, even Minnie shuddered. "I hate trolls!" she exclaimed.

I could only nod at the sentiment. Trolls! What else could go wrong on this Quest?

"At least it stopped raining," Bain muttered.

Yes, well, there was that.

CHAPTER EIGHT

We trudged south toward troll country. I had never seen a troll before, so I thought it best to see if my companions knew anything about these cruel creatures of the interior. When I broached the subject, Bain spoke up first.

"I've never seen one, but my father has. He told me stories. He says they're rather stupid—much more so than the elves—but they are vicious. They eat people. They have rock-hard skin that my father says our swords will be useless against."

"That doesn't sound promising," I muttered.

Silence descended. I looked at Minnie to see if she had anything to add and noticed something peculiar about her expression. "Minnie, what's wrong?"

Her thin face stretched into an expression I could not really recognize. It disturbed me as it once again reminded me of the injured look I had frequently been the main cause of. Finally, she said in a voice barely above a whisper, "A troll killed my parents."

Oh. Both Bain and I looked away. The pain evident in her voice troubled both of us. I had not known that. My lips compressed as I abruptly remembered teasing her about being a troll.

Minnie continued, her voice barely above a whisper, "I was only six when it happened. We used to live in one of the fishing villages to the east of Khol. That particular year, the Phoenix's Rebirth turned everything to desert, making the farming bad and even the fishing was bad, for some reason. My parents decided to move to Khol to see if things would be better.

"We were crossing a single mountain ridge to reach Khol when a troll attacked." She shuddered. "It was awful. I was sitting next to my father on our wagon when we saw it. I'll never forget it. That year, the trolls were shorter than the average man, but they were still incredibly strong. This one was strange. It had reddish skin—like a rash. From what I know, this is unusual. That's all I remember of it before my mother shoved me into a hidden compartment in our wagon. I could hear their screams as the troll killed them. Maybe it didn't know I was there or maybe it was satisfied with my parents—I'm not sure, but it finally left. A man traveling along that way found me two days later and took me to Khol. If it wasn't for him and King Emeth's generosity, I would be dead too."

We walked in silence, not sure what to say. My guilt for all the things I'd done to Minnie blossomed enormously. What a jerk I'd been!

Minnie, cleared her throat. "Anyway, I hear they like mountains best."

Bain agreed. "That's where my father fought one. In the year he went on his Quest, the entire north was covered by a huge mountain range that he had to transverse."

"How did he kill it?" I asked.

"He didn't. He tricked it and got away while it was confused. He said his sword only scratched the troll's hide."

Still looking troubled, Minnie asked, "Do they live in groups or singly, then?"

Bain shrugged. "I don't know. My father only encountered one. Maybe they are loners. We should be able to handle one at least."

"If we do find one," Minnie said, her eyes dark, "feel free to kill it anyway you can."

I started at the pure vehemence in her voice. I swallowed, but privately, I thought it would be better if we didn't encounter one at all. "How big was it?" I asked Bain.

"The year my father fought it, it was only about the size of the elves we just left, and even that size was too much for my father to handle easily. He said it just kept coming and coming, no matter what he did to it. Who knows how big they are this year."

I fervently hoped they were small—very small. Tiny even.

The conversation dropped off. We were all bruised, hurt, tired, and somewhat cranky from our experiences with the elves. Bain and I had taken the brunt of the physical attacks, and my body ached with every step. Pain crippled my steps so that I began staggering, more than walking. Bain still walked with a limp, and my ribs hurt from where I'd been punched a number of times. The punches themselves hadn't been too heavy, but there had been many of them.

Minnie noticed our slowing pace but didn't say anything until later that day when we finally came across the north-flowing river Eddie had told us about. "All right," she said briskly. "Time for a break."

Neither Bain nor I felt much like arguing. We sank down beside the river, uttering groans and deep sighs in the process. Minnie shook her head and set about making a small campfire.

"It's getting late anyway," she said to no one in particular. "We'll camp here for the night. You two look like you could use the rest."

I just nodded, content to let Minnie take charge. I felt beat up and exhausted. If I ever saw an elf again, it would be too soon!

We spent the night there at the edge of the river. At one point, Minnie walked downstream for a ways to clean herself up, allowing Bain and I to do so where we had made camp. I must admit, getting clean, even in the cold water of the river, did make me feel much better.

The next day, after another breakfast of eggs—I still didn't know how Minnie found them—we reluctantly shouldered our packs and began following the river south. I felt somewhat better, but my sore muscles protested every step and my ribs protested every breath.

From the few patches of sky we could see, a thick layer of clouds had rolled in. So far, it hadn't started to rain again, but none of us held out much hope that it would stay that way. This was, after all, a rain forest.

We progressed south slowly. Our injuries still hadn't quite healed—Bain's face sported one ugly bruise! The underbrush near the river was also thicker. It got thinner only where there was no direct sunlight under the canopy of trees. We didn't feel like wandering too far away from the only landmark we could be sure of, knowing that the river, at least, would lead us straight south. Just to be safe, we frequently consulted the compass.

We only managed a handful of miles before camping for the night again. Still, we were making progress, and I was in no hurry to encounter a troll.

And of course, that is when we did.

Three days after leaving the elf holt, we rounded a bend in the river and spotted a gigantic creature sitting at the water's edge scooping out seemingly buckets of water with a single, hairy, gigantic paw. It slurped loudly as it drank.

We froze. The creature easily outweighed Bain and I put together, and though it sat on its hairy haunches, I knew that it would stand at least several feet taller than me once it climbed to its feet.

Then, without looking, it reached up and tore a thick branch off a nearby tree with so little effort that a chill ran all the way down my spine. It began gnawing on the bark, and even over the roar of the water, we could hear the snap as the branch broke in its enormous and clearly powerful jaws.

So much for little trolls! I didn't know what to do. We might be able to slip back and circle around, but I felt distinctly uncomfortable about not being absolutely certain of where it was. I'd hate for it to pick up our trail and track us. I had no confidence at all that Bain and I could handle such a brute face-to-face. At the moment, it didn't know we were here, so we had the element of surprise.

Slowly, I drew my sword. Bain, sweat dripping from his face, saw and slowly drew his sword too. We knew that the troll's hide would be impervious to such weapons, but both of us felt better for having the weapons in our hands. If we had the chance, we would take it.

I glanced at Minnie, but she looked petrified with fear. And no wonder! One of these beasts had killed her mother and father.

A deep-seated anger spread throughout my body. This troll had killed her parents! I knew that wasn't exactly true, but I felt irrational at the moment.

I returned my eyes to the enormous troll. I licked my dry lips and gripped the hilt of my sword tightly. If I got the chance, I'd kill this monstrosity.

For Minnie.

Then the troll stood up, and I nearly wept in fearful frustration. It was gigantic! Its forearms looked twice as thick as my thighs! I'd never seen any creature so large before. The troll then did something peculiar. It tossed away the partially gnawed branch, shifted its feet to get better balance, and then leaned way over the river's edge. Maybe it was attempting to snag a fish or something.

The river at this point cut through a steep gorge and moved rapidly toward the north. It looked deep here and treacherous. Suddenly I saw our chance. If we could push the troll into the water while it was off balance, it would be swept downstream. If it survived the trip—hopefully it would not—it would still be too banged up to chase us.

Without giving it any more thought, I lunged into a silent charge. Bain, startled at my sudden action, followed after I'd already gained a good ten yards. I ran as fast and as silently as I could, hoping that my added weight would be enough to unbalance the troll and send it crashing into the raging river.

Fortunately, the river once again covered the sound of my approach. The troll loomed ever larger in my sight as I barreled toward it. When close enough, I let loose a war cry and flung myself against the troll with as much speed and power as I could muster.

And bounced right off.

The impact set my teeth to chattering and my eyes to cross. I hit the ground flat on my back, having made no impression on the troll at all. My breath left me in a rush, and despite all the air around me, I couldn't get any of it in my lungs. I gasped like a fish out of water.

Then Bain flew over me in a similar attempt. He too bounced right off the troll's hide. He slammed into the ground next to me, looking as if he had just eaten something poisonous.

"Huh?" the creature grunted. Ponderously it turned around.

I gasped—or as well as I was able—and looked frantically around for my sword. It lay several feet away. I tried reaching for it, desperate to try to at least go out with a fight.

Then I felt myself being lifted quite easily off the ground by my pack straps. The hairy troll stood before us, having lifted each of us easily off the ground with a hairy finger hooked under our pack straps. Bain and I dangled several feet off the ground, helpless.

"Little men," the troll boomed, "are you hurt?"

I gaped speechlessly. Well, mostly that was because I still couldn't get my breath. Still, that was the last response I'd expected from a monstrous and vicious troll. The beast's flat and hairy face even managed to look concerned.

Minnie came running up. "Roy, Bain, that's not a troll! I recognize him now. He is a hibagon!"

A hibagon? I tried to remember my school lessons. I'd heard the name, but I couldn't really place it.

Minnie continued, "They are kind creatures. He won't hurt us."

The hibagon, nodded slowly. "I won't hurt little men." His voice came out surprisingly clear and concise, assuming you overlooked the growling sounds added to each word. He set us back on our feet, where both Bain and I swayed unsteadily.

Minnie walked up and, without any hesitation, placed a hand on the ape-like creature's arm. The hibagon suffered it without complaint or fear. "They're solitary creatures," she explained, "but they have always given aid to travelers in need."

The hibagon settled back on his haunches and regarded us with his smallish eyes. "You seek the Phoenix," he said.

I was still too unsteady to be startled. I sucked at the air around me, hoping some of it would fill my lungs. I felt like I'd run into a brick wall.

Minnie answered for us. "Yes. Roy here is on a Quest to see if the Phoenix will give him a Gift so he can be renamed."

The small eyes shifted directly to me. "You seek to be worthy?"

I finally got my breath back. I said—after several attempts—"I do. Without the Gift, I will be nothing more than a vagabond for I have been Named Delinquent."

"Then I shall aid you." The hibagon reached out and placed a huge hairy palm on Bain's and mine heads.

I felt a tingle that spread through my body, radiating downward. My aches disappeared, my weariness dissipated, and my cuts healed. I felt completely rejuvenated. "Hey! You healed me!" I exclaimed.

"Me too!" Bain shouted, looking himself over in wonder.

I glanced at him and noticed that the bruise on his face had completely disappeared. I then regarded the hibagon in a whole new light. "How did you do that?"

He shrugged ponderously. "It is what all hibagons do. We can heal anything but ourselves." He reached over and gently brushed Minnie. Her eyes widen and the weariness fled from her face as color flooded in. She didn't even look so skinny anymore, not that anyone else would be able to tell. She sighed in pleasure and patted the hibagon on the arm thankfully.

"I feel I must apologize," I said slowly. "I thought you were a troll."

The hibagon chuckled, causing his huge shoulders and head to jingle in mirth. The effect reminded me of an avalanche I once witnessed. "I do not look like a troll. This I can assure you."

"Sorry. We don't really know what trolls look like, and the elves warned us that we were heading into troll country."

The hibagon considered this at length. Finally he said, "This is true. Trolls infest the mountains to the south, but I am curious why the elves would have warned you of this. The elves generally steal, not warn strangers of potential hazards."

"This idiot here Named one of the elves," Bain interjected, waving a hand at me. "The elf became king, and apparently he let us go in gratitude."

The hibagon's eyes widened in surprise. He turned to look at me more fully. "You did this? Truly?"

"Seems like it," I admitted uncertainly.

"Tell me."

So I told him the story.

When I finished, the hibagon shook his great head in wonder. "This is remarkable. To Name a creature of the wild, such as I, can only be done when three conditions are met. First, it must be given freely without having been asked for. Second, there must be an element of faith in the creature upon whom the Name is bestowed upon. Third, the Name must be given with no intent upon the Name itself. In other words, the Naming could not have been made with any thought of possessing power over the one Named. It has to be a Name free of any reputation or intent—a blank slate as I think you call it."

My face scrunched up in confusion. "You're saying I did all of that?"

"You must have, else you could not have Named the elf."

"I just did it because calling him 'elf' seemed so ridiculous!"

"That meets the third qualification," the hibagon pointed out. "You must have also believed in the elf."

"Well, I figured he was our only shot at recovering the compass. It was either him or nothing."

"Apparently, that was enough."

"What does it mean?" I felt a deep chill run down my back. My lips felt unusually dry. "Did I break the world or something?"

The hibagon chuckled deeply. "No, but I fear it will cause you or your kind trouble in the future. The lack of identity has kept the elves from thinking beyond their own basic nature. But with a Name, that particular elf may begin grasping at things that were once beyond his care. This could cause great grief."

"Told you it was a mistake, dolt!" Bain muttered.

"How was I supposed to know?" I demanded, throwing up my hands.

"Names have great power," the hibagon continued. "Names build a reputation that gives them meaning. A Name with meaning shows intent and often the character of an individual. It is nothing to take lightly."

I worried my bottom lip. It seemed my own Naming as a Delinquent was indeed defining me. *Ashes!* Why couldn't I do anything right now that I wanted to do something right? I looked at the hibagon and saw wisdom in his features I had not noticed before. Tentatively, I asked, "Do you have a Name?"

"Alas, I do not. Many of my kind do, but I am young and still making my way in the world. Maybe one day."

Minnie nodded. "Of all the creatures on the island, the hibagons are the least effected by the Rebirth of the Phoenix. They are also among the fewest—except for possibly the unicorns. Many of the hibagons have earned Names. The only other creature of the island with Names are the unicorns, but I hear they are harder to find than hibagons."

The great face of the hibagon nodded. "Unicorns are very rare, very special. They only appear to men in times of great grief. They are born with names, and this gives them a special kind of empathy." He shrugged his great shoulders. "Alas, my kind must earn ours."

I looked at the hibagon, a notion seeping into my mind. "I would give you a Name," I declared.

The wise face looked a bit sad. "I greatly appreciate the gesture, but you may not. You would Name me because of my assistance to you—to fulfill a debt you perceive, even though there is no debt. Your Naming would have no power. You would not see it as being freely given."

I knew it was true, but I struggled with the justice of it all. The hibagon deserved a Name much more than Eddie had, and though I gave the thieving elf a name, I couldn't give this kind hibagon one. "It's not fair," I complained.

"It is of little importance at the moment," the giant hibagon said. "I am young. I have plenty of time to find my Name."

"Just how old are you?" I asked.

"Seven hundred and twenty-four."

I choked. "What? That's young?"

"A mere babe," he replied seriously.

I opened my mouth to ask how old others of his kind were, but snapped my mouth shut. I really didn't want to know.

"Rest here for the night," the hibagon offered. "I will see that no harm comes to you. In the morning, you may continue with your journey. I must, however, warn you. There are indeed trolls in the mountains to the south. They are not so amicable as I. I would advise you to stay clear of them, but if you seek the Phoenix's nest, you may have difficulty avoiding them."

Minnie smiled and kissed the hibagon on his hairy cheek. "We accept your kind offer."

With so much hair, I couldn't tell for sure, but I could've sworn the huge hibagon blushed.

"Rest then," the creature said. "In a day hence, you will find yourself in troll country."

That was something he could have left unsaid.

He looked at me as if perceiving my thoughts. "I see the Blessing upon you, Roy of the humankind. Perhaps it will see you through the difficult times ahead."

The word 'perhaps' had an ambivalent ring to it that I didn't like.

CHAPTER NINE

A day later, we reached the mountains and, unfortunately, troll country. "Now what?" Bain asked, looking up the sharp ravine from which the river descended in a torrent of white water. "We can't go up that way."

Trees still covered the mountains, but they didn't seem to be as thick as what we had traveled through over the past four days. The mountains rose sharply out of the earth and ranged in a southeasterly direction—which was not exactly the direction we wanted to go since we knew that the Phoenix nest lay directly south of Khol.

The three of us looked first up the steep slope of the mountain, then to the northwest, and finally back down the range to the southeast.

"I vote we follow the mountains southeast until we find a pass that will let us go right over the mountains," Minnie said.

Bain nodded. "That does sound best. I wish we knew if there was an easy way around. For all we know, the mountains end just to the northwest of here."

"It is a problem," I agreed. "But we can only take the route that is presented to us. We go southeast along the mountains."

Naturally, we were on the wrong side of the river, so we had to backtrack a ways until we found a suitable place to cross. Having done so with only minimal drenching—I fell in partway to the amusement of the other two—we proceeded to follow the mountain range.

"The hibagon warned us that this is troll country," Bain spoke up. "We need to take precautions."

"What are you suggesting?" I asked.

Bain seemed to be working up to something. He glanced at us and then at the mountains. "One of us should scout ahead. Trolls are stupid. If we have enough warning, we should be able to either elude them or trick them. What we can't afford to do is get in a fight—we'd lose for sure. One person is harder to spot than three and makes less noise. I do have some experience in tracking and hunting—my father insisted that I learn—so I'm volunteering to scout out the way."

I glanced at Minnie. We had only been traveling together for slightly over six days, but I'd come to trust Minnie's judgment. "What do you think?" I asked her.

"I don't really like the idea of splitting up," she replied.

"Neither do I," Bain said, "but I like falling prey to trolls even less."

They both looked at me. The burden of leadership was not something I was used to. When I was with Seth and Vin, they looked to me because I was the most clever at devising fun—the trouble we got into was always incidental. Being responsible for people's lives and well-being was a burden I had never before had to carry. I wasn't sure I liked it. Still, I didn't want to look like a complete fool, so I said, "Do it. But we need a way to keep in touch. Wait for us every hour so we can compare notes. However, come back and find us the moment you see anything that is dangerous." I looked around. "I'm not so sure that trolls are the only thing we need to worry about."

That didn't seem to put Bain at ease, but he straightened up even more and nodded. "I can do that."

"Oh, and I'll carry your pack while you're scouting. You don't need the weight slowing you down."

Bain looked surprised by my offer. He shrugged out of the pack and handed it to me. "I appreciate that."

"No problem."

With a wave, Bain loped on ahead. Soon he completely disappeared from view.

"Here," Minnie said moving closer, "let me help you with the packs."

"Thank you." With her help, I was able to secure both packs somewhat comfortably about my shoulders. The weight didn't seem as bad as I had expected, but certainly more than I really wanted to carry. Well, leaders had to make sacrifices, I supposed.

That brought to mind Beth Chalom's prophecy, my second boon: *"Your way shall be fraught with danger, this is easy to see, but your fate shall be decided when you give up that which you hold most precious for that which you hold in disdain. Failure may be the path to success, and success may lead to failure. The choice will be yours."*

I felt surprised that I could remember it so well. Apparently, the prophecy had been seared into my brain. That figured. I tried to relate the sacrifices I was making to that of giving up what was most precious to me and came up with nothing. I didn't even know what was most precious to me.

I shook myself and tried to brighten up. Looking at Minnie, I grinned. "Well, Skinny Minnie, it is just you and me now."

Her own smile slipped away like bubbles in a river. "Why do you call me that?" she demanded as her face turned red and her eyes went hard. She brushed a stray hair aside viciously. "It's mean. It's ugly. It's hateful!"

My mouth dropped. *What have I done?* "What did I say?"

Minnie practically bared her teeth at me. "*Skinny Minnie! Skinny Minnie!* I know I'm skinny! I know I'm ugly, but you don't have to rub my face in it!"

My jaw dropped even further. "Uh—"

"Shut your face!" she roared.

I snapped my jaw closed.

"You've made me the laughingstock of the entire city. Everywhere I go, that is all I hear, 'Skinny Minnie!' I hate it! And it's all your fault. You started it. You're the one who did this to me. No one can look at me without thinking, 'Skinny Minnie!'" She burst into tears. Sobbing, she turned and hurried away in the direction Bain had gone, leaving me in astonishment.

I watched her go, paralyzed. I never knew she had felt that way. It had seemed an innocent thing to do, calling her skinny. After all, the girl *was* very skinny. I started to run after her, but I shuffled to an uncertain stop. I didn't know what to say to her. For some reason, I doubted that a simple apology would work in this case.

And then it hit me. I had Named her. Without intending to, without realizing what I had done, I had given her a Name and, with it, a reputation that had clung to her much like my own Naming now clung to me. I recalled the first time I had called her Skinny Minnie.

We were just kids then. She was perhaps a year older than I, but at the age of ten, I already had a mischievous streak in me. I had known of Minnie, seen her around, but in this case, she had—for the first time that I knew of—tried to interact directly with kids her own age. Before, she had always shied away or avoided us.

There must have been about a dozen of us loitering around the old city gates during the annual Phoenix Festival. I happened to notice her shy approach and instantly recognized an opportunity for a bit of fun. We had all mentioned how skinny she was, so I just upped and yelled, "Hey look! It's Skinny Minnie!" All of the boys and girls took up the chant with me, laughing and pointing. Minnie had fled in tears, much as she just had, so many years later. That had been the first time I'd made her cry, and it certainly hadn't been the last.

Looking back on it all, I realized just how big of a jerk I had been. I never even considered looking at it from her perspective. Since I wasn't physically hurting her, it never even occurred to me that I was really harming her in anyway. To me, I was just playing, goofing off.

My unintentional Naming of Minnie that day had haunted and hounded her ever since. She was friendless, more or less, but I always thought that was her fault, not mine. I had seen her as flawed, imperfect…wrong somehow. To me, she was fair game for whatever mischief I could come up with. The other children had simply followed my lead.

Burn it all to ash! I screamed into the vaults of my mind. What had I done?

More to the point, how could I fix this? Honestly, I didn't know, and it made her decision to come with me even more mysterious and baffling. At first, I thought she may have wanted revenge for my latest prank with the manure, but there were years of resentment she could be harboring against me.

Feeling like scum, I shambled into a walk, the packs weighing on me more than they should. I didn't try to catch Minnie. I didn't even know what to say to her. For the first time in my life, I finally had some idea how Minnie must have felt for all those years.

It was surely an eye-opening experience.

I don't know how long I walked, lost in my own thoughts and generally feeling both sorry and angry at myself, when someone shouting my name brought me up short. I stopped walking and looked around.

Before me hung two nets from two different trees. Each net jerked about as if some large, wild creature had been caught in it. From these nets, two muffled voices yelled at me.

"Roy, watch out! It's a trap!" That sounded an awful lot like Minnie.

"Watch where you step!" another voice shouted, sounding suspiciously like Bain.

The situation finally penetrated my foggy brain and clarity erupted into my thinking.

"What happened?" I shouted back, thinking it too late to be quiet with my companions already thrashing about and shouting.

"I got caught in a trap," Bain's muffled voice shouted back. "When Minnie tried to rescue me, she got caught too. We don't know how many more of these traps are around here, so be careful."

Slowly, I set the two packs I carried on the ground and took a good look at my surroundings. The mountains rose sharply to my right as we had been following its meandering base for some time. The trees in the area had thinned out some, but vines hung down from many of them. The ground was covered in loose debris—leaves, vines, low bushes, rocks, and so forth.

Minnie and Bain had been neatly scooped up by some ingenious nets obviously set out to capture large animals. I squatted down to get a better look at the ground around me and soon spotted another net off to one side. It had been cleverly concealed by the debris, making it look as if it were part of the terrain. I traced it to several ropes that had been cleverly made to resemble the natural vines hanging from the trees. One wrong step, and I would be caught too.

Next, I looked around for signs of life. Clearly, someone had laid this out to catch something. If that someone was unfriendly, I wanted to know about it. But I saw no one. Other than the constant swarm of bothersome insects, I saw and heard nothing else.

"Hang on," I said to my friends. "I'm going to try to find a way to cut you down."

"Hurry," Bain called. "Who knows when the owner of these traps will come back."

"I know. I know already," I grumbled. Once the third net had been spotted, I stepped around it easily. The mountains came down in nearly a sheer cliff face at this point, scalable only with the right equipment and training. Still, the ground next to the cliff face would afford a safe passage to where I could cut down the ropes holding my friends.

"How did this happen?" I asked Bain, trying to distract my mind as I made my way along the cliff face.

"I just walked into it. Never even saw it."

"Who do you think put the traps here?"

"Don't know. It had to have been recent though. The Phoenix's Rebirth was only about a couple of weeks ago. Could be anyone."

"You think humans are living out here?"

"Maybe, but the interior of the island is very dangerous. Most people can't live out here very long."

That left one of the species of creatures who inhabited the interior. I tried to think which species had the intelligence to pull this off, but nothing came readily to mind—other than trolls, and I doubted they could do this.

At that moment, I reached out along the cliff face to steady myself and placed my hand on someone's nose. The owner of said nose promptly bit my fingers.

"Yeow!" I cried, jumping away. Fortunately, I had cleared the third net, so I didn't get caught in it. I spun to face the cliff and watched incredulously as a somewhat short, pudgy bald man seemed to emerge directly from the cliff.

In fact, dozens of short, pudgy bald men were emerging from trees, bushes, and the very ground all around me. They looked so much like their surroundings that, if they had not moved, I probably would never have seen them. Each wore a pair of odd patterned shorts that their somewhat ample stomachs hung over, and many of them had their faces painted with yellowish swirls.

And they all orientated on me.

Suddenly, they each held a weapon of some kind. Swords glinted in the sunlight, knives flashed maliciously, and knobby clubs waved menacingly at my face.

I hastily backed away, trying to draw my own sword, when the ground under me suddenly gave way. I let out a startled cry and plunged down amid a torrent of dirt and debris.

I struck the hard bottom, rolled, and hastily covered my head as still more dirt, branches, and twigs fell down atop me. I had fallen in an altogether different kind of trap—a hidden pit.

When the dirt finally stopped falling on me, I slowly pushed myself up and brushed off the dirt as best I could. Looking up, I could see yellowish eyes from dozens of the men staring down at me. Finally, I recognized them.

"Gnomes! You're gnomes!" I cried, feeling greatly relieved. No other creature of the island fit the profile, and everyone knew that gnomes were generally peaceful creatures.

One of the gnomes peered down at me. "That is the skinniest troll we've ever captured," he commented to the others. The others nodded knowingly. He then addressed me. "What are you and your fiendish companions doing by the front door of our gnome home?"

"What?" I asked, bewildered.

One of the other gnomes nudged the speaker. "Told you they were stupid. They must be trolls."

"Hey!" I yelled back, offended, "I'm not a troll!"

"Yeah?" the accuser shot back. "Prove it!"

I thought about that for a moment. "Would a troll spot your trap and try to avoid it?" I asked.

"Well, you did get caught anyway."

"That's because one of you bit me and scared me half to death!"

"I dunno," another one demurred. "Could he be right?"

"Look," I interrupted, wanting to put an end to this, "would a troll get scared at all?"

The gnomes exchanged a series of glances. "Probably not," one of them admitted grudgingly.

I hit myself in the chest. "I'm a human! Can't you see that?"

"We don't see so good in the daylight," another gnome explained. "We live mostly in the mountain, not outside. It's hard to see in all this light."

"Well, trust me; I am not a troll."

The gnomes murmured among themselves for a bit. "Okay," one called down. "We're convinced that you're not trolls, but you and your friends carry weapons. This concerns us greatly. Are you trying to invade our gnome home? Humans aren't much better than trolls," he finished brandishing his weapon at me.

I blinked. "Have you seen what's out there? The weapons are for self-defense!"

"You're not on your way to ally with the trolls then?" another asked suspiciously.

"Of course not!"

"Why should we believe you?"

I gaped at them. What could I say that they would believe?

It was Bain who came to our rescue. He cut in, "We hate trolls. A troll killed our friend's parents."

"Whose parents?"

"Mine," Minnie said softly. "A troll killed my parents when I was very young."

The gnomes muttered among themselves for a bit. Finally, one of them asked, "You sound like a female. Is this true?"

"Yes. My name is Minnie."

More muttering. I heard someone say something about a Name and trolls, but I couldn't quite make it out. "Is there any more of you?"

"No," I said.

"Okay. We'll cut you down." He looked down at me. "And get you up. But be warned. No funny business or we'll have to hurt you."

"No funny business," I promised, holding up my hands in surrender.

In a surprising amount of time, all three of us had been released from the traps and stood before an array of nervous gnomes. They kept fingering their weapons and glancing anxiously at each other and us.

One of the gnomes stepped up. "I am a gnome watcher, and the rest of these are gnome guards. We must take you to the gnome council to decide what is best to do with you."

"But we are on a Quest," I protested. "I need to find the Phoenix's nest."

"I'm sorry," said the gnome watcher, "but we can't let you go any farther. Trolls control the land in the direction you are going, and since we are at war with the trolls, we can't take the risk that you would be captured and tell them of this entrance to our gnome home."

I idly wondered if a troll would bother to interrogate their prisoners. From what I knew, trolls would simply kill us, cook us, and eat us. These gnomes, however, seemed awfully paranoid and jumpy. Best not to get them riled up, I decided.

"Fine," I said since it was obvious that Bain and Minnie were leaving the talking to me. "Take us to your leaders."

I had always wanted to say that.

The gnomes moved over to the cliff face. One of the guards did something, pushing at various parts of the cliff wall, and suddenly a section of the cliff swung ponderously inward, revealing a cave that led off deep into the mountain. Torches casting dim light were jammed into the walls at various intervals.

"Let's go before some real trolls show up," one of the guards muttered nervously.

The watcher turned to regard his fellows. He pointed. "You, you, and you. Seal the front door behind us, reset the traps, and then keep watch."

The three chosen for the job reluctantly stepped back. I realized that none of the gnomes had specific names. They seemed to be identified with their particular tasks, not any individuality. Looking closely at them all, I had a hard time discerning any distinguishing features. Some sported scars and various weapons, but they all wore those strangely patterned shorts and no shirts. Their skin, however, tended to take on the coloring and hue of whatever they happened to be standing next to. I was only really able to distinguish them when they moved. I figured if they all stopped moving and held perfectly still, I would easily lose sight of them. They had perfect camouflage.

"Let's go," the gnome watcher ordered. The gnomes arrayed themselves around us like an honor guard—or as prison guards—and we all walked into the tunnels.

Fortunately, the tunnels were tall enough that neither Bain nor I had to bend over. Darkness swallowed us up as we walked. Only the dim pools of light from the scattered torches gave us anything to focus on.

I grew somewhat nervous myself. I had never been in a cave before, and the feeling of being enclosed bothered me. I shoved the feeling down and glanced at my two friends.

"Are you two okay?" I asked softly.

Bain nodded. "Just a bit embarrassed."

"Minnie," I said carefully, "what about you?"

"I'm fine, Roy. Thanks for asking."

I thought about apologizing again, but stopped, realizing how lame it would be at this point. I wanted my actions to be the apology. "What do you know about gnomes?" I asked her instead.

Minnie relaxed a bit. Clearly, she had been expecting something else from me. "Gnomes, as we are discovering, love to live underground. They can generally be found wherever there are mountains, and I guess they are natural enemies of the trolls."

"I wouldn't say that," the gnome watcher interrupted. "We've lived in peace with the trolls before, but this time they somehow found one of the entrances to our caves. They've been sending raiding parties into our tunnels to hunt us down. We've become their main source of food, so we now have to fight back."

"You mean you don't normally fight the trolls?" I asked.

"No one *normally* fights trolls—at least not in their right minds. Normally, we just stay out of their way and hide. That works well when they don't know about our tunnels or they are too big to fit inside." He thought for a second. "Or when we are huge and they are tiny. But this time, they are about your height and they can easily navigate the dark tunnels. So we have to fight back."

The ominousness of that little speech seemed to hang heavy in the air, so we all fell silent as we walked.

The air began to cool as we descended into the bowls of the mountains. We came to several branches, and, occasionally, the gnome watcher took one of these side passages without hesitation. I became confused and wondered if I could find my way back out if I had to.

Eventually we came to a huge chamber. Stalagmites and stalactites littered the floor and ceiling. A luminous fungus growing on the walls shed enough light in the room for us to see the vastness of it, and I was appropriately awed. I never knew such things existed!

Neither Minnie nor Bain could refrain from trying to see everything at once as we wound our way through the stalagmites on the cave floor. Drips of water fell in various places and added to the height of the sharp spires of stone. If I hadn't known better, I would say that it would take thousands of years for something like this to form, but I knew that all of it had come into existence overnight when the Phoenix was reborn.

It startled me. The power of the Phoenix must be much greater than I ever imagined. All my life it was a normal, natural thing for the Rebirth to simply remake the island. We didn't consider it a miracle at all since it happened every year without fail. It was predictable. But seeing all this, the intricacy, detail, and majesty of this underground world, I began to get a glimmer of the miraculous nature of what I had simply taken for granted before.

We left that chamber for another tunnel that eventually brought us into another huge cavern, again, illuminated by the strange fungus. This one, however, was filled with gnomes working industriously. Much of what they were doing was lost on me. Some wheeled carts full of rocks, others carried tools such as shovels and picks, and still others looked to be working in a garden of sorts. How anything other than the fungus could grow down here was beyond me. Some of the gnomes were obviously female. They wore a shirt in addition to the shorts, but on the whole, they were as pudgy and bald as their male counterparts.

The gnome watcher turned to us all and said, "We are almost there. The council will decide what will become of you, but I must warn you. The council really doesn't like humans. Our memories are long, and humans have not always been kind to us."

"You mean they might decide to kill us?" I demanded, appalled.

"Oh no!" the gnome watcher exclaimed, likewise appalled. "We would never do something like that. That isn't in our nature!"

"Then what?" Minnie asked, confused.

The gnome watcher shifted as if embarrassed. At length, he muttered softly, "They might send you into the tunnels controlled by the trolls."

All three of us stared at him, aghast. He looked suitably embarrassed. I didn't know what to say. Minnie, apparently, didn't know what to say either.

Bain, however, summed it up rather succinctly. "That may very well be a fate worse than death."

CHAPTER TEN

T he gnome council consisted of eleven members. Apparently, from what little I could gather, each member represented a particular working class among the gnome society, thus giving each segment of their society a say in the decisions of the entire tribe.

Minnie, Bain, and I stepped into a round chamber. We were made to stand before a long curved table carved out of solid stone, behind which sat the eleven gnome council members. Though still bald and peering at us with typical yellowish eyes, each wore a long, white robe. They varied little in height or physical features that I could tell, though subtleties in the dim lighting made it clear that they, at least, could easily tell one another apart. The seats, much like the table, looked to be made from solid stone. I idly wondered how they had accomplished all of this work in two weeks since the Phoenix's Rebirth.

One of the gnomes, a female, who sat in the exact center of her fellow council members, nodded in a bobbing manner, almost nervously, as we shuffled to a stop before them. I noted wryly that no chairs had been provided for us. Like every gnome I'd seen so far, this one appeared pudgy, not exactly fat, but certainly not lean like the elves had been. She looked us over with her yellowish eyes, and I felt a bit uneasy. A scared gnome was a dangerous gnome, as the saying went. The gnome watcher's warning that we might be tossed into troll-controlled tunnels rang in my thoughts.

"This is our gnome home," the female gnome began, eyes flickering to her fellows. She cleared her throat. "We are at war. In normal circumstances, we would simply send you on your way, having never shown you to our tunnels, but since we cannot risk you revealing another one of our entrances to the trolls, we have detained you. Do you understand our reasons?"

I glanced at Bain and Minnie, but both of them remained silent, letting me do the talking. I cleared my throat and stepped slightly forward. "We understand." Actually, I didn't. I would have never known of the entrance if they hadn't opened the cave mouth.

"Good. We have several options available to us as to what we will do with you. First, we can keep you here until the war is over. Second, we can turn you back if you promise to return to your human city." I heard doubt when she said that. "Third, we can release you into the troll-controlled tunnels. This last choice amounts to a death sentence—something we would like to avoid. They will kill you and eat you. Do you understand this?"

I nodded again. "We do, except for one point. If you aren't worried about releasing us into the troll tunnels, why were you concerned about us continuing on into troll-controlled territory outside?"

"All trolls are not equal, human," another one of the councilors explained. He was male and sported the yellowish tattoos I had seen on some of the other gnomes. "The males are vicious and incredibly stupid. The females are smarter, but just as equally vicious. Only the males roam the tunnels, as they are the primary fighters, being generally bigger and stronger than the females. The females, however, control much of the surface land in these mountains. If you'd continued on your way, the odds of being captured by the more clever females was much greater. They would have tried to get information out of you, but in the tunnels, you will just be killed by the male trolls and eaten."

That seemed too pat to me; but true or not, the gnomes absolutely believed it. "Well, I'm hoping there is a fourth solution," I said. "I am on a Quest to the Phoenix's nest. Is there a way south that avoids the trolls and gets us out of your hair?"

The gnomes glanced at each other. None of them had hair, so maybe I had just confused them. One of them, another female, leaned forward. "There are tunnels going in that direction. Some are already controlled by the trolls and the others have yet to be explored. Every year, we get an entirely new cave complex…sometimes it is in mountains such as now, but other times it is deep underground. We usually explore them all, but we haven't had time to do so yet. The war with the trolls is slowing everything down."

Minnie stepped up next to me. "How bad is this war?"

The councilors all looked grim. "We have lost eighteen gnomes. Three of them were children playing in one of the tunnels. They were the first to fall."

Minnie looked sick. "What about now? Are you winning?"

"We aren't good at killing," another of the councilors, a male, said. "It isn't in our nature. We try to block off tunnels, but the trolls are strong, and they are constantly seeking to dig through those areas we've blocked. We've managed to bury a few, but who knows if they were killed or not. More than likely, they just dug themselves out."

"So you are losing the war then?"

The gnomes all glanced uneasily at each other. The female in the center cleared her throat. "I guess you could say that."

Two gnome guards burst into the room. Every eye in the room turned to rest on them. I had begun to pick up the tale-tale signs that differentiated the various gnomes. The guards all carried weapons, but they also had their faces painted in swirling yellow lines. Each gnome had the ability to perfectly blend in with his surroundings, and, apparently, the paint aided to the effect in some way.

The lead gnome came to a gasping stop. "Trolls in tunnel thirty-six B!"

"What?" cried the councilor with similar markings. "That tunnel was cleared two days ago! How did they get in there?"

"We don't know, councilor!" the gnome guard said, wringing his hands. "We don't have any traps or defenses set in that tunnel—we thought it was clear!"

All the councilors were standing by this time. One said, "That tunnel leads right to the heart of the gnome home. We are going to have to evacuate! Hurry, gather everyone in the central chamber—"

"Hey!" Bain cried, surprising everyone, including me. "You're running away?"

"We must! The trolls are coming!"

Bain looked at the gnome guards, his voice taking on a tone of command that effectively silenced everyone else's. "How many trolls are there?"

"Two."

Bain blinked. "You're running away from two trolls?"

"Have you ever encountered a troll before?" one of the councilors demanded.

"Well, no, but—"

"Then you have no idea. We must evacuate before it is too late!"

By then, many of the gnomes were wringing their hands and talking all at once. I guess gnomes were not among the bravest of creatures.

Bain surprised us all again by stepping forward. He clapped his hands hard, startling the scared gnomes. "You can beat two trolls. Why not collapse the tunnels before they get here?"

"Not those tunnels!" another gnome, a female, cried. "Those tunnels are unstable. If we bring them down, it could bring the entire mountain down on all of us. There is a fault that runs through that area—don't you know anything? We could breech a magma flow below and flood the gnome home with lava! Are you trying to kill us?"

All three of us humans stared at the female gnome as if she had sprouted two heads. The level of paranoia they exhibited amazed us.

Bain tried again. "Then look, they are stupid creatures, right? My father fought one and was able to trick it. All we need to do is deceive these trolls into going elsewhere. Once they are gone, you can block the tunnel, build your defenses, or do whatever you need to do to make it safe here."

That got the gnomes attention. "You say your father fought a troll before and lived to tell about it?"

"Yes."

The gnome councilors gathered together and a hurried whispering campaign began. Finally, the female that had first addressed them stepped close. "We want you to lead our guards into battle, human."

Bain blinked, surprised. "You want me to do what?"

"Your father fought a troll, so it stands to reason his son can fight one too. We will still organize an evacuation in case you fail, but you can take the guards and fight the troll." She wrung her hands. "Please, human, we do not want to leave our gnome home!"

Bain started to back away, his hands out in front of him. "No. No, I can't do that. I'm not my father…"

I stood still next to Minnie, trying to understand what was going on. Bain seemed sure that he could defeat the trolls, but now that he had been placed in charge, he seemed as nervous and panicky as the gnomes did. The gnomes would never make great warriors. Their nature seemed fearful. They needed someone to take charge, to help them find their courage, to show them the way.

I also knew that if the gnomes abandoned their home, they would no doubt abandon the humans to the advancing trolls. Our best bet for survival was to help the gnomes defend their home, and Bain was our best chance of doing that.

I stepped over to Bain and placed a hand on his shoulder. "Bain, you can do this."

His wild eyes sought my own. "What?"

"You can do this. You can defeat the trolls and save the gnomes. The gnomes are looking to you, and of us all, you have the greatest experience when it comes to battle. I believe in you."

Minnie picked up on my cue, and she added her own support. "I do too, Bain. You can do this."

He looked frantically from me to Minnie, and then back to me. Whatever he found in our eyes steadied him. He stood straighter, and his shaking hands settled down. He allowed his tongue to wet his dry lips. With newfound resolve, Bain gave us a barely perceptible nod before turning to the desperate gnomes.

"Very well. I will save your home, but afterward, you must help us complete our Quest."

The gnomes all nodded their pudgy heads frantically. "Yes! Yes! We will do as you say, warrior human."

"How long do we have before the trolls reach the central chamber?"

The gnome guard considered briefly. It seemed that his panic decreased the moment he had a specific task to do. "Trolls don't move fast. They'll be here in an hour."

Bain looked perplexed. "How did you get word of them so quickly then?"

"We have a communication system based on echoes. Our forward watchers sent word."

"Fine. How many gnome guards can you give me?" Bain asked.

"I can get around thirty in short order."

Bain shook his head. "I want six. Too many of us and we'll just get in each other's way. We need to trick them, to lead them away." Bain glanced over at me. "I don't know anyone who has pulled more tricks than you, Roy. Up for a bit of mischief?"

I grinned. "Knew that skill would come in handy someday."

Minnie rolled her eyes. "All that practice on me better pay off."

Reminded of my guilt, I swallowed my grin. I looked at her sheepishly. "Sorry," I muttered.

She gave me a slight smile, but her eyes went flat and determined suddenly. "Go get those trolls, boys. I'll stay here and try to keep everyone from running off."

I raised an eyebrow at her tone. For someone dead set against killing, she seemed unusually content to shed troll blood.

Seeing that her parents had died at the hands of a troll, it was understandable—it just seemed out of character to me.

"Right," Bain said. He looked at the gnome guard. "Do you have a map of the tunnels?"

"No. Gnomes don't need maps. Besides, the tunnels change every year."

"Well, can you sketch something out for me. I need to see what I have to work with."

"Good idea, Bain," I said, turning my mind back to the problem at hand.

The gnome nodded and took out a knife. He walked over to one of the walls and began etching white lines into it with the point of his knife. He worked for several minutes. "These tunnels here are lower than those there," he said pointing. "The trolls are coming up this tunnel here." He indicated with another white line.

Bain and I studied the map. "Any ideas, Roy?" he asked me.

I nodded. "The tunnel the trolls are following forks here. If we can get them to take the left fork, it will circle back to those lower tunnels and lead them away from the gnome home."

The gnome guard shook his head. "Trolls have incredible sense of smell. They will know where the main cavern is. They know to follow the smell of our peat moss farms."

Minnie, who had followed us over to the wall, asked, "You have peat moss that grows in caves?"

"It is a different variety than what grows outside," the gnome explained. "We use if for many applications—some varieties are even edible."

"Coming back to the matter at hand," Bain murmured, "how then do we get them to go the wrong way?"

I pursed my lips. "They need to have something more attractive and probably more readily available to go after."

"You mean live bait. We're going to have to go down there."

"Probably."

The gnome suddenly looked nervous. "But that means we'll have to face the trolls! We can't do that! They'll kill us and eat us!"

"We will have to go down there," Bain stated again. "Roy, what will you need?"

I looked at the gnome guard. "What about gnome smell? Can the trolls smell you too?"

"If we don't mask our scent. We can mask our scent as readily as we can mask our bodies. It's part of our nature."

"Is there any place in these lower tunnels that we can trap the trolls?"

The gnome considered his map. After a moment, he pointed to a spot. "This tunnel widens into a large chamber. There are two sinkholes there—this is where a thin layer of rock separates a larger empty space below. We've bored a few holes in the thin rock and echoes indicate that they are about two to three hundred feet deep."

"Would a fall like that kill a troll?"

The gnome shrugged nervously. "We could always drop boulders down on top of it if we had to. They're tough, but not invincible." His worried face belied the confidence in his words.

I nodded. "That's where we need to get the trolls to go," I told Bain. "If we can get them there and trick them into falling into one of the pits, then our problem is solved."

"My thoughts exactly," Bain agreed. He turned slightly to the gnome. "We have to kill the trolls. We can't let them return and show more trolls how to find you. We also need some of your watchers to backtrack the trolls' progress and find out how they got in that tunnel in the first place. You may need to close it off."

The gnome nodded and called over a fellow gnome. He gave the watcher instructions and the gnome hurried away. Bain seemed to be doing well. In fact, he was a better leader than I had suspected.

I glanced at Minnie to see her reaction to Bain's declaration that we would have to kill the trolls, but she said nothing. In fact, her eyes showed agreement. I felt vaguely disappointed. I didn't know why this bothered me. After all, I had no objection to killing the trolls. I was very much for it. Still, I felt disappointed in Minnie.

Bain turned back to the map while talking to the gnome at the same time. "How do you collapse tunnels and walls?"

"We have an explosive powder that we make out of sulfur and other ingredients. We bore a hole, and then insert a container of the powder attached to a string. We light the string, and when the fire reaches the powder…boom!"

Both Bain and I exchanged a long glance. Both of us had heard of gnome powder before, but its specific properties and the secret of making it was wrapped in legend. No human had ever mastered the art, despite the fact that the occasional human who washed up on the beach claimed to know the secret. Apparently, they could not find the right ingredients to duplicate it. Only the gnomes knew how. I suspected it had something to do with their nature.

"We need some of that stuff," Bain told the gnome.

"Sure. We have plenty."

Bain and I exchanged another long look. With power like that, they should be winning the war, not losing it. The gnomes were not exaggerating when they said that killing wasn't in their nature. Apparently, they never even considered the powder as a weapon source.

"Arm everyone with spears," he told the gnomes. "We need something to keep the trolls at bay." Another gnome took off. Looking around, Bain rubbed his hands briskly together. "Okay then, we better get a move on."

In short order, half a dozen gnomes, each carrying a single metal canister and a spear, led Bain and I through the dark tunnels toward the oncoming trolls. The gnomes all seemed jittery and nervous, stopping ever so often to tap the walls and listen. Bain and I stopped with them, but we never heard anything.

The tunnels twisted and turned, occasionally branching off into other tunnels. Some of which looked worked and others more natural. The amount of work the gnomes had accomplished in only two weeks astounded me. My amazement aside, I quickly became lost despite trying to visualize the map of lines the gnome had etched into the council-chamber wall. Nothing resembled what I could remember. I just had to trust the gnomes, who seemed to have an unfailing sense of direction and understanding of the caves.

Finally, we came to a juncture that looked no different than others we'd passed. The rocky walls looked natural enough, but the ground had been worked, providing a smooth path among the rocky rubble and uneven ground. "This is the fork we spoke of," the gnome leader said softly. "The one to the right goes down and circles around to the chamber with the sinkholes."

"Where are the trolls?" Bain asked.

Another gnome pointed straight ahead with a shaky finger. "That way." He paused to listen, worrying his bottom lip. "I can hear them. They'll be here in ten minutes."

"Good," Bain said, rolling his spear between his hands.

I noticed that the gnomes trembled slightly, but Bain seemed to be holding up better now that he was in charge. Responsibility did that to some. Give someone a chance, and they could very well surprise you. I, however, detested responsibility.

"Three of you go set up the trap with the sinkholes," Bain instructed. "The rest of us will lure the trolls in that direction. Make sure you mark the traps. I don't want to fall into another one."

A gnome chuckled at that, but the rest just shifted nervously. "Uh, who gets to go set up the trap?" asked the gnome guard who I'd quietly decided was the leader. I had no intention of naming him deliberately or accidently.

I could see that all of them hoped to be on that detail. None of them wanted to be the bait that led the trolls to the traps.

Bain randomly pointed out three of the gnomes. "You, you, and you. Go set the traps."

Relieved, the indicated three jogged down the right tunnel, their stomachs jingling as they went. They took no more than a few steps, however, before they seemed to disappear, blending in completely with their surroundings.

Bain turned to the remaining gnomes. "Okay, fellas, here is what we're going to do." He outlined the plan for us. I liked it and added a few details that might make things easier. The gnomes, however, grew increasingly upset as they listened. They began to come up with objections.

"What if the trolls take a different path?"

"Why would they?" Bain countered. "Wouldn't they have to backtrack first?"

"Well, what if the trolls catch us?"

"Why should they? You said they were slow."

"Well, what if I fall down?"

"Blend in and mask your smell."

"What if the troll steps on me?"

"Then hold your breath," Bain suggested.

I didn't know how that would make any difference, but Bain apparently didn't care. He held up his hands forestalling any more protests.

"Something might go wrong, but you must begin thinking about all the people who are counting on you and not just about yourselves. Trust me on this. When you realize that many more gnomes will die if we don't succeed, you will understand how important this is. The risk, my friends, is worth it."

The gnomes fell silent, absorbing the short speech. They did seem a bit braver—if only marginally. They nodded. Two of them trotted a ways down the tunnel toward where the trolls would come and jammed a pair of torches into the tunnel walls, providing us with some light for when the trolls appeared. The three remaining gnomes moved into the right-hand tunnel. Instantly, they disappeared, blending into the rocks. Bain and I each found a good-size rock to throw and took our positions squarely in the center of the tunnel. We were the bait, even more so than the gnomes.

We waited tensely, not saying anything, knowing that at any moment the trolls would loom into view and the fight would be on. I gripped my spear tightly in my left hand and the rock in my right. Together, we waited.

We didn't have to wait long. Both Bain and I could hear them coming long before they stepped into the pool of light provided by the flickering torches. Their heavy breathing made it sound like an army approached. Their loud footfalls set the very floor of the tunnel to vibrating under my boots.

Could the gnomes have mistaken the number of approaching trolls?

Then two creatures marched into the pool of light. They stood easily as tall as either Bain or I, but were massively stocky with muscles bulging under their iron-gray skin. Warts sprouted over the trolls' faces and body like patches of diseased grass, and their squat, bulbous noses looked as if they had been repeatedly punched into a fat, flat disc. Their mouths, however, were full of huge teeth with two oversized incisors projecting upward, overlapping their upper lips and nearly poking into their fat noses. Four beady eyes glinted in the torchlight, sunk deep into their large brows. Each wore a loincloth of sorts and carried a huge club that didn't look very wieldy in such close quarters as the tunnel offered.

It took a moment for Bain and I to react. Neither of us had ever seen a troll before, so the mere sight of them set us back on our heels. Suddenly realizing what I was about, I nudged Bain, and we yelled to get the trolls' attention. Then we wound up and threw our rocks as hard as we could at the trolls. We could hardly miss. Their bulk took up most of the width of the tunnel.

But that was when everything started to go horribly wrong.

CHAPTER ELEVEN

My rock struck the rightmost troll square in the stomach without any effect at all. In fact, I wasn't even sure the troll noticed. Bain's rock struck the leftmost troll in the nose. This brought the troll up short, forcing his companion to stop as well. The troll on the left began rubbing his nose and taking deep, gulping breaths.

The troll sneezed.

The sound was deafening in the tunnel. Goopy snot shot out and splattered on the floor at the troll's feet. He rubbed his nose, and then sneezed again, nearly knocking himself off his own feet.

"Eh?" the second troll asked. He looked to be a bit taller than his companion. Short, brownish looking hair stuck out of the troll's head in seemingly random directions.

"Mi nose was tickled," the first complained, rubbing vigorously at the offending body part. I realized in horror that if the troll had rubbed my skin like that, he would have rubbed off a good chunk of my muscle along with the skin.

"What tickled it?" the second asked, evidently curious.

The first troll peered down the corridor to where Bain and I stood. "Man-thing there." He pointed.

The second troll looked, spotted us, and frowned. He looked puzzled. "No man-things in gnome tunnels. Those be skinny gnomes."

Bain and I stared in astonishment. We couldn't even move, so surprised were we. The situation hadn't developed at all how we'd envisioned it. We'd hoped to enrage the trolls to the point where they lumbered after us, not even thinking about the gnomes anymore.

"I's a tellin' you, they be man-things," the first troll disagreed with alacrity. "And it tickled mi nose!"

"What we do then? I came to eat gnomes, not skinny man-things."

The shorter one peered more closely at us. "They do be awfully skinny." He sniffed deeply. "Moss be that way." He pointed right at us. "Fat gnomes be that way too. We go."

They trampled on, right at us. I realized they intended to either walk right over us or simply swat us out of the way. Apparently, they only had room in their brains for one thought at a time, and eating a fat gnome was the one thought that currently had dominance.

What to do?

An idea crept into my mind. I ducked down the side tunnel, letting my free hand trail along the wall until I encountered something soft. "Here!" I cried, grabbing the gnome ear I had found. "Look! I have a fat gnome!" I hauled the terrified gnome away from the wall and shook him so that the trolls, now coming even with the fork in the tunnel could see.

The gnome in my grasp whimpered pathetically, and it was all I could do to keep him from running away. I hated to do it, but I had to get the trolls' attention somehow.

Bain had leveled his spear at the trolls and was slowly backing up in the direction we had first come from, cut off from me and the other gnomes. I appreciated his valiant effort to stand between the trolls and the gnome home—even if I thought it foolish.

The trolls hardly seemed to notice the skinny man-thing, but at my cry, both trolls turned to look in my direction.

"Hey," the shorter of the two trolls exclaimed, "man-thing has fat gnome!"

"Ooh! Yummy," the second one proclaimed, rubbing his belly.

I stared. They sounded like children!

Bain saw an opportunity and thrust with his spear. He hit the second troll squarely in the chest with the sharp point, but the impact drove Bain back a few steps.

"Hey," the troll bellowed, "man-thing tickling me again."

Uh-oh. That didn't sound very childlike. I shook the gnome in my hands again until his teeth chattered. "Look! Fat gnome! Come and get it!"

The gnome squeaked and tried to pull away, but I hauled him back. He never even tried to hit me or pry my fingers away.

Bain tried to strike with the spear again, but they ignored him, taking a slow step in my direction. The spear made contact with one of the troll's arms. The troll absently reached over with his other hand and scratched the spot.

The first troll hesitated, eying me speculatively. "There be only one," he complained. "There be two of us. We need two fat gnomes."

"You can eat skinny man-thing," the second one offered generously.

The first smacked the second upside the head. The blow would have killed a human, but it merely knocked the taller troll back a step or two. "Not fair! Me want fat gnome too!"

I realized that if I didn't give them a better offer, they would just continue on up the tunnel in the direction where they dimly determined there would be at least two gnomes to consume.

I dropped my spear and reached out blindly, trusting the Blessing, and grabbed another gnome. This one, at least, tried to bite my fingers in desperation. I griped him around the neck and yanked him into the center of the tunnel. "Two fat gnomes!"

"Hey!" the troll cried, brightening. "The man-thing has two fat gnomes now. One for each of us."

Now the trolls seemed more interested. They stepped into the side passageway, coming my way. I began to back up, pulled along by the frantic gnomes.

"Do trolls have any weak points?" I asked the walls around me.

The remaining hidden gnomes said, "They have sensitive eyes and ears. Are you really going to feed us to the trolls?"

"No! Find the others, but don't mask your scent. We want the trolls to follow us. Run!"

I released the gnomes, and they both turned and ran as fast as their chubby legs would allow down the tunnel. The last gnome broke from his hiding place and darted after his fellows.

"Hey! They be getting away!" one of the trolls hollered, his gravelly voice echoing.

They hesitated, so for good measure, I picked up my fallen spear and swung it like a club at one of those sensitive ears. I contacted solidly along the side of the face of the larger of the two trolls.

"Ouch! Man-thing bit me!" he cried, grabbing at his smarting ear. He turned his beady eyes on me, and they narrowed into barely perceptible slits. "Kill!" he roared, lumbering in my direction.

I let out a squeak of fear, turned and ran as fast as I could down the dark tunnel. The gnomes, fortunately, had placed torches often enough along the tunnel to prevent me from smacking into one of the walls when the tunnel made a turn or stumbling too much on the uneven ground.

The enraged trolls rambled along behind us, like an avalanche gaining momentum. The gnomes in front of me scampered ahead with surprising agility. Only belatedly did I realize that Bain had been caught behind the trolls. Well, Bain would just have to follow as best he could.

By the time we reached the chamber with the trap, I could hardly run. I took great heaving gasps of air as I stumbled to a stop. I could hear the trolls pounding toward me, so I knew the trap still had a chance. So far the trolls had not really reacted as expected, but hopefully they would still fall prey to our trap.

I looked hastily about me. Luminous fungus clung to the walls and ceiling, casting an eerie yellowish-green light around everything. The chamber we stood in was large, but the walls were smooth, as if something liquid had once passed through it. I knew that to be impossible since the chamber itself was only two weeks old, but who really knew what went on in the world while everyone slept during the Rebirth. The ground before me was slightly uneven, as if gentle waves of the sea had been petrified somehow.

Two circles of glowing fungus outlined the sinkholes, revealing the trap locations. The gnomes had bored holes into the thin layer of rock atop the sinkholes and inserted their canisters of powder. I could make out a string or thin rope of some kind leading off each of the canisters to a spot next to one of the few boulders in the chamber.

I couldn't see him, but I suspected one of the gnome guards lay in wait there, prepared to light the fuse—as the gnomes called the string.

Now, to get the trolls to step into the trap.

The gnomes had assured me that the thin layer of rock would hold my weight, so I ran into the nearest circle and turned around, holding my spear out before me. Sweat beaded my brow and my hands shook. I had never before seen anything so monstrously strong and unaffected by my efforts. No wonder people hated trolls!

The trolls lumbered into the chamber, spotted me, and charged. The bigger one took the lead, his huge fists sweeping the air before him. If he connected, I would be pulverized.

A spark of brilliant light caught my attention and a flash of fire flared toward me, following the string. I saw that the fire would reach the canisters about the same time the lead troll got there too. Good. The trap would work!

Only then did I realize that I still stood right over the trap myself. I began to backpedal, struggling to get my spear up to slow the charging troll down some.

I felt awfully clumsy all of a sudden.

I made it to the perimeter of the trap and took several more steps back, still holding my wavering spear point up in the direction of the troll. The larger troll lumbered into the trap and raised one hugely muscled arm to slap the spear out of its way when the world exploded.

The force of the explosion picked me up and flung me, the spear, and any rational thoughts I'd retained through the air. A cloud of dirt, rock, and dust followed me, and everything seemed to slow.

Through the debris cloud, I still managed to see the dim outline of the troll flailing desperately as it fell into the hole beneath it. The trailing troll had been hit with the same force of the explosion as I had, but he'd merely rocked back on his feet, hardly deterred.

Then I hit the cavern floor and seemed to roll forever. I came up against a smooth, curved wall, rolled partway up it, and then fell back. My ears rang, my body ached, and my brain threatened to shut down as blackness nibbled away at the edge of my vision.

I shook my head groggily and slowly pushed myself to my knees. The dust cloud dissipated enough for me to clearly see the second troll peering down into the sinkhole where his companion had disappeared.

Ah, ashes, I muttered internally. *We didn't get both of them.*

The remaining troll scratched at his head in confusion. "Where troll-friend?" he inquired generally. He looked down into the hole and hollered, "Halloooo! You down there?"

No response came back.

The troll looked around, saw me, and asked, "Man-thing, what you do with troll-friend?"

Honestly, I couldn't answer even if I'd wanted to. I heard him, but it still didn't register, what with my ringing ears and disorientation.

The troll growled low in its throat and strode around the sinkhole, coming in my direction. I saw that it would avoid, either accidently or intentionally, the other trap. And I was in no condition to run.

That's when Bain came out of the darkness and flung himself on the troll's back, his dagger digging into the creature's right ear.

The troll bellowed in pain as the dagger actually cut deep into the earhole, one of the few vulnerable spots on a troll's body. With sudden speed, the troll snatched Bain from off his back and flung the hapless young man in my direction as one might swat at a bee.

Bain rolled to my feet then rose shakily to his knees beside me. We regarded each other, knowing what was coming next. If the troll wasn't angry before, it surely was now.

"Quick," Bain said, "help me with this spear."

I dimly realized that my spear had followed me across the cavern—or I had held on to it somehow as I'd been blown through the air. I got painfully to my feet and helped Bain pick up the spear.

Meanwhile, the troll had lunged into a fearful charge, intending to kill his tormentors. We got the spear upright and Bain wedged it into a small depression against the wall. "Keep it straight," he warned me. "It has to be straight!"

We both held the spear, Bain closer to the head and me closer to the wall. I didn't really understand what was going on, but at that point, I trusted Bain. We held the spear as steady as we could, and the troll simply impaled himself on it in his rage.

I could feel the force of the impact on the spear shaft, and the butt of the spear actually embedded itself farther into the wall as a crack ran up the entire spear shaft. I realized then that if the spear had been at an angle at all, the troll would have simply snapped the spear in two the moment he struck it. But because it had been held level to the charging momentum, the point had enough force—provided by the troll—to actually penetrate the troll's skin.

The troll came to a sudden stop. He blinked his beady eyes as it took a moment to realize he had run into something that actually hurt. He looked down to see the spear embedded deep in his chest. An expression of wonder crossed his face, and he reached out one thick hand to touch the spear shaft almost delicately.

Then the light left the troll's eyes and it slumped forward onto its knees. Since the spear haft was still braced in the wall, the troll didn't even fall all the way over.

It was dead.

My body began to shake as I let go of the spear and fell back against the cavern wall. Bain joined me, breathing hard. He had a look of satisfaction on his face.

"There, Father," he whispered to no one in particular, "I did it. I killed a troll—something you never did."

The gnomes were coming forward slowly, their own spears held out before them. They poked at the troll body gently, as if afraid of waking it or something; but when the troll didn't react, they started to cheer, dance around, and clap each other on the back.

My breath had begun to catch up with my body, and though I ached something terrible, I felt alive. With the ringing in my ears dissipating, it registered what Bain had just said. I glanced over at him and felt a camaraderie that I'd never expected to have with the prince. "What was that about your father?" I asked.

Bain shrugged. "It is the reason I came on this Quest with you, Roy."

He seemed to be fighting with something internally, so I just waited. I figured he would tell me when he was ready, and I took the opportunity to get my breath under control. Surprisingly, I didn't have to wait long.

"My father is king of Khol. Do you know how he got the job?"

Job? I had never considered it a job. "Not really. I guess I just assumed he inherited it somehow."

"His own father was not king. My father was an orphan—the details of which I know little about. He never told me the whole story." He sighed. "There are a lot of things he never told me. But as a young man, he went on the Phoenix Quest, the only man in Khol alive today to have actually survived a trip to the Phoenix's nest. He became king because of that. He was given the surname of Emeth, but I bet you don't know what his given name is?"

"Not a clue. I've only ever known him as King Emeth."

Bain nodded. "His given name is Garret. Few remember him that way—mostly because he has discouraged any mention of it. Before he became king, replacing the old king, he was known as Crazy Garret."

That rang a bell. "I remember something about that. Crazy Garret was supposed to be the wildest, craziest, and best warrior of the old guard under the old king."

"That's my father."

I took a deep breath. "I didn't realize they were the same person."

"They aren't. The Quest changed my father. He came back a much gentler, more stable, and kinder man—or so he claims. Do you know what his surname means? It means 'truth.' I don't know what he went through in his Quest, but his encounter with the Phoenix changed him profoundly. Mind you, I only learned of this years later. I wasn't even born when all this happened. Mostly I learned of it from the older soldiers in the King's Guard, and usually when they were too drunk to realize what they were doing."

I frowned. "So what does this have to do with you coming along on my Quest?"

Bain took a deep breath and let it out slowly. "My father is a brave and powerful warrior. Despite his surname, he still retains all his bravery and skill—well most of it anyway. He is getting older. But I'm different. I grew up in the palace, not on the streets or in the Guard as he did. I learned how to use a sword and various weapons, but that is because I'm a prince, not a warrior."

"You want to be a warrior? This is why you came along?"

"No," Bain disagreed. "I want to prove that I am not a coward."

That took me by surprise. I looked at the dead troll and wondered why he or anyone else assumed he was a coward. "I don't understand."

"I'm not like my father. I don't want to be a warrior. I don't like fighting. I would rather run away." He sighed again. "I don't even like confrontations. But those are not the qualities of a prince or the son of a warrior. My father never expressed disappointment in me. He never even compared me to what he was or used to be. But I did. Every time I saw him wield a sword or spear, every time I watched him spar, every time I listened to a story about him from one of the older guards, I compared myself to him, and I always fell short in my own eyes."

I was finally understanding. "So when I chose to go on a Quest and your father would not let Minnie come with me unless someone else did, you decided this was your chance to prove that you could be like him?"

"Pretty much. I suspect it was why my father didn't put up much of a fight when I volunteered. I think deep down he wants me to follow in his footsteps. I think that he is hoping that your Quest will become my Quest." Bain shifted his position a bit to look me in the eyes. "You probably never even realized this, but if you complete this Quest, you may very well be our next king."

"What!" I sat up straight, adrenalin flooding my system all over again. "What are you talking about?"

"Khol law states that anyone with a Gift must be a public servant in some capacity, but only someone who has completed the Phoenix Quest can be king. Right now, that is my father—but there is no one else. The last man to attempt one never returned. You are the first one to go on a Quest in three years. If you succeed, and there is no one else who does, you will be king next."

"Hold on now. I don't want to be king."

"Neither did my father. I think, however, that he would like me to follow him—to be king after him. But to do that, I must go on the Quest myself. I must survive. In a way, if we survive this, then both of us will have completed the Quest, and I will be as eligible to ascend to the throne as you will be."

"Well, let's hope we both survive then," I said briskly. I thought of something. "What if there is no one who has completed the Phoenix Quest, who then becomes king?"

"Those who have the Gift in the city will form a council from among themselves and rule until someone qualifies for the throne, but I don't think you still quite get it. I didn't come so I could be king—that's my father's reason for letting me come. I came because I needed to prove I wasn't a coward. I want my father to see me the way others saw him." Bain's lips firmed. "I don't want to disappoint him."

"You think you have?"

"I think deep down he's disappointed. That's why I came to help you, Roy. To be honest, I wouldn't dare go alone...I just don't have the courage for that. But when I realized I could go on the Quest with you—even if it was yours—I jumped at the chance. Though to tell you the truth, I was scared to death. Still am, really."

"Well, that makes two of us," I said, smiling.

"What do you think Minnie would make of this?" Bain asked, matching my smile.

"Honestly? I don't think anything scares that girl."

"Except maybe trolls."

"Well, yes, there is that," I agreed.

Bain chuckled lightly, and I felt our friendship bond in unexpected ways. Then I thought about our conversation a bit more. To think, I might one day be king! I analyzed the possibility from several angles, not sure how I really felt about it.

Suddenly, a thought struck me with the force of an epiphany. "Bain, if both of us complete this Quest, we will be in line to become king, right?"

"Yep. That's the way it works. Khol law."

"What if Minnie completes the Quest?"

Bain's eyes widened, and he stared at me as if someone had gut-punched him. "No way! Do you think—"

"She might want to become—"

"And that's the reason she came along—"

We stared at each other, not really knowing what to believe, what to say, or what to think.

"No way!" we said in unison.

CHAPTER TWELVE

The gnomes set out to make us heroes. Being a hero might be all well and good for Bain, but for me, I didn't care for the expectations that went along with the title. I had, up until this point, lived by the philosophy that the lower you keep everyone's expectations, the less work anyone requires of you.

Bain reveled in the roll of being the hero, quickly becoming the unofficial leader of the gnome defense effort. Over the next three days, while both of us recuperated some from the battle with the trolls, he organized the gnomes into teams and sent them out into the tunnels to set up traps, block passages, and otherwise shore up their defenses against the trolls. The gnomes, for their part, agreed to any of his suggestions enthusiastically. As long as they didn't have to actually fight with any of the trolls, they were satisfied to follow Bain's directives.

I tried to ignore them all, spending all three of the next days trying to get as much sleep as I could. The grateful gnomes had given me one of their sleeping chambers, a round, cave-like hole carved or formed into the wall of the main cavern. Only a curtain separated me from the din outside, but in truth, I could sleep through anything.

And I needed the rest. The gnome explosion had left me bruised, seemingly, over every inch of my body. Perhaps some healing residue leftover from the hibagon remained in my system, for by the third day I was feeling pretty good. But I was in no real hurry to get on with my Quest.

The trolls were still out there, and to get to the nest, we would need to go through the trolls.

It was easier just to sleep and forget about all of it. However, on the fourth day, Minnie bustled into the chamber and immediately pinched her nose. "Roy, you need a bath."

"I need sleep more," I countered, disgruntled. I didn't smell anything.

"No, you definitely need a bath, and this place needs to be fumigated."

Apparently she wasn't going to go away. I sighed and pushed myself up from the pile of blankets. I glanced over at the remains of what passed for food with the gnomes: an edible moss, mushrooms, and meat of some cave dwelling creature that I thought it best to remain nameless. It looked to have been more of an overgrown rat to me. Maybe that's what smelled.

I ran my hands through my hair—which had lengthened noticeably since the Quest had begun—and it came away greasy. Okay, maybe I did need a bath. "You win. Point the way and I'll get cleaned up."

"There is an underground stream not far away. The gnomes use it for many things, but it will do nicely. Here, catch." She tossed me a bar of soap.

"Where'd you get that?" I inquired.

"Brought it with me."

That pack of hers must have room for half the city of Khol in it. I shrugged and struggled to my feet. "Which way?"

"Go to the small end of the cavern and ask any gnome there where the stream is. They'll point the way out to you. I'd remain downwind of them, though. No sense in poisoning them with your fumes."

I fixed her with a baleful stare. "Ha. Ha."

"But hurry, the gnome council is assembling in an hour to decide how best to help us on your Quest."

And so reality decided to intrude once again. I thought about quibbling, making some excuse, and returning to bed, but as nice as the gnomes were, I didn't relish living in these caverns. I wanted to return home. To do that, I would need to complete my Quest. "Very well. I'll be there."

I left, found the stream—the water must have been near freezing—and washed up. I'd brought along a change of clothes, which I struggled into, and then spent fifteen minutes or so washing out the ones I had slept in over the last three days. They still had my blood on them, but I scrubbed hard and got most of the stains out. Despite the frigid water, I did feel invigorated after having cleaned up. There was just something special about being clean.

I made my way back to my room, but the moment I stepped near the blanket that covered the small entrance, I could smell the foul odor of the place. I decided not to go in for the moment and went looking for the council chamber.

Minnie and Bain were already there when I appeared. The gnome council sat in their eleven chairs behind their curved table, regarding us with the same mixture of fear, dread, and hope that had been evident during our first meeting.

I nodded to Bain and sidled up to Minnie's side. She said, "You smell better."

"I feel better too," I remarked. "But that water was freezing!"

She looked mildly surprised. "Oh, I use the hot springs on the north side of the cavern."

I gave her a steady look. "You didn't mention any hot springs."

"I didn't?" She blinked at me innocently. "Oh my. It must have slipped my mind."

Yeah right. I decided to wrap what was left of my dignity around me and ignore her. I focused on the council members.

The female gnome in the center stood when she realized she had my attention. "We are grateful for the assistance you have given us in turning back the trolls and helping us to prevent further incursions into our gnome home. You have done so at great personal risk, and one among you," she gestured at me, "has been gravely injured in defending us."

I opened my mouth to explain that I hadn't been that hurt, but Bain, standing on my right, nudged me with an elbow. I kept my mouth shut.

Bain stepped forward and addressed the council. "We thank you for your kindness over the past several days. It was our honor to fight for you."

The female gnome continued, "Yet we feel we are still in your debt. We would repay this debt if we are able. We know that you are on a Quest to reach the Phoenix's nest, and we will aid you if we can. We know of no tunnels that will get you by the trolls, and the path you must take leads through the troll tribe that controls this mountain. We have discussed the matter and have come up with only one way to aid you. You must go see the hermit."

All three of us humans exchanged confused glances. I cleared my throat and asked, "What hermit?"

"There is a human who lives in the mountains above us. He has power over the trolls—this we have seen with our own eyes. We find his presence there strange for a number of reasons. First, humans rarely live in the interior of the island. Their structures tend to fall apart, and the Rebirth often makes life difficult for any human who tries to build a permanent structure. Second, this human has lived here for nearly eight years—much longer than other humans who have tried it. Third, he can control the trolls."

"Why do you call him a hermit?" Minnie asked.

The female spokesperson shrugged. "This is how he describes himself to any who comes near. He says, 'Don't you know what a hermit is? It means leave me alone! Go away!' We have granted him his wish and left him alone."

Bain leaned over to me. "Ever hear of this hermit?"

"Nope. You?"

"Me neither. Minnie?"

She shook her head.

Bain cleared his throat and spoke louder. "You say he has control over the trolls? How is that possible?"

"When one comes near his tower, he orders it to go away and it does. The trolls never bother the hermit."

This sounded promising, but suspicious as well. I decided to question this further. "Is he their leader or something?"

"We don't think so. From what little we have observed, he just tells them to go away and they do. We approached him once to see if he would be willing to aid us in our war."

"What happened?"

"He told us to go away too."

I glanced at Bain and then asked, "What did you do then?"

The gnome representing the watchers said, "We went away of course."

"You went away," I said slowly. "Just like that?"

"Well, he told us to go away."

Gnomes were not known for their bravery, so they very well may have just gone away upon being told to do so, but I found it incredible that they would have given up so easily. Who was this hermit? "Did he ever harm any of you or the trolls?"

"Not that we know of. He just keeps to himself in his tower."

Minnie suddenly looked more interested. "He lives in a tower?" she asked. "How did he build a tower out here?"

"That is a mystery to us. One year it wasn't there and the next it was and he was living in it." The gnome speaker considered. "Though I believe he was forced to rebuild it three years ago. He may even have used the trolls to aid him."

I wasn't sure I liked the sound of that. I wanted to ask more questions, even though it seemed the gnomes lacked a thorough sense of curiosity.

Bain beat me to it. "So you think he will help us get by the trolls?"

"He is human. You are human." The gnome speaker shrugged. "Why would he not help you?"

We could think of a dozen reasons, but we let it pass for the moment. Bain continued the questioning. "How do we find this hermit?"

The female gnome in the center gestured and two watchers stepped forward. "These gnomes will show you the way. There is a tunnel that opens up near his tower. You must be careful, however, for trolls regularly pass through the area. Though they do not bother the hermit, I fear they would kill and devour you."

Bain, Minnie and I put our heads together. "What do you think?" I asked.

Minnie shrugged. "I don't know what choice we have. You beat two trolls, sure, but that was more a result of foolishness than anything else."

I felt slightly offended by that.

She continued, "Or perhaps it was the Blessing given to Roy. Either way, I'm not sure we want to fight an entire tribe of trolls."

I worked my sore arm. "I didn't feel very Blessed," I complained.

Minnie gave me a flat look. "You're still alive, aren't you?"

Bain jumped in. "I agree with Minnie. Two trolls were hard enough. It would be suicide to tackle any more. If this hermit can help, then I say we should try to talk to him. He doesn't sound dangerous, just protective of his privacy."

"But don't you find it strange that he lives out here?" I asked. "I've never heard of anyone who lived this long in the interior."

"As Bain said," Minnie interjected, "he doesn't sound dangerous. We wouldn't lose anything by asking."

I gave in. I didn't really trust this hermit, but I didn't know of another way to get by the trolls. "Fine, but it is too dangerous for you to go, Minnie. I want you to stay here until Bain and I get back."

Bain nodded his agreement, but Minnie shook her head. "That is very sweet of you, Roy, but if the hermit agrees to help, you might not be able to come back here. We need to stay together. Besides," she added, looking at the gnomes, "I think the gnomes are hoping we all will go."

Neither Bain nor I could come up with a suitable counterargument. Well, leadership wasn't my strong suite anyway.

Bain said, "We go together." He turned back to the gnomes. "We would be pleased if you showed us the route to the hermit."

The female gnome in the center nodded, looking relieved. "The two watchers will take you. Gather your things and go with our thanks."

That sounded much like a dismissal. I suppose that even heroes wore out their welcome, but if we were to get on with this Quest, we needed to leave anyway. So we gathered our things—I was grateful to leave my foul smelling room anyway—and followed the two gnome watchers into the tunnels.

Daylight flooded through a hidden entrance that the two watchers had opened. The device to move the slab of stone from the entrance was canny, consisting of a series of pulleys, stout ropes, and counterweights. None of it made sense to me, but it amazed me how quickly the gnomes had moved to find all the entrances to their gnome home and block them off in one way or another. Those that had already been detected by the trolls were collapsed or permanently sealed, but those that the trolls hadn't discovered yet were cleverly hidden.

I peeked out of the cave and squinted painfully in the bright daylight. "It's bright out there," I complained.

"Your eyes have adjusted to the darkness of the caverns," Minnie explained. "It'll take us time to adjust to normal daylight." She edged past me and took a quick glance outside, shielding her eyes as she did so. "I can't see the sun because of the trees, but it feels like late afternoon to me."

"How can you tell?" Bain asked curiously.

"It's just a sense I get."

"Well, there is no time like the present," I said. "Let's go."

We stepped out into the light, and I squinted, trying to get my bearings. The two gnomes followed us out cautiously, trying to look everywhere at once. One pointed up the slope. "The tower is at the top of the peak."

I blinked, surprised. "How did he build a tower all the way up there?"

The gnome shrugged, seeming on edge. "Last year the tower was in the middle of a valley. Who knows what the terrain was like when it was built."

Of course. I should have figured that.

"Thank you for your help," Minnie said.

The two gnomes nodded nervously, looking around for any danger. "You're welcome. We will go now." They darted back inside the cavern and the stone block that cleverly concealed the entrance ponderously closed behind them. It shut with a hollow, final sound.

"Guess we're not going back that way," I muttered.

"The gnomes did all they could," Minnie said, defensively. "We can't expect any more from them."

"Perhaps not," I agreed grudgingly, but for the past four days, I had felt safe. I didn't relish leaving all that behind to traipse around in the wilds again. Oh well, best man up and get on with it.

We picked our way up the slope, at times detouring around the steeper parts. Occasionally, we would get a view of the vista around us. When I could, I would look north through the trees toward our home. I noticed the others doing it too, and once we thought we spotted the sea, but mostly we just saw trees.

At the top of the peak, we were greeted by a rocky clearing and a tower built precariously at the edge of a mind-numbing drop-off on the south side of the peak. The tower itself had been built with grayish-black looking blocks of stone. The round structure looked like a finger jutting out of the earth to about thirty feet high. A squat doorway built of stout wood was the only entrance I could see, and that, naturally, sat right at the edge of the cliff. A tiny window at the top overlooked the entrance.

We walked up to the door and only then noticed a sign had been nailed to the wood. It read: GO AWAY! We exchanged glances.

"I'm not so sure about this," Minnie said softly. "In all the stories, hermits are dangerous people."

"What stories?" I inquired.

"You know—stories."

Well, I didn't know. "I guess I don't read much."

She gave me a withering look. "Well, in the stories, there is a reason hermits come into the wilds to live. They don't like people."

"Now she tells us," Bain muttered, echoing my sentiments exactly. "Should we go back then?"

Now that I was here, I was in no mood to go back. I reached out and rapped on the wood. "Hello?" I called. "Anyone home?"

"Don't you know what a hermit is?" a ragged voice shouted out of the window above. We looked up to see a thin face framed by long, ragged black hair peering balefully down at us. He fixed us with one of his startling green eyes and shouted, "It means leave me alone! Go away!"

We promptly turned around and started away. We'd made it perhaps a hundred feet away when something about the whole situation bothered me. *Why am I leaving? I don't want to leave, do I?* I looked down at my feet, which were walking briskly away of their own accord. Coming somewhat to myself, I began to fight each step, trying to impose my will on my own body.

I slowed and then stopped. Bain and Minnie kept on walking. I frowned at them, trying to think. We needed to talk to the hermit, so why were we walking away? I shook my head, trying to get rid of the cobwebs that seemed to have shoved my consciousness down into the back of my brain somewhere.

I realized that the hermit must have done something to us, compelled us in some way. It didn't feel at all like what the elves had done. This felt more invasive, more personal. With the elves I had felt like I was in a trance, but this felt as if someone had hijacked my body.

I took a deep breath and came out of it. My body was mine again. "Hey," I called after Bain and Minnie, "stop."

They didn't listen. I ran after them, grabbed Bain by the shoulders, spun him around, and slapped him hard. It worked.

He blinked and recognition flooded his eyes. A hand went up to his stinging cheek. "Did you just hit me?"

"Maybe," I demurred, "but you, uh, needed to wake up. Look at Minnie." We glanced at her as she continued to walk away. "We've got to wake her."

"You gonna slap her too?" Bain asked doubtfully, blinking a bit in confusion as he slowly regained control over himself.

I didn't want to. Despite my rather checkered past—particularly when it came to Minnie—my father had drilled into me that if I ever laid a hand on a woman, he would kill me. I believed him. "No. You do it."

"What? No way. She'll kill me."

"We've got to wake her somehow!"

Bain thought about it. "You just need to startle her, right?"

"I think so."

"Well, maybe you could kiss her."

I choked. "Then she'd kill me!"

Fortunately, neither of us had to risk our lives at Minnie's hands. She stopped another fifty feet away and shook her head slowly. Looking around, she saw us arguing. "What are you guys waiting for?" she demanded impatiently. "Let's go."

We looked at each other and then at her. "Uh, where are we going?" I asked, carefully.

"We need to find a way through the tribe of trolls. The hermit isn't going to help us, so we need to find our own way."

"How do you know he won't help us?"

"He told us to go away. So let's go. We need to hurry!"

I realized that some of the mind control still lay on her. She was obeying whatever command the hermit had instilled in us. Bain and I hurried to her side and by mutual consent, each of us grabbed an arm, picked her up, turned her around, and started walking back toward the tower.

"What are you doing!" she yelled, struggling in our grip. She wasn't a match for our strength, and we were able to manhandle her without hurting her. "Let go of me!"

"We're going back to talk to the hermit," I told her firmly.

"We can't! He told us to go away!" It seemed the closer we got to the tower, the more control she lost.

"Uh-huh," Bain agreed, wincing. He seem to hesitate too.

"What are you going to do?" she demanded.

"Well," Bain said lightly, shaking his head as he fought with whatever was going on inside him, "we're debating on whether to slap you or kiss you."

"You wouldn't dare!" she cried, shocked. She hesitated then, as if perhaps reconsidering part of that declaration. After a moment, she said, "You can put me down now."

I glanced at her. "You're not going to walk off?"

"No. The compulsion is gone—mostly."

We set her down, and she rubbed her shoulders, shivering. "That was worse than what the elves did! How did he do that?"

We stopped some distance from the tower, not ready to risk confronting the hermit yet.

"It has to be the Evil Eye," Bain remarked thoughtfully. He rubbed his head. "I've heard about it, but I've never seen it before."

"But that power comes from the Dragon," I protested. "It's a legend. The Dragon doesn't really exist."

The Dragon—Nachash—was a bedtime story spoken by parents to scare their children into obedience. I had never before seen any evidence of a creature that, according to legend, was the equal of the Phoenix in power and was as much evil as the Phoenix was good.

Bain shook his head. "My father believed the Dragon existed. I don't know much, but I think I remarked once that the people of Taninim worship the Dragon. To them, the Dragon is very real."

I recalled that conversation, frowning. "So you're saying that this hermit is a Dragon worshiper?"

"I don't know. It just explains how he did what he did."

I cleared my throat. "Then do we want to have any dealings with him? He sounds kinda dangerous to me."

We considered each other for a moment. Finally, Bain said, "I don't see that we have much choice. He might be the only person who can see us safely through the trolls in these mountains. Without his help, we'll have to either turn back or risk the trolls alone. I'm telling you again, I'm not real keen on going up against an entire tribe of trolls."

Minnie sighed. "I agree with Bain. The hermit might be dangerous, but he doesn't seem to want to hurt us. All he told us to do was go away. If he wanted to, I bet he could have made us walk right off the edge of the cliff."

That gave both Bain and I an uncomfortable start. I hadn't thought of that. My desire to face the hermit plummeted noticeably. Bain looked as if he might just very well change his mind altogether, but I hadn't come all this way to be stopped. I shored up my courage, straightened my shoulders, and began walking back to the tower. The others followed more or less because they had to. "All right then," I said briskly, "best one of us not look him in the eye then—no matter what."

Minnie nodded, a shudder running the full length of her body. "That would be me. I'm not looking in his eyes again if I can help it."

"You know what to do if either Bain or I are entranced?"

A sly smile graced her thin lips. "Oh, I'll think of something."

I stared back at her uncertainly. Already I felt a sting on the skin of my face, and she hadn't even slapped me yet. Minnie seemed altogether too certain of herself in that respect.

I turned away from them and regarded the wooden door of the tower as we walked back up to it. I pounded on it again, none too gently. I didn't feel very neighborly at the moment.

"What is it now?" roared the voice from above. "Didn't I tell you three to go away?"

This time, all three of us kept our eyes averted.

"We just want to speak to you," I called. "It's very important."

"Nothing is more important than my privacy," the voice complained. "Look at me when I'm speaking to you!"

I felt a tug on my will, but I successfully fought it off. "If it is all the same to you," I answered, "we'd rather not."

There came a pause from above. "Oh, very well. I can see that I'm not going to get any peace until you've said everything you want to say. Come on in then. The door is open."

Bain tried the door, and, sure enough, it opened without so much as a squeak. We stepped inside to find only a flight of stairs that wound around the inside of the tower. We took the stairs until we came to a well-lit room at the top, cluttered with books, potions of some kind, a few caged animals, and a musty smell that I couldn't quickly identify.

In the center of the room, hands firmly planted on his hips, stood a tall man, perhaps in his midforties, wrapped in a green robe that matched his eyes. He looked thin, though the robe effectively hid any lines of his frame. The one thing that really stood out to me was the size of the man's ears. On a bird, they would double as wings! Deep lines marred his face, like a prune; but even if his face was smooth and clear, nothing would be able to mask the pure annoyance that practically radiated from him.

Minnie looked deliberately away, but I decided to meet the hermit's gaze. I had defeated his spell before, I figured I could do it again. Bain tried to look, but his eyes kept falling away nervously.

The hermit regarded us each in turn, his eyes piercing. When they came to rest on me, they narrowed perceptibly. "Ah, now I see. You have the Blessing upon you."

I jumped, startled. "Uh, yes."

"Very well. You are here. What do you want?"

"Um, I'm Roy, this is Bain and Minnie. I am on a Quest to the Phoenix's nest, but we need a bit of help getting by the trolls. The gnomes told us that you have some degree of power or influence over them, so we came to ask your indulgence and help."

He tugged at one of his phenomenally large ears and licked his lips as he thought about my words. "Interesting. My name is Jairus Ramah, and this is my home."

I blinked, startled. "You have a surname!"

"I do. What of it?"

"I just—well, that is I…um…"

He snorted. "You're from Khol. You think everyone that has a surname needs to be enslaved to the general well-being of everyone else. Well, not me. Here, I serve no one. I am free."

None of us knew what to say, so we just stood there, shifting from foot to foot.

"However," he remarked, "that does not mean that I will not help you. Come, let us talk about it." He gestured to a small bench and another chair. He rubbed his hands. "I have a feeling that we have much to discuss."

ROY'S JOURNEY THUS FAR
Dotted Line = Roy's Journey

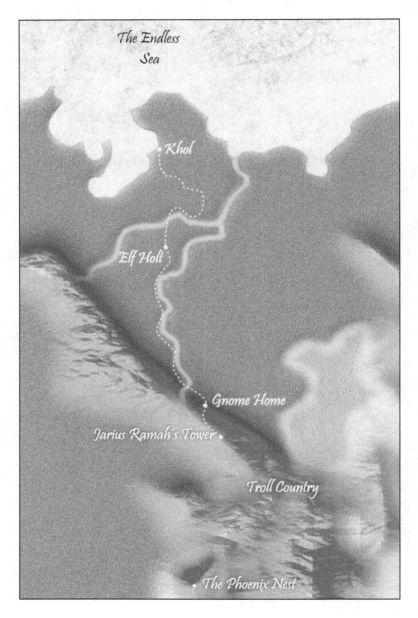

CHAPTER THIRTEEN

"**Y**ou've set out on a fool's Quest," Jairus stated bluntly. I didn't really know how to respond to that. I glanced at Bain and Minnie, but they carefully kept their eyes elsewhere, leaving the negotiations to me. I cleared my throat, shifting uncomfortably on the wooden chair I'd accepted.

"The wisdom of my Quest is not as important as the fact that I am determined to see it through," I responded, thinking myself clever.

"Very foolishly stated," the hermit drawled. "You seek my help. What is it that you think I can do for you?"

"We hear that you have power over the trolls, so we are hoping you will guide us through troll territory."

"Hmmm. What will you give me in return for this service?"

That set me back. In Khol, anyone with a surname performed public service and never required payment. The throne saw to their needs. I licked my lips. "Uh, what do you want?"

"I want to be left alone. I've told you that already."

"What if we promise never to tell anyone in Khol that you are out here?"

"Why would any idiot from Khol come way out here?" he demanded, eyeing me meaningfully. His gaze seemed to burn right through me.

Something pushed at the edges of my will, but I bit my lip and fought it off. "Surely there is something else you want," I said lamely.

Jairus Ramah sat back in his oversized chair and tapped his fingers on the armrest. I idly wondered how he managed to get a chair all the way out into the middle of nowhere. He regarded me for some time, much like a cat watches an unwary mouse. "You present a challenge to me," he said at last, "and I haven't had a challenge in a long time."

"I'm afraid I don't know what you mean."

"The power of the Blessing upon you is significant. The Blesser must have been very powerful. Few have ever resisted my Evil Eye."

I started. "Bain was right! You do have the Evil Eye."

Jairus smiled, pleased. "I do. Perhaps I need to explain the nature of the Gifts to make clear my interest in this interruption of my solitude. This will help if we are to proceed—or if I am to help you." He settled more thoroughly in his chair, and then snapped a look at Minnie. "You. Girl!"

Minnie looked at him reflexively.

"Fetch some water!" Jairus ordered.

Without so much as a whimper of protest, Minnie stood bolt upright and went over to a bucket of water in the corner. She dipped a cup full of water and brought it immediately over to Jairus.

He accepted it much as a king would accept his due. "Good. Go sit down."

Minnie did. The moment she sat, she blinked as if coming to herself. Once she realized what Jairus had done to her, she flushed deeply, turning her face away.

I scowled at the hermit, my fists clenching. He chuckled and wagged a finger at me. "That was just a demonstration and will serve as a starting point for this discussion."

He took a sip of water, and I wisely held my tongue, though I wondered if my knuckles would have enough force to flatten a dozen of the man's wrinkles. He winked at me as if he had read my thoughts.

"All Gifts," he began, "have one of two sources: the Phoenix or the Dragon."

Once again, here was someone who believed in the Dragon. I began mentally rearranging my perceptions. It seemed my disbelief in this instance was foolishness. In fact, the almost emphatic way Jairus spoke of the Dragon probably convinced me of the truth of it more than anything else could. I still held on to some doubts, but they were slowly fading.

Jairus continued, "Personally, I feel that the Phoenix's Gifts are rather pathetic in comparison to the Dragon's, but regardless, the strength of the Gift always depends upon the spirit and strength of mind of the individual who wields the Gift. No Gift, even those of similar nature, is equal. I possess the Evil Eye, but so do others. They, however, do not have my level of power. Some can only make suggestions and others can only affect weak minds. My Gift is powerful, because I am powerful. Do you understand?"

I nodded slowly. His words sounded right, but I suspected that if I was receiving this lecture from someone with a Gift from the Phoenix, it would have a different tone or flavor to it.

"Your friend there has a very strong mind," Jairus continued, indicating Minnie, "but my Gift can override her will and dominate it. I can make her a slave to my will."

"I was able to resist you," I pointed out somewhat arrogantly.

"And that is the challenge you present to me. Whoever bestowed the Blessing upon you was powerful, perhaps even my equal in strength. Even so, the Blessing is a fickle power, for though it can be granted, much of its strength is derived from the person upon whom it is bestowed. Despite the Blesser's individual power, the strength of the Blessing upon you is, in part, because of you." He leaned forward, his eyes boring into me. "It makes me wonder what the real nature of this Quest of yours is all about. Bestowed upon someone else, I doubt the Blessing would be so strong."

"I just want a different Name. I've been Named a Delinquent—"

"Ah. And so you are outcast in Khol much as I am in Taninim."

That surprised me. "You have been Named Delinquent too?"

"Don't be absurd. We don't have such petty and archaic practices in Taninim. I was exiled. My power made...others uncomfortable, let's say. Jealous, they conspired against me—but that is a story for later. You then are on a Quest to see if the Phoenix will find you worthy enough to grant you a Gift and thus a surname. Is this it?"

"Yes," I said, chagrined. Putting it like that made my entire Quest seem absurd.

"Ha! You are a fool! You really think the Phoenix will grant you a Gift merely for showing up at his nest? You are naïve if you believe that!"

"I don't understand."

"Of course you don't. You're a simpleton—with a surprisingly strong spirit." Jairus shrugged. "Guess it takes all kinds. Listen, the Phoenix only grants a Gift to those who will work in his interests. This is the fallacy of the Phoenix's Gifts. Those with Gifts serve his designs only. Failure to serve means you can have the Gift stripped from you."

I didn't know that—or rather no one had ever explained it to me in that way. Minnie finally looked up, agitation written all over her face. "You make it sound as if that is a bad thing. Why? You imply that the Dragon's power is superior."

"It is, my dear girl. The Dragon grants Gifts upon those who have the strength of will and desire to wield it. He doesn't require service. I serve myself and only myself. That is true power. That is a true Gift. Those in Khol who worship the Phoenix are deceived. If our two cities ever confronted each other, Taninim would crush Khol easily."

"But I was able to defeat your Evil Eye," I protested, not liking where this conversation was headed.

"And yet you need my power to get you past the trolls, do you not?"

That stumped me. I fell silent.

"If you had my Gift, dear boy, you would not need me at all. You could walk among the trolls without fear, dominating their puny wills, and making them into your servants if you wished."

Minnie rose to the challenge. "Then why don't you do that?" she demanded.

Jairus laughed. "Why would I want to? I want peace and quiet while I plan my return to Taninim. Trolls hanging around all the time would be an inconvenience, not to mention quite smelly. The point is, the Dragon's Gifts are much more practical." He returned his eyes to me. "I sense that you could be powerful in your own right if you ever came to understand this truth."

To be honest, something about this appealed to me. I could see how his power would benefit me much more than the Blessing would. With his power, I could cut right through troll country without fear. With his power, I could protect Minnie and Bain easily.

Still, something about it bothered me. I didn't believe for a second that he was telling me the entire truth. I shook my head. "Perhaps you're right, but I doubt it is for me. My Quest is to the Phoenix's nest. There I must go."

Jairus contemplated me silently for a few moments. In some way, he looked pleased rather than disappointed. I didn't know how to take that. He said, "Do you know how the Dragon bestows his Gifts?"

"No, sir."

"It is quite different than that of the Phoenix. The Phoenix bestows his Gifts on those who are willing to serve his will. They must be chosen or proven worthy first. This is why so few actually possess such a Gift. Have you noticed this?"

I nodded. "I have. In Khol, I guess there are maybe less than a hundred who have a Gift."

"Correct. This is not true with the Dragon. In Taninim, there are thousands with Gifts. The reason for this is simple. The

Dragon gives freely to any who seek him. There is no payment or cost to receive a Dragon's Gift, merely the will to use it."

I found myself curious despite my attempts to dismiss his words. I asked, "So how do you get such a Gift?" Out of the corner of my eye, I could see that Bain and Minnie looked troubled by my question.

"You must brave the Abyss. That, in truth, is the only real requirement. The Abyss has two entrances. One is always found in Taninim in the Temple of the Dragon, but the other entrance moves from year to year, at the whim of the Phoenix's Rebirth—it could be anywhere. One must merely enter the Abyss and deal with the Dragon. All who do so and can find their way back out are granted a Gift. Only the weak and uncertain are unable to find their way back." He shrugged again. "This weeds out the riffraff, which is so unlike Khol, would you not agree?"

I nodded because I thought he expected it, not out of agreement. I had never been to Taninim, so I couldn't rightly say this outcome was better or not.

"Indeed," the hermit continued, answering his own question. "In Taninim, a surname is not so rare."

I perked up at that. "Really?"

"Naturally not. The Dragon represents power, my boy, and he is very liberal with his Gifts."

I honestly gave thought to changing course and heading straight to the southern city. If nothing else, I wanted to verify the hermit's words, prove the truth of them for myself. However, I knew that neither Minnie nor Bain would agree to such a course of action. They were committed to my cause, my Quest. To abandon that now would be to abandon them. This I could not do. Regardless of their reasons for coming, they had become my friends—true friends—and that meant something to me now. I didn't want to lose that.

So I shook my head and said, "Sounds nice and all, but I still need to finish my Quest, and we still need your help through troll country."

Jairus Ramah drummed his fingers on the armrest again. "You are an interesting challenge all right," he said mostly to himself. "What year is this?"

We glanced uncertainly at each other.

"Well? Speak up! What is it? I've sorta lost time. Is this the Year of the Swine, Bull—what?"

"It's the Year of the Lamb," Minnie answered.

"The Lamb huh? That represents subservience and dependence. Perhaps that is a good omen. That would also mean that the next year is the Year of the Dragon, right?"

We nodded.

He mused a bit more and then nodded. "Very well. I will help you, but there is one thing I will require in return."

"What's that?" I asked, feeling more relieved than I'd suspected I would.

"I want your promise."

That shut me up. I really didn't want to make any promises with this hermit, but then, refusing to make promises was more in my nature than any particular suspicion about Jairus. I had always been reluctant to make any promise. I didn't like commitments that made demands on my life.

"It's nothing major," the hermit continued, seeing my reluctance. "I am only asking that if—and only if—your Quest fails, that you return here and finish this conversation with me. It may be that I might be able to offer you a better alternative than what you would be given at Khol." He leaned forward. "It will be a significant improvement over being an outcast and a vagabond, this I assure you."

"But you are an outcast already," I pointed out.

"Unlike Khol, Taninim doesn't count things in such a manner. I have a plan to return and assume my rightful place there. You might be able to help in that. You would find a place of honor and wealth if you did."

I hesitated again. Jairus had read me correctly. If I failed in my Quest, I wasn't sure I could return to Khol. He was offering me a better life than anything I would be able to get in my home city or in any of the villages that hailed to Khol.

"Roy," Minnie said, "don't do it."

I glanced at her and noted the concern in her face and was touched by it. I looked at Jairus. "Only if my Quest fails?"

"Only if. If you succeed—which I find highly unlikely—you need not ever return here. Think about it, boy. You lose nothing, even if you do come back here. All I'm asking is that you allow me the chance to finish this conversation with you. You make no promises outside of that."

"The Dragon cannot be trusted," Bain interjected. "Why should we trust you?"

"You already do, boy. You are here, seeking my help. You would not be here if you didn't trust me to some degree. I have nothing to prove. You all may go away and leave me in peace—as I wanted you to do in the first place."

"The Dragon still cannot be trusted," Minnie echoed firmly.

The hermit smiled indolently. "Ha! You hardly even believe in him! What matter is it then?" He snorted. "You do not need to trust him anyway. He cares not what we do with his Gifts, only that we have the will and strength to wield them. Trust has nothing to do with my proposal. If anything, it is I who am trusting you to keep your word. It is all I ask." He looked cunningly at Minnie. "Do you want my help or not?"

She fell silent as did Bain. Their objections had been effectively silenced. Both knew that we needed the hermit's help, and all I had to do to get it was make a promise. If we succeeded and I obtained a Gift and a surname, we would be free from this promise. Failure, however, meant that I would return—assuming I lived—to Khol as nothing more than a vagabond, having earned a reputation that would follow me around for most of the rest of my life. As much as I hated to admit it, that reputation was something I had earned. My Naming had been of my own creation.

True or not, I wasn't sure I wanted to return to Khol under the cloud of failure and a negative reputation. I looked up and stared directly into Jairus's eyes. "I promise to return if I fail to be granted a Gift from the Phoenix," I said emphatically.

He clapped his hands in glee. "Good. Very good. Well then," he exclaimed, jumping out of his chair, "you will stay the night, as evening is now upon us. We will start tomorrow." He cast his eye at all of us. "Be ready."

CHAPTER FOURTEEN

We set out at first light, heading directly into the heart of troll territory. Jairus Ramah walked quickly through the trees atop the mountain ridge, his long cloak swishing noisily with each step. I didn't know how he could stand to wear the thing in the stifling heat and humidity. Sweat broke out all over my body within the first hundred yards, but an hour later, the sky clouded over and it began to rain. Now the cloak made more sense, though I doubted I could be convinced to wear one.

Minnie, Bain, and I followed Jairus, and none of us seemed overly inclined to talk. My friends and I watched Jairus as much as we watched our surroundings for trolls. Having witnessed the hermit's power, we felt safe, but until the first troll had been met and turned aside, we all fretted.

I still wore my traveling clothes as did Bain, though how Bain had managed to keep his soft leather cap through everything seemed nothing short of miraculous. I could see a few tuffs of red hair poking out just above his brow, damp in the rain. Minnie had changed into a rather fetching light blue travel dress, darkened slightly due to the rain. I had never seen it before and doubted she could have carted it in her pack along with everything else, but no other reasonable explanation presented itself. I promised myself to take a careful look at her pack someday, just to assure myself that it was normal.

Suddenly, Jairus stopped atop a rocky outcropping that jutted out over the southern cliffs. The trees found no purchase here, allowing for a stunning view to the south. We gathered around him, staring at tree-covered mountains that seemed to stretch out toward the south. The drizzle affected the view some, and a few of the more monstrous peaks disappeared into the clouds above.

Lifting one robed arm, the hermit pointed solemnly toward a tall, cloud-shrouded peak at the western edge of the mountain range. "Behold," he half whispered, "there lies the Phoenix's nest."

I felt a chill run up my spine as I beheld the journey's end of my Quest. I studied the mountain, wondering exactly where the nest would be located.

Bain asked the question first, "On that tall peak there?" he shook his head. "At the top?"

"I suspect so," Jairus said. "Or not. It could even be inside the mountain."

"It could be inside? Is that possible?" I asked.

"Of course. Wherever the center of the island is, that is where the Phoenix's nest will be."

"What is the best route to take to get there?"

He pointed straight down the cliff. "I will show you a path that will take you into the valley below. It is all I've really had a chance to explore in the three weeks since the Rebirth. The valley looks to empty out into the rain forest to the west of the mountain range, there." He shifted where he was pointing. "I would go that way and skirt around the mountains until you reach the peak. I suspect you will find the entrance to the Labyrinth there."

We all looked at each other in confusion. "Labyrinth?" I echoed slowly. "What are you talking about?"

The hermit gave all of us a condescending look. "You mean no one warned you about the Labyrinth?" He snorted. "You are woefully unprepared for this Quest. The nest is always surrounded by a maze. The maze, like everything else, takes various forms after each Rebirth. To reach the nest, you must solve the riddle of the Labyrinth and of the Guardian that hunts within it."

"Wonderful," I muttered dryly.

Jairus chuckled. "As I said, I am very doubtful that you will complete your Quest—let alone survive it. Regardless, if you fail and happen to survive, remember your promise."

"I haven't forgotten," I muttered.

"Good then! Let me show you to your doom!" He strode briskly off into the trees beyond.

"He's a cheery fellow," Bain grumbled, wiping moisture from his brow. He looked around sourly. "I hate the rain."

Since I agreed, I just nodded and trudged after the hermit, my heavy, waterlogged clothes chaffing at my skin.

Progress along the mountain ridge slowed as the terrain became rockier, and the rain became harder. The slick stones made handholds unpredictable and footing treacherous, but the slow pace and the fact that everyone kept their miserable thoughts mostly to themselves, allowed me to ponder the trials still before me.

I hadn't known of the Labyrinth. I knew that a Guardian protected the nest, but in all honesty, I had convinced myself that the Guardian would present no trouble to us. We were supplicants, not invaders. Why would the Guardian see us as a threat? Jairus made it sound as if the Guardian would kill us the moment we ventured into the Labyrinth.

This bothered me on a number of levels. First, why hadn't King Emeth warned us about these dangers? Why hadn't he adequately prepared us? For a moment, I wondered if the king was targeting me specifically, but King Emeth had not given this information to his own son either. There was a mystery there, but my irritated mind could not decipher it.

Second, I didn't understand why the Phoenix made it so difficult to reach him. Why surround the nest with a maze and a monster—by all the stories—that would kill anyone or anything caught? Since it was a benevolent creature, this made no sense to me. In fact, if the hermit was telling the truth at all, the Dragon was much more accommodating. Why would this be?

I began to wonder if I had been deceived all my life. Was everything my parents taught me a lie? Had I been living under a delusion? I gnawed away at these thoughts, turning them over and over in my brain, trying to understand what I was walking into and found my faith shaken.

Suddenly, I didn't want to go. Why risk my life for something that may be based on a lie? Even more, why waste my time?

I glanced surreptitiously at Minnie and Bain. They trudged on behind me, following me because this was my Quest. Did they have faith in this Quest or did they have faith in me? Then I wondered if it mattered.

I hesitated long enough for Minnie to catch up to me. The day had passed slowly and, thankfully, without any signs of trolls. The rain continued to fall unabated, and at the moment, it merely drizzled. I was wet, hungry, and irritable, but my mind was consumed by these thoughts. I needed someone to talk to. I glanced at Minnie's thin face, and she cast me a slight reassuring smile as she moved stringy strands of her hair aside. Encouraged, I asked, "Do you wonder if all of this is just a fool's Quest as he says?"

Her smile slipped into a sharp frown. "Don't let Jairus get to you," she said. "He serves the Dragon."

"Does he?" I disagreed. "Seems to me he serves only himself."

"I'm not sure what the difference is, Roy. If serving himself furthers the Dragon's ends, what does it matter? It is the same thing. That which makes no difference is no different."

I chewed on that for a time. Finally, I asked, "Will you tell me why you are really coming on this Quest with me? You seemed so sure of yourself, and all the reasons I thought you had for coming along I've since discovered are not true."

She raised a thin eyebrow. "What did you think I came for?"

"Honestly?"

"That would help, yes."

"I thought you were just looking for a way to get back at me."

She smiled at that. "I guess you might think that. But no, that is not the reason."

"Well, I've figured that much out," I said.

"I suppose if you boiled it all down—and to be honest with myself—I am here for the exact same reason you are here. I want to change my reputation...I want a new Name."

This surprised me. "But you were never Named," I protested. Then I snapped my mouth shut, realizing that this wasn't true. As I had already discovered, I had Named her years ago and that Name had stuck with her since that time. "Skinny Minnie," I said softly. "That is what you are wanting to change."

She nodded shortly, adverting her eyes. I could see the emotions swirling in her face, and I suspected that more than rain was wetting her cheeks.

"This is all my fault, isn't it?" I asked heavily. "I Named you all those years ago—not even thinking when I did it."

A slim smile flashed across her lips. "You seem to be good at that."

"Eddie the elf," I agreed. "Yes, it seems that even my own Naming is a result of me not thinking. But I would think that I would be the last person you would want to go with or follow."

Minnie stilled her features and looked steadily into my eyes. "You Named me, Roy. I am hoping that by aiding you in your Quest for a new Name, you will be able to give me a new one as well."

"Me? Why not the Phoenix?"

"I don't think the Phoenix will grant me a Name," she responded softly. "Not all my reasons could be considered pure."

That stroked my curiosity. "Oh? Like what?"

"Sorry, Roy, but a girl has to keep some secrets."

I fell silent, keeping my eyes on the next step before me. Bain continued to follow and the hermit pranced ahead of us, seemingly unconcerned about the sheer drop on our right or the steep slope on our left.

I had to ask, "Then am I a fool for going on this Quest? My reasons are purely selfish."

"Perhaps, but you've changed since we began this, Roy. The Quest is more than just the prize or the nest, it is the journey. Look at Bain. He told me why he came along and what happened with the troll in that cavern. For him, his Quest has already succeeded. In his eyes, he has become like his father—even better than his father. Haven't you noticed that he is more confident now?"

"Not really. But I don't doubt it. I don't pay much attention sometimes."

"Really? I hadn't noticed."

"Oooh, that was a low blow," I muttered, a smile playing along my lips.

She returned the smile and that, more than anything, showed me that she had forgiven me. "I want to apologize for all I did to you. I was wrong, and it grieves me that I have caused you so much pain."

"I know, and for me that has made this journey worthwhile. We've all changed, Roy. This Quest, despite the dangers, has made us better people."

A realization dawned on me. "It's not that we went on a journey, is it? It's why we went on this journey and what each of us was hoping to find that made all the difference. If we had begun this to find treasure or something, our greed would have torn us apart, wouldn't it?"

She looked surprised. "I never thought of it that way. You could very well be right. Our chosen purposes complemented each other, forced us to grow together. And that is a good reason to continue on this Quest, don't you think?"

I glanced at Bain again, mentally including him in the discussion and in my emotions. Yes, it was a very good reason to continue. "Thank you, Minnie. For a moment there, I was lost, but you brought me back."

"You may not have realized this, Roy, but you have already done that for both Bain and me. So you are welcome...with pleasure."

I now had a reason to continue on the Quest—besides the worry of having to keep my promise to Jairus. Although, I still had doubts about the full truth of the Phoenix and the end result of my Quest, at least the journey itself was profitable. I'd just have to wait and see about the rest of it.

"Ho!" Jairus cried, coming to a stop. "We have company."

We hurried to him and looked to where he was pointing. In the trees ahead, we could see a trio of trolls stomping toward us. They carried clubs with which they bashed limbs and branches out of their way. The trolls were making their way over what my father termed a saddle. This was a slightly mild rounding of the land between two sharper, jutting peaks in the long mountain ridge. Periodically, we had encountered one and the going always got easier for a time—unless one happened to be occupied by trolls.

"Do they see us?" I asked nervously.

The hermit shrugged. "Let's find out." He raised his voice. "Hey, wart-face! Do you see us?"

I nearly choked as the three trolls lifted their smallish eyes and stared at us. One grunted. "Man-things there," he bellowed, pointing.

The other two nodded sagely. "How many you see?" asked another, his voice carrying above the patter of the rain.

"More than one...I think," the third responded, scratching at his head, undecided.

That answer appeared to be enough. "Kill and eat, then," the first replied, raising his club over his head.

"Kill and eat!" the other two echoed enthusiastically, likewise raising their clubs.

They began a lumbering run in our direction. Bain and I hastily drew our swords and stepped in front of a terrified

Minnie out of reflex. We braced ourselves, knowing that our swords would be practically useless against the thick hides of the trolls, but the terrain behind us narrowed significantly, and we knew that retreat would not be an option. I stared in horrified fascination as they bore down on us. I could see drool dripping from the corners of their fat lips, and their two tusklike teeth jutting out of their mouths made them all that more ferocious in my eyes. My grip on my sword became slick.

But our heroic gesture was in vain. The moment the trolls got close, Jairus looked at all three trolls and said, "Stop."

The trolls practically fell over themselves coming to a clumsy stop, but stop they did. They stood there, chests straining as if they couldn't believe that their bodies were refusing to obey their own commands. They snorted in protest, but they did not move.

"You see," Jairus pointed out casually, "my power is far superior to anything the Phoenix could give you."

Despite my intense relief that I would not necessarily be killed and eaten, I found myself very annoyed at the hermit's words. "There is a constable back home who can do the same thing," I said. "He made me 'stop' once."

"Oh?" Jairus asked. "A Word of Power. Impressive. Could he do this?" Turning his attention back to the trolls, he fixed them with his eyes and commanded, "Fight each other."

There then commenced the most appalling brawl I'd ever witnessed. One of the trolls swung his club in a powerful sideways blow that picked his fellow troll up and sent him flying fifteen feet into a medium-size tree. The impact obliterated the tree, splintering it into deadly shrapnel.

While the first troll watched, admiring his cruel work, the third troll took a double-handed grip on his own club and brought it crashing down on the distracted troll's hard head. The wet dirt and rocks around the first troll's feet jumped a few inches into the air from the impact, and the club shattered, sending splinters everywhere.

"Ouch," protested the struck troll, his eyes blinking a bit cross-eyed.

The third troll tossed his broken club away and punched the standing troll in the nose, knocking him to the ground. By that time, the second troll returned to the fray, but having lost his own club, he commenced to use his natural weapons, punching and biting his fellow trolls.

Now that they were warmed up, the three trolls really got into it. My mouth fell open as they pulverized each other, trees, and even boulders. I'd never witnessed such strength before. Then one went down, having received simultaneous punches to either side of his head. The troll's eyes rolled up in his head, and he fell over as if poleaxed.

"Stop!" Jairus cried. The trolls turned, blurry eyed, and focused on the humans. "Stop!" the hermit ordered again. The two remaining trolls froze. Turning to look at us, I could see the merriment in the hermit's eyes. "Could your constable do this?" He turned back to the trolls. "Throw that one over the cliff," he ordered.

Minnie gasped and I felt my heart lurch, but the two standing trolls obediently picked up their unconscious fellow, walked by us to the cliff, and casually tossed him over. I watched, my heart beating harshly in my chest, as the thrown troll fell silently into the misty depths, disappearing from my vision.

"Why?" Bain demanded. "Why did you make them do that?"

The hermit spun around and fixed Bain with his eyes. Bain tried to look away, but Jairus held him. "That troll wanted to kill you and eat you, boy. Only my power stopped it. Why would you care about the fate of a creature whose only goal in life is to make a meal of you?"

"It…I don't—it wasn't fair."

"Fair? What is wrong with you, boy? That troll could tear your limbs off without hardly flexing its muscles. What's fair in that?" The hermit glanced at Minnie. "And didn't I hear you say something about trolls having killed your parents, girl? Would you see kindness shown to such vile creatures?"

I didn't know how Jairus had found out about Minnie's parents, but my eyes, like everyone else's, went to Minnie. She stared at the remaining trolls with haunted eyes, her body trembling with reaction. A war raged within her, and I suspected she was reliving the horrible moment when her family had been attacked and killed by a troll.

Finally, she shook her head. "No," she whispered.

"Good girl," the hermit muttered, turning away. "She at least has a head on her shoulders."

Frankly, I didn't know what her response meant, but I wondered if the hermit wasn't wrong in his interpretation of it.

"It wasn't right," Bain mumbled softly, refusing to look at Minnie. He looked pale, unsteady on his feet.

Jairus ignored us and looked at the other two trolls. "Go your way and forget about us."

The two trolls lumbered away without even once glancing back at us.

When they had disappeared, Jairus took us all in with a single glance and a cruel smile. "There. Aren't you glad I came along?"

I couldn't come up with any suitable response to that. Even Minnie looked petrified by what had just happened. I didn't even know how to process it. No doubt about it, Jairus was incredibly powerful. I idly wondered why the trolls hadn't snapped out of it at the first punch. When I had slapped Bain, that had startled him out of whatever Jairus had done to him, but with the trolls, they just continued to fight.

"Come along," the hermit beckoned impatiently. "There is a suitable campsite in the next saddle or so. We'll find it and get some rest for the night. The way into the valley is not far, but we must pass through the troll village to reach it."

Still not quite sure what to do, we obediently followed. I didn't much like staying in Jairus's presence, his attitude grated on me, but I was forced to admit that without his power, we would never have gotten this far. For that, at least, I was grateful. Plus, I didn't relish the thought of trying to sneak through an entire troll village without his power to back us up.

Tomorrow was already shaping up to be another interesting day.

I hated interesting days!

CHAPTER FIFTEEN

Around noon of the next day, we approached the troll village. The mountains flattened out here, providing a large, level area among the peaks for the village. Most of the trees had clearly been uprooted by the trolls and fashioned into crude huts that stayed together mainly by brute force and dried mud. I warily watched the huge fire pit that marked the center of the village. Something large had been spitted and was slowly being roasted over the fire. I hoped it wasn't a human.

From our position behind a group of boulders near the top of one of the surrounding peaks, we watched perhaps a hundred trolls roam around the village. Mostly, I couldn't tell what they were doing. To me they looked to be lounging randomly, seemingly unaffected or bothered by the constant drizzle. A fight between two of the trolls was being cheered on at the edge of the village, but other than that, very little activity was taking place.

"The way into the valley is there," Jairus said, pointing to the thickest concentration of huts on the south side of the clearing. "We will have to go through the village to reach it."

"Why can't we just go around?" Bain asked.

The hermit leveled a withering look at the young prince. "There is no way around. The way down is through a ravine in the cliff face that begins there. So, unless you plan to jump, we will have to go through the village. Trust me. Have I led you astray yet?"

We didn't answer, but in truth, the hermit had been of tremendous value so far. We'd encountered three other troll hunting parties on our way to the village. Each time Jairus Ramah simply told the belligerent trolls to go away and forget about the group of humans. They had, so we were able to continue on our way unmolested.

"There is nothing to fear," the hermit explained. "All we need do is walk right on through. I'll take care of the trolls. There is a ledge—more of a crack, really—in the cliff face that goes all the way to the valley floor. Once you are on this path, my task is done. I'll return to my tower, and you can continue on with your foolish Quest."

The prospect of getting rid of the grumpy hermit appealed to me. I liked his power, but not his attitude. No wonder the citizens of Taninim had exiled him.

"Then let's get on with it," I decided, standing up and striding forward. I would be burned to ash if I allowed Jairus to show us up.

Bain stepped forward with me, leaving the hermit and Minnie to follow us. I felt good about that, and Bain winked at me in approval. I could hear Jairus grumbling to himself, but he didn't try to take the lead.

It didn't take long before a group of trolls spotted us. They hooted and bellowed to their fellows, and, suddenly, a hundred trolls came running in from every direction. They seemed amazed that prey would so boldly walk into their village, and so for the moment, they just stood in front of us, waiting for us to come to them.

I slowed enough to allow Jairus to take the lead. He sniffed audibly as he passed me, but I wasn't offended. He could sniff all he wanted to as long as he dealt with the trolls.

The hermit stared at the mass of trolls and bellowed, "Make way! You will allow us to pass unmolested!"

I couldn't rightly be sure that the trolls even understood what the word "unmolested" actually meant, but the group in the center obediently stepped aside, making a path through their midst.

I wondered aloud, "Are you sure you can control so many at once? They look a bit agitated."

The hermit glanced at me. "I am very strong. Besides, this lot is easy. Their brains are small, and they are easily overwhelmed. It is nothing. You should consider this fact, boy. You could do a lot more good with a Gift from the Dragon than you ever could with one from the fickle Phoenix."

Actually, I had begun to suspect this may be true. I couldn't say for sure, but watching what Jairus could do was rather convincing. It didn't matter though. My reasons for continuing the Quest had changed. I glanced at Bain and Minnie, particularly Minnie.

As we approached the trolls, I pulled my mind back to the matter at hand. "How long can you control them?"

"The effect varies. With trolls, my commands usually have enough force of will to last a few days. You'll be long gone before then."

The trolls snarled and growled as we came up to them. I could see their natural instincts warring with the hermit's will.

They didn't move toward us, but they drooled hungrily as we passed.

Once we'd passed, the trolls fell in behind us and followed us to the southern edge of their village. I didn't like it and, apparently, neither did Minnie. "Why are they following us?" she demanded.

"I didn't tell them not to," the hermit replied absently.

"Well tell them to go away."

"Why? They aren't bothering us."

"It's just—unnerving," she admitted.

"It isn't my job to comfort your insecurities, girl. Just ignore them."

Not an easy thing to do. The village ground had turned to mud in the rain that stuck to our boots and hindered our progress. I looked back, hoping the trolls had lost interest in us. No such fortune. The barefoot trolls plowed through the mud with ease, seemingly unconcerned with the mud or the rain. They made no sounds other than breathing heavily and grunting.

A few of the trolls looked different than the ones I'd seen before. I focused on these in an effort to distract my mind. Slightly smaller and wearing actual clothing—if you can call a tunic that fell to the knees and nothing else, clothing—they often pushed themselves to the front of the larger trolls. I thought this odd. The new trolls typically had longer hair, though they looked uglier by far. Their faces bore a torrent of warts that ranged in size from a pimple to the size of my thumb. Their tusklike teeth were also shorter, barely protruding from their lower jaw. At first, I thought them to be juveniles, but upon closer examination, I determined them to be females.

I nudged Minnie who walked close by. "Look, females."

"I saw," she whispered back. "Remember what the gnomes said. They are more intelligent." She glanced at Jairus. "So they might be harder to control."

I hadn't thought of that and my nervousness increased. I put my hand to my sword and Bain mimicked my gesture. I didn't like this. Why didn't Jairus just send the trolls away. Was he trying to intimidate us? If so, it was working.

We reached the edge of the village at last. The trolls, unbothered by such basic emotions as fear, had built many of their log huts right next to the cliff edge. The rain and cloud cover obscured some of the view, but it was every bit as spectacular as my first glimpse of the mountains to the south and the peak that was home to the Phoenix.

A descending ledge—a scar in the cliff face, as Jairus had described—ran a ragged line diagonally to the valley floor below. It looked steep, but passable at the same time. A few trees clung to the ledge here and there, but other than that, only the obvious footprints of trolls spoke of anything that might be on the trail below.

I studied the tracks. "Jairus, what about any trolls down in the valley below?"

The hermit looked around and picked out a particular female troll. "You, come forth."

The female shambled forward, glowering dangerously at all of us, but she stopped several feet away. I saw that she wore a headdress comprised of bird skulls. I shuddered. Trolls were weird.

"Tell me the truth. Are any trolls on the path down or in the valley below?"

"No," she growled out, sounding like a thwarted avalanche. "Valley sacred."

"See?" Jairus said, turning to us. "No trolls."

"Wait a moment," Bain said, stepping forward. "What does it mean, 'sacred'? Is there something about the valley we need to know?"

The hermit sighed. "There are a lot of things you should probably know, but knowing them will not change the essential thing."

"What's that?" Bain challenged.

"Your stupidity. Trolls live in the mountains, so valleys are sacred to them. Occasionally they go down there and leave a sacrifice to appease whatever superstition they hold most dear."

Bain opened his mouth to protest, but snapped it shut again. I agreed with Bain's reticence. Bantering with the hermit was a losing proposition. Jairus's reasoning did strike me as a bit odd though. If the trolls preferred the mountains, then why didn't they hold mountains to be more sacred than valleys? Ultimately, I decided, it didn't matter—as long as there were no trolls down there.

"Look," I said, anxious to get a move on, "I believe him. He commanded the troll to tell the truth. Why there are no trolls down there is irrelevant. Let's just go."

Bain still looked troubled, but Minnie nodded. Her thin face looked unnaturally pale. No wonder—surrounded by trolls, her childhood nightmare, I was amazed she'd kept it together this long.

We started toward the crack.

"Remember your promise, Roy," Jairus said sternly. "I expect you to keep it."

"Only if I fail," I responded just as sternly.

"Oh, there is no doubt of that. The question is when will you give up? There is a better way to get what you want, you know."

I didn't know. Turning my back on him, I led my two friends into the ravine.

If a colossal giant could wield a monstrously huge knife and carve a thick line in the cliff face from the top all the way to the valley floor at a fairly shallow decline, it might explain what we found ourselves navigating. Resembling more of a crack in the cliff than a ledge, it meandered down toward the valley floor at an angle we found manageable, if not downright scary.

Within moments, we left Jairus Ramah and the trolls behind and moved slowly down the fissure in the cliff. Bain and I let Minnie take the lead while we nervously listened for any signs of pursuit. If the trolls decided to come after us, there would be very little we could do, at any rate. They couldn't come at us more than one at a time, but that one would hardly need to fear our swords. We would be lost, but Bain and I silently agreed we would buy Minnie time to escape if need be.

But nothing followed us down. Because of the nature of the crack, we were protected from the rain here and there, but in many parts, the rocks were wet and slick, making footing dangerous. A small stream of water followed our route down the fissure, adding to the precarious nature of our descent. Still, in four hours, we reached the base of the cliff.

"Oh, I never thought I would be so happy to be on level ground again!" Bain cried, falling to his knees, and then prone on the wet ground. He stretched out, uncaring of the mud. "That was terrible!"

I couldn't agree more. Minnie and I sank down to the ground under a protective tree, leaning back against the trunk. I pulled out my water flask and took a longer drink than perhaps I should have. I didn't worry about it too much. We were in a rain forest. Water abounded.

Neither did we worry over much about the drinkable state of the water we would find. The Rebirth typically purified all water sources each year, though the water became progressively fouler as the year progressed. Travelers from beyond the island who'd been marooned here sometimes spoke of the dangers of disease and poisoned waters at all times of the year, but the waters on the island were, in general, safe to drink at the beginning of a Rebirth.

Minnie shifted her pack around and pulled out a wrapped package that the gnomes had given her containing dried meats and mushrooms. We ate sparingly since we didn't really know how long our food would last, but soon my stomach stopped rumbling and my body stopped complaining.

The sun had begun its descent and evening would soon be upon us. The rain, at that moment, spent itself at last, and the jungle floor began to come alive as insects and birds emerged to announce their presence. I swatted at a huge mosquito, but I didn't complain. I looked very much forward to sleeping dryly this night.

"We need to make camp soon," Minnie said, echoing my thoughts.

"And change into something dry," Bain added.

"But not here," I said, looking at the crack we'd climbed down. "I don't trust those trolls to stay away forever. We need to find a safer place for the night."

Bain groaned, but climbed back to his feet. Minnie offered him some of her food before packing the rest away and standing also. "Which way should we go?" he asked.

I pulled out the compass and consulted it. "I suggest we go southwest for a time until we cross the valley. Jairus suggested that we then head west out of the valley before turning south again and following the mountain range to the nest."

"Sounds good to me," Bain approved.

Minnie nodded and we all set off across the valley. We didn't know how large the valley was, but I figured we would just travel until a suitable campsite presented itself.

The farther we walked, however, the more uneasy I became. I couldn't pinpoint exactly what caused this feeling, but soon I was so jumpy that even Bain noticed.

"You okay?" he asked as he came up alongside of me.

"I don't know," I admitted. "I just have this feeling that something is wrong."

"Well, I don't feel anything. You, Minnie?"

"Not really," she replied, looking at me in concern. "Well, I'm still worried that those trolls might follow us down here."

"That's not it," I said, looking around. My skin felt prickly and the hairs on the back of my neck rose. Something was wrong. Something dangerous. My mouth went dry. "I just have this feeling that something is waiting for us."

"Like what?" Bain asked.

"I'm not sure. I've never experienced anything like this before."

Bain looked around. "It's getting darker. If we don't find some place to camp soon, we'll be in real trouble. Roy, I think you're just jumping at shadows. That hermit really got under your skin, didn't he?"

"No, he didn't," I lied. "Fine. Let's keep moving."

We started out again, but this time I kept my hand on my sword, gripping it to the point where my knuckles showed white.

The feeling got worse, and finally the trees fell away to reveal a clearing and a rocky protrusion at its center. The rock formation looked as if someone had haphazardly tossed together a bunch of huge boulders in one spot. Only it wasn't a solid mass of stone. The mouth of a dark cave at the mound's base practically glared at us the moment we came upon it. We came to a stop, staring at this oddity.

"What's that?" Bain demanded, squinting in the failing light. "More caves?"

My bad feeling only intensified the more I looked at the cave. I could hardly even take a step in its direction. My body trembled to the point where my teeth started to chatter. "I don't know," I stated, struggling to keep my teeth from clacking together. "But something is very wrong about it."

"It's just a cave," Bain insisted. "Maybe it's one of the tunnels the gnomes haven't explored yet. Wouldn't it be nice to find a way back to the gnomes that bypasses the trolls completely when we come back?"

"Look at the trees," Minnie said softly, "They stop in a perfect circle around the rocks."

Sure enough, the tree line ended so abruptly that it couldn't be natural, forming a perfect circle around the clearing and the cave. For fifty feet from the trees to the rocks, absolutely nothing grew. Enough light lingered in the day to see that much.

"I don't like this place," I muttered, partially pulling my sword from its sheath. "I think we should go."

A figure suddenly moved out of the shadows on the far side of the clearing and strode just to the cave mouth. His appearance came so suddenly, that we just froze where we stood, watching. The cloaked figure turned at the entrance and drew back the hood and looked right at us. "No need to go, Roy," said Jairus's familiar voice. "Come here."

Bain and Minnie immediately stepped forward, walking briskly toward the cave.

I took three steps and stumbled, fighting a will that sought to control my body. I clapped both hands to my head and screamed in primordial rage at the intrusion into my mind.

Falling to my knees, I snarled angrily, "Jairus, release me!" My head cleared instantly. I looked up to see the hermit's smiling face just as my two friends walked up to him and stood absolutely still.

Betrayal!

I leaped to my feet, my sword appearing in my hands.

"Stay your hand, Roy," Jairus ordered.

I snarled, brushing aside his will on my mind, but he held out a warning hand, forestalling me with something much worse.

"Don't make me command Bain to kill you," he said sharply.

I froze in place, my heart thumping. I stood there, breathing hard, unsure what to do. Then more shapes moved into the clearing, and I realized that Jairus hadn't come alone. He had brought the trolls.

They surrounded the clearing, leering, and drooling hungrily. I turned a slow circle, my sword waving unsteadily in front of me. Fear crept into my heart, making my grip slick. My throat constricted and my thumping heart accelerated, but I stood my ground, snarling back at the hungry trolls.

I rotated back around to face Jairus. "What is the meaning of this? How did you get here?"

The hermit tugged at one of his large ears, grinning with the satisfaction of one seeing his plans all come to fruition. "There is more than one way down into this valley, Roy. I warned you that you would fail, and you will—either here and now or later. It doesn't matter. In one sense, I'm saving you quite a bit of time—and perhaps even your life."

I stared at him. "I have no idea what you are talking about."

Jairus gestured to the cave entrance. "Do you know what this is?"

"No. And I don't want to know. Something is wrong about it—dangerous."

"Hardly," Jairus responded with a half-smile. "What you feel is the Blessing's reaction to the Abyss. This is the entrance to the Abyss, the Dragon's sanctuary."

I slowly gripped my sword with both hands. "I don't believe you," I lied. I knew the truth of it. I could feel it. The Blessing was indeed warning me.

"Liar," the older man said, amused. "Every year, upon the Rebirth, I set out to seek the second entrance to the Abyss. I can feel it, much like you do now—though in my case, it calls to me. Fortunately, for this year, it appeared close by my tower."

"What has that to do with me?"

"Only that I knew where to steer you, to bring you here. You see, Roy, there is something you can do for me, but you aren't ready yet. Only after you have met the Dragon will you be able to help me. Trust me, Roy. What I am offering you is a much better choice than what the Phoenix or those fools in Khol will ever give you. I am offering you freedom and a Name. You have one of the strongest spirits I've ever encountered. Aided by the Dragon's Gift, you could become very powerful."

"I don't want anything to do with you," I protested. "Let me and my friends go!"

The hermit only looked mildly disappointed. "I expected as much. Clearly you need something else to motivate you." He fixed his eyes on a few of the trolls and gestured toward my friends. "Take these two. You may return to your village and eat them." Four trolls surged forward to obey.

"No!" I cried, rushing to intercept.

"Hold him!" Jairus yelled.

Another troll stepped in front of me. Enraged, I swung my sword. It raised an arm casually to parry the strike, and my blade clanged off as if having struck metal. My hands went numb and the sword fell from my grasp.

The troll reached out to grab me, but I balled my fists and ducked under the creature's arms. I came up inside of his reach and boxed his ears as hard as I could.

The troll howled and turned in circles, his thick hands reaching up to try and comfort his sensitive extremities.

I snarled in glee at that, but found my body lifted harshly off the ground by another troll behind me. I dangled in the air, thrashing uselessly. "Let me go!" I raged.

I watched helplessly as the four other trolls each grabbed an arm of my friends. The squeezing grasp shocked them from the hermit's control. Both of them went berserk, biting, hitting, and kicking. It did no good. The trolls merely walked away, lugging their captives with them.

I could hear Minnie's panicked sobs, and tears began running down my face. I twisted to look at Jairus. "Don't do this," I pleaded. "Let them go!"

"Why? I have no reason to."

"I'll do whatever you want! Just don't hurt them." Hot tears stung my eyes.

"Not yet. You aren't ready. Not until you face the Dragon."

"You were supposed to help us!" I cried, desperately. "You were supposed to be our friend!'

He snorted. "You don't know what my surname means, do you? Ramah means betrayer." He gestured to the troll that held me. "Throw him into the Abyss. Let the Dragon have him."

I screamed in rage and panic, but nothing I did even fazed the troll. He walked right up to the entrance and threw me in.

I fell into darkness.

CHAPTER SIXTEEN

I fell. The darkness of the Abyss consumed all. In a split moment of eternity, I came to know all and nothing. I became all and nothing. Past, present, and future merged, and time became meaningless—a moment that never passed, but was gone in an instant.

I landed on a pedestal of stone; an island in a sea of flame.

I rolled to a stop in the exact center of a perfectly round stone pedestal, uninjured by either the fall or the landing. I climbed to my feet, my heart still thumping wildly, desperate to get out and help Minnie and Bain. But I could see no exit. Above me swirled inky darkness, rippling as if something was slithering just out of my eyesight.

Fire roared up all around, giving light to my surroundings, but refusing to penetrate the darkness I had fallen from. Circling stairs led down into the sea of flames all around the pedestal; but looking into the fire, I could see no bottom—only flame. I stood on an island in the middle of a sea of flame.

I ran a hand through my hair, turning in useless circles. I felt utterly helpless. I couldn't get out. I couldn't help my friends. I had indeed been tossed into the Abyss.

Strangely, I felt no heat from the fire. In fact, a chill settled over me and I shivered. I dared not touch the flames, though, I knew deep down that they would still burn me.

From this flame, the monstrous head of a black dragon emerged with the suddenness of a piercing arrow. I fell back in terror, but my entire body went rigid, refusing my commands to run.

Ridges of razor-sharp spines ran from a sharp spur near the nose of the Dragon all the way back along the head and down the neck. Black scales absorbed the light of the fire, reflecting nothing. Two red eyes the size of wagon wheels regarded me lazily, while a sinuous tongue flicked through teeth the size of my entire body. Two giant, black wings fanned out from the body, and the Dragon lifted itself up to tower above me in all its majesty and glory.

My legs gave out and I collapsed to the cold stone. I found myself shivering uncontrollably as I stared in abject terror at the monstrous form of the Dragon.

STATE YOUR PETITION, a voice sounded in my head.

The power of that voice rang through every fiber of my being, testing me, sifting through my character, desires, and needs.

"I—I don't understand," I replied shakily. "Where am I?"

YOU KNOW THIS ALREADY, ROY OF KHOL. YOU ARE IN THE ABYSS AND ALL WHO COME HERE HAVE DESIRES THEY SEEK TO FULFILL. THEREFORE, STATE YOUR PETITION.

Some of my courage and sense returned to me. "Who are you?" As if I didn't already know.

I AM NACHASH, THE DRAGON OF THE ABYSS.

"This is what the Abyss looks like then?" I asked inanely since I could see it very well for myself.

ONLY TO YOU, ROY OF KHOL. ALL WHO COME HERE SEE WHAT THEY EXPECT TO SEE. THIS IS WHAT YOU EXPECTED TO SEE. IT IS A WORTHY EXPECTATION OF MY POWER, THUS I HAVE DECIDED TO GRANT YOU YOUR PETITION. WHAT IS IT THAT YOU MOST WANT, ROY OF KHOL?

I could hardly believe my eyes and ears. I never really accepted that the Dragon was real, but this…if such a creature really existed, this was exactly how I imagined it would look. This was a creature of vast power indeed.

So what was it that I most wanted? Without hesitation, I replied, "I want to save my friends."

The Dragon flowed around the pedestal, forcing me to turn to follow it. Flame swept in its wake, licking at the Dragon's wings and scales. It reared up again and giant foreclaws reached out and took hold of the rocky top of the pedestal to either side of me. Massive black claws dug into the rock, sending little puffs of pulverized dust into the air.

I staggered back, coughing and absolutely terrified. It would not take much to be cut in half by the smallest of those claws.

I CAN GRANT YOU THE POWER TO SAVE THEM. IS THIS YOUR WISH, ROY OF KHOL? DO YOU TRULY DESIRE MOST TO SAVE YOUR FRIENDS?

"Yes," I cried instantly. Having observed what Jairus could do, I knew I would need something equally powerful to defeat him and the trolls. The Blessing had proven woefully inadequate to the task. I needed something more. The Dragon's offer fed my hopes.

PERHAPS, BUT YOU ARE NOT YET READY.

I licked my lips, struggling to control my fear and allow hope to take over. "How do I get ready then?"

A POWER RESTS UPON YOU THAT WILL DENY MY GIFT, ROY OF KHOL. UNTIL THIS POWER IS FORSAKEN, YOU CANNOT ACCEPT MY GIFT.

"What are you talking about?"

THE BLESSING, ROY OF KHOL. YOU MUST FORSAKE THE BLESSING OF THE PHOENIX. OUR TWO POWERS ARE NOT HARMONIOUS, AND THE TOUCH OF THEM BOTH WITHIN YOU WOULD BREAK YOUR MIND AND SHATTER YOUR BODY.

I paused, thinking that such an end would be most uncomfortable. On some level, this made sense. The two, the Phoenix and the Dragon, were enemies—maybe not on the scale or in the realm of understanding that I could relate to, but the friction certainly existed. The Blessing, however, had been helpful on my journey to this point. Giving it up would seem like a betrayal. Swallowing hard, I cleared my voice. "Is there no other way?"

The huge head, filled with all those awful teeth, lowered, coming level with my head. *THERE IS NOT, ROY OF KHOL. THE POWER I GRANT YOU MUST NOT BE SHACKLED BY THE BLESSING, OR YOU WILL NOT BE ABLE TO FREE YOUR FRIENDS.*

I licked my lips. I had expected that. "Okay, but what's the catch?"

The red orbs blazed brightly, and I stumbled back from them, suddenly scared. *I OFFER NO DECEPTION. I TOUCH THE WORLD THROUGH ALL WHO BEAR MY GIFTS. THAT IS ENOUGH FOR THOSE WHO HAVE THE STRENGTH AND WILL TO WIELD SUCH POWER. DO YOU POSSESS THE STRENGTH AND WILL?*

I straightened up and dared to look the Dragon right in the eye. "I do." Then I hesitated, suspicious. "Don't I have to serve you or something?"

I REQUIRE NO SERVICE. THE POWER WILL BE YOURS TO USE AS YOU SEE FIT. IS IT YOUR WISH TO WIELD MY GIFT IN THE AID OF YOUR FRIENDS?

I made up my mind. "Yes," I replied firmly.

THEN YOU MUST FORSAKE THE BLESSING.

"How?" I'd expected this, but I had no idea how to accomplish it.

YOU MUST DENY IT WITH A CURSE. ONLY THE STRENGTH OF YOUR DENIAL CAN DISPEL IT. IF ANY PART OF YOU STILL ACCEPTS THE BLESSING, IT WILL REMAIN AND YOU WILL LEAVE HERE POWERLESS.

I thought about that. On one hand, the Blessing had served me well. Too many so-called coincidences had happened along the way for me to deny its existence and its help; but on the other hand, it wasn't going to save Minnie and Bain.

In this, I agreed with Jairus. Despite his betrayal, we had still needed him and his power to get through the trolls—the Blessing could only do so much. The hermit's power was undeniable. With power like that, I could save my friends.

Thinking back across my journey so far, I realized where such power as given by the Dragon would have been much more useful than the Blessing ever had been. I would have been able to saunter through the elf holt without getting captured or beaten. I could have easily defeated the trolls in the cave beneath the mountain and saved the gnomes by myself—Bain would have never needed to risk himself.

In fact, with such power, no one in Khol would dare call me Delinquent. I would've never had to go on this stupid Quest in the first place!

The more I thought about it, the madder I got. I'd been deceived right from the first! The whole Quest was a sham; a means to control people who do not toe the line and conform to someone else's sense of morality.

With steady hands, I looked at the Dragon. Most of the denial had already begun in my heart, now I just needed to declare it. So with as much conviction as I could bring forth, I pronounced my curse on the Blessing. "I deny the Blessing and all it entails—the Dragon take it and burn it to ash!"

A flash of warmth sped through my body, leaving a deeper chill in its wake than before. It was done. I could feel it. The Blessing was gone.

The Dragon reared up far above me, its oily black scales changing to a golden hue.

THE BLESSING IS NO MORE. I NAME THEE OSHEK. OPPRESSOR. AND GIFT TO THEE THE POWER OF THE CHAOS CURSE. GO. FREE THY FRIENDS.

I blinked, finding myself standing at the entrance to the Abyss within the circle of trees. Everything looked pretty much the same. The large boulders hadn't moved, and the line of trees retained its exact distance from the cave entrance. Even my sword remained where it had fallen during my scuffle with the trolls.

Only two differences were obvious. The sun had set, leaving the world in darkness and indicating that a certain amount of time had passed since I'd been thrown into the Abyss. The other difference came from a few torches that someone had set out around the tree line; the light cast eerie shadows wherever I looked.

Jairus stepped out of one of those shadows and walked toward me. My eyes narrowed the moment I could make out his mocking grin. "So, you survived," he began knowingly. "You could have only done that if you had forsaken the Blessing."

"You intended this to happen, didn't you?" I accused him. I hadn't moved or tried to reach for my sword a dozen yards ahead of me on the ground.

"Of course. I saw the potential in you right away. All you needed was the right motivation and opportunity." He shrugged easily. "I gave it to you, is all. Now, with my advice, you can truly become a power to be reckoned with. Tell me, what surname did the Dragon give you? After all, isn't that what you most wanted?"

The Dragon's voice echoed through my mind: *I Name thee Oshek. Oppressor.* Something deep in me stirred, making my stomach ache. Power. A slow grin made its way onto my lips.

I ignored the hermit's question by asking one of my own. "Where are my friends?"

"Likely they will be breakfast soon, but why speak of them? They were only chains about your neck. You are well free of them."

I didn't answer that. I let my anger and rage bubble up within me. I could sense the change deep within. A new power stirred there, straining to be released, chomping at the bit to make its mark on the world around me. *Oshek. Oppressor.* Only I didn't know how to release it. I could feel the power pushing at me, trying to explode out of me, and that's when I saw Jairus try to fix me with his eyes, try to snare me with his power.

"The Dragon take you to the Abyss!" I cursed him, throwing up a hand to break eye contact.

Something happened.

I felt power explode from me, not like an arrow shot deliberately from a bow, more like the widespread explosion of the gnomish powder we used to blow open the sinkholes in the cavern during my battle with the trolls.

A large tree snapped in half and fell directly toward the hermit. He whirled around, cried out in surprise, and dove out of the way, barely clearing the crashing tree. A small flock of strix came out of nowhere, diving frantically at the hermit, biting any available flesh. Jairus flailed about him, desperately trying to knock the carnivorous birds away. He yelped when one took a nasty bite out of his cheek.

I grinned, thoroughly enjoying it, seeing as the hermit could not use his power on something moving so quickly or that didn't have enough brains to command.

The hermit managed to either stun the strix or drive the remaining ones away. He stood next to the fallen tree, panting heavily. "The Chaos Curse," he said in a voice that resounded with satisfaction. "Very rare. Very powerful. Well done, boy." He looked into the shadows. "Take him!"

Three trolls lumbered into the clearing, snarling as they oriented on me and charged. I looked at them and pursed my lips. The power continued to stir in me. This called for another curse.

"Thy way be thwarted!" I cried, cursing them.

Immediately, two of the trolls' feet got tangled together and they tripped, falling headlong onto the ground where they bounced slightly from the impact. The third made it two more steps before his foot sunk in a small hidden hole. Such was the power of his stride that his leg snapped, sending him howling to the ground, clutching desperately at his injured limb.

Ants crawled out of a nearby den and quickly swarmed over the other two trolls, getting in their mouths, ears, nostrils, and anywhere else they could find. The trolls rolled on the ground, slapping at their own bodies, howling in pain and anger. Finally, they climbed to their feet and ran into the woods, bouncing off trees and running headlong into boulders in their desperate attempt to flee these sudden terrors.

I learned something about my power at that moment. The strength of my curse depended on how angry I was at the recipient. Mildly annoyed resulted in an annoying, if satisfactory, curse; but a curse of rage would bring about acts that could kill. Oh, I could have used this growing up. This would have been really fun.

Smiling in satisfaction, I turned my attention back to Jairus. For him, I felt a deep abiding anger. I snarled, preparing to curse him again, but he backed away, laughing. "Don't waste your time on me, boy. Save your friends if you can. We will meet again— when you're ready to listen." He slipped beyond the torches and into the shadows.

Reminded of Minnie and Bain, I immediately set out for the crack in the cliff face, snatching my sword off the ground as I passed it. I didn't really think I'd need it, but it belonged to me, so I didn't see the sense in leaving it lying there. I cast the treacherous hermit from my mind. I needed to arrive at the troll village before sunrise if I was to save my friends.

* * *

I reached the village at the top of the cliffs just as the sun broke through some scattered clouds in the east. I knew from the gnomes that trolls typically didn't kill their prey until just before they cooked it. They tended to like their meat as fresh as it could be. This gave me hope that my friends would still be alive when I arrived.

During my long climb, I carefully nursed my anger into a simmering rage. I loathed the trolls for threatening the lives of my friends. I despised them for terrorizing the gnomes. I hated them, one and all, for murdering Minnie's parents. I planned on issuing a powerful curse.

I surveyed the village. Trolls moved here and there, sluggish in the morning, but in the middle, near the fire pit, I saw a makeshift cage. Inside I could see the ragged appearance of my two friends—alive, if worse for wear.

The trolls milling around finally caught sight of me and hooted as they alerted their fellows to my presence. A score or more emerged from their huts and started toward me, their greedy eyes focused on me and drool escaping from the corners of their mouths.

Rage flashed through me, white hot.

Oshek, the oppressor.

Throwing my arms out and tilting my head back, I cursed them. "Die!" The power fairly exploded out of me, leaving a sense of emptiness and desperate need behind. I slumped and then fell to my knees, empty of energy and emotion.

But my curse fell upon the village like a consuming fire.

A section of the village, built near the cliff face, broke off, carrying a half dozen trolls and several huts over the cliff. I smiled as their screams faded away.

The trolls heading my way all fell afoul of something. Some tripped, their faces smacking hard into the muddy ground. One fell headlong into the fire, knocking burning embers every which way as he thrashed about in desperation. A wind picked up out of nowhere, carrying the embers into huts where they quickly caught fire, blazing up much worse than would be expected.

I laughed as chaos erupted all around me. A pack of wolves dashed into the village, biting and nipping at the trolls' feet, legs, and eyes. Soon the entire troll population milled about in absolute confusion. Fights started everywhere as the dim-witted trolls blamed their neighbors for some misfortune. A few were even thrown over the cliff in rage by their fellows.

I struggled back to my feet, my rage spent. I then walked down through the middle of the village toward the cage holding my friends. Whenever a troll tried to interfere, something happened. A spear thrown in rage happened to skewer another troll heading my way. A dozen wolves attacked another, overwhelming the troll momentarily, but ignoring me completely.

The fact that something was terribly wrong began to sink into the thick skulls of the brutish trolls. A female began shouting for everyone to flee into the jungle until a male, trying to pull out some reptile that had managed to climb deep into its ear, clipped her on the jaw, spinning her about and driving her into one of the mud huts. The hut exploded, sending logs rolling everywhere, tangling the feet of more trolls. Some still heeded the call and began running for the trees. Even they knew something was wrong.

I reached the cage, feeling as if I'd walked the entire length of the island. I felt sick. Not only did my stomach threaten to heave out its last contents, but being forced to watch the continual destruction of the troll village had left a bad taste in my mouth. I hadn't realized it would be quite like this. Suddenly, I felt uncertain about my new surname.

Bain and Minnie watched the chaos in stunned amazement. It took them a moment to notice me.

"Roy!" Minnie cried happily. "What is going on?"

I sucked in my breath, trying to renew my strength, but I could hardly stand. "I'm trying to rescue you," I replied in a somewhat giddy voice. Strangely, I started to hiccup. "I just need (hic) to (hic)…"

Mind you, I've never felt overly heroic, but being beset with the hiccups during a rescue was downright embarrassing. I fumbled with my sword, but I lacked the strength to do much with it.

Bain saw, reached through a space between the logs, and drew the sword himself. He nearly sliced my hand off when I hiccupped again right at that moment, but we got the sword leveraged correctly against the ropes that bound the cage shut, and soon both of my friends stepped out of the cage, free.

"We need (hic) to go," I said, finishing with another, somewhat high-pitched, hiccup. I glanced at Minnie, embarrassed.

But she, like Bain, stared out at the chaos going on around them. Minnie's confusion showed in her eyes, but Bain's sought mine. "You're doing?" he asked softly.

I nodded, hiding my chagrin behind another hiccup.

Frowning, Bain took another look at the bedlam and took me by the arm. "We'll talk about it later." He nudged Minnie. "Minnie, grab our stuff!" He pointed.

Startled, Minnie turned back, saw my condition, and nodded. Their packs had been tossed haphazardly near one of the other mud huts nearby. She ran over, grabbed them, and hurried back; her thin arms strained under the load. By then, Bain was hauling me toward the cliffs, my hiccups hindering the effort somewhat.

I lacked the strength to tell them that we didn't need to finish the Quest, so I just let them half drag me back down our original path. Soon we left the chaos behind and began our descent.

We made it only part of the way down the ledge before I collapsed completely. Bain located a somewhat wide spot and half dragged me to it, laying me down as gently as he could.

"Why's he so tired?" Minnie asked as she worked to make me as comfortable as possible.

"I doubt he's even slept since we were taken," Bain responded evasively.

She frowned at that. No doubt neither of them had slept much either. My eyes closed, and soon the entire world faded away as I slipped into unconsciousness.

CHAPTER SEVENTEEN

I slept the entire day and into the night. The next day I managed to get to the base of the mountain where my strength gave out again, so we spent two days near the Abyss while I regained my strength.

Neither Bain nor Minnie realized how close we were to the entrance of that evil place, but I could feel it, like a steady tug. This, at least, explained how Jairus had been able to locate it so readily. The Dragon's Gift acted like a compass, pointing right to the Abyss. And with the absence of the Blessing, I no longer felt uneasy at its presence, which, at least, allowed me to get some needed sleep.

We never heard from the trolls or Jairus during the time we remained in the valley. Apparently, both had had quite enough of us, so we were able to rest and recoup in peace. Even the rain stayed away.

But on the morning of the third day, we picked up our packs, broke camp, and began walking west out of the valley. We knew that a spur of the mountain range jutted out some into the heavy rain forest to the west. All we needed to do was round the spur and head south, directly to the peak and the Phoenix's nest.

"If we don't run into any obstacles," Bain predicted hopefully, "we should reach the base of the mountain either tonight or sometime tomorrow." He glanced at us. "This Quest may be over in just a few days."

"And then we have to go back home," I muttered, not looking forward to the return trip.

"No sense in worrying about that," Minnie said. "Let's focus on this task first." She smiled at me. "Are you excited about this, Roy? Soon we'll get you to the Phoenix, and you can petition him for a Gift—and a surname. I'm certain you'll get one. After all you've done for us, I just know the Phoenix will have to give you a Gift."

The word petition sounded ominously like what the Dragon had said to me. I forced a smile and nodded my head. "It's what I came for," I said.

I didn't know what else to say. Having attained a Gift from the Dragon, I wasn't all that keen on trying to win my way to the Phoenix. In many respects, my Quest was over. I had gained a Gift and a surname. The only worry was my promise to Jairus. He had betrayed us, so did I have to keep my promise? I gnawed on that. In one sense, I felt no obligation since the hermit hadn't really helped us at all.

So why did I feel so uncomfortable?

Oppressor.

That's what my new name meant. To be very honest about it, I really didn't like it. To be sure, anything was better than being Named Delinquent...but Oppressor? That bothered me.

I could still feel the power of the Chaos Curse within me. But in the absence of my anger, it lay like a coiled serpent, ready to spring forth when my anger called upon it. At the moment, it just stirred restlessly deep within like a man plagued by a nightmare.

Indeed, now that my anger had faded entirely, I found that my ability to call the Chaos Curse forth had also diminished in equal proportions. Yesterday, when no one was looking, I'd tried to curse an innocent butterfly just to test out my power, but I could feel no animosity toward it, no anger; so the most I could conjure was an erratic flight path, and since most butterflies flew erratically, I wasn't all that sure I had actually accomplished anything.

Thus, I learned of another limitation to my power. In the absence of anger or animosity, I would be powerless.

In truth, I wasn't sure how I felt about that. I guessed that in dangerous situations I would find the necessary anger to call the Chaos Curse forth, but on the other hand, I didn't relish having to be angry all the time in order to manifest my power. Despite all the trouble I'd managed to get myself into growing up, I really wasn't an angry person.

I felt disappointed, cheated in a way. I had all this power—and if the evidence of what happened in the troll village was an adequate indicator, I had a lot of power—but I could only use it when hatred, anger, or animosity called it forth, and I just didn't have much of that.

Troubled, I fell silent. Minnie chatted away with Bain and me. If she noticed my reticent answers, she decided not to comment on it—for which I was grateful. Bain, however, threw me several concerned or suspicious glances throughout the day. That evening, while he and I ventured out to gather firewood, he broached the subject.

"Roy, we're close now. Tomorrow we'll arrive at the base of mountain where the nest is, and if Jairus didn't lie, the Labyrinth.

I need to know what is going on with you. What happened after we were taken from that clearing in the woods?"

I sighed, knowing this conversation was inevitable. "What do you remember?"

Bain shrugged. "I remember Jairus. I guess he snared us with his Evil Eye because the next thing I knew, I was being hauled away by the trolls. Minnie was screaming. You were being held by a different troll. They took us away."

"Nothing else?"

"No. Nothing."

"You didn't hear what Jairus said about that cave in the clearing?"

"No. What was that place?"

I considered lying. Bain had heard nothing, which meant Minnie had also heard nothing. They didn't know, so I could hide it and say whatever I wanted. But why did I feel the need to hide it at all? Why did I feel ashamed? I didn't understand these emotions that swirled around inside of me. Taking a deep breath, I decided to tell Bain. If anything, maybe telling someone would alleviate this feeling of guilt.

"The cave was the entrance to the Abyss—the second one that Jairus told us of."

The prince's mouth fell open. "You're serious?"

"I am. I don't know what Jairus was trying to accomplish, but he had that troll throw me inside. I don't want to go into all the details, but I faced the Dragon."

Bain's eyes widened even further. "The Dragon is real?"

"Oh yes. Very, very real. He is huge, monstrous, worse than any of the stories you've heard."

"But you're still alive. He didn't kill you."

"Obviously. The Dragon isn't like that. He didn't want to kill me. He wanted to give me a Gift."

Bain, who had been in the act of picking up a stick from the ground, froze. He straightened, looking at me in an unrecognizable way. "And he gave you one, didn't he? That was you in the troll village. You did all that."

I nodded. "Yes. I have the Gift of the Chaos Curse. Apparently, it brings chaos upon anyone I curse. I was so desperate to save you and Minnie, so angry…I hated the trolls—well, for everything. I cursed them all. You saw what happened."

"You practically destroyed the entire village. You were kinda out of it there at the end, so you may not have really seen, but most of the huts were either on fire or destroyed. That curse destroyed the whole village. I saw many of the trolls running into the forest, but the village itself was destroyed."

I took a deep breath, feeling miserable. "I know. I didn't realize how powerful this Gift is. I was just so angry. They were going to kill you and eat you—I couldn't let that happen. The Blessing wasn't enough to save you. We needed something more powerful, so I agreed to accept the Dragon's Gift. To do so, I had to forsake the Blessing on me."

"I'm not sure you should have done that," Bain said slowly.

"It was the only way to save you!" I snapped. "What did you want me to do? Let you die?"

"I'm in no hurry to die, Roy—and I am grateful—but I'm unsure of the cost. What you did—now we don't have the Blessing. I just—"

"We don't need it," I interrupted, feeling angry. "I have enough power to complete this Quest without it. Now we don't need someone like Jairus. Now we have me!"

Bain fell silent, worrying his lower lip with his teeth. I could see he wasn't convinced and that he thought what I had done was a mistake. After everything I'd done to save him, why wasn't he more grateful?

Irritated, I decided he needed a demonstration. I snapped, "Confound thy doubt!" The curse brought forth my power, which fell upon Bain immediately.

The pile of sticks he carried shifted, causing him to lose his grip. He staggered forward, trying to catch them, but he tripped over a root and fell sideways, his ankle caught fast. He cried out in pain as he fell.

Immediately, my anger fled, and the power coiled back inside me, waiting for the next call. I rushed to Bain's side, dropping my own pile of sticks. "Bain! I'm sorry! Are you okay?"

I reached out for him, but he slapped my hand away. "Stay away from me," he hissed, pain showing in his face.

"I didn't mean it." I stood there, desperate to help, but uncertain as to what to do. "I just got angry that you doubted me. I just wanted you to see—"

"You cursed me, didn't you?"

"Just a bit," I admitted, ashamed. "I just wanted you to see that I could take care of you and Minnie—"

"And now my ankle is twisted," he said tightly. "You're doing a wonderful job."

I looked. He still wore his boots, so of course I could see nothing, but the pain in his face was plain enough. I felt like a total idiot. "Bain, I'm so sorry. I didn't mean for that to happen. Let me help you up—"

He held his palm out, forestalling me. "Wait. Just wait." He took a deep breath, and I assumed he was trying to calm his own anger down. "Roy, what is the point in going on? Why should the

Phoenix give you a Gift when you already got one from the Dragon?" He paused. "I assume he Named you as well."

I bit my lip. "Yes. Oshek—it...it means oppressor." I winced. Even I didn't like the sound of that—particularly when it was spoken aloud.

Bain stared at me for a long moment, and I grew decidedly uncomfortable under that gaze. He was my friend. I didn't like the fact that he was either disappointed in or frightened of me.

"Yes, the surname is an apt description of what I saw," he finally said. He shook his head. "Regardless, what is the point in going on?"

I sat down beside Bain and picked up one of the loose sticks. I began poking the ground with it. The lingering sun cast enough light to see by, though a constant cloud cover, the canopy above, and an occasional drizzle obscured much of it. But I could see Bain and his carefully composed face.

I gave some serious thought to what Bain had asked. For the first time since the Quest had begun, I truly wished my father was here. I needed his wisdom and counsel. At seventeen years of age, I'd finally gotten myself into a type of trouble I couldn't easily talk my way out of. At length, I spoke, "I asked myself the same question, but I'm not sure I have a good answer. At first, I didn't see the point in going on. Completing this Quest...well, it seemed rather redundant. But now, I'm not so sure. There are several reasons, one being my promise to Jairus. I...I don't want to go back to him."

Bain frowned. He shifted around, tugged off his boot, and examined the ankle. I could see that it was swelling. He leaned back against a tree and stretched his legs out. I knew the injury would likely slow us down tomorrow, but my irritation was mostly aimed at myself. I had caused this. This was my fault.

Bain asked, "What other reasons?"

"Mostly I feel I need to complete the Quest. It is what I set out to do…and what you set out to do with me—and Minnie too. I guess if I don't complete it, I feel I will be letting both of you down."

"But how can you complete it, Roy? Why would the Phoenix Gift you anything?"

"I don't know."

"Do you want this Dragon's Gift?" Bain asked, looking more troubled than at any other time since I'd known him.

And that was the crux of the situation. I considered. "I like what I can do with it, but I don't like how it makes me feel or how I must feel in order to use it."

Bain shook his head. "I'm not even going to pretend to understand that. I just want to know if you want it. Is this what you were looking for?"

Asked that way, I immediately responded, "No. It's not what I was looking for. I can't tell you exactly what I wanted to find when we first started out on this Quest, but this wasn't it. I'm not sure those I care about would understand this new power and surname. I don't want the Name of Delinquent, but I'm not sure that the Name, Oppressor, is one I would like to be known by either."

"That, my friend, is good to hear," Bain said, sighing. "You need to make a choice. I don't know if the Phoenix will Gift you, but regardless, maybe—as Minnie says—it is the journey that is important. Maybe, what you are looking for can only be found by completing your Quest—regardless of the outcome." He paused. "Know what I think?"

"Tell me."

"Reputations can be earned in many different ways. Maybe, just completing the Quest is the thing you are really looking for."

My second boon came to mind: Your way shall be fraught with danger, this is easy to see, but your fate shall be decided when you give up that which you hold most precious for that which you hold in disdain. Failure may be the path to success, and success may lead to failure. The choice will be yours.

Maybe I had to give up the my desire to be Gifted. Maybe this was the sacrifice I needed to make. I struggled with it. This was the problem with prophecies. You could twist them around to fit many different situations. How do you succeed by failing? That part of the prophecy still bugged me—well, actually, all of it bugged me.

I echoed Bain's sigh and nodded, determination steeling through my mind. "Okay. Let's complete this Quest. I owe it to all of us."

"Good. Help me to my feet."

I stood while he carefully put his boot back on. Then I grabbed his offered wrist and hauled him to his feet. Slowly, Bain put his foot down and winced. He took a few steps, hobbling with each one. "Okay. I think I can walk—if I take it real slow."

"Maybe Minnie knows something we can do. Hopefully it'll be okay by tomorrow." I grimaced. "I'm so sorry, Bain."

"I know. Grab some of that wood. Minnie will be wanting it."

I backtracked, picked up my load and Bain's, and then followed him as he hobbled back toward camp.

Minnie saw him coming and stood upright over the small fire she had managed to get going. "What happened, Bain?"

"Twisted my ankle. Anything you can do for it?"

Minnie retrieved her pack, rummaged around inside, and pulled out a long bandage. "Thought this might come in handy. The bandage has been soaked in a herbal remedy that should ease the pain and swelling some." She glanced at Bain. "Your father's physician gave this to me. Want to know what's on it?"

Bain slumped down next the fire and began to carefully remove his boot. "No. If Artimas had anything to do with it, knowing will just give me nightmares. Did you know that he once mixed pig fat in a poultice of six different herbs. I'm telling you, it smelled something terrible."

Minnie sniffed. "You have no appreciation for the sciences."

"That's not science. Honestly, I don't know why my father keeps him around. He needs someone with the Touch, not that charlatan."

"We'll see if you continue to think that in the morning. If you can walk, then you'll be thanking me—and him."

"Minnie," Bain said, his voice dropping an octave. "I'm already thanking you."

She paused to look at him in surprise. They exchanged something that I found to be unreadable. I dropped my bundle of sticks and cleared my throat. They both started at the noise, looking away from each other. I sat down and fed the flickering fire a larger piece of wood.

"Bain thinks we'll reach the Labyrinth tomorrow," I said to them, feeling a tad disgruntled. "I'm thinking I should go in alone."

"Absolutely not," Minnie said. "This Quest is now all of ours—and don't try to argue with me."

Relief, like a cool drink of water, washed over me. I had hoped for nothing less, but I didn't feel I could ask for it. "Thank you," I said softly.

"The problem," Bain put in, "is not the Labyrinth. It is the Guardian. I think we must assume that the Guardian is real and presents a very real danger."

Minnie raised an eyebrow. "Oh? What changed your mind? I seem to remember you thinking the Guardian was nothing more than a myth."

Bain exchanged a brief glance with me. "Jairus contributed to that, I guess. His power is clearly not of the Phoenix, so that leaves only the Dragon. If the Dragon is real, then why not the Guardian? I think in that, at least, Jairus was telling us the truth."

Minnie seemed to consider that as the last of the light faded and the forest closed in around us, hot and humid. The fire cast faint light on the thick trees; and some of the vines moved, making me think we were surrounded by snakes.

Minnie finally spoke, "What happened in the troll village...was that Jairus?"

Bain's eyes flickered to me, but I remained silent. He said, "The Dragon was behind that, I believe. I don't know to what extent Jairus was involved."

Minnie had been watching both of us; and being no idiot, she finally stopped her preparations for dinner, put her hands in her lap, and looked me right in the eyes. "Okay, Roy, I've waited patiently for you to tell me what happened with Jairus. I thought you would tell me when you were comfortable, but I think maybe I should know now—particularly if we are going to finish this together. I'm sorry. I didn't want to push you, but—"

I waved a hand, dismissing her apology. I looked at Bain, "I think she should know."

He nodded. "It will be for the best."

So I told her what happened, trying not to gloss over anything, while not lingering on anything either. I told her of my encounter with the Dragon, my new power, what I had done at the troll village, and, finally, my conversation with Bain and my decision to finish the Quest.

She didn't interrupt once. She sat very still, staring into the flickering fire. I grew nervous as I saw no reaction from her. I half expected her to get angry, to despise me, but no emotion showed on her features. I finally came to a halting stop, feeling helpless.

"What does Oshek mean?" she asked in a quiet voice, still not looking right at me.

I swallowed. That had been the only thing I hadn't told her. "Oppressor."

She gave a single nod in acknowledgment. Another pause persisted while I fidgeted silently. Then she shifted a bit, took both of my hands, and folded them between her own. She looked up at me and said, "It doesn't suit you, Roy. The Dragon misnamed you. That is not who you are. That is not what you do."

A pleasant sensation rippled through my frame. I am typically not a sentimental person, but hearing those words said in that way from someone who could, in all honesty, claim I'd oppressed her, brought tears to my eyes.

Perhaps nothing could motivate a person more than someone's belief in him. I never had someone believe in me like Minnie did at that moment. Something fundamental shifted in our relationship, and for the first time in my life, someone's good opinion of me mattered—really mattered.

"I—I'm not sure what to say, Minnie. Thank you."

"That's good enough."

I could see matching tears in her eyes, and that, more than anything, convinced me of her sincerity.

Bain reached over and placed his hands over ours. "Perhaps the Blessing hasn't deserted us entirely," he said. "Maybe, just maybe, we'll see this done."

It would be a moment I would undoubtedly remember for the rest of my life. For starters, I determined to forsake this new Name and Gift from the Dragon. I would seek out one from the Phoenix, but even if I failed to gain one, in the eyes of these two, I was no longer the Delinquent.

For the moment, that was enough.

The Labyrinth and the Guardian could wait until tomorrow.

CHAPTER EIGHTEEN

The next morning, we set out for the Labyrinth. Not knowing what form it would take, we wondered if we would even recognize the Labyrinth when we saw it. I suppose it was possible that it was built on such a grand scale that we could enter it without even realizing it, and that thought made me jumpy as I looked around suspiciously.

Clouds rolled in, dark and ominous, and thunder boomed distantly. A storm was brewing, and I hoped we could avoid it somehow. *Not likely,* I thought ruefully. *Not the way things have been going.*

Bain's ankle was much improved, thanks in part to Minnie's ministrations. He still wore the bandage around his ankle, giving him extra support, but despite his noticeable limp, we moved steadily toward the peak we believed harbored the Phoenix's nest—if slowly.

Three hours later, we emerged from the jungle to stand before the Labyrinth. We stopped to stare at it in awe. In our wildest dreams, we never imagined such a thing could even exist.

"Will you look at that," Bain breathed. "It's massive."

"And it goes all the way to the mountain," Minnie added.

"And halfway up," I whispered, stunned. "How are we ever going to find our way through that? It's impossible."

The entrance to the Labyrinth slopped away between two mountains toward a valley beyond where we could see a maze of cliffs climbing toward the towering peak beyond. Yellow light radiated from a huge cavern-like hole halfway up the towering peak beyond the maze; the light glowed against the clouds from some unidentifiable source, a soft counterpoint to the harsh lightning that crackled around the peak from the storm brewing above. The cliffs that formed the entrance looked slick and unscalable. Nothing grew within the maze of ravines. It was completely devoid of the jungle we had fought through, providing a clear level pathway that was perhaps fifty feet across, the intent of which was unmistakable.

One of my neighbors had once created a small maze out of some hedge groves that had appeared on his land after a Rebirth. What lay before us resembled his efforts. Only this maze had been fashioned out of solid rock walls.

"Do you think that is where the Phoenix nest is?" Bain asked, pointing to the giant glowing cavern in the peak beyond the maze.

Neither I nor Minnie answered him. The answer seemed self-evident. Getting there was another issue altogether. From where we stood, we could see two other possible entrances to the Labyrinth, one to the north and the other to the south. I suspected that there were others, but these three seemed to be the ones for this section of the maze. We moved deeper into the entrance of the one before us.

The cliffs were sheer and tangled with growth toward the top, impossible to climb. Deeper into the ravine, the path appeared to narrow to twenty feet across, maybe a bit wider. The ravine ran straight toward the maze covered valley beyond before curving away to the right and losing itself deeper into the Labyrinth.

"What do you think?" I asked. "Should we try this one or one of the other entrances?"

"Does it matter?" Bain asked.

"Well, this one might be a dead end."

"If it is, we can always retrace our steps," Minnie said, "and try one of the other entrances."

I squinted, peering down the ravine. "What if we get lost? There's no telling how many twists and turns we'll make before coming to a dead end. What if we just miss the right path?"

"More importantly," Bain said, his voice cracking, "where is the Guardian?"

"Good question," Minnie murmured.

I hadn't realized it until now, but I'd thought there would be only a single entrance to the Labyrinth and that the Guardian would be camped out at that one entrance. So in one respect, multiple entrances made it impossible for one creature to guard every entry point. That gave me an idea.

"Okay, if there is a Guardian, it has to be able to move through the maze to block any portion of the maze from intruders, right? That means it doesn't matter which entrance we take; there is a way to the top."

"Not unless only one of the entrances goes to the top," Minnie disagreed. "All of the others could be dead ends."

"But then only one of them will have the Guardian in it," I pointed out. "If we see no sign of the Guardian, then maybe we can just come out before going too far and try one of the other entrances."

Minnie frowned. "Maybe that'll work."

"Personally," I added, "I'm hoping my idea is right. That'll at least give us a chance to sneak by the Guardian."

Bain nodded. "I like that option." He cast around until he found a likely rock, picked it up, and moved over to the rock wall next to the entrance. He scratched it against the wall, leaving a white chalky line behind. "Good. We can use this to mark where we have been at least."

"Good thinking, Bain," Minnie said.

"All right, let's walk up the path a bit and see what we can see," I suggested.

For some reason, we all came to a halt just at the entrance threshold. Standing side by side, we gazed ahead into the rocky corridor that sloped downward into the valley around the mountain that housed the Phoenix nest.

"This is your Quest, Roy," Minnie remarked. "You go first."

I shrugged. It didn't make any difference to me. I took a step forward, crossing some invisible line that marked the entrance.

Something roared deep within the Labyrinth. The sound echoed through the many ravines, seemingly coming from every direction at once, and here and there, sand shifted down from above. The sound struck a chord deep within my being, and I felt as if, without anything being present, I was being physically rebuffed.

I quickly stepped back and shared a nervous look with my two companions. "I think that answers the question as to whether or not there is a Guardian," I muttered.

"Uh-huh," Bain agreed. "Maybe we should try one of the other entrances."

"I don't think it'll matter," Minnie said. "I think the Guardian will know the moment we enter the Labyrinth and will know exactly where we are at any given time."

"You're not helping," I said, wincing. "How am I supposed to get by something like that?"

"You haven't even seen it yet, Roy. Its roar could be much worse than its bite."

I stared at her like she'd just grown a second head.

She managed to look sheepish. "Okay, it wouldn't be much of a protector if all it did was roar. I'll give you that."

Bain bit his lower lip. "I still think we should at least look in one of the other entrances before we go in. I'll do it. Wait for me here." He turned around, putting feet to his thoughts. He hobbled away, favoring his injured ankle.

Minnie and I stood together, afraid to cross the invisible line that marked the boundary to the Labyrinth. My imagination conjured up all sorts of giant, hungry beasts that could roar like that.

"Would the Guardian really kill us?" I wondered aloud after a moment. "I mean, the Phoenix is supposed to be a good creature, right? Why would the Guardian be evil?"

Minnie nodded, following my logic. "Maybe it's not good or bad. Maybe it just is. It could defend the Phoenix's nest from everyone—regardless of the nature of their character."

"I wonder if it would really try to hurt someone who had the Phoenix's Gift already."

Minnie shot me a quick look. "And by contrast, you're wondering if the Dragon's Gift will make the Guardian more inclined to try and kill you."

"Exactly." I put a hand on my sword. "It roared the moment I stepped in."

"You were the only one to step in," Minnie pointed out. "We don't know if it would have roared regardless."

I gave her a courtly bow—well, a bow anyway—sweeping my arm toward the maze. "Be my guest, mi'lady. Let's see if the monster roars."

Bain came back about that time.

"Hey, Bain," I called, "we're about to test a theory."

Bain didn't say a word as he hobbled up, but the moment he got close, he jerked his sword from its sheath and swung it at me. If I hadn't been looking right at him, he would have cut me down right then and there, but I managed to fling myself aside, and his sharp blade zipped through the air where I had been standing.

"Bain!" Minnie screamed. "What are you doing?"

Bain ignored her, reorienting on me as I rolled to my feet some distance away. He shuffled after me, his weak ankle keeping him from following too quickly.

I felt confused. At first I wondered if he had seen something—the Guardian perhaps—that caused him to think he needed to kill me. Then I wondered if he had never really accepted my explanation about the Dragon's Gift and had planned on killing me for having made a deal with the Dragon.

He stabbed at me again, and I leaped away, barely avoiding having myself skewered. I dropped my pack, pulled out my own sword, and held it before me, trying to emulate Bain's grip and stance. We had spent over two weeks together, and he had never offered to teach me how to use a sword. I had never asked, not really wanting to know.

That oversight became clear to me as he proved to be the superior swordsman. I tried to parry his next swing, but he stepped into the blow, nearly tearing the sword from my grasp. I staggered back, my hands tingling.

"Bain," I panted, "what's wrong? Why are you doing this?"

He said nothing as he launched a series of strikes that only missed because I kept backing up, and he could not follow quite as quickly with his bad ankle.

I looked around for something to help. If I could disarm him, I could probably wrestle him to the ground. Although we were of similar size, the years I had spent on the farm and roughhousing with my friends gave me a distinct edge in unarmed fighting. I was stronger, but until I could get the sword away from him, he had the real advantage.

Minnie stood off to the side, watching the fight with a mixture of bewilderment and fear. Clearly, she didn't know what to do either, and I wasn't about to risk her getting too close, lest Bain turn on her.

And that's when I saw Jairus Ramah standing near the tree line watching the fight. Instantly, I knew what had happened.

I jumped away from Bain to clear some room and yelled, "Let Bain go, Jairus!"

His laughter accosted me. "Not likely, boy. You see, I know something about the Chaos Curse. I know that you can't curse what you aren't angry at, and you can't be angry at Bain. This isn't his fault. It's mine. But if you try to curse me, he will kill you." He laughed again.

He was right. I could find no hatred, anger, or animosity for Bain. My power was useless against him, but if I turned toward Jairus, Bain would likely kill me, being under the hermit's command.

"But why kill me? I thought you wanted my help!"

The hermit nodded. "If you can die that easily, then I am at least relieved of a fool."

I grunted, not sure of the logic, but I figured the hermit was a tad crazy anyway. I refocused on Bain. I needed to neutralize Bain first before I could deal with the hermit.

I went on the attack. I jumped forward, swinging a powerful overhand strike at Bain's sword, hoping I could whack it from his grasp, knock him down, and immobilize him.

None of that happened.

Bain took the blow at an angle on his own sword, shifting the attack away from his body. This brought him in close enough to me to smash an elbow into my face.

I reeled back as my teeth cut through my lips and blood began pooling in my mouth. I let out a hoarse cry of pain and only managed to avoid another one of Bain's swings by flinging myself violently away. I rolled on the hard ground and came to my feet, spitting blood.

"There's another option here, boy," Jairus called. "I'll let both of your friends live if you promise to help me."

I backed away from Bain who stalked me slowly, hindered by his ankle. "What exactly do you want, hermit? I'm not in the mood for any of your games."

"Stop," Jairus ordered. "Stay prepared to attack."

Bain came to a stop, but his eyes remained steady on me. I could see the silent struggle going on in prince's eyes. I knew he was fighting, and I knew he didn't want to hurt me.

"If you try to curse me," the hermit warned, "I'll still have time to order Bain to either kill you, the girl, or himself. Don't be a fool."

I gritted my teeth, biting back the curse on my lips. I had never really met an evil man before—though Vin, my partner in crime back home, did come to mind—and I didn't really have any experience in dealing with such profound evil. I spit out, "Tell me what you want."

"I want my rightful place restored in Taninim. Those fools ran me out when I gained more power than they had. But with your help, Roy, I can retake my rightful place. The rewards will be great, boy. You'll have a place of honor. You'll be respected. You'll be revered. You'll have wealth—a life of ease—and your pick of any woman you want. What do you think you'll get in Khol, even if you do return successful? Become a servant, a slave to the whims of a moral code you neither agree with or understand?"

"I do agree with it!" I protested.

"If that was true, boy, you would never have accepted the Dragon's Gift."

That stung, but I couldn't deny the truth of it. Instead, I asked, "Why do you need me? Why can't you find someone else?"

"I need your power, not you. I saw what you did to the troll village. It was a work of raw destruction, a true display of power. You are still untrained with it, unfocused. I can hone your anger to direct your power in ways you cannot possibly imagine. With it, we can rule Taninim. That's what I want. I want to overthrow King Kasaph. And you're going to help me do it."

"I'll agree once you let them go," I said, eyes narrowing.

He laughed, his huge ears wagging like small wings. "I'll let them live, not go—at least not right away. I'll keep one of them with me, the girl perhaps, to ensure you keep your bargain. She'll die if you betray me."

"Roy!" Minnie shouted, drawing closer. "Don't listen to him. Don't—"

"Be quiet!" Jairus roared.

Startled, Minnie involuntarily looked at the hermit who then latched onto her with his eyes and snapped, "Be still. Be quiet."

Minnie stopped dead in her tracks, falling silent. I fumed. The hermit had had years to perfect his power and knew all the little tricks to get people to fall prey to his Evil Eye. In contrast, I was nothing more than a novice with a lot of raw power.

I could feel my rage building. I would be burned to ash rather than let Jairus win. I would curse him and hope for the best, but then I looked into Minnie's eyes and saw them silently pleading with me. I knew two things right then.

First, if I cursed the hermit, the hermit would still compel my friends to do something that would destroy me. I couldn't bear to have their blood on my hands, and I really didn't want to die. Second, Minnie didn't want me to use my power, even if there was a chance I could save her.

I took a deep breath, trying to calm myself down. I lowered my sword and dared to look Jairus in the eye. "No," I said calmly.

He looked startled. "What?"

"No. I'm not going to help you. I want nothing to do with you or your greed."

His eyes narrowed, and I glanced away quickly lest he try to snare me. I knew he couldn't compel me to use my power, even if I was under his control. The power required my anger, not his. He could not control the Chaos Curse or the degree to which I used it. Only if he had my cooperation could he win.

The hermit glanced at Bain. "Kill him," he snarled.

Bain leaped forward, his sword slashing murderously at my throat. I was ready for that, so I ducked and danced out of the way. I had to find some way to loose Bain from Jairus's control. I engaged Bain then, only coming close enough so that our swords would meet, but not getting my body near enough for a full strike.

We exchanged ineffectual sword blows, and nothing I did could jar him enough to be free of the Evil Eye. I would need to get closer; I would need to actually cause physical pain.

I spit out more blood, feinted right and went left, but Bain was a canny fighter, and he saw right through the ploy. His sword swung easily to deflect my swing, forcing me to retreat.

That's when a rock hit me in the back. I cried out, staggered forward a step, and flung myself to the side once again as Bain came to meet me with his stabbing sword. A long, thin, bloody line appeared on my arm. I got to my feet and saw blood on Bain's sword.

I didn't have time to even take stock of the wound on my arm as I dodged another rock. This time I saw who'd thrown it.

Minnie.

She cast around for another stone. I swallowed, realizing how complicated this had just become. I couldn't defeat both of them. I couldn't even really harm them—they were my friends!

That's when an idea seeped into my brain. I rarely gave ideas a great deal of thought. When one came, I usually just acted on it. So I acted.

I charged Bain. He stood his ground and prepared to meet my charge head on. I swung wildly and he parried it easily. I danced around until I found myself caught exactly between Bain and Minnie. Now came the dangerous part. I too stood my ground as Bain moved in to engage me.

I needed to keep this position long enough for Minnie to throw another stone. My heart thudded as Bain finally engaged me within killing range. His sword blurred through the air, and I brought my own up in a desperate gamble. I succeeded in blocking the first strike and the second, but the second one knocked my blade out wide. I was wide open to a killing strike.

Bain brought his sword around for the blow, and I realized there was nothing I could do to stop it. But then he hesitated, just slightly, just enough to give me time to duck.

And Minnie's rock sailed right over my head and hit Bain square in the chest.

He grunted and stepped back, a look of shocked pain crossing his face. His eyes cleared and I knew Jairus's control had been broken.

"Bain!" I cried, stepping forward and dropping my sword. "Don't look at the hermit." I shielded him with my body.

He nodded, quickly coming to understand the situation, but I saw the blood draining from his face as he realized what he had nearly done—my blood still dripped from his sword. That, or the rock, must have really hurt. Having been the recipient of one such missile myself, I knew how he felt. I helped him to sit on the ground where he began shaking horribly.

Seeing that he would be okay—mostly—I whirled around to go after Minnie. She lacked a weapon—other than rocks—so I felt I could snap her out of Jairus's control easily enough. Then I would be free to deal with the hermit in my own fashion.

But she was gone. And so was Jairus.

He had taken her.

CHAPTER NINETEEN

"He took Minnie," I shouted. "Get up! Hurry!" Bain looked up from his slumped sitting position on the ground. He said nothing, merely shaking his head. I started to protest, but then I got a really good look at Bain. His face had lost a lot of color, making his hair look even redder—somewhere during the fight, he had lost his cap. He clutched at his chest, breathing raggedly, and I didn't even need to look to know that his ankle had gotten worse during the fight.

"I can't do this alone," I protested through split lips. I spit out another glob of blood. Bain's elbow had really done a number on me. My face ached something fierce. "Come on, Bain. I need you."

He shook his head again, pulling in a ragged breath. "I'm really hurt, Roy. I'll just slow you down."

"But—but you could die here alone!"

He nodded, accepting the fact. "Maybe—probably. It doesn't matter. You must rescue Minnie. Go. Please."

I took two steps away and froze. I couldn't leave. I don't know why, but on some level, I knew Bain was in more trouble than Minnie was. I felt so torn about what to do that I finally just screamed. The sound reverberated into the rock walls of the Labyrinth, echoing eerily in the stone corridors.

And from somewhere inside, the Guardian roared in response. My heart thumped at the sound. Emotionally drained, I slumped down and collapsed near Bain.

He looked up, coughing. "What are you doing? Go get Minnie."

I shook my head. "We go together, Bain."

"I just—"

I cut him off with a weak wave of my hand. "Minnie is fine—she'll be okay. Jairus won't hurt her."

"You can't know that, but even if that's true, he's getting away. You must go now."

"He won't take her far," I said.

"How do you know?"

"Because he wants me to follow."

Despite his obvious pain, Bain managed to look perplexed. "But he could go anywhere. How will you find him?"

I nodded absently, thinking. "That shouldn't be a problem. I already know where he's going. Taninim. But he'll make sure that I'm following before trying to get too far ahead. What we need is a plan...and I need you for that."

Bain seemed to lose interest in the argument, conceding with a sigh and a perplexed shake of his head. "Then help me to my feet so we can start," he said.

"Not yet. Let's figure out what's wrong with you first."

He coughed again. "I'm not sure. Did you punch me in the chest or something? There's this pain here." He touched the middle of his chest.

"Actually, you got hit by a rock."

"A rock?" He blinked. "You threw a rock at me?"

Now it was my turn to blink. I smacked my head. "I'm such an idiot! I could've thrown a rock at you from the first!" I looked at the bloody slice on my arm ruefully and shook my aching jaw, which was attached to my aching head.

Bain frowned. "You mean you didn't throw a rock at me?"

"No. Minnie did."

He grimaced. "Why'd she throw so hard then?"

"She wasn't aiming at you." I moved over and squatted down beside Bain. "Take off your shirt." I helped him to remove his pack, and he struggle out of his shirt. I examined the ugly blue and black bruise.

"Why did Minnie throw the rock then?" he asked persistently.

I paused, confused. "Did you get hit in the head?"

"I don't think so. Why? You hit me in the head too?"

"No, but you don't seem to be talking right. She was trying to hit me, not you."

"You?"

"Yeah. I think you're going to be okay. Your chest is bruised, but I don't see any real damage."

"Is that what happened to your lip?"

I glowered at him. "No, that was you."

"Oh." A pause. "Why'd she throw a rock at you?"

"Bain," I said exasperated, "does it matter?"

"Did you do something to her?"

"Of course not! She was under Jairus's spell. He was making her throw rocks."

"Oh."

"Come on. Let's try to get you on your feet and test that ankle of yours." I slipped my arms under his and hauled him to his feet.

He leaned against me heavily, breathing hard. I could see that each breath caused him physical pain, but he toughed it out and gingerly placed weight on his injured ankle. He winced, but bore it stoically.

"Give me a minute to catch my breath, and then we can go," he said. I nodded. After a moment of silence, he asked, "So why did she hit me instead of you?"

I rolled my eyes. "Bain, you're impossible. I ducked when she threw it at me, okay? It hit you instead. It was the only way I could think of to wake you up."

"So she wasn't really trying to hurt me?"

"Oh brother," I breathed. "Here, drink some water. It should help. We'll eat on the way."

He nodded and took a fairly long pull on the water flask I fished out for him. I said nothing. I took a swig myself, swirled it around my mouth, and spit the bloody water out. Already, my lip had begun to swell. I was grateful we didn't have a mirror. This was one injury I didn't care to inspect.

Bain eased back into his shirt and bent down to pick up his pack. He lifted it with effort, but I took it from him when he nearly toppled over. I would carry both packs for the time being. Shortly, we were ready to go.

As predicted, we found Jairus's trail easily. The footprints led due south, again, as anticipated, disappearing into the thick jungle. "Yep, he's going to Taninim," I said. I nodded to a smaller pair of prints in the soft dirt. "And he's got Minnie."

"Then let's get the betraying, troll-loving coward," Bain muttered under his breath.

"Right."

We moved off, following the trail at a slow pace. Bain walked on his own power, but he had to stop often to catch his breath and rub his chest. I led, pushing aside tree branches, ferns, and trying to find easy routes over moss-covered logs and rocks. I helped where I could, but we practically crawled through the trees.

I glanced back at the Labyrinth only once. To be honest, I was glad I didn't have to venture in there yet. The Guardian's roar unnerved me like nothing I'd faced so far. Even my encounter with the Dragon had not affected me in such a way. That, perhaps, had more to do with the unexpectedness of the encounter. I suppose had I known what I would be facing ahead of time, I would have been quite a bit more nervous. At least the Dragon had a reason to keep me alive. The Guardian had no such need.

A couple of hours later, the trail led us to another river. This one ran to the southwest. It came out of the mountains via a series of gigantic falls, down into a narrow gorge that cut deep into the earth as it continued downhill. I could see no way to cross it. Indeed, Jairus's and Minnie's footprints turned to the right here and followed the river into the jungle.

We drank our fill, washed our wounds, refilled our water flasks, and pushed onward. When the sun set out to dip below the horizon, we stopped on a small knoll in the foothills below the mountains and watched as the river lazily wound its way through a dark valley below. Pushing aside an inconvenient branch, we could see some distance downriver from this height.

We stood there silently for perhaps half an hour as the landscape below us darkened and finally fell into near blackness. Only a partially full moon shed any light below, and most of that reflected off the river in soft shades of silver. Still we waited. Soon the tiny flare of a distant campfire came to life near a bend in the river. Only the way the bend worked and where the fire was located allowed us to see it through the dense jungle. We studied it, knowing who had made it.

"He'll be expecting you to try to get her tonight," Bain said slowly. "He'll have a trap waiting for you."

"I know," I replied in a calm voice. "But I won't let him have her for another day."

"Good man," Bain said. He paused while we both stared at the fire below. It looked to be about a mile away or so, maybe an hour's walk through the uncertain terrain in the darkness. Bain spoke up again, "I've given this a lot of thought. There are only two ways that I can think of that will get him to leave us alone."

"You mean, kill him," I said. I had already come to that conclusion, distasteful as it was.

"Yes, that is one of them. The other, which may be more palatable to you, is to blind him."

I started, frowning. "That would work?"

"I think so. If you could blind him, then his Evil Eye would be useless."

I worried my lower lip as I tried to think it all the way through. "It would be better than killing him. I—I tried to kill him when I first came out of the Abyss. I was so angry..." I trailed off, swallowing hard. "But Minnie doesn't believe that I am that person. I would like to prove her right. As bad as he is, my ma says everyone has a soul—so I guess he does too. So blinding him? I'm for that. But how?"

I could only see Bain's outline in the moonlight, but his voice sounded sad. "You're going to have to use your power."

"You want me to curse him?"

"His eyes, yes. Curse his eyes. Maybe it will blind him. That or you'll need to stab him with your knife."

I balked at both suggestions, but cursing the hermit just might work. I certainly had the anger to accomplish something like that, and using it in that manner would spare me from having to try to kill the man again—or stab him in the face. It would, however, require me to use my power—breaking my vow not to use it again.

I shook my head ruefully at my own hypocrisy. I had been fully prepared to use it on the hermit when he was controlling Bain, and now I wanted to keep my vow? Apparently, my promises were fickle things. *Welcome to my life,* I thought bitterly.

My lips firmed and I straightened my shoulders. There had to be a way to do this without using my new powers. There just had to be. Well, maybe it would come to me later.

"What do you suggest we do?" I asked. "We could probably try to sneak down there, but to be blunt about it, I don't think you could travel at night. You'd likely hurt yourself worse. Plus, trying to thrash my way through the jungle at night will no doubt make way too much noise."

"Build a fire," the prince said. "I'll stay here."

"But then he'll know where we are," I protested.

"He already knows where we are, Roy. But if he sees a fire, he might not think to look for you if you try to sneak in. He'll think you're here—or at least coming from here."

"You've got a plan, don't you?"

"Yes."

I hesitated. "I'm not going to like it, am I?"

"Probably not."

I groaned. "Tell me."

"How good of a swimmer are you?"

"In the river? In the dark? Are you crazy? You did hit your head. I knew it!"

"I'm not the one going to try to swim in a fast-moving river at night. You are."

I choked.

I couldn't see Bain's smile, but I knew it was there. The crazy prince meant to get me killed for letting that rock hit him!

"I got a good look at the river before the sun went down," Bain continued. "The going is a bit rough for about half a mile, but then it slows and is rather placid out near where that campfire is. It's still going fast enough that you'll need to make sure you are near the bank or you'll most likely be swept right past them. But I doubt he will be expecting you to try to reach him from the river. It's your best shot. If you can get to Minnie before he realizes it, you'll be able to free her and then deal with Jairus."

"You still think I should curse him, don't you?"

"I don't know another way to make sure he doesn't come after us. Whatever he wants from you, he is going to unusual lengths to get it. Do you think he'll just give up?"

No, I didn't. I nodded in the darkness, and then set about to make a fire. The moon helped. Otherwise, we would have been floundering around trying to find anything. At last, a merry little fire flickered in a small hole we'd dug out.

I pulled off my ragged shirt and stuffed it into the bag. This particular climate didn't do clothing much good and things tended to fall apart easily in all this humidity and heat. My boots were sturdy, but I had long ago wished for some stout sandals instead since my feet always felt wet and soggy. For this, however, I would go barefoot, so I removed the boots as well. I set aside my sword since I didn't want the weight dragging me down while I rode the river downstream.

Soon, I stood by the river, ready to begin. The water continued to cut through the wide gorge here, moving swiftly and turbulently toward where the land flattened out some. It would widen then and slow down, giving me a chance to reach the bank where the fire was. My only concern was that the campfire was built so that anyone in the river would never see it. I didn't want to miss it. Sighing, I studied the moonlit river, counting two bends before the campfire. That's what I would use to determine when I needed to get out—at the third bend.

"Roy, bring her back, please," Bain said.

"Count on it."

"Then may the Phoenix bless you."

I doubted it. I had already denied the Blessing, so I no longer had it on me. With a start, I realized that this was a situation where the Blessing would be much more useful than my own power. Irritated all over again at my continual stupidity, I shunted all such thoughts out of my mind and focused on the task at hand.

I sat down on the bank. The water rushed by just under my feet, roaring loudly like an enraged beast. From what I remember, it looked deep enough and devoid—mostly—of rocks. I hated to think what would happen if I hit one.

Taking a deep breath, I jumped into the rushing water. It gleefully snatched me up like a leaf and bore me rapidly downstream.

Within moments, I got so turned around in the darkness that I lost all sense of direction. I was a pretty good swimmer, but in the darkness, I felt completely out of control. I tried to stick my feet out in front of me, so I could deflect off any obstacles in my path, but the water kept dragging me askew and several times I ended up going under the water upside down. I nearly panicked each time, fighting to get my head above the water.

My foot touched something hard and buckled against it, but then I was carried by too fast to even try and use it to stabilize my descent down the river. I gasped, swallowed a mouthful of water, and came up spitting as the river suddenly dipped without warning, increasing my velocity.

I heard an even louder roaring sound ahead. I ignored it, trying to fight the current, but it finally dawned on me what the sound might be.

Waterfalls.

I began fighting my way desperately to the bank. I kicked hard and nearly hit my head against the wall of the gorge. My hands scrabbled against the dirt, tearing loose chunks of it off. The roaring of the falls grew louder. I panicked.

I tried to claw my fingers into the dirt wall of the gorge, but nothing I could do would arrest my momentum, and then I found a root or something sticking out. I grabbed it tightly, and nearly had my shoulder wrenched out of its socket as I finally brought myself to a halt. Immediately the force of the river shoved me under the water. I gasped, swallowing more water.

I lacked the strength to pull myself up against the force of the water, and if I stayed here, I would drown.

I let go.

Moments later, my body shot out over the falls. I flailed as I fell, spinning through the air, end over end. Fortunately, the fall wasn't far, and I landed in a fairly deep pool. I hit the water, plunged under, and scrambled around as I tried to figure out which way was up. Finally, I managed to get my head above water and gulp down great chunks of the air around me.

My heart throbbed painfully; and every instinct in my body told me to get out of the water that very instant, but Minnie's thin face intruded into my panic. I forced myself to calm down and take a real evaluation of the situation.

I floated now in relatively calm water. The river, its rage sated, expanded here to perhaps a hundred feet and moved along at a much more sedate pace. I forced my beating heart to slow down some.

Okay, you're alive. Don't panic. I repeated that to myself like a mantra. Finally, I calmed down enough to pay attention to my surroundings. I had no clue if I had gone around the two bends in the river I'd marked out. I hadn't expected the trip to be so terrifying. The darkness had made it so much worse, but now I needed to focus on finding that campfire.

Sometime later, I spotted it to my right. I slowly made my way to the edge of the river and just floated easily, letting the water take me to my destination. At length, I came abreast of the campfire. I pulled myself ashore slowly, careful not to splash the water as I moved through some reeds growing at the edge.

I parted the vegetation and peered carefully at the fire. I could see no one. Taking a careful breath, I inched my way out of the river and moved as stealthily as possible toward the light. Perhaps in retrospect, moving directly to the fire was not the wisest move, but I thought Minnie would be near the fire if she was anywhere.

I got there and stopped. Something was wrong. I could see no real signs that someone actually had made camp. I saw only the fire, not even extra wood to last through the night. *What?*

"Halloo! Roy, is that you?"

I knew that voice. My muscles tensed, and I slowly turned toward the river. The voice came again—from the other side.

"I'm glad that you care enough for the girl to attempt to rescue her. I needed this little bit of verification before I left."

"Let her go, Jairus," I cried across the water.

He laughed. "You're so predictable. Consider this part of your training, Roy. I only speak this as a courtesy, so listen carefully. I am taking the girl to Taninim. That is where you will find her. If you fail—for whatever reason—she will be of no more use to me, and I will kill her. Tell me you understand."

I struggled mightily to get my anger under control. I couldn't see Minnie, and Jairus appeared only as a black shadow against more shadows. If I tried to curse him, he could still kill Minnie, and we both knew it.

"I understand," I bit out bitterly. "Just don't hurt her."

"I have no wish to hurt her, boy. She is merely a means to an end. If you do your job well, I'll give her back to you." He retreated back into the trees, but his voice floated over toward me once again. "It won't be so easy to track me now, boy. Follow as you may. We will meet in Taninim."

I stood there and only the sound of the river filled my ears. I could probably ford the river here, but I would be swept downstream for some distance before I could get to the other side, meaning I would have to make my way back up. Even then, I wouldn't know which direction he had taken. I couldn't track him until the morning, and then, I suspected, he would make good on his threat to hide his trail.

My heart sank. I had failed.

I collapsed next to the fire, tears streaming freely down my face. Anguish beyond anything I'd ever experienced before pierced my soul. I cried bitter, hot tears until sobs racked my body, and I curled up next to the dying fire, unable to stand, unable to sit, unable even to think.

"Oh, Minnie," I sobbed, "I'm so sorry."

I cried and cried until nothing else would come. Only then did something come over me and drag me into sleep.

I dreamed strangely.

CHAPTER TWENTY

I woke to a long, wet tongue that glided over my face. Startled, I scrambled to my feet and spun in a full circle, looking for danger. I stopped and put my hands to my head, closing my eyes tightly while trying to recall what in the world I was doing all by myself near a river.

Then it all came back to me like hammer blows. I stiffened, recalling Minnie's plight and my dreams from the previous night.

Something had called to me in my desperation, whispering to me in a haunting voice that pulled me into a deep, restful sleep. It had felt like wisps of fog trailing along the edges of my consciousness, calming me and comforting me. I had never experienced anything like it in my life.

One phrase had come through clearly only once: "Trust the finrir."

Finrir.

I snapped my eyes open and beheld a good-size dog sitting on the ground at my feet, its tail wagging. The thing looked like a massive brown fur ball. I suspected if I shaved it, it would only be half of its original size. The only thing that differentiated it from other dogs I'd known were the greenish tuffs that grew out of the top of its long, pointy ears. A black nose, two great big brown eyes, and black paws made up the rest of it.

"You're a finrir?" I asked hesitantly.

The dog barked once, its tail wagging furiously back and forth, sweeping aside loose leaves and twigs. I rubbed the side of my head again, unsure. I knew what finrir could do. They could find anything—some said that they could even find hope. Nice, if true. Fairly rare, finrir resisted making attachments to people, but if one was made, it was a lifetime bond.

Someone had sent the finrir. But who? I scouted around the small clearing looking for evidence. I found only the marks of a horse's hooves. I knelt down to examine them.

They were deep, and they roamed around the campsite where I'd had slept. Other than my own prints, I saw nothing to suspect that a human had ridden in on a horse. How could a horse even move effectively in this jungle anyway?

I was baffled. Then I thought of the unicorns. A unicorn? They were reputed to help travelers on occasion. Could it be?

The dog bounded over and licked my face. Startled, I sat back on my heels and regarded the animal. "Did a unicorn send you?" I asked.

He cocked his head, his tongue lolling out.

I sighed wearily. I'm talking to a dog now—and expecting an answer. Well, why not? Standing to my feet, I addressed the finrir. "I'm to trust you, eh? Okay, I can do that. Are you going to help me find Minnie?"

He barked again and suddenly ran around in two complete circles before sitting back on his haunches and regarding me with his friendly brown eyes. I could hardly see the eyes for all the hair. Even the nose looked to be swallowed by the mass of fur.

I looked around. Jairus's decoy campfire had been built on the edge of the slow-moving river. All in all, it would've made a decent campsite. I turned and looked across the river. No one stood there, and I could see no signs of either Jairus or Minnie.

"Bain!" I suddenly cried. I'd left him alone all night. I turned to the finrir. "Come on, boy. We've got to go find Bain."

He barked once and darted off into the trees before I could even point out the way. Well, at least he was headed upstream. That was good.

I ran to the stream, dunked my head in, and took a long pull of the refreshing water. Reinvigorated, I bounded to my bare feet and set off after the finrir. The shaggy head of the dog popped out from behind a tree some distance ahead. He barked at me as if to say, "Hurry up, stupid human!"

Admittedly, I added that last part, not feeling particularly pleased with myself. I trotted after the dog, grateful that I was used to running around outside without any shoes on.

My sorrow of the night before had been replaced with tentative hope. The finrir did indeed find hope.

Three-quarters of an hour later, we found Bain. He was lying next to the remains of a smoldering fire. I rushed over to him, fearing the worst, but the rise and fall of his chest assured me. I gently shook him awake. "Bain, get up. We've got to be going."

He groaned as he sat up and stretched. He eyed me, the dog, and then looked around. "Where's Minnie?"

"I didn't get her, Bain. It was a trap. Jairus was waiting on the other side of the river. He told me that he was taking her to Taninim."

Bain got to his feet and looked at me suspiciously. "You were gone all night. Why?"

"It's a long story, and I'll tell it to you on the way. But we got to go. This finrir here will help us find her."

The dog barked and ran around in another circle.

"That's a finrir?" Bain asked astonished. "I've never seen one before." He reached out a hand, and the dog suffered itself to be patted on the head. "Except for the ears, he looks like a regular dog to me."

"Well, the unicorn said he could find Minnie. At this point, I'm willing to try anything. How are you feeling?"

Bain was staring at me. "You saw a unicorn?"

"Well—not exactly. I might have dreamed of one though. Maybe. Does it matter? Can you travel?"

Keeping one skeptical eye on me, the prince examined himself. He pushed lightly on his chest. "It still hurts, but it is much better. I can walk, just not at speed."

I frowned. "We've got to move fast, Bain."

"Perhaps not. If you are right and this is a finrir, then all we need to do is follow it."

"We're already behind," I explained patiently. "Even if they are traveling slow, it will take us some time to catch them."

Bain looked like he wanted to say more, but he just nodded. "Then I'll go as fast as I can."

I put my shirt back on, found my boots and pulled them on too. I retrieved some food the gnomes had left us, and we decided to eat the jerky as we walked. We would forage for nuts, berries, and fruits along the way.

In short order, we were ready to go. I turned to the finrir. "Okay, boy, I really don't know how this is supposed to work, but find us a quick way to Minnie."

The dog barked twice and darted away, heading downstream. We followed as quickly as we could. Amazingly, the finrir found the easiest path down various rocky declines, over knolls, around trees, avoiding ferns, and dodging vines. I hadn't noticed this on the way back to Bain, being worried about him, but now I realized that the dog found ways to navigate the terrain that saved us a lot of time.

My hope grew. Maybe we would be able to catch Jairus after all. I dreaded to think what would happen if we had to actually go into Taninim to find them. The stories all said that the people who lived there were evil, worshipers of the Dragon. Having encountered the Dragon myself and knowing now that there was indeed a price to the Dragon's Gifts, I could believe the reports. I didn't want to go there.

Thinking of my power stirred it deep in my spirit. It writhed, anxious to be unleashed, to touch the world with its destructive power. I clamped down hard on my feelings, denying it permission to manifest. It settled down, coiling up much like a viper would.

We soon came to the waterfall I'd gone over the night before. Looking at it in daylight, I wasn't all that impressed. Under normal circumstances, I would love to go back up the river and ride it over those falls again. It fell for perhaps twenty feet into a wide pool that then flowed southwest at a much slower pace. Birds darted around it, basking in the mist and providing welcoming music. A snake slithered away at our approach, and some of the ferns shook as various critters retreated into the jungle.

The finrir barked to get our attention and darted toward the falls, disappearing behind them and emerging on the far side, wet but very anxious to continue on its journey.

"Oh, that'll cut time down," I said. "Let's go."

The prince and I made our way down to the river's edge and found a narrow ledge that ran behind the waterfall. Mist made the rocks slick, but we made it through easily enough. Other than getting wet—something you had to expect in a rain forest anyway—we had forded the river in a fraction of the time it would have taken us otherwise.

Instead of following the river, the finrir darted into the jungle, more southward than westward. The dog immediately found a game trail, used by deer or elk perhaps, and began following it. Trusting that the creature knew what he was doing, we hastened along behind him.

And so it went. The finrir knew how to find the path that offered the fewest obstacles. Once, the dog left a wide game trail entirely. We could see the dog moving through the thicker underbrush. Unsure, we hesitated, wanting to continue on down the current easier path.

Something large grunted somewhere down the path, sounding suitably dangerous and irritated. We decided to follow the finrir.

Bain did slow us down some, but the finrir's choice of paths more than made up for it.

Along toward evening, the dog led us out of the jungle and into the foothills of the mountain range that rose up majestically to the east. The trees continued to grow thickly here, but the rise in elevation afforded the occasional view of the land below. To the southwest, I caught a glimpse of the ocean.

No maps existed of the interior for obvious reasons, but the general outline of the island never changed. Having studied a few maps, I knew that a large bay could be found directly to the south. To get to Taninim, we would either have to cross the bay itself or skirt around it to the east until we could travel south again.

If the finrir was truly tracking the evil hermit, then Jairus had elected upon the secondary option. A fishing village may exist along the coast in the vicinity of the bay, but I suspected that Jairus Ramah had no intention of announcing his return to its inhabitants until he could appear like an oncoming storm.

At last, the finrir stopped, his nose pointing straight ahead and one foot lifting. We looked, but the sunlight was fast fading, and we could see nothing in that direction.

"They are up there?" I inquired, softly.

The dog yipped quietly, and then lay down.

Bain sank down too, looking exhausted and pale. "We've got to be getting close," he said, breathing heavily.

I had not heard a single complaint from him the entire day. Whatever discomfort he felt from his injuries, he'd chosen not to say anything. Anxious to save Minnie, I hadn't inquired either; afraid I would be obliged to stop.

"I think so too," I agreed. "They are up there, somewhere in the mountains."

"Well, it looks like the finrir has decided this is as far as we go today. Perhaps we should get some rest, but I wouldn't light a fire tonight. If they are close, we don't want to give ourselves away."

So we made a cold camp that night. We ate some more of the jerky and finished off some of the berries we'd found along the way, washing it down with water from our flasks.

I felt edgy. I knew that I would face the hermit once again, and I felt sure tomorrow would see that confrontation. My anger stirred at the thought, waking the power in my spirit. I clamped down on it again, afraid of it, afraid of my anger.

We slept fitfully that night. I woke dozens of times and scanned the darkness around me nervously. The dog lay at my feet, seemingly unconcerned. Each time I glanced at the finrir, my uneasiness was assuaged a bit, and I was able to return to an uneasy sleep.

The next morning, Bain and I stretched cramped muscles and quickly prepared to move out. "Okay, boy, find Minnie," I said to the finrir. "It's time to go."

The dog lay down and began licking at one of its paws, taking no heed of me. Bain and I stared at the creature, stumped. We tried again, each of us, but the dog refused to budge.

"What do we do now?" I demanded.

Bain considered. "I haven't got a clue."

Frustration began to build in my spirit, stirring the power. The dog glanced at me with its large eyes and immediately I calmed. Taking a breath, I said, "Maybe there's a reason why the finrir doesn't want to go on."

"Are you suggesting that we somehow got ahead of Jairus and Minnie?" Bain asked.

"Maybe, but I doubt it. I can feel we're close, but I think they're up there, ahead of us." I motioned to the slopes of the mountains that we could see through the trees. "That's the way the finrir pointed last night."

Bain pursed his lips. "Those mountains look difficult to navigate. Maybe they're up there, but can't find a pass through the mountains."

The dog began to wag its tail.

"So," I concluded, "they would have to come back through here—right here."

The dog yipped softly.

"It seems the finrir agrees."

My faith restored, I turned to the dog and knelt down next to him, stroking his thick fur. "Thank you, boy. If this is where we should be to find Minnie, then I free you of any obligation you may have. You're free to go."

The dog bounded to its feet, licked my face, yelped playfully, and then darted into the trees in the direction we'd come from. Soon, the dog had disappeared, leaving the prince and me alone.

"Now it's our turn to set a trap," I said, standing back to my feet.

Bain remained sitting, hunched over his knees. "If we can catch him unprepared, we have a chance," he agreed. "I still think you're going to have to curse him."

Up to this point, I had tried not to think about it. I really hoped there would be another way other than using the Dragon's Gift. Without the Blessing, I had no direct protection against Jairus's Evil Eye. The Chaos Curse was more than its equal in power, but it would mean that I had to strike first—from ambush. Bain saw my Gift as a tool, but he didn't have to live with it, nor did he really understand it.

"I don't know if I can," I said dubiously. "My power is sort of all encompassing. I'm not sure I could wield it like a knife."

"It's either that or kill him," Bain said grimly. "If we don't take care of this now, he will just follow us and create more mischief."

"I know," I said, frustrated. "Let me think."

But in the quietness, we heard the shuffling feet of something—or someone—approaching. I cocked my head to the side and listened carefully. After a moment, I could pick out the sounds of two sets of footfalls crackling over the jungle undergrowth.

Bain and I had slept the night just below a small rise in the land. Whoever was coming was coming from the other side. The moment they crested the hill, they would see Bain and me.

We exchanged glances and hurriedly moved as quietly as we could behind some trees. After a moment, we could hear someone talking.

"Stupid mountains. No way across. Burn it all to ashes." A pause. "Come on, girl, pick up the pace. I haven't got all day. Waste of time going this way. Burn the Phoenix—a pox on the bird! Changing everything every year. Stupid."

I easily recognized Jairus's voice. He was coming directly at us, and it sounded like he would pass between the two trees that Bain and I hid behind.

The moment was upon us. I could not just stand here and do nothing. I couldn't see Minnie, but I imagined her looking haggard and worn from her experience with the evil hermit. Anger bubbled up within me. I let it come.

But strangely, my anger wasn't at the hermit. It was directed at what he was doing. This seemed strange—like a different texture of wood on a familiar table. Interestingly, I found myself unable to be angry at the man himself. In fact, I felt pity for the hermit.

Living alone for all those years, harboring resentment and plotting revenge on all those he believed had wronged him had burned out something wonderful inside of him, poisoned it until it became folly and madness. He understood my friendship with Minnie as only something to manipulate, to take advantage of. He could not comprehend love, compassion, and the strength that comes from such a relationship.

In a way, I was him for so many years—living a life where the thrill of teasing Minnie or someone else became my entire existence. My friends—or so-called friends—only echoed my insolence and desire for trouble. When I needed them, they had turned their backs on me. Even in this, I could find no anger. Before this Quest, I would have done the same in their shoes.

So when I stepped out from behind the tree to curse Jairus, my anger had morphed from hatred of the man to pity for a wasted life. I had a focused anger that lashed out at his deeds, the tragedy—but not the man. The power within me balked, like being forced to drink a foul-smelling tonic for an ailment that didn't exist.

But I had enough anger to call the Chaos Curse forth, even if the anger itself lacked the necessary evil.

I stepped out in front of Jairus, who at first didn't even notice me as his eyes were fixed upon the ground. When he did look up, surprise and fear warred to control the expression on his face. And before he could use his own power, I used mine.

"Burn your eyes!" I cried.

CHAPTER TWENTY-ONE

The moment the words left my mouth, the power sprang forth like a viper. Jairus staggered back, his tanned face draining of blood. He turned toward Minnie, preparing to command her, when he stiffened. His eyes rolled up inside his head and he fell to the ground. He started to spasm violently.

I watched in fascinated horror as the hermit flailed about, his fingers and limbs curling inward like crooked sticks.

Then Minnie, who had until this point stood silently behind Jairus, blinked and came out of her stupor. She looked around, taking in Bain and me; a bemused smile spread across her lips. Then she looked down at the hermit and whatever instincts existed in her took over.

"Get me a piece of wood," she ordered sternly as she fell to her knees beside the shaking hermit. "Quickly, before he bites his tongue off!"

Bain cast about, found a piece that looked serviceable, and tossed it to her. She picked it up and quickly stuck it between Jairus's teeth.

"There," she said, taking a deep breath. "He's having a seizure. I've seen this before with one of the women I helped back home. It will pass—I hope."

I took a long look at Minnie. Her dress looked ragged, and her hair hung off her thin face in stringy strands. Her face had dirt smudged on it, and she looked even more emaciated than normal.

I walked over, pulled her to her feet, and gave her the most relieved of hugs possible. "You're okay," I whispered, pushing her back at arm's length. "You're okay."

She looked from me to Bain, and then back to me. A faint flush graced her cheeks as she realized something was terribly amiss. She glanced around. "Where are we?"

Bain came over and gave Minnie a hug of his own. She seemed embarrassed by all the affection, and for the first time that I could remember, she stuttered over her own words. "Wha—what happened?"

"Jairus happened," Bain explained. "What is the last thing you remember?"

"You two fighting…" she trailed off. "Oh." She glanced at Jairus in dismay. The hermit's seizure had begun to lessen. At any moment, the attack would stop.

"Maybe we should get going," I urged. "I'd like to put as much distance between us and him as we can."

"We can't leave him like this," Minnie protested. "It would be the same as murder."

I hadn't considered that. Bain and I exchanged knowing glances, and I rubbed my jaw, careful to avoid my barely healing lips.

Minnie saw our hesitation, and her own lips firmed into a thin line. "Don't even think about it," she warned.

"We can't take the risk," Bain said. "Come on, Minnie. He made me try to kill Roy. We can't trust him."

A shaky voice interrupted our argument. "I can't see."

We turned to look.

The hermit stared blankly into the sky. The stick Minnie had placed in his mouth, lay to one side, deep teeth marks visible in the wood.

"I can't see," he repeated in a trembling voice.

Minnie bent back down and put a hand on the hermit's shoulder. "Let me look," she said softly. She peered into his eyes, and I held my breath. If he used his power on her, I would intervene in any way necessary. I could not stand to have her taken again.

But nothing happened. She glanced back at us. "He's blind."

Jairus sucked his breath in. "What did you do to me, boy? What did you do?"

I came over and steeled my voice. "You know what I did. I cursed your eyes."

Minnie glanced up at me sharply, her eyes narrowing.

I plowed ahead. "You threatened my friends, turned us against each other—against our wills—and kidnapped Minnie. I could not let that pass."

Jairus's face turned red, and he began to flail about, this time in rage. Minnie ducked a wild swing and hastily backed away.

"Where are you?!" he screamed. "I will kill you! I swear upon the Dragon's Breath, you will die for this!"

"You left me with no choice," I retorted, irked that he would blame me for his own doings. I put steel in my voice. This had to end. "Know this, Jairus Ramah. If I see you again, it will be your death. I give you this fair warning only once. On your head be the consequences if you threaten any of us again."

"Curse you, boy! Curse you to the Abyss!"

My lips tightened. "By the way, this nullifies my promise to you. Succeed or fail, I will never return to you. Do you hear me?"

The blind hermit spat something out at me better forgotten. The man looked ready to foam at the mouth. Shaking my head, I turned away from him and addressed Minnie. "Come. He has chosen his fate. Let's go."

This time she made no protest. Gathering our things, we began to walk away from the raging hermit. We could hear his voice for some distance.

"This is not over! Your curse lacked heart, boy! I can feel it! It is weak, pathetic—your anger defused! It will fade and I will find you. I will move heaven and earth to find you, boy! Do you hear me! I will find you! I will see again, and when I do, I will bring the full force of my power upon you and your friends! Do you hear me? I'm coming for you!"

I looked over at Minnie. "Is he right?"

"Probably," she replied in a troubled voice. "Seizure blindness is often temporary."

"Ashes," I mumbled. "Just what I wanted to hear. How long before he can see again?"

"I don't know. Hours maybe, but it could take days."

Bain shrugged. "We left him with plenty of water and food. That is all we can do for him. He brought this fate upon himself, as Roy said. I feel no guilt."

"Neither do I," I added.

Minnie nodded shortly, but I could see she was still bothered.

We said nothing further as we walked away. The hermit's sputtering, raging voice followed us like a plague until, at last, we could hear him no longer.

"Where to now?" Minnie asked after about an hour of walking.

"We know of a shortcut back to the river," I said.

"River?" she asked, perplexed.

"Yes, another one. We will go there first. We can get cleaned up, relax a bit, and then...and then we finish this. It's time I saw the Phoenix."

I could sense approval radiating off both my friends, and I basked in it. Life is best experienced with people you love. If nothing else, this journey had taught me that.

We reached the waterfalls late in the afternoon. Minnie immediately took her pack and went downstream to freshen up while Bain and I set about getting our own selves cleaned up. I dove into the pool beneath the falls, scrubbed myself off with a piece of Minnie's soap, and then cleaned my soiled clothing as best I could.

Then I lounged around the water's edge, enjoying myself as Minnie and Bain set out to prepare a solid meal for a change. I don't know how, but Minnie managed to find more bird eggs, and she even somehow caught some fish that she fried.

It was paradise. I couldn't even feel the Dragon's Gift within me. It was as if it had vanished.

No one even said anything about my lounging.

The next day, we hiked with renewed energy back to the Labyrinth, determined to finish this. Only one more interruption awaited us to derail the completion of our Quest. And in a very real sense, it succeeded.

"Are you ready to do this?" I asked as we stood, once again, at the threshold of the Labyrinth.

"You're not going to give a speech, are you?" Bain demanded suspiciously.

"Me? Nah, but I am feeling somewhat sentimental. We've come a long way—"

"He's going to give a speech," Minnie muttered.

"I knew it," Bain said, sighing.

I looked from one to the other and choked down what I wanted to say. I grinned sheepishly. "Can't blame a guy for trying."

"Can too," the prince shot back.

"He's right," Minnie added. "We can too blame you. Let's get on with it."

I don't believe in fate or anything like that, but I can't help but believe that some sense of humor existed in the universe that ensured that moments like these always went awry in some way. The very instant I prepared to take a step into the Labyrinth and finally complete my Quest, an angry voice from behind us interrupted.

Jairus Ramah.

"Come back here and face me!" he shouted. "Curse your bones to the Abyss!"

I jerked noticeably, but didn't turn around. "Ashes! The man doesn't give up!" I ground my teeth together and steeled my heart for what I must do. I still didn't feel anger toward him, and I determined not to use the Dragon's Gift. This time, I would take him without it. "Don't look at him," I warned both of my companions. "Bain, we're going to have to somehow get close to him without looking."

"It's direct eye contact," Bain whispered. "Use one hand to shield yourself from his face, but keep him in your general line of sight. Understand?"

I nodded and we both drew our swords.

"Be careful," Minnie whispered, standing resolutely with her back to Jairus. "Try not to hurt him. He's just a lonely man."

"He's an evil man," I replied steadily. "And I did warn him what would happen."

"Face me, boy!" the hermit roared. "Let us test the strength of our Gifts—a duel to the death."

Bain and I separated, using one hand to shield our eyes from a direct line of sight. I could see Jairus walking toward us. He used a knotted staff as a walking aid. From what I could tell, he looked worn and beaten down—but angry, oh so angry. His hair stood out in all directions, and I could see a variety of rips in his long green cloak.

I circled to the right while Bain went left. We put the hermit between us, and with one hand still raised, we moved slowly in on him. It was awkward. I could see where he was, but I couldn't get a sense for what he would do, so when he suddenly leaped at me and swung his staff at my outstretched hand, it caught me completely off guard.

Whaack! Whaack!

He hit my out raised arm first, and then the arm that held my sword. I yelped in pain as both of my arms went suddenly numb. My sword dropped from nerveless fingers, and my blocking hand fell to my side. With nothing to block my view, I looked right into the hermit's eyes.

I felt a stab of fear that overrode the pain in my arms. I wanted to look away. I wanted to raise my hand again to block his gaze, but he held me with his power, and I knew I was lost.

Bain saved me. He came rushing in, yelling at the top of his lungs, his sword leading. Jairus spun around to deal with the threat, cursing. Somehow the hermit managed to parry Bain's swinging sword and snap out a blow of his own. Bain danced awkwardly out the way—curse that weak ankle of his!

I darted forward, thinking to leap onto the hermit's back, but the wily man spun around, swinging his staff in a dangerous arc. I averted my gaze and jumped back. Jairus turned to face Bain, now the more dangerous of the two of us.

Bain did much better than I, but with one hand raised to block his gaze of his opponent's face, his attacks looked sloppy and uncoordinated. I stooped to pick up my sword and help, but my tingling fingers couldn't grasp the hilt with any degree of strength.

Frustrated, I left the sword and circled the two combatants, trying to stay at the hermit's back. To my surprise, Jairus wielded the staff like he knew what he was doing with it. Soon, he had Bain retreating, barely able to keep himself from being pummeled by the older man's whirling staff.

Then somehow Bain got his sword tangled up with the staff and the two were pulled close together where they grappled with each other. Bain looked to be stronger, but he had his eyelids tightly closed, lest he inadvertently look into the hermit's eyes.

I saw my chance. I ran toward them and leaped on Jairus's back, bearing everyone to the ground. I heard a grunt, a gasp of pain, and suddenly blood appeared on the ground as we rolled around.

"Hold him!" Bain yelled, sounding strangled.

I shifted my grip and slowly drew the hermit's struggling arms to his body, pulling with all my strength.

"Let me go!" Jairus snarled, jerking manically at my arms. "Face me!"

The prince freed himself and staggered back a few steps. "Hold him still," he panted, looking at some spot directly over where I'd wrestled with the hermit.

I grunted with the effort. He was a man possessed! I could not believe the strength in his thin frame. Someone needed to do something! I could hardly feel my hands, so I had no idea if I could really hold him.

Then Bain arrived and delivered a powerful kick to the hermit's head. The impact drove the man's head into my chest, knocking the wind out of my lungs. I gasped as all my strength left me, but Jairus no longer presented an immediate threat. He lay beside me, out cold.

I pushed the man away and rose shakily to my feet, wheezing hard. I'd never been so physically abused in my life— adding up all the scrapes, bruises, and blows I'd taken since the journey had begun. I decided I didn't really care for Quests. I would rather read about them than live them. But that was foolish. Everyone had adventures—that was life.

Minnie ran over and bent down to examine the hermit's unconscious form. After a moment, she nodded. "Out cold, but he'll be okay in time."

"Hurray," I muttered.

She ignored me. "What do we do now? We can't leave him like this. Either he'll die or he'll come after us."

At least she finally understood that. I had begun to wonder. I looked down on the hermit, considering my options. "I told him that I would kill him if he returned," I said coldly.

Minnie looked up at me. "Not like this."

I nodded, knowing she was right. "Not like this, but we can't let him be either. Maybe we could just tie him up?"

"That would be the same as killing him. Something is bound to come along with the scent of all this blood." She stopped abruptly, frowning. Then she checked the hermit more thoroughly. "He's not cut. Where did all the—Roy, are you hurt?"

"What? A little. He hit my arms pretty hard. They're still tingling a bit."

She whirled around to look at Bain. One look convinced both of us that something wasn't right. Bain held a bloody dagger in one fist, and he swayed unsteadily on his feet.

He offered us a half smile. "Yeah, he got me. He had a hidden dagger on him."

He then collapsed into a sitting position, and we could see all the blood soaked into his shirt and trousers. Minnie let out a little cry of shock and rushed over to him. I arrived a step behind her.

Bain had been stabbed low in the left side. Blood still bubbled up out of the wound. Minnie grabbed my hands and pressed them to the bloody gash. "Hold it tight," she ordered. "Help me get him on his back." We leveraged the injured youth to a prone position, and then Minnie dashed away.

I studied Bain's pale face. In the fight, I hadn't noticed the knife or the stab. I cursed myself for being a fool once again. For the prince's sake, I forced a smile on my lips and teased, "There are easier ways to get a girl's attention, Bain."

"Don't I know it," he replied weakly, "but sometimes it's the heroic gestures that work best." He coughed weakly. "Have you noticed that she's quite a girl?"

I nodded, relieved that Bain was lucid, but feeling odd about the direction the conversation was taking. "I have." In truth, Minnie had completely surprised me. I can't say that I would ever be physically attracted to her, but in every way that mattered, Minnie was quite a girl.

Bain looked at me with serious eyes, as if reading my thoughts. "To me, she's beautiful." He coughed again and his face looked even whiter. "Promise me that you'll protect her."

"You can do that yourself," I retorted lightly. "She doesn't like me much."

"Not quite true," he whispered. "But I fear I won't be in much condition to help—" He stopped short as Minnie rushed back.

She brought more bandages, a water flask, a needle and thread, and some linen cloth—more stuff from her pack, no doubt. She had me strip away Bain's shirt and upper tunic so she could get at the wound.

"It looks deep," she commented to no one in particular, "but at least the blood is slowing already. It doesn't look life threatening. I'll stitch it up before it gets any worse."

"You're saying I'm not going to die a hero?" Bain asked softly.

She shot him a sour look. "Not if I can help it. If I have my way, you'll die an old man in bed surrounded by your great-great grandchildren."

"Ah, you take all the fun out of life," he complained, his eyes closing as he winced in pain. "Do you have to sew me up like a bag of potatoes? That hurts!"

"Men!" she said to the air as she worked. "Fools, every one of them. Stop moving or you'll pull the stiches out."

Her comment about men irked me for all of a moment and a half, but I could not really protest. I fit her idea of men to the letter.

She finished at last and wrapped the bandaged around his midsection, and then she had me help Bain to a shady tree where we propped him up next to it. Taking a long breath, she glanced up at me. "He can't go on like this. He's lost a lot of blood…he can't afford to do anything strenuous."

"Then we stay here and nurse him back to health," I stated firmly. "We aren't leaving him behind. If we have to take him back to Khol, then that is what we'll do. The Quest can wait."

Minnie's eyes shone with gratitude, and I considered her in the light of Bain's earlier comments. Was there something growing between them? And if so, I wondered how I really felt about it.

Bain interrupted my musings by saying, "No. You need to finish this, Roy. You and Minnie go into the Labyrinth and find the Phoenix. Complete the Quest."

"No, Bain," Minnie said softly, "we won't leave you behind."

"You must. I know I can't follow, not like this, but there are two reasons why you need to leave me and go on."

"Like what?" Minnie asked skeptically, fully prepared to argue any point he brought up. Women were good at that, I noticed.

"First, someone has to stay behind and make sure the hermit doesn't interfere. I have enough strength for that as long as you tie him up for me."

Minnie opened her mouth, but Bain held up a warning finger. She closed her lips, irritated.

"Second," he continued, "the return trip is bound to be much more dangerous now that I am injured to this degree. If we are going to survive, we need to see the Phoenix. I have a sneaking feeling that, unless we complete this Quest, none of us will come out alive."

"You can't know that," I said, bending down.

"But I do know that the Phoenix can help us quicker than anyone else can. You need to get to the Phoenix."

It did sort of make sense. Minnie didn't think that Bain was in any danger of dying, but how long would we have to stay out here before he was well enough to travel? Without the Phoenix's help, could we even get home? I thought of the troll village we would have to go through. I shuddered as the power within me stirred at the memory of the chaos I had wrought there. Could I do that again? What would such a thing do to me?

I found Minnie's eyes. "What do you think?"

"I…I don't know. I don't like it, but we've come through so much. We have no reason to believe the return trip will be much easier." She sighed again. "Oh how I wish the hibagon was here. He could heal him."

"Me too. But I think Bain's right. We need to finish this."

She nodded. "Fine, but maybe I should stay with Bain."

I felt a surge of fear at that—and a tinge of jealousy. I didn't want to go alone, but then an honest and frank thought crossed my mind. "No, you need to go with me. This Quest is no longer about me. This is also about you. You need to see the Phoenix as much as I do."

Something in my tone must have convinced her, for she sighed and nodded. "Are you sure, Bain? You'll stay here by yourself?"

"Ha. I won't be alone. I've got an evil hermit to keep me company." He hesitated. "But, uh, I would appreciate if you would tie him rather firmly to a tree—and blindfold him too.

Yes, a blindfold would be nice…and a fire? Maybe a little food and water too."

Minnie rolled her eyes. "Anything else, Your Majesty?"

"Hmmm…I'm sure to think of something."

In short order, we got Bain as comfortable as we could, leaving him with enough firewood, food, and water to last a couple days if necessary. The hermit we tied up nearby and put a stout blindfold tightly over his eyes.

So an hour later around midafternoon, Minnie and I once again stood at the threshold of the Labyrinth. I couldn't help but feel a sense of rightness about it. My Quest largely came about because of what I'd done to Minnie. It was right that she be there to witness the fruits of my change of heart.

"Together," Minnie said, grabbing my hand.

I held it tightly, feeling the thin bones of her hand in mine. I felt protective and relieved at the same time.

"Together," I echoed.

We stepped into the Labyrinth.

ROY'S JOURNEY THUS FAR
Dotted Line = Roy's Journey

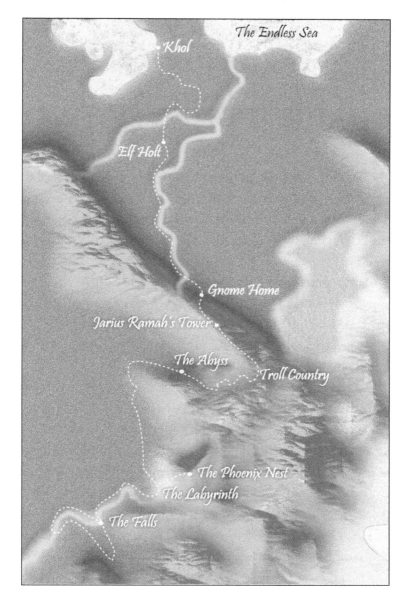

CHAPTER TWENTY-TWO

The Guardian's roar of outrage at our intrusion caused the hairs on the back of my neck to stand up. The sound echoed up and down the ravines, making it impossible to get a clear fix on the original direction from which the sound had come.

I shuddered, squeezing Minnie's hand. "I don't think he's happy we're here," I said quietly, my eyes darting about to make sure the beast didn't burst upon us that very moment.

"Maybe we should move along before he shows up," Minnie suggested.

"Agreed." I released her hand and slowly drew my sword, taking the lead.

We walked up the first channel, which was cut into the rock like a wide hallway, the floor so smooth and uncluttered that I knew it could in no way be natural. We walked for ten minutes before coming to the first fork. I looked right, and then slightly to my left.

"Any suggestions?" I asked.

"No."

I would have to choose then. Fine. I could do that. "We go left," I said decisively. "That seems to go more toward the mountain." I could still see the peak rising above the maze as we began our descent into the valley. At least I had a reference point.

Minnie said nothing, so we angled into the left-hand channel and walked forward. Minnie used a stone to scratch a white arrow in the cliff wall to mark our passage and indicate the way back. The maze branched again not long after that. We consulted and decided to continue on in the one that went generally toward the distant mountain. We did this several times over the next hour or so with no visible progress—except that my legs had started to ache. Minnie marked each path we took, but I was beginning to get irritated with her seemingly senseless efforts. Then a couple of hundred feet later, we came to something of a crossroads. Six ravines, cut into the rock floor of the valley, branched off here, leading in all directions.

"That's not good," I said, nervously. My emotions felt more on edge as I looked hastily down each one to see if the Guardian was bounding toward us. I saw nothing.

"No, it's not good," Minnie said with a tremble in her voice. She pointed to the exact center of the intersection.

I looked and saw several white objects scattered around. Bemused and somewhat perturbed at having my thoughts interrupted, I moved over to look. I stopped short, staring. "They're bones," I said, now understanding her fear. I spotted a skull. "Human bones."

Minnie bit her lower lip. "I think this is the Quester who left Khol three years ago and never came back."

I sniffed. "There's no way to know that. This could be anyone for all we know."

She scowled at me. "Then how you do explain the ring there."

I followed her skinny finger to a skeletal hand sticking up out of the ground as if trying to claw its way free. One of the fingers bore a ring engraved with the Khol city crest of a spread-winged, red Phoenix. "It's a ring," I said, unwilling to concede the point yet.

"That ring is only given to the King's Guard. The man who went on that Quest three years ago was one of the Guard."

I did seem to remember something about that. I shrugged, dismissing it entirely. I couldn't debate her on it even though I desired to. "Fine. It's the lost Quester. It doesn't mean anything."

"It means that we can die in here!" she snapped at me.

Some of her fear seeped into me, and I glanced nervously around. I went over and examined the bones. Sure enough, they looked gnawed on and a few were even splintered as if crunched between large jaws. I didn't like this.

Gingerly, I removed the ring and put it in my pocket. We could at least take the ring back. Maybe the man had a family. Besides, the ring looked to be made of gold. No sense in leaving something valuable like that just lying around.

Minnie rubbed her shoulders briskly, looking as jumpy as I felt. "Pick another one," she ordered. "Let's get out of here."

I considered, somewhat annoyed at her clipped tone. "Don't rush me." I studied each ravine in turn and made a decision. "Let's go back. I'm tired of this aimless wandering about. I want to check out the first fork and go the other way." Actually, now that we had found the human skeleton, I wasn't that interested in going forward.

She nodded curtly, and we walked back down the ravine from whence we came. It seemed to me that we came to the previous fork much quicker than we'd left it. Strangely, this intersection split off into four different directions instead of the two I remembered. None of them looked familiar.

"That's not possible!" I exclaimed, fear and frustration eating at the fringes of my mind. "I know this was the way we came."

"My mark is gone too," Minnie said, pointing.

I looked to where the mark should have been. Indeed, it was gone. I ran my hands through my hair, feeling trapped. "We couldn't have come the wrong way. Let's go back to the other intersection. Maybe we went down the wrong path accidently."

We did, but this time, after a few hundred feet, the ravine forked ninety degrees to the right and left, leaving us facing a blank, uncaring wall—the six channels of before were gone. So were the human bones.

"It's the Labyrinth," Minnie said, sounding somewhat disgusted. "It's changing on us. When we make a choice, we cannot go back."

I grunted noncommittally, realizing the truth of it. "This is just getting better and better!"

"I wish Bain was here," Minnie mumbled.

"Why? You don't think I'm up to the challenge? You think I'm going to fail or something?"

"How should I know?" she shot back. "I just know that three of us are better than two." She kicked violently at a loose rock. "I could kill that stupid hermit!"

I snorted. "Now she tells me. You know, the only reason I didn't kill him before is because of you. If it were up to me, I would have skewered his sorry eyes long ago—but no, you had to go all soft." I shook my head in despair. "I'll never understand women."

"That's the truth, Roy the Delinquent," Minnie said, mockingly adding a glare to top off the insult.

I gaped at her, my ire rising. I don't know why I got so angry, but I did. I exploded, "Oh, that's just fine coming from you, Skinny Minnie!" I gleefully watched as she paled. Oh, this felt just like old times. I snarled, "You blame me for everything wrong in your life, and then you tag along on my Quest and expect *me* to somehow make *your* life all better. Well I got news for you, you little strix. I ain't your salvation! Burn you to ash, woman! Why couldn't you just stay home and stay out of my life!"

The angry words burst out of me, uncontrolled, unmindful of the consequences. I knew distantly that these were emotions I'd abandoned since this Quest had begun, but for whatever reason, they were all coming back. And it felt so good to tell her—right to her face—exactly how I felt.

Minnie's face turned ashen, but where she would normally just burst out into tears and run away, she did something completely unexpected. She slapped me. Hard.

The blow on my already tender jaw sent waves of pain up my neck and deep into my brain. I spat out a bit of blood and turned back to Minnie, my fists clenched and muscles tensed.

She confronted me, practically sticking her nose in my face, and yelled, "How dare you! You're an awful excuse for a man. The way you treated me all my life is deplorable. You're nothing but an ugly, stupid, cowardly brute! You're no better than a troll!"

"Am not!" I retorted, so angry I could think of nothing else to say. I even tried to reach for the Chaos Curse, but it was strangely elusive, unresponsive.

"Are too!" she shot back, the veins in her neck throbbing.

"Am not!"

My mind could still not conjure up anything more profound in retort. Maybe Minnie realized that something was wrong as well, for she withdrew, still looking very, very angry, but she did seem more in control of herself. She glared about her and shuddered, rubbing her thin shoulders vigorously.

She muttered, "Something about this place...it—"

That's when the Guardian burst upon us, all teeth, rage, and ferocity. I only had time to shove Minnie away and swing my sword with all my strength. I hit the beast on a massive shoulder. It screeched in pain and rage, swiping at me with a huge paw. I ducked but got clipped anyway and was sent spinning haphazardly to the ground.

Adrenalin pumped through my body, shrugging off any pain. I leaped to my feet and backed away, holding my sword out before me.

The Guardian hesitated, realizing that it now stood between two different prey. In the initial attack, I had shoved Minnie one way, but I had tumbled in the other. We were separated.

"Run, Minnie!" I yelled, both incredibly scared for her and angry at her at the same time. The woman should've had enough sense not to get separated!

Minnie turned and ran without even a wave or the slightest hesitation. She didn't even look back!

Figures.

She did exactly what I'd asked her to, but for some reason I expected something that would reflect more...concern? I growled in frustration. Her quick compliance angered me.

The manticore, for now I recognized the Guardian for what it was, turned to face me, letting Minnie go. I snorted ruefully. Now I got to be the bait.

Figures.

The beast had a massive head of a lion, wings of an eagle, and a tail of a scorpion. I'd only read about such things in storybooks. The beast stood twice my height and probably three times as long, and it had muscles that rippled along its legs, back, and neck. Golden fur covered the body except for the wings. It snarled, baring teeth the size of my forearm and growling with a lust of destruction I could hardly comprehend.

I reached for my power again. Surely, I had the anger to call it forth, but the Chaos Curse slipped from me like an eel. Maybe the way I had used it on Jairus had somehow offended it. I didn't know if it was even sentient, but whatever the reason, I was now powerless.

I started to inch slowly backward, waving my sword warningly in front of me. My sword had done some damage already. Blood dribbled down the Guardian's shoulder, but it hardly seemed enough to even faze such a terrible beast.

Its tail whipped around and stabbed at me, missing by inches. I saw the barbed tip and the icky fluid that seeped from it, no doubt deadly poison. I stumbled back, but it followed, its paws jabbing ahead of it like a pugilist, and its wings spread out for balance.

I lost what little bravery I had. I panicked. Spinning around, I ran.

Honestly, I didn't expect to escape. I just felt this desperate need to run away. I ran blindly down the ravine, having dropped my sword in my terrified desire to get away.

The Guardian roared in fury, and I could feel the ground tremble as it leaped after me in pursuit.

More fear enveloped me, like nothing I'd ever experienced before. I began to lose control over my own body as my mind became numb with terror. I staggered to the left when my feet suddenly refused to respond properly, and that's when I saw the crack in the smooth wall of the ravine. Beyond it lay another ravine, another part of the maze. The crack looked barely big enough for one dumb human, but certainly too small for one ferocious manticore.

Without thinking of it further, I leaped through. The rock wall bulged dangerously the moment the manticore struck it at full speed, dislodging rock and dirt that nearly buried me. A paw snuck through, catching my pack and ripping it open. The blow thrust me forward, and I smacked into the opposite wall of the ravine with enough force to jar every bone in my body. I fell back into a sitting position, temporarily stunned.

After a long, long moment, I became conscious of the fact that the manticore was still trying to get through the crack in the ravine wall. It was throwing itself at the weakened wall with a gusto that boarded on a frenzy. Loose dirt spilled into my side of the ravine and dust rose lazily into the air.

It would only be a matter of time until it managed to claw its way through. Staggering to my feet, I picked the first direction my body came to face and jerked into an erratic run.

Soon I left the manticore and its rage behind me. Eventually, the only thing that followed me was silence. I stumbled on, walking for hours until darkness fell, and I could go no farther. I slumped down against the ravine wall, having no idea how many turns and twists of the maze I'd taken and no idea where I was or where Minnie was. I slumped there, breathing heavily and still overcome with terror and fear, until mercifully, I fell to the hard ground and unconsciousness overtook me.

* * *

Bright sunlight stabbed at my eyes, intruding upon my temporary escape from reality. I opened them, blinking into the brilliant light. I pushed myself up against the wall and looked up and down the ravine. I saw nothing. The Guardian hadn't found me in the night, but then neither had Minnie. I was alone. I hated being alone.

If Minnie hadn't run off like that, if she would've been loyal, then I wouldn't be in this mess. I was sure of it. My thinking had become muddled, but I was in no condition to recognize it.

I ran my dry tongue over chapped lips and tried to dry swallow. It hurt. I needed water. I reached back and pulled off my pack and stared at it in dismay.

Sometime during the battle, the manticore had shredded my pack. There was nothing in it now, just a bunch of useless, torn fabric. My water and food were gone.

I threw the pack from me in rage. Pulling myself to my feet, I looked around, unsure of which direction I'd come. It didn't matter. This sadistic maze would never let me go back the way I'd came. I ran my hands through my pockets, finding only the ring taken from the skeleton hand. I almost threw that away too, but stuffed it back in my pocket. With irritation gnawing away at my mind, I started walking, picking a direction at random.

I don't know how long I walked, but eventually my parched throat began to make swallowing difficult, and my body began complaining from the lack of water. I desperately wished for water. What I wouldn't give for water at that moment! And as if my desperation had somehow conjured it, right in front of me was a pool of clear water.

I didn't even think to test it to see if it was drinkable or even wonder how it got there. I fell flat on my face, stuck my head in the pool, and drank greedily. I drank too much, but I didn't care. I drank even more, splashing the water on my face and body to cool it off in the sweltering heat and humidity.

At length, I rolled over, my body half in and half out of the cool pool of water. I slept for a time, satiated on the water, but eventually my stomach began rumbling, and I decided I needed to go find something to eat.

But so far, I'd seen nothing growing in the Labyrinth—not even a blade of grass. The odds of finding something were incredibly low, but my stomach insisted, so I grudgingly climbed back to my feet, picked another direction at random, and began walking.

Eventually, my hunger pains became so acute that I even vomited much of the water out of my stomach. I didn't even know a person could do that—it wasn't natural. I needed something to eat—something sweet, perhaps—but anything would do.

Again, just as before, as if my desperation had somehow conjured it, there before me grew a low bush overburdened with ripe looking green fruit of some kind. I didn't know what it was—I'd never seen it before, but I didn't care. I hastily plucked one off the bush, half worried it would vanish into thin air before I could eat of its succulent flesh. I bit into it and sank down next to the bush as a feeling of euphoria overcame me. This was the most delicious thing I had ever eaten.

I ate one after another until I was so full that I could hardly move. If the manticore had come along then, I would have been easy prey, but I hardly cared at that moment. The only thing that mattered was that I wasn't starving. I leaned back in the shade of the bush and let weariness overtake me.

Night came and went.

I woke beside the bush, feeling somewhat better. I ate some more of the fruit, sucking out as much juice as I could. I might have stayed there longer, not anxious to leave the bush as long as fruit still remained, but the roar of the Guardian sounding awfully near sent me to my feet in an instant, stark terror overwhelming me.

A cold sweat flushed my face, and my eyes darted this way and that, looking in dread for the Guardian to come. And as if I conjured it, it came. This time, I saw it a long distance down the ravine, but it saw me too. I screamed, turned, and ran, terror-stricken.

It roared in triumph and bounded after me. I looked back once, screamed again and ran even harder. But I couldn't outrun it. It took a single leap for every fifteen steps of my frantic sprint. It would catch me, kill me, and eat me.

Desperately, I wished for the exit to this cursed place. I had to get out. I needed to get out!

And there it was, the exit to the Labyrinth right there in front of me. I could see trees beyond the threshold tangled in leafy vines, moss, and wide-leafed ferns—the jungle. I couldn't see Bain or any indication of another human, so maybe this was a completely different exit, perhaps on the other side of the mountain.

I didn't know. I didn't care. I lowered my head and ran harder. Behind me, the manticore roared in rage and redoubled its effort to catch me. It was still some distance behind me, but closing fast.

I'd almost reached the threshold when I slammed to a sudden stop of my own accord, my heart beating wildly.

Minnie!

For all I knew, Minnie was still deep in the Labyrinth, alone and lost. Two sides waged a war in my spirit—a war I would never have suspected existed until this moment. Minnie's insight regarding the maze suddenly became my own. This place, this Labyrinth did something to a person. It brought out all the worst in me.

I shook my head. "I can't leave her," I said aloud, trying to bolster my courage in the face of the monster fast closing in on me. "I won't leave her."

Another ravine, one I hadn't noticed before for some reason, branched off to the right. Gathering what little courage I could find, I pivoted and darted toward that branch of the maze.

The manticore passed me at full speed. Surprised by my sudden change in direction, it roared in fury. It then tried to mimic my pivot by spreading its wings wide to slow it down, but it was going too fast. It did swipe at me with a paw and the scorpion's tail stabbed at me, but I managed to avoid them both. The Guardian lost its balance and tumbled over and over before abruptly crossing the threshold of the maze.

And vanished.

I blinked. *Huh?*

Somewhere deep in the Labyrinth, the Guardian roared in frustrated rage. The echoes set my teeth on edge, and the familiar horror began to rise within me. I stomped it down and sighed in relief. Apparently, the Guardian couldn't leave the maze. That was good to know, but that still put the beast between me and the Phoenix's nest.

I turned and looked back up the ravine that I'd just run down. It looked like the most direct route through the valley and to the cavern carved out of the peak beyond. This time, I meant to get there. This time, I realized, I needed to get there. If I didn't—if I left, I would most likely abandon Minnie to her death. It was up to me, I figured. There was no one else to save her, so I had to be the hero.

With this need foremost in my mind, I turned and marched resolutely up the ravine. I ignored all the side passages, and the one I followed never wavered from going straight down the valley and the angled up to the cavern in the mountain. Before I knew it, I reached the mouth of the cavern and was awash in a fiery light that nearly blinded me. When I could see again, I nearly swallowed by tongue. For there before me, sitting sedately on the ledge of the cavern about ten feet above my head, was a huge nest.

It rustled as something inside stirred, and then the Phoenix rose up before me in all his majestic beauty. He stretched his wings out wide and they burst into a blaze of fire that somehow drowned out the other ambient light.

WELCOME, ROY OF KHOL.

CHAPTER TWENTY-THREE

I fumbled for the right words to say. I had finally made it to the Phoenix's nest. I'd completed my Quest! The Phoenix hopped up on the edge of the nest and shook his wings back over his body, the flames dying out as suddenly as they'd burst into life. The bird was huge. Colored in hues of fiery red, the Phoenix resembled in many ways an eagle, but with softer lines—perhaps less of the predatory look that most would associate with the eagle. The bird looked to be about the same size as the manticore, which meant he probably didn't weigh as much, being a bird, but he possessed claws that looked to be as powerful as the Guardian's. The red feathers framed a narrow face and a beak that looked like it could crack boulders. The head resided on a long sinuous neck that shone in red tones. Despite the obvious uses for his claws and beak, I felt no fear.

In fact, a peace settled around me, washing away my terror, my animosity, and my uncertainty. I straightened my shoulders and addressed the Phoenix. "I have come," I stated.

SO THOU HAST, replied the bird, his voice resonating pleasantly in my mind.

I waited for more, but the Phoenix merely blinked at me, turning his head nearly all the way over. I cleared my throat. "Um, aren't you supposed to give me something?"

WHAT WOULD THOU THAT I GIVE?

I scratched my tender jaw. Was this the right bird? This one seemed awfully ignorant of what was supposed to happen. I tried again. "Are you the Phoenix?"

I AM.

"Do you bestow Gifts?"

UPON WHOM?

"Upon those that come here to your nest."

NO.

"What?" I said, shocked. "You don't give Gifts?"

THAT IS NOT WHAT THOU HAST ASKED. I DO NOT GIVE GIFTS TO THOSE THAT COME HERE.

"Then what is the purpose of all this?" I demanded. "Why did I have to come all the way here?"

THOU DOST NOT KNOW?

"Of course not!"

IF THOU DOST NOT KNOW, the bird said, sounding slightly amused, *THEN WHY DIDST THOU COME?*

"I…I wanted a Gift, I guess."

THOU SEEKEST ONE IN ERROR, ROY OF KHOL. A GIFT MUST BE OFFERED FREELY AND THEN ACCEPTED FREELY, NOT DEMANDED OF OR TAKEN. HOW CAN IT BE A GIFT IF THOU MUST WIN IT? IT WOULD BECOME A PRIZE, NOT A GIFT.

That stumped me. I never saw it that way before. I thought that all I had to do was prove myself worthy, and then I would be granted this elusive Gift. I had worried, obviously, that it would be the Dragon's Gift that ultimately sunk me, not the fact that making it to the Phoenix's nest would somehow invalidate my Quest entirely. A notion crept into my mind.

"But the Dragon gave me a Gift."

YES, I SENSE THE TAINT OF IT IN THEE. The Phoenix said nothing more about it, which seemed ominous to me.

"What if I deny the Dragon's Gift?"

THAT WOULD BE NO EASY TASK, ROY OF KHOL. THOU ART WELL SUITED TO THE DRAGON'S GIFT.

I sucked in my breath. I didn't like hearing that. "What do you mean?"

THOU SEEKEST MORE THAN A GIFT. THOU SEEKEST A NAME TO REPLACE THE ONE OF DELINQUENT ALREADY BESTOWED UPON THEE. THINE ENTIRE QUEST HATH BEEN ABOUT TRYING TO CONVINCE OTHERS TO THINK OF THEE DIFFERENTLY THAN WHAT THOU REALLY ART. EVERY STEP THOU HAST TAKEN WAS, ULTIMATELY, A SELFISH ONE BORN IN PRIDE THAT DEMANDED OF OTHERS TO THINK OF THEE DIFFERENTLY THAN THE REPUTATION THOU HAST RIGHTLY EARNED FOR THYSELF. THIS ATTITUDE IS WELL SUITED TO THE DRAGON'S GIFT WITHIN THEE.

"But I'm not that person anymore," I protested, irked.

ART THOU NOT? WHY THEN DIDST THOU COME HERE INSTEAD OF SEEKING MINNIE, THY COMPANION? THOU COULDEST HAVE FOUND HER AS READILY AS THOU FOUNDEST ME.

I opened my mouth, and then snapped it shut. Taking a deep breath, I said, "I knew that if you gave me a Gift, I would be able to save her. That's why I came here."

A NOBLE AMBITION, ROY OF KHOL. DO YOU KNOW THE NATURE OF THE LABYRINTH?

"No."

I WILL TELL THEE THEN. The great bird seemed to settle upon the nest edge, a perch that no doubt spoke of patience. My inner turmoil continued to seethe within. I didn't want an explanation. I wanted help! *LONG AGO, THE DRAGON LAID A CURSE AROUND THIS, MINE NEST, TO KEEP SEEKERS FROM FINDING ME. FROM IT SPRUNG THE LABYRINTH, AND THE CREATURE THOU KNOWEST AS THE GUARDIAN. THE MAZE EVOKES THY BASE LUSTS, FEARS, AND AMBITIONS, FEEDING OFF THEM, AND THEN FEEDING THEM BACK TO THYSELF. IT SEEKS TO BRING FORTH THE SIDE OF THINE HEART THAT IS MOST DEMANDING, AND THEN GRANT THEE THOSE REQUESTS. RECALL THE WATER, THE FRUIT, AND THE EGRESS OUT OF THE LABYRINTH? THESE WERE THY LUSTS, THY BASE DESIRES THAT THOUGHT OF NOTHING ELSE, NOT EVEN THY FRIENDS. EVEN COMING HERE, TO ME, WAS ONLY GRANTED BY THE LABYRINTH WHEN THOU BECAME DESPERATE TO BE THE HERO. THOU ART NOT HERE TO SAVE MINNIE. THOU ART HERE TO CHANGE HOW MINNIE DOTH PERCEIVE THEE. THY TRUE DESIRE IS TO BE THE HERO AND RETURN TO KHOL IN TRIUMPHANT VICTORY.*

My mouth fell open as the Phoenix's words hammered home into both my brain and my heart. I traced my journey from Khol to this point. I can honestly say that I'd changed, that I'd become a better man for the journey and for the friends I'd made. But it was also true that much of my ambition had been rooted in the desire to make everyone see me as something other than a Delinquent, something better, something to be honored and respected.

I was devastated. Facing the truth about one's self rarely creates change, it often creates self-pity, and that was where I found myself: lost in my own failure and ultimate, if hidden, depravity.

These words hath caused thee pain, the Phoenix said, his long neck bobbing down to look me closer in the eyes. This pain may help thee to see thy path more clearly, if thou dost not succumb to it.

I nodded. "What about Minnie? Can you do nothing to help?"

SHE IS FACING HER OWN TRIALS AS THOU HAST, ROY OF KHOL. IT IS NOT FOR ME TO INTERFERE.

"But the Guardian will kill her!" I protested. The full reality of the situation had finally dawned on me. I'd failed, and in my failure, Minnie would die.

THERE IS NOTHING TO FEAR FROM THE GUARDIAN, EXCEPT FOR THAT WHICH LIES WITHIN YOU. THE GUARDIAN REQUIRES A PRICE FOR ENTERING ITS TERRITORY. DEATH NEED NOT BE THAT PRICE.

I wondered if the Phoenix was talking about the Chaos Curse. Could I use that to save Minnie? "If you will not bestow a Gift upon me, may I leave to find Minnie?"

GO AND SAVE HER IF THOU WILT, ROY OF KHOL, BUT GO WITHOUT MY GIFT.

I nodded curtly, turned my back on the majestic creature, and walked out of the cavern and back into the twisting maze of the Labyrinth.

Within moments, I was lost.

I glanced back once, but the nest and the Phoenix had disappeared. Only the glow of the cavern shown over the cliffs around me. I looked around. Finding something in the maze depended upon desperate desire. I'd already discovered this, and the Phoenix had articulated it for me. Now that I understood it, could I use it to find Minnie?

I closed my eyes, trying to summon up desperation for Minnie. But I could not. I was still wallowing in a shallow pool of self-pity. I tightened my eyelids, trying to form a picture of Minnie in my mind. I'd failed, but that didn't mean she had to fail did it? The success of her Quest wasn't dependent upon mine, was it? I refused to believe that it was. Minnie had come because she wanted, much like me, to shake off a reputation.

Hers, however, had not been justly earned. Hers had been given to her by me in my own mean-spirited, arrogant, and selfish pride. I realized belatedly that she wasn't out to get a new reputation, but to reach out to me, someone who she could rightly consider an enemy.

I thought back to the day when her voice, the only one among so many, rose to volunteer to accompany me on my Quest. Had she done it out of some foolish pride to prove to me and herself that I was wrong? Possibly. Maybe even likely, but her method had been unique. Where most would have simply let me go and suffer the probable consequences of my own foolishness, she had elected to help me. I wouldn't have done it in her place, but she had. Perhaps she had done it out of her own pride, but she had also done it out of the kindness of her heart.

That heart deserved a better Name than the mocking one I'd labeled her with. The stigma of all the things I'd brought down upon her had clung to her, aided in large part by my persistent persecution of her. She had been mightily wronged.

I found out in that moment that reputations, rightly or wrongly gained, were not so easy to change. But maybe I could change Minnie's. There was nothing that I could do for myself, but there was something I could do for her.

Sudden, desperate need to make things right with Minnie welled up inside of me. It had, strangely, nothing to do with me at all. It had everything to do with Minnie. I would just have to live with my well-earned reputation, but Minnie shouldn't have to.

I could Name her anew.

And this need rose up in me like a rising tide, and I opened my eyes.

Minnie emerged from one of the ravines, her eyes haggard, her hair harried, and her strength exhausted. She turned, saw me, and staggered toward me with her hands outstretched in desperation. Her own need and mine had found each other.

A triumphant roar bellowed out of the channel Minnie had just fled from, and the manticore came bounding out, its tireless energy giving its prey no quarter. It turned and spied Minnie.

Minnie gasped, took three of four more steps in my direction, and then collapsed in the middle of the smooth, squared ravine.

Abruptly, the power within me stirred, straining to be released upon the Guardian. The Chaos Curse had finally awoken and wished to do battle. Anger tried to accompany it, but I could find nothing to vent it upon. I now knew the nature of the Guardian. I knew how to save Minnie and give her a last gift, from me.

Like a thwarted thunderstorm, the Chaos Curse simmered and seethed as I shoved it far down within me. I would not need it.

The Guardian was nearly upon Minnie when I spoke, casting my thoughts along with my words at the Guardian. "Desist, Guardian. Stay your hunger for but a moment."

The giant beast stopped as surely as if it had run into a solid wall. It stared at me in utter malevolence, its tail lashing back and forth in agitation, wings spread wide, and teeth gleaming in the dull light.

YOU MAY NOT STAY MY WRATH, HUMAN. THERE IS A PRICE TO WALK THE HALLS OF MY HOME. YOU CANNOT REFUSE ME.

I walked forward until I stood between Minnie and the manticore. I was close enough that if the beast so desired, he could rip my head off with one swipe of his massive paw.

"You will have payment," I said steadily. "The cost has already been determined."

The Guardian regarded me intently, then it abruptly sat on its haunches, folding its great wings along its back. *BE ABOUT IT THEN, HUMAN. I HUNGER.*

Turning, I went back to Minnie. She lay curled into a ball, shaking like a leaf. I reached down and gently drew her up, keeping her steady. Hot tears of relief flowed down her cheeks. "Oh, Roy! It was awful. I lost myself." She swallowed hard. "I lost you."

"I know. I did too, but we've found each other. It is over."

She looked over my shoulder at the Guardian. "What did you do, Roy?" she whispered hesitantly.

I smiled at her, my desperate need reasserting itself. Much like she'd done for me around the campfire upon learning of my dark secret, I gathered her hands between my own and held them tightly together. "Minnie, you came with me on this foolish Quest of mine to get me to see you in a different light. It may have been slightly bullheaded and irrational on your part," I permitted a small smile to show on my lips, "but you did it in a way few would. You did it by showing love to someone unworthy of that love. Through this entire Quest, you have become my anchor, the single real truth in my life. I made it this far, made it to the Phoenix, all because of you."

She sucked in air and her eyes became liquid soft. "You saw the Phoenix?"

"I did, and he *did* give me a gift…though it was not the one I expected or desired. It was, however, what I needed. Through it I came to understand some things. Mostly about you, Minnie. I have done you real harm, saddled you with an undeserved reputation, and spoiled potential friendships as a result of it. I can't undo it, but I can give you something, Minnie. I can give you to everyone else in the same way you gave yourself to me."

I paused then, knowing that the moment I did this, everything would change. It would be the end of me, but it would give Minnie a future.

"I Name you Hope. For all that you are and have been, you have always given me hope. Minnie Hope, I thank you."

I could feel her tremble with emotion, and tears carved groves down her dirty cheeks. I gently reached up, lowered her brow gently, and gave her a single farewell kiss of brotherly affection on her forehead. Then I pushed her back, my task done, and turned once again to the manticore.

Taking a few steps closer until within range of its paws, I said, "I am ready. Take my life as the price." *Death need not be the price,* the Phoenix had said. But this wasn't for me. This was for Minnie. I knelt down, bowed my head, and closed my eyes.

Minnie only then realized what I meant to do. I heard her sobbing as she struggled to reach me. She would not be in time. This had to be done.

I heard the Guardian rise to his massive paws. *FOOLISH HUMAN, DID YOU THINK I WOULD NOT TAKE YOUR LIFE?*

Something whipped around, and then punched me in the stomach. Pain lanced through me so sharply that my throat constricted, cutting off my scream of agony. My eyes snapped open, and I saw the manticore pivot mockingly and stalk slowly off. In my mind, it gave me one last taunt. *THE POISON WILL SOON KILL YOU, HUMAN, AND THEN I WILL RETURN TO FEAST ON YOUR FLESH. A PAUSE. AND HER PRICE IS TO WATCH YOU DIE.* I heard soundless laughter in my head as the Guardian moved away.

Poison? Oh, the Guardian had struck me with its scorpion tail. I could feel the poison working, stiffening my limbs. I toppled over and curled up as best I could, fighting unsuccessfully the pain as it ran like stabbing knifes up and down every inch of my body.

"Roy!" Minnie fell to her knees beside me, her tears spattering on my cheeks and forehead. "Roy! No, you can't die. You can't!"

"It's okay," I managed to whisper. Talking was hard, and I could feel my body shutting down under the poison's assault. I didn't have much time. "You are Hope," I whispered. "Find Bain and return to Khol. What we did here today will change the world—you will change the world."

"Oh, Roy, this isn't what I wanted to have happen. I did want you to see me differently because others saw me as you did. I just wanted to show you that you were wrong."

"I know." The words barely crept out. I could speak no more.

"This can't be the end," Minnie said softly. She looked up into the air. "Please."

And that's when a shadow passed over us, and the piercing cry of a great bird split the sky, fire blazing from his feathers like the sun.

CHAPTER TWENTY-FOUR

*B*E AT PEACE, ROY OF KHOL. The Phoenix's voice resounded in my head, bringing me peace. I tried to speak, to thank the Phoenix for showing me the truth about myself and helping me find the way to help Minnie, but my mouth refused to work.

Something huge and unfathomable settled down beside us. The temperature dropped to a comfortable level, smothering the stifling heat. My eyes had begun to glaze over, so I couldn't really see the Phoenix, but I could feel his presence.

THY JOURNEY IS NOT YET DONE. TARRY A MOMENT AND ALL WILL BE WELL.

That I could do. I surely wasn't going anywhere. My vision darkened further, but the Phoenix's voice came again, piercing through the fog of the poison. This time, however, the Phoenix addressed Minnie.

WOULD THOU HEAL HIM, MINNIE?

"Oh yes, if I could!" Minnie cried.

Strangely, I could hear just fine, though I could feel nothing else of my body or see anything.

THOU CAN, MY DAUGHTER. I GIFT THEE THE TOUCH. HEAL HIM.

I heard Minnie gasp in surprise as if discovering something amazing within herself. Then I felt two points of radiating warmth, one on my head and the other on my shoulder. The warmth spread through my body, purging it of the poison and healing all the damage it had done. My eyes cleared and I could see again. Breath flowed into my lungs and energy surged through my body.

I looked up. Minnie knelt over me, one hand on my head, and the other on my shoulder. Her eyes were closed in concentration. Soon she sat back, looking tired but pleased.

I sat up in astonishment and poked myself first in the arm, then in the leg, and then in the chest. Minnie lost her smile, watching me. "Roy, what are you doing?"

"Making sure you didn't miss anything," I said absently as I poked the other leg. She punched me in the shoulder. I grunted. "Ow! Hey, that hurt."

"Brute," she said teasingly.

"Skinny," I shot back smiling.

This time, her answering smile told me that that particular injury had now been healed.

WELL DONE, MY DAUGHTER, the Phoenix said in our heads. I focused on the Phoenix in time to see the bird's long neck twisted around to look at us upside down. *FEW HAVE THE STRENGTH OF SPIRIT TO PURGE OUT THE GUARDIAN'S POISON. THOU ART STRONG.*

"Thank you," she whispered, pleased.

I NAME THEE SAYBER AND SEND THEE FORTH WITH MY BLESSING.

Minnie gasped again in surprise, but then she looked over at me. "If it is all the same to you," she said to the Phoenix, "I'd rather keep Hope. I like that Name."

That warmed me immensely. I never knew how much such approval could mean to me. I smiled and gave her a slight nod of thanks.

The Phoenix wasn't finished yet. *KEEP IT THOU SHALT, MY DAUGHTER. SAYBER MEANS HOPE. ROY HATH NAMED THEE WELL.*

A foolish grin spread across Minnie's face. Now it was my turn. I looked at the Phoenix. "Thank you for showing me something about myself. It is a gift, one I hope to use wisely."

The Phoenix twisted his head around again and bobbed it up and down. Then he spread his wings and stood upright. I gaped in awe at the pure majesty of the bird even as flames burst forth from his feathers, burning and yet not burning. He was full-grown now, since only in the first four weeks of the Rebirth did he have his infancy.

IT IS A RARE INDIVIDUAL WHO CAN SEE SO DEEPLY WITHIN HIMSELF AND ACCEPT HIS FLAWS, MY SON. I AM PLEASED. I GIFT THEE THE BLESSING.

I started, staring at the bird in utter surprise and wonder. "I didn't expect that!" I exclaimed, part protest, part excitement.

THIS IS WHY I COULD GIFT IT TO THEE. THE BLESSING CAN BE A POWERFUL THING AS YOU KNOW, BUT WITHIN THEE, THOU SHALT ONLY BE ABLE TO BLESS OTHERS, NOT THYSELF. USE IT WISELY, FOR MANY WILL SEEK THY BLESSING OUT OF GREED AND PRIDE.

I felt something change deep within me, a power of a different origin and feel waited contently for me to bring it forth. I felt awed and then baffled. "But I thought you wouldn't give me a Gift because of the Dragon's Gift." I hesitated, thinking. "Does this mean I no longer have the Dragon's Gift?"

THOU HAST BOTH, MY SON. THOU ART UNIQUE, FOR I CAN RECALL NO TIME IN MY LONG YEARS WHERE A MAN HAS HAD BOTH GIFTS.

"But the Dragon said that the two powers would tear me apart!" I said worried.

THE DRAGON LIED. DOES THIS SURPRISE THEE? the Phoenix asked, sounding amused.

My eyes narrowed. "No. Not really."

THOU ART WISE. THE TWO POWERS WILL BE IN CONFLICT, THAT MUCH IS TRUE. THOU SHALT BE IN CONSTANT BATTLE OVER WHICH ONE TO BRING FORTH, FOR THEY ARE, BY THEIR NATURES, OPPOSITES. THOU CANST CURSE OR BLESS. IT IS NOT THE POWERS THAT WILL DESTROY YOU, BUT THE STRUGGLE TO CHOOSE WHICH ONE TO USE.

"Oh, I never plan on using the Chaos Curse again!" I stated vehemently.

THAT IS NOT A PROMISE THOU ART LIKELY TO KEEP, the Phoenix contradicted, sounding amused again. *TIME SHALL TELL. STILL, THOU NEEDEST A NAME, SO I NAME THEE YASHA.*

My eyes widened again in surprise, but then I narrowed them thoughtfully. "Might I ask what that means?"

CANST THOU NOT GUESS, OPPRESSOR?

I winced at the use of the Name given to me by the Dragon. Apparently, I was not going to be getting rid of it any time soon. Names followed you around either as a curse or a blessing. Curse. Blessing. Oppressor. Then it dawned on me. "Deliverer."

VERY GOOD, ROY OSHEK YASHA. THOU ART OPPRESSOR AND DELIVERER. UPON THEE RESTS THE BURDEN OF WHICH COMES FORTH FROM WITHIN THEE. DO NOT THINK THAT THOU ART

ALONE IN THIS, MY SON. ALL CARRY A SIMILAR BURDEN OF CHOOSING ONE NATURE OVER ANOTHER, TO DO RIGHT OR TO DO WRONG, TO BE GOOD OR EVIL. ONLY IN THOU, THIS AFFLICTION IS NAMED AND THUS, PERHAPS, CARRIES A WEIGHTIER BURDEN OF RESPONSIBILITY.

I liked the new name, if not the responsibility that came with it. Oh well. I squared my shoulders and decided it was time to grow up a bit. "I will carry this burden and learn wisdom."

THUS THE PROPHECY HAS BEEN FULFILLED.

I blinked. The prophecy. Without thinking, I recited it out loud, "Your way shall be fraught with danger, this is easy to see, but your fate shall be decided when you give up that which you hold most precious for that which you hold in disdain. Failure may be the path to success, and success may lead to failure. The choice will be yours." I looked around until my eyes found and stayed on Minnie's. "All I wanted was for people to respect me."

She placed a hand on my shoulder. "You gave that up for me, didn't you?"

I nodded, unsure if I could really speak. Finally, I said, "I just came to accept the fact that my reputation had been justly earned and that to change it would take more than a simple Quest. Responsibility. I never wanted to take responsibility—I hated responsibility. But then I decided to stop focusing on myself and focus on you. I thought I could help you by taking responsibility for my own actions."

The Phoenix's head bobbed. THUS YOU LEARNED THE TRUE MEANING OF HUMILITY, MY SON. IT IS ENOUGH FOR NOW. COME, CHILDREN, THERE IS ANOTHER THAT WE MUST SEE TO.

Both Minnie and I looked down the ravine and saw the exit to the Labyrinth. Indeed, this one came right out where we had started. And there, still sitting under the tree was Bain. Minnie and I ran to him as the Phoenix launched himself into the sky and circled above us, a trail of fire following in its wake.

I reached Bain first, and my heart leaped when his eyes popped open and he saw us coming. "'Bout time," he grumbled. "I've had to put up with this fool for two days! He never stops talking!"

I glanced over at Jairus, still bound and blindfolded. He evidently heard our approach, for he began yelling, "Untie me, curse your bones. This is no way to treat your betters!"

By mutual agreement, all of us ignored the hermit. Bain looked wan and pale. Even his reddish hair looked faded. I couldn't imagine what it must have been like to be saddled with the hermit for two days and having to listen to the man rant and rave. Bain had certainly suffered his own trials on this journey.

Minnie fell to her knees beside him. "Be quiet," she admonished him. "Let me work." She placed her hands on his injured side and closed her eyes. He winced at first, but after a moment, his eyes widened in wonder. The transformation was evident even to my eyes. The scrapes, cuts, and bruises all disappeared as if they had never been. His pallor changed to a healthy hue and energy surged through his body.

He sprang to his feet and touched his side, tested his ankle, and then did a skip and a jump just to show he could. "Minnie!" he cried, coming back to where she sat, looking very tired. "You have the Touch!"

She smiled at his enthusiasm.

Then the Phoenix landed beneath the tree, and the prince fell back, startled. The flames flashed out, leaving the red feathers unsinged and the bird unharmed. Bain recovered enough to stare in dumbfounded amazement. He glanced at me with one eye, keeping the other firmly fixed on the great bird. "Is that the Phoenix?" he whispered.

Something about the situation stirred my natural mischievousness. "Nah, that's his kid brother," I said with a straight face. "You should see the big one." I held my hands out as wide as I could get them.

His face struggled with his imagination, for the bird before him, even sitting, towered above us all; his long sinuous neck turned this way and that as he regarded Bain.

"Th...this is the sm...small one?"

"Yep," I replied.

After a moment, Bain's eyes narrowed. "Wait a moment. There's only one..."

INDEED, HE IS JESTING THEE, MY SON. I AM THE PHOENIX.

We all heard the voice, even Jairus, for he shut up as surely as if someone had gagged him.

Bain regained his composure and bowed regally to the Bird. "I greet you in the name of my father, King Emeth, and thank you for aiding my friends."

I REMEMBER THY FATHER, YOUNG ONE. HE HAS USED MY GIFT WELL OVER THESE YEARS. I AM PLEASED. The bird's attention shifted to Minnie who continued to sit in utter exhaustion on the ground. THE TOUCH COMES AT A PRICE, MY DAUGHTER. HEALING THY FRIENDS HATH EXACTED A TOLL ON THY BODY. MUCH OF THY POWER IS BOUND TO THY SPIRIT AND THE LOVE THOU HAST FOR THE ONE THOU TOUCHEST, BUT THOU SHALT SHARE THE PAIN WHEN THOU DOST HEAL NEXT. I HAVE SPARED THEE MUCH OF THIS FOR THOU AND THY FRIEND'S SAKE.

Minnie looked up and nodded her understanding. "I will be careful next time."

The Phoenix's attention shifted back to Bain. *I AM PLEASED WITH THEE, BAIN OF KHOL. TO THEE I GIFT A WORD OF POWER: VALOR. WHEN THE HEARTS OF THINE FRIENDS FAINT OR WHEN THOSE AROUND THEE FALL PREY TO FEAR, THOU SHALT BE ABLE TO BOLSTER THEIR SPIRITS AND RALLY THEIR COURAGE. SPEAK BUT THE WORD OR A VARIANT THEREOF WHEN THOSE AROUND YOU ARE IN NEED OF COURAGE.*

Bain bowed his head, humbled. "This is a great Gift," he said, "but it is my own heart that too often falls prey to fear."

WHERE IS THE TRUE SOURCE OF THY COURAGE, MY SON? IS IT NOT IN THOSE WHOM YOU SURROUND THYSELF WITH? THOU HAST FOUND THY COURAGE BECAUSE THOU HAST FOUND TRUE FRIENDS. WHEN THEY ARE STRONG, THOU SHALT BE STRONG. There was a pause as the Phoenix drew himself up even taller than before. *I NAME THEE MEREA, A TRUE FRIEND.*

Bain nodded soberly, accepting the Name. "I will endeavor to do the Name honor. Thank you."

FAREWELL, MY CHILDREN.

With that, the huge bird launched into the air, fire bursting forth from his feathers once again. He circled once and then winged off over the mountains. We watched the Phoenix go until we could see him no longer. Then we all turned to look at each other.

"I got a surname," Bain said excitedly. "And I can feel the power inside of me."

"Me too!" Minnie said.

"Me too!" I echoed.

We laughed. Enjoying the moment, enjoying each other's company—until the gravelly voice of the hermit intruded.

"Release me this instant," he ordered. "When I'm free, I'll kill all of you! A pox on your Names! A plague upon the Phoenix!"

Minnie and I exchanged a troubled glance. What were we to do with the hermit now? But Bain walked over and said, "We've nothing to fear."

And suddenly, we knew it was true. Bain had bolstered our courage. Indeed, our trust in Bain had also deepened immeasurably. I realized that this was a powerful Gift for a leader. When Bain became king, everyone around him would become fiercely loyal to him, but I also knew that the strength of his Gift depended directly upon his love and loyalty toward us. What we felt was a reflection of what he'd already given us, and this only intensified our bond to him.

Bain reached down, untied the hermit, lifted him to his feet, and removed the blindfold. "You are free to go," he said firmly.

All three of us dared to look him unflinchingly in the eye. The hermit scowled, glowering at each of us. His power came up against mine and recoiled. He flinched, backing away. "Burn you all," he muttered. "I will have my revenge."

I sighed. I had had quite enough of this. "Be gone, foul one, but go with my Blessing."

Jairus reeled back as if suffering a physical blow from the power of the Blessing that enveloped him. He clutched at his chest, panting heavily and glaring at us as if we had just sprouted two heads. "No," he whispered. "No!" he cried more frantically. He staggered away, and then ran into the jungle and shouting over and over, "Curse you! Curse you!"

I knew we would not see him again.

"At last," Minnie said, looking a bit less tired. "I thought we would never get rid of him."

"Curious," Bain said, "what will the Blessing do to him, I wonder?"

I shrugged. "I have absolutely no idea. From the way he acted, he didn't appreciate it very much."

"Right." Bain turned to us squarely. "Now then. I want to hear about all of it. What happened in the Labyrinth?"

We told him. Minnie went first, and I listened, fascinated to hear of her adventures during our separation. Apparently, she suffered many of the same things I had—though in different ways—but didn't encounter the manticore again until right there at the end when I'd intervened.

Then I told my story, and Bain's eyes widen when I told how the manticore had stabbed me with its stinger, poisoning me, and then how the Phoenix had arrived and Minnie had healed me.

"Be honest with me, Roy," Bain said after I'd finished. "Were you hoping the Phoenix would show up and save you at the end there?"

I grinned sheepishly. "I guess there might have been that hope in the back of my mind. I really didn't want to die, but I couldn't think of anything else to do for Minnie. I'm glad it got the Phoenix's attention."

"Uh-huh. I knew it. You're a sneaky dog, Roy."

I shrugged. "Perhaps."

"He couldn't have known," Minnie said defensively. "Not after being rejected by the Phoenix."

I shook my head. "I wasn't rejected. I was shown the way. I really don't understand it all. All I know is that after meeting the Phoenix, I found my way. That perhaps is the best gift I could've gotten."

Bain raised an eyebrow. "Yes, well, it all worked out in the end, but now what? Our Quest is over."

"We go home," Minnie said firmly.

I agreed with that. "But," I added seriously, "I doubt our Quest is over."

That got their attention. "What do you mean?" Minnie asked, a hint of suspicion lacing her words.

The prince nodded, his eyes narrowing. "Yeah. What she said."

I grinned. "I seriously doubt that the Phoenix gave us these Gifts just so we could sit around and do nothing. I bet we're meant to do something with them. If we can't make a difference, then what is the point of having this power?"

The smile on Minnie's thin face suddenly matched my own. "You've really matured, Roy. You definitely aren't the spoiled brat I knew in Khol."

"For the first time, I realize I have a responsibility I'm willing to undertake. And what is maturity if not taking responsibility for your responsibilities?" I gathered both of my friends in with my eyes. "I suspect that our Quest—our life—has just begun."

Bain grimaced. "You know, that might be a bit more maturity than I care to contemplate right now. Why don't we concentrate on one thing at a time, like getting home first? I've about had enough of elves, trolls, evil hermits, and Dragons. I could use a real bed to sleep on too."

Actually, that sounded good to me. "Well, at least you still have your bedroll," I pointed out. "I lost everything when I fought the Guardian."

"Ha!" Bain exclaimed, pointing a finger at me. "You didn't fight nothing. You ran away!"

"Probably the single greatest act of wisdom I've exhibited on this entire trip," I agreed ruefully.

"We'll get it figured out," Minnie said. "But if it's all the same to you, I'd like to put some distance between me and the Labyrinth."

Bain immediately took charge. That too was a change. Before, he was content to let me lead things, his own fears keeping him from bearing the responsibility of leadership. And now, I was content to let him lead. I trusted him. On some level, I knew it was his power manifesting, affecting Minnie and me, but since the strength of his power was but a reflection of his trust in us, I had total confidence in his leadership.

Together, we gathered up a few spare things, and then began our long trip home.

CHAPTER TWENTY-FIVE

T hankfully, our trip home was uneventful—more or less. We skirted the Abyss, and this time my two companions could feel it's presence like one might a sour stomach. For me, I had mixed feelings. The Chaos Curse reached out, trying to pull me toward that evil place, while the Blessing recoiled, leaving me slightly out of sorts. It was like two snarling dogs unhappy in each other's presence.

I felt relieved when we began our ascent out of the valley toward the troll village. There may have been, as Jairus claimed, another way over the mountain range that wouldn't take us through troll country, but we didn't know of it. We talked it over and decided that between us, our Gifts would see us safely through. We didn't have much choice. We would need to take things on faith.

It turned out that our fears were all unnecessary. The troll village was deserted. Apparently, the superstitious trolls figured the place was cursed and had moved on. They weren't far off in their thinking. I hurried through the village, feeling sick from the total devastation that I'd caused. Hardly a hut stood, and here and there I could see what might be the remains of a troll left to rot.

We made sure to stay away from Jairus's tower and found a way over the mountains and down to the northern slopes of the mountain range. From there, we walked west through the tangled jungle until we found the river near where we had met the hibagon all those weeks ago. It seemed like forever, and we had all lost track of the exact number of days we'd been gone.

I'd used the Blessing to bless our return trip—specifically Minnie and Bain's return trip, hoping to benefit from it in a residual way—and it seemed to work, for we were able to avoid King Eddie and his elf holt. I don't think he would have been pleased to see us, and I wasn't at all sure that we would be pleased to see what he'd done with his newfound authority.

That would be a problem for another day.

And so, maybe ten days after leaving the Labyrinth, my family's farm came into view between the trees just outside of Khol. Minnie had insisted that we come here first.

I found my father chopping down trees near the house. He would sell the wood to the mills—though with all the trees available this year, he would not get a premium price for his labor—and use the cleared space to farm.

The moment we came into view, he spotted us, dropped his axe from nerveless fingers, rushed to me, and gave me the strongest bear hug we'd ever exchanged. I'd never been overly impressed with my father, but being away from him for so long had greatly changed my attitude. I was glad to see him.

I squeezed back. "Hi, Pa. I'm home."

He pushed me back to arm's length, a single tear escaping his eyes. He wiped it away and shook me gently. "'Bout time, Son. 'Bout time. Been gone a month, Son."

I blinked. "A month?"

"Thirty-two days," he looked at the sky, "and about five hours to be precise. I've missed you, boy."

A scream of happy surprise came from the house. I turned to see my mother barreling down on me, her skirts flapping out behind her, and a stained apron whipping about her waist, clinging to her desperately by a single tie. She hurdled a stump and slammed into me, nearly bowling me over.

"You're safe!" she cried. "Thank the Phoenix! My son is safe."

"Hi, Ma," I said, hugging her close. "I missed you."

She sobbed in happy relief for a moment then pulled back and wiped her eyes with her apron. "Just look at you. You're a mess." She spared a glance at Minnie and Bain too. "You're all a mess. Come inside and get cleaned up and eat something. Come on."

We let ourselves be pulled into my home. The moment I entered, the smell of the place assaulted me with memories. I took a deep breath and let it out slowly, feeling truly safe for the first time since we'd set out on our Quest. It was good being home.

We did as my mother requested, tolerating the fuss she made over us. Soon we were cleaned up. Since Bain was practically my size, we found a change of clothes to suit him. My mother found an old dress from her younger days that fit Minnie—more or less. My mother had never been *that* skinny.

Finally, Bain stood to his feet after having eaten some of my mother's cooking—oh that had been the best meal ever! "I want to thank you," he said, "and I'm sure you want to hear all about our adventures, but it is time that Roy, Minnie, and I return to the city. We must meet with my father and have the Quest declared ended."

My father nodded. "We're going with you. I'm sure we'll hear all about the Quest in due course."

I smiled, grateful. I wanted them to be there at the end.

Together, the five of us set out for the city. A couple of guards at the Moon Gate saw us coming. One blinked in surprise, leaned over the wall to get a better look, did a double take, and immediately ran to a horn attached to a pole. He took a deep breath and blew.

The deep sound reverberated out and over the city. One blow meant warning. Two blows meant danger. Three blows meant happy tidings. Four blows—never before heard in my lifetime—meant a Quester was returning. We entered as the fourth horn sounded over the city. In the distance, the bells of the Singing Cathedral began to peal. A shiver of happiness ran down my spine.

We made it perhaps twenty feet through the gate before the city turned out to meet us. They came running from everywhere, lining the streets and cheering wildly. I was somewhat intimidated by it all. They couldn't know if we'd succeeded or not, but apparently coming back alive was reason enough to rejoice.

Then Minnie spied a child limping along the edge of the street, trying her best to keep up with our pace. We could all see the girl's bruised knee. Minnie, of course, detoured right over to the girl. Bain and I stopped to watch, knowing what she meant to do.

"What happened to your knee?" she asked the girl.

Awed that one of the Questers would speak to her, the girl stammered, "I...I fell."

"I can relate," Minnie said. She knelt down and gently touched the wound, her eyes closing. In no time, the bruise and scrape disappeared.

The little girl wiggled her leg in amazement. "It's all better!" she exclaimed.

Immediately a murmur spread through the crowd. I caught the fringe of it. "The Touch! She has the Touch!"

Well, if there was any doubt of the success of our Quest, Minnie had dispelled it. Then I remembered something else. It had been a long time since someone with the Touch had significant strength to do what Minnie could do. A few with the power could heal minor things, like a cold or a scrape, but Minnie had something special—the city just didn't know it yet.

Minnie rejoined us, walking gingerly. She had assumed the girl's pain. I nodded respectfully to her, and she smiled back.

We resumed our walk to the palace, paced by the cheering throng of people. We had to pass through the old city gates first, and the throngs followed us right up to the palace. The gates to the palace stood wide open. A line of city guards lined the pathway down the long corridor that led to the throne room. The people gave way before us, but followed us in as we passed through the doors.

One or two of the guards nodded to Bain, who returned a grave nod and the simple phrase, "Stand tall, men." I saw them straighten noticeably as if eager to please their prince.

We reached the double doors that led to the throne room proper, and they were pushed open by another pair of halberd-wielding guards. One stepped forward and announced, "Your Majesty, the Questers come!"

A hush descended on all present. I could see the king sitting on his throne, but he looked ready to burst right out of the throne and run to his son. Only his sense of kingly decorum or perhaps convention kept him in his place. Even I could see how relieved he was to see his son safe and sound.

However, three specific individuals awaited us down the middle of the main throne room aisle, spaced evenly apart. This was the traditional ending of the Phoenix Quest. We would be examined by each in turn before being presented to the king who would finally declare the Quest ended.

We paused to give the crowd time to filter in around us and fill up the two wings of the throne room. After a time, we instinctively knew to move to the first examiner.

The first to await us was Justice Holly Yosher. She possessed the Inner Eye and would look into our very souls to determine our current character and demeanor. We stopped before her.

She looked a little frazzled as if called hastily to the throne room. She brushed her hair back and looked into Bain's eyes first. I sensed her power move, and I was pleased when a radiant smile formed on her lips.

"My prince," she said, curtsying. She then raised her voice for all to hear. "Welcome home, Prince Bain Merea, friend and heir to the Phoenix Throne."

The crowd lining the room erupted into cheering and applause. They liked Bain and perhaps some of his power had something to do with their enthusiasm.

Holly turned to Minnie and looked her in the eye. Another smile blossomed on her lips. She came forward and lifted Minnie's hands up in her own. "Welcome home, Minnie Sayber, hope and heir to the Phoenix Throne."

Another, somewhat more subdued, round of cheering came from the crowd. It was unprecedented to have two heirs to the

Phoenix Throne presented at the same time. A hush soon fell over everyone as Holly turned to me.

I steeled myself, knowing what she would see.

She looked into my eyes, and I knew instantly that I had the power to shut her out with the Chaos Curse. The Dragon's power stirred uneasily. The Blessing within me, however, embraced her sight.

She started, a perplexing frown showing on her lips as she discerned the nature of what lay within me. She shook her head, as if coming out of a daze, and then she smiled, putting me at ease. She laid a hand on my shoulder. "You have come a long way, Roy. I can't say that I am altogether pleased with what I see in you, but the Phoenix has Gifted you and that says a lot. I am proud of you, Roy." She raised her voice so all could hear. "Welcome home, Roy Oshek Yasha, oppressor, deliverer, and heir to the Phoenix Throne."

A faint cheering went up, but for the most part, the crowd began murmuring to each other in general confusion as they sought to understand what had just happened. No one in their history had ever had two surnames or had three heirs to the Phoenix Throne presented at the same time. They did not know what to make of it.

I joined them in that. I didn't know exactly what to make of it either.

Justice Holly Yosher stepped aside and bowed. Then we proceeded on to the next examiner. This was the man who'd Blessed me, giving me my first boon. We shared a similar power now. He would determine if the Blessing remained on us and our Quest.

We walked up to him and he bowed. He then sucked in his breath and closed his eyes. I never did get his name—though I meant to find out. I had a thousand questions. I was also a bit worried. I had the Blessing, but I no longer had *his* Blessing. Would that make a difference?

He opened his eyes and looked at Bain, sensing the Blessing upon him. He glanced at Minnie and saw the same thing. He raised a curious eyebrow since he knew he had not bestowed it. When he looked at me, he squinted as if unsure of what he saw. He could sense the Blessing in me if not upon me. Finally, he shook his head in wonder, winked at me, and spoke loudly. "Welcome home, Questers. The Blessing remains upon you."

The crowd clapped again.

Then we came to the third examiner, Beth Chalom, the seer who had prophesied my failure and my success. She would now give another foretelling, following the conventions of the Quester's Ending. She wore the same white dress as before—or at least a similar one—and her smile looked as radiant as ever.

We stopped in front of her and she curtseyed, somehow managing to keep her white staff from tipping in the process. "Welcome home, Questers. It is an auspicious ending that all of you have returned to us safely. Shall we see what this foretells?"

We nodded and she closed her eyes. She spoke, her voice soft, "To have come this far and suffered so much speaks well of your strength, dedication, and faith. I see a future that is both sure and tangled. Much still awaits you and much is still hidden. Only one thing of you each is plain—though I know not to whom they pertain. I see that one among you shall rule us all, another shall leave to save us all, and the third shall fall or doom us all. This is all my sight can see."

No one spoke. No one even knew what it meant. The last part of the prophecy didn't sit well with anyone. It seemed clear to me that Bain would be the ruler, and I had an ominous feeling that I fit the third part. I shifted uncomfortably.

Beth opened her eyes and smiled. "Foresight rarely means what you think it means," she said, looking me squarely in the eye. "You, Roy, should know this better than most." I thought of her first prophecy and how it had been fulfilled in ways that worked out but were completely unexpected.

I nodded. "I do."

"Then," she said, addressing the king and moving out of the way, "I present the Questers to the Phoenix Throne, Your Majesty."

The king rose smoothly to his feet and came to the edge of the dais. The three of us moved closer, side by side. Bain and I bowed and Minnie curtseyed. The king studied each of us in turn, though his eyes lingered longest on Bain. I could sense his pride in his son and felt his satisfaction. My own parents, standing behind us, radiated a similar pride.

"Welcome home, Questers," the king said in a raised voice. "I greet you in the name of the Phoenix. You have been tested before us and found true in your Quest and purpose. You have returned to take your place among us and to serve the people. We therefore declare your Quest to be ended on this day in the Year of the Lamb, the thirty-third year of King Emeth's reign." He beckoned to the people. "Come! Let us rejoice! Our Questers have come home!"

The crowd of people collapsed in on us. Bain darted out a step ahead of the throng of people and made it to his father before anyone could intercept him. They embraced long and hard. My view was cut off as others suddenly surged around us, most following Bain and crowding around the father and son.

Many of the ladies surged toward Minnie, and she was soon whisked off as everyone demanded the story from her.

I was left in an island of relative calm. Many glanced my way, but they seemed nervous, unsure. I just stood there, unsure myself, not knowing if I should try to leave or if I was required to stay.

Eventually, I spotted a familiar figure push through the crowd toward me.

Seth.

He stood uncertainly, looking downcast.

"Seth!" I cried, happy to see him. "I'm so glad you're here!" I jumped forward and clapped him on the back and pumped his hand, glad someone had taken note of me. This wasn't exactly how I'd envisioned the end of my Quest.

"You are?" he asked, looking miserably hopeful.

"Of course I am. Why wouldn't I be?"

"Well, you're famous now, Roy. You've got powerful friends—I just thought that..." He trailed off.

I understood. "You worried that you let me down by not volunteering to come with me on the Quest, is that it?"

"Yeah. I should've done it, Roy." He smacked a fist into his palm. "I just got so scared. I'm sorry. I almost tried to follow you the day after you left, but Vin said I would be a fool to go. I didn't know what to do."

I placed my hands on his shoulders and forced him to look at me. "Seth, you are my friend. I'm not sure I was ever a good friend to you, but I don't fault you for not coming. Honestly, if our roles had been reversed, I probably would have done the exact same thing you did. Listen to me, Seth. I've learned some things on this trip, but one of the things I've discovered is what real friendship is. You, me." I smacked him on the shoulder. "We're friends."

Seth's grin took up his entire face. "Friends?"

"Friends," I agreed.

He sighed. "Thanks."

"Yeah, well, speaking of friends, where's Vin?"

Seth shrugged. "He refused to come in. He said that he didn't want to be part of anything that honored Skinny Minnie."

I lost my smile. "That's not her name," I said firmly. "Her name is Minnie Sayber...Minnie Hope. Do me a favor and drop the Skinny."

Seth looked surprised. "Wow, you really have changed."

"For the best," I assured him. "Let Vin know, if you see him again, that he had better leave Minnie alone. Trust me, he doesn't want to mess with any of the three of us."

Seth grinned. "Sounds fine with me! Vin has been nothing but a pain in the Phoenix's eye since you left."

I nodded. "Yeah, he would be."

That's when King Emeth pushed through the crowd into the island of calm that surrounded Seth and me. He laid a hand on my shoulder. "Son, it seems people aren't too sure what to make of you."

I shrugged. "It's understandable. My surnames are a bit of a contradiction."

"Yes, but having completed the Phoenix Quest myself, I think I have a bit of a clearer prospective on things. Come, I want to hear all about your Quest. We shall retire to the north antechamber." He looked at Seth. "You're welcome to come too, Seth."

Seth swallowed. "You know who I am?"

King Emeth laughed. "I do. Come. Roy, bring your parents."

I gathered up my parents and all of us followed the king through a door into a smaller, but more private, room set behind the throne.

Bain was already there, seated around a large oval table. Next to him sat his lovely sister, Princess Kyrin. I remembered her from when our Quest had first started, but now that I had the chance to really look at her, I was startled by how pretty she was. My heart skipped a beat when she smiled shyly at me.

Minnie came in next, accompanied by Holly Yosher, Beth Chalom, and the man who had Blessed me.

"Please," the king said, pulling off his crown and tossing it into an empty seat, "everyone sit down. Justice Yosher, are you prepared to transcribe?"

"I am, Your Majesty," Holly said, finding a chair around the table and setting down a thick stack of loose paper, a quill, and an inkwell.

"Excellent." The king waited until the rest of us had found a seat. "Now then, I want to say a few things before we hear your story—mainly to you, Roy."

I sat up straight, my heart thumping.

The king continued, "I had my doubts about you and this Quest, but I also knew that if you survived it, you would become an honorable man. It happened to me. It is why I did not forewarn you of the Labyrinth. Some things must be faced alone, and the Labyrinth, I fear, is one of those things. I apologize for this, but I felt it necessary." He glanced at Bain. "Even for my son. But know that I am pleased by what I see in you, and even if half of the things my son tells me are true, you are a worthy heir to the Phoenix Throne." A tear escaped his eyes, and I found my own eyes misting over. "I am pleased, Roy, for all you've done for both my son and for Minnie. I am in your debt."

The king cleared his throat and held up a hand to forestall me from talking. "The Phoenix must decide which one of you shall ascend to the throne one day, and since there are probably a few years left in these old bones of mine, none of us need worry about that right now. I will have the official documents drawn up and announcements made. We will also find suitable occupations within the palace for each of you. But now, I think we are all anxious to hear of your Quest. Roy, this started out as your Quest, why don't you tell us the story and Holly will write it all down."

I felt strange. The king's approval made the people's uncertainty about me meaningless. I stood to my feet, and, strangely, my nervousness fled the instant I did so.

I looked around the table, my eyes finding Bain's, and he smiled in encouragement. Then I looked at Minnie. This Quest had ended up more about her than about me. The finrir was supposed to help find hope, and for me, the finrir had more than succeeded. I saw Bain and Minnie exchange lingering glances as they waited for me to start, and I smiled. I was pleased.

In my pocket, I fingered the ring I'd recovered from the bones of the lost Quester. I had no idea why that man had failed, but I knew why I had succeeded. Looking around the table one more time, I began to tell my story. A story of friendship, sacrifice, and hope.

THE END

ABOUT THE AUTHOR

G reg S. Baker lives in the southwest with his lovely wife and four children. An avid reader and writer, this series is his first venture into the young adult arena. Inspiration for the Isle of the Phoenix novels came from an honest dismay at the lack of clean, wholesome, adventure stories for his children.

Figuring he would just write them himself, he developed the concepts of the Island with the purpose of being able to produce dozens of adventure stories for his children to aid them in the transition into adulthood while instilling Christian values at the same time.

He believes that being a husband and a dad is his greatest calling, and writing has become an outlet to share his understanding of life with those closest to him—while having quite a bit of fun doing it.

For information on upcoming books, to access interactive and exclusive content, and to help shape the unique and miraculous world of the Phoenix Island, go to www.IsleOfThePhoenix.com.

CPSIA information can be obtained
at www.ICGtesting.com
Printed in the USA
LVHW042346141019
634128LV00007B/2277/P